THE PRIVATE MEMOIRS
AND CONFESSIONS OF A
JUSTIFIED SINNER

THE PRIVATE MEMOIRS AND CONFESSIONS OF A JUSTIFIED SINNER

written by Himself
with a detail of curious traditionary
facts and other evidence by the Editor

◆

James Hogg

Introduction and Notes by
DAVID BLAIR
University of Kent at Canterbury

WORDSWORTH CLASSICS

First published 1997 by Wordsworth Editions Limited
8B East Street, Ware, Hertfordshire SG12 9HJ
Introduction and Notes added 2003

ISBN 1 85326 188 2

Wordsworth® is a registered trademark of
Wordsworth Editions Limited

2 4 6 8 10 9 7 5 3 1

Printed and bound in Great Britain by
Mackays of Chatham, Chatham, Kent

CONTENTS

GENERAL INTRODUCTION

Wordsworth Classics are inexpensive editions designed to appeal to the general reader and students. We commissioned teachers and specialists to write wide ranging, jargon-free introductions and to provide notes that would assist the understanding of our readers rather than interpret the stories for them. In the same spirit, because the pleasures of reading are inseparable from the surprises, secrets and revelations that all narratives contain, we strongly advise you to enjoy this book before turning to the Introduction.*

General Adviser
KEITH CARABINE
Rutherford College
University of Kent at Canterbury

INTRODUCTION

James Hogg's *The Private Memoirs and Confessions of a Justified Sinner* (hereinafter *Confessions* for short) was published in 1824. Hogg was then fifty-four years of age, and had a literary reputation more for his poetry than for his fiction. He was part of an Edinburgh literary circle that had grown up in the 1810s, although Hogg, born in Ettrick Forest, a remote part of the Borders region of Scotland, had had little formal education and had spent his early years in farming. He had established a character as a shepherd-poet, rather as Robert Burns in the previous generation had allowed himself to be a ploughman-poet, the idea of the untrained rustic Muse being congenial to a certain kind of Romantic literary fashion; and when, late in life, in 1832, he at last visited London, Hogg found himself

---

* In the case of the present volume, however, the first half of the Introduction (to p. xvi) is designed to be read *before* the reader reads the novel itself. The second half should be read afterwards.

something of a literary celebrity. Before *Confessions*, he had published some prose fiction – *The Brownie of Bodsbeck* (1818), *The Three Perils of Man* (1822) and *The Three Perils of Woman* (1823). None of it had drawn much attention or acclaim in its own time; nor did *Confessions*: its heyday has occurred in the last decades of the twentieth century, when, after being 'rediscovered' in the 1940s by André Gide,[1] it has come to be seen as a remarkable, formative work of nineteenth-century fiction which in part anticipates the ideas and methods of Modernism.[2] It is, however, at root a very Scottish novel.

In *Confessions* an anonymous Editor, possessed of a document, part-printed, part in manuscript, dating from more than a century earlier, writes a reconstructed account of some of the circumstances with which it deals. Then he reproduces the document for the reader. Finally he tells the reader how he came by it. The whole book is, in a sense, written backwards.

That is not its only peculiarity, as will be discussed later. But the book is thus framed by the experience of a man of the 1800s confronting and attempting to understand events from Scottish history of the late seventeenth and early eighteenth century. This, in essence, although very differently conducted, was what had driven the novels that Walter Scott had written between *Waverley* in 1814 and *A Legend of Montrose* in 1819, before he turned away from recent Scottish history to explore the English Middle Ages in *Ivanhoe*. None of these novels – neither Scott's nor Hogg's – with their knowing and intricate reconstructions of the Scottish past, can live fully for a reader today unless she or he has some understanding of the extraordinary social, political and doctrinal tensions which had shaped that past. This understanding cannot be taken for granted in a twenty-first-century reader outside Scotland, and probably no longer pertains for many a reader inside Scotland. I am therefore devoting the first half of this introductory essay to an explanation of the historical situation with which Hogg's *Confessions* deals and to a brief account also of the religious doctrines in which its central character, Robert, is embroiled. This, I hope, will enhance many

---

1 Gide wrote an enthusiastic Introduction for an edition of the novel published by the Cresset Press in 1947.

2 See, for example, Robert Kiely's description of it as 'an early form of symbolist fiction in which various configurations of imagery *suggest* several things at once and "stand for" nothing but themselves' (Kiely, p. 226). For publication details, see the Select Bibliography which follows this Introduction. Most subsequent references to items in the Bibliography will give simply the author and page number in parentheses immediately after the citation.

readers' experience of this thrilling novel. I trust that others, who know this background well, will, if they do not skip these pages altogether, pardon the inevitable simplifications and omissions that attend upon such a short account of such complex matters.

The problems that the Scotland of Hogg's novel had experienced in the seventeenth century arose in large part from the differences between the Protestant Reformation as it had occurred in Scotland and in England – or, rather, from the politicisation of those differences. The immediate occasion of England's break from the Church of Rome had, of course, been King Henry VIII's wish to change wives. The Pope would not agree to it; so Henry severed the cord with Rome and established in 1533–4 a Church of England of which he was head. This is not to say that there was no theological (as distinct from political) drive in Anglican Protestantism, but the Church of England was not a radically reformed Protestant church like those which had emerged in other parts of Reformation Europe. It retained, in modified form, much of the liturgy of Roman Catholicism, much of its dress and ritual; and it retained episcopy – that is, the hierarchy of authority in the church headed by archbishops and bishops (*episcopus* being Latin for 'bishop') under the Crown. The relatively cautious nature of these reforms was later to be a matter of sustained contention between the mainstream Church of England and its more radical, Puritan wing; but it is with Scotland that we need to be more concerned.

The Protestantism that had emerged in Scotland in the sixteenth century had been the more uncompromising Protestantism inspired by Martin Luther and, more especially, by John Calvin, some of whose doctrines will be discussed later in this Introduction. In Scotland its principal local advocate was the fiery reformist polemicist, John Knox. This more 'European' Protestantism was more politically radical as well as more theologically rigorous than the English version, challenging established theories and practices of power which had been predicated on the association of kingly authority with divinity. Its rejection of Catholicism was theologically root-and-branch – one celebration of the mass, Knox famously asserted, is worse than a cup of poison – and in those parts of Scotland where it had taken hold – mainly in the Lowlands and Borders – a new, reformed Church of Scotland had been established. Although this allowed itself to be presided over by Scottish bishops appointed by the Crown – an uneasy compromise negotiated during the minority of King James VI in 1572 – it had a popular base in a more militant form of Presbyterianism. Along with jettisoning the liturgy, the ornaments and the ceremonial of Roman Catholicism, Presbyterianism wanted to set its face against episcopy and to assert its freedom ferociously against any incorporation of Church and State. The only government of a Presbyterian Church was in theory through the pastors and 'presbyters' or the elders of the congregations.

When in 1603 James VI of Scotland became James I of England on the death of Elizabeth I and united the two kingdoms thereby, he found himself monarch of a single country with two principal reformed churches of very different characters. Under the four male Stuart monarchs who reigned during the century – James I (1603–25), Charles I (1625–49), Charles II (1660–85) and James II (1685–88) – this situation became increasingly perplexed and volatile for three related reasons. One was the monarchy's underlying wish to unite the kingdom under a single church. The others were the Stuarts' political tendency towards an absolutist style of monarchy and their personal tendency towards crypto- and finally outright Catholicism, which from the beginning was regarded with profound suspicion and hostility by English Puritans and Scottish Presbyterians alike.

In 1637 Charles I and his Archbishop of Canterbury, William Laud, who had already antagonised the Puritan wing of the church in England by reforms which appeared to pull the church back in the direction of Catholicism, attempted to impose the English *Book of Common Prayer* on the Church of Scotland. There was rioting in Edinburgh when it was introduced, and in reaction to infringements of their beliefs and autonomy, a group of Presbyterians gathered in Greyfriars Churchyard in Edinburgh on 22 February 1638 and drew up a declaration of their principles known as the National Covenant. This became a defining moment in the history of the reformed church in Scotland, and the issue of absolute adherence to the terms of the Covenant became a galvanising one. Those who, through thick and thin in the decades that followed, stuck militantly by the principles of 1638 became known as 'Covenanters', a label that comes up several times in *Confessions*, although among Covenanters there were varying degrees of militancy (see Note 126).

The Covenanters were the natural theological allies of the Puritans in England, and saw themselves as such. Accordingly, when hostilities were in progress in England between Charles and the Parliamentarian and Puritan forces, the Scots entered into a Solemn League and Covenant (1643) with Charles's opponents. They understood in so doing that the Parliamentarians in England would, if successful, guarantee Presbyterianism in Scotland and facilitate its establishment also in England. When the Parliamentarians then appeared to go cool about this arrangement, elements in the Scottish Presbyterian movement were prepared to get into bed with Charles himself: in 1647, Charles, in return for Scottish military assistance against his English enemies, agreed to the terms of the Solemn League and Covenant. In 1649, however, Charles was defeated and executed; and when his son was crowned as Charles II at the Restoration in 1660, after eleven years of the Commonwealth, the new king made it clear, in spite of having himself signed up to the Covenant and the National Covenant, that he did not intend to be bound by the deal his father had cooked up under duress with the Church of Scotland. Once again episcopy was imposed by force in Scotland. This time the result was in effect a sporadic civil war which lasted from the 1660s until the 1680s. Congregations and militant clergy who refused to accept episcopy were banished from their churches and, often worshipping outdoors, were regarded as outlaws: violent repression by the government was met with violence. This era became enshrined in Presbyterian mythology as 'the killing times' and those who suffered death fell as martyred saints. In *Confessions*, Robert on the first page of his memoirs alludes to what his mother had suffered during 'the persecution of the saints' (p. 67), and the gaoler in the Tolbooth wryly recollects the imprisoned 'saints' of thirty years earlier (p. 103). In various other ways too the memories of these years pervade the world of the novel and help to locate loyalties and attitudes. The Editor tells us of the old Laird of Dalcastle (pp. 15–16) that during those 'dreadful times' he had 'leaned to the side of kingly prerogative', thus avoiding any penalties, but 'without taking any active part in suppressing Covenanters'. Experience of his wife's religious temper, however, now drives him into full political alliance with the 'Cavalier party'.

With the death of Charles II in 1685 and the accession of his brother James, an avowed Catholic, events moved quickly in both Scotland and England. James endeavoured to secure the passing of a bill declaring religious toleration, which would have been fine for Scottish Presbyterians had it not extended to the detested Roman Catholics. But in 1688 James's regime in England effectively collapsed and he was ousted by Parliament, a constitutional milestone which became known as the 'Glorious Revolution'. In his place, his (Protestant) daughter, Mary, and her husband, William of Orange, were installed on the throne. By 1690, William had granted religious toleration to all but Catholics and Unitarians, had ended episcopy in the Church of Scotland, and Presbyterianism had been officially established.

The dethroning of James II, however, had other, more divisive consequences. Elements in England and, more entrenchedly, in Scotland, refusing to recognise the constitutional status quo after 1688, retained a loyalty to the cause of the exiled James and then to his son, styled James III after his father's death in 1701. These Jacobites (Jacobus being the Latinisation of 'James') drew support from the Highlands in Scotland, which had largely remained Catholic and feudal, and from those sections of society which had identified their interests with the Stuart court and also doctrinally with the cause of episcopy. In *Confessions*, George Colwan and his young friends are identified as Jacobites, and sit talking treasonable talk and drinking treasonable toasts (see p. 37 and Note 47). A brief Jacobite rising had taken place in Scotland soon after the 1688 Revolution, and in 1715 and 1745 northern Scotland would be the starting-point for full-scale armed rebellions led by the exiled Stuarts to restore them to the British throne. The Editor alludes to the 1715 rising at the end of his first narrative (see p. 66 and Note 71).

While the situation after 1689, then, allowed the Church of Scotland to re-establish itself on Presbyterian principles, free from state persecution, the Scotland of the early 1700s in which *Confessions* takes place remains fraught by these events. Old tensions still run deep, especially for those who can remember the martyrdom of the 'saints' or who, like Johnny Dods, were present at the Battle of Bothwell Bridge (see p. 149 and Note 143). In other ways, however, the alignment of loyalties and hostilities in Scotland at this period goes beyond issues of worship and runs deep into the social and political fabric. The marriage with which the novel begins, between the Episcopalian Laird of Dalcastle and the Presbyterian Miss Orde, takes place not just across a division of religious persuasion, but across an embedded social division between a Borders landowner, a gentleman who identifies his interests with the court party, and the daughter of a middle-class city merchant. The merchant stands to gain social prestige and the Laird stands to gain the Orde fortune on his father-in-law's death – as well, probably, as a handsome dowry. Such marriages could function as a means of effecting the transfer of funds from the newly enriched, thrifty merchant class to the often hard-pressed, extravagant, old country gentry: the Editor pointedly notes that the old Laird is 'supposed' to be a rich man (p. 3). Hogg places this marriage at a historical cusp, in 1687, during James II's brief reign, when years of internecine bloodshed were giving way to peaceful coexistence. Even though the Editor has little sympathy for Lady Dalcastle, we can still see, however, how these new 'marrying times' can create martyrs just as the old 'killing times' had done. Now they are young women, sacrificed 'in still and blooming beauty' (p. 4) by their fathers.

Some of the complexities of these social/political/religious alignments can be gleaned by looking, for example, just at one page of *Confessions*, page 19, and at the variety of labels used to designate the two 'parties' gathered in the Black Bull tavern. There, the Presbyterian side is referred to as 'the Revolutionist faction' (i.e. its adherents are supporters of the 1688 Revolution) and as 'the Whigs'. The latter term, which is used intermittently throughout the novel, is probably a contraction of 'whiggamore' (a cattle drover) and was first used contemptuously of the Presbyterians by their opponents in 1648, when a faction from the west of Scotland marched on Edinburgh. Meanwhile the other group are variously described as 'Jacobites', 'Episcopalians', 'Cavaliers' (as Stuart loyalists had been designated in the English Civil War, although it also denotes a whole style of dress and life), the 'High-Church party' and the 'prelatic party' (i.e. supporters of prelates, or church hierarchy). The term 'the court party' is also used by the Editor (p. 3), and Robert uses it again in contradistinction to what he calls 'the country party' (p. 98); and, as applied to the hard-line Whigs, the term 'Covenanters' is still current in the world of the novel, as is the more general term, 'reformers'.

The Black Bull episode in the novel, with its ensuing riot, is set against the background of the 1703 Parliament in Edinburgh. The circumstances of this 'famous session', as the Editor calls it (p. 16), reinforce the continued ferocity with which religious faction determined politics in Scotland. The old Laird is returned to the Parliament under the 'influence' of Lords Seafield and Tullibardine. The former (born James Ogilvie), appointed Lord High Chancellor for Scotland in 1702, was by political inclination Whiggish, but needed to win the support of the 'High-Church party' in the 1703 session. Accordingly he used his patronage to secure the office of Lord Privy Seal for Tullibardine (born John Murray) who had changed his political allegiances from Whig to out-and-out Jacobite. The Whig/Presbyterian party in the Parliament was at odds with the government in London over matters of religious conformity, the succession (the queen, Anne, being childless) and the very issue of the sovereignty of the Edinburgh Parliament *vis-à-vis* Westminster. As the novel's account of events suggests, political plotting and counter-plotting extended well beyond Parliament itself: when word reaches the Reverend Wringhim of Robert's imprisonment (p. 20), he is at dinner with the Marquis of Annandale, then Lord President of the Privy Council; and we have earlier been told that Mr Wringhim is cultivated by the Duke of Argyll, the most powerful member of the Whig aristocracy in Scotland.

In this way, then, Hogg enmeshes the fictional material of the novel in the real historical details of religious and political division, just as he enmeshes it in the real geography of Edinburgh and the Borders, as explained in some of the notes at the end of the text. He also, of course, enmeshes it in the doctrines of the Reformers, and it is to a clarification of this issue that the last contextual part of this Introduction will be given over.

Scottish Presbyterianism was not a single, uniform movement, any more than English Puritanism was. It had from the beginning encompassed different degrees of religious militancy and different degrees of pragmatism. Moderates had been happy with a limited form of episcopy and had been prepared to go along with the Stuarts' proposed reforms in the seventeenth century: not all Presbyterians – not even a majority – were Covenanters and saints ready for martyrdom. Theologically too there were moderates and extremists. *Confessions* takes us into the heart of the most extreme form of Calvinist faith; and the positions adopted by and opposed to this form of Calvinism are central to the novel. As it goes on, the nature of these beliefs is rehearsed often enough to become reasonably clear; but some brief explanation at the outset may help.

Two principal and related doctrines are prominent in the novel: the idea of justification by faith, and the doctrine of the absolute predestination and infallibility of the elect. The novel's title throws 'justified' at the reader in a way that is intentionally disconcerting, inviting us to see simultaneously what might ordinarily be meant by the phrase 'justified sinner' – in which 'justified' would mean 'vindicated by circumstances' – and what the term signifies in the technical language of Calvinist theology. Here 'justified' means, in effect, 'cleansed of sin and made just through grace'. Like much of Calvinist theology, the idea of justification through faith derives from St Paul's Epistles, here particularly the early chapters of Romans. The argument presupposes that no number of good works can qualify man to enter the Kingdom of Heaven, because the stain of original, endemic sinfulness cannot be eradicated by man's pitiable endeavours at moral 'goodness'. Rather, that stain can be undone only through Christ's absolute freedom from sin and his sacrifice of himself for the salvation of mankind, his free gift of grace. Men must be 'justified' in and through Christ by trusting absolutely in him and in his life, death and resurrection; and here Paul, in a way that is echoed by Wringhim and Robert in the novel, identifies a standard link between the 'promise' made by God to Abraham in the Old Testament and Christ's promise to man:

> For the promise, that he should be the heir of the world, was not to Abraham, or to his seed, through the law, but through the righteousness of faith. For if they which are of the law be heirs, faith is made void, and the promise made to none effect . . . Therefore it is of faith, that it might be by grace; to the end the promise might be sure to all the seed . . .
>
> [Romans 4:13–16]

Taken to one conclusion, this results, as it does for Robert in *Confessions*, in a profound contempt for all Christian teaching that urges moral 'works', as this is seen to be based on a fatuous theological fallacy, implying that man can seek to achieve grace through the pursuit of moral righteousness rather than 'the right-eousness of faith'. In a text which Robert himself quotes (see p. 78 and Note 90), man's good deeds are seen merely 'as filthy rags'.

In the Book of Revelation, St John sees the beast which, he is told, 'shall ascend out of the bottomless pit, and go into perdition: and they that dwell on the earth shall wonder, whose names were not written in the book of life from the foundation of the world' (17:8). It is one of several references in Revelation to the Lamb's 'book of life'; and Robert in his memoirs (see p. 79 and Note 94) recalls this powerful image of the idea of predestination, whereby it is proposed that those who will be saved are an elect established from the moment of Creation by eternal and unalterable decree. Of the various forms of this idea that exist in Christian theology, the doctrine adopted by the extreme Calvinism practised by Wringhim in the novel is the most rigorous. It proposes that God has predetermined from eternity whom he will save and whom he will damn, regardless of their love, merit, goodness or vileness in life. This, in a sense, takes the idea of justification by faith a step further: here faith is not just faith in Christ's grace generally, but is a specific faith in the certainty of one's own justification through it. Once one has arrived at that faith, by whatever means of assurance, one joins an 'elect' whose spiritual destiny cannot be altered, 'the society of the just made perfect' (p. 79 and Note 92). These are, literally, God's chosen, and the analogy with God's 'promise' to Abraham and the 'covenant' with the Israelites is emphasised by language used in *Confessions* by characters who think of themselves as being of the elect. For Robert, the assurance of his election is followed immediately by his first meeting with the mysterious Gil-Martin (pp. 80–1).

Furthermore, taken to one logical conclusion, this assurance frees the elect from any adherence to morality or to the laws laid down by kings or by society. The seeds of this can again be detected in St Paul's Epistle to the Romans – 'Who shall lay any thing to the charge of God's elect? It is God that justifieth' (8:33). In *Confessions* this idea – sometimes called 'antinomianism' – is present from the earliest pages. 'How delightful,' the Editor reports Lady Dalcastle as saying (p. 11), 'to think that a justified person can do no wrong. Who would not envy the liberty wherewith we are made free?' The reader is likewise free to infer that this 'liberty' facilitates an adulterous liaison between her and Mr Wringhim, of which Robert is the result. In Robert's memoirs, the infallibility of the elect is a constant dilemma for him as he wrestles with his sinister mentor, Gil-Martin. On their first meeting (p. 80) and again on their second (pp. 84–5) the absolute nature of predestination and therefore of infallibility is insisted upon by Gil-Martin. Robert, however, anxiously calls infallibility 'the least tangible of all Christian tenets' (p. 101) as he ponders Gil-Martin's murderous promptings, and he constantly experiences pangs of doubt about this for which he then is reproved and reproves himself.

In this context, the phrase 'justified sinner' is a complex play of different meanings created by the specificity of the term 'justified' to Calvinist theology and the complex relationship between different ideas of 'justification' and different ideas of 'sin'. Between Robert's use of the phrase on the title page of his memoirs in 1712 (see p. 175) and the Editor's reuse of it on the title page of his publication in 1824, it has accumulated layers of historical dust and dark irony, which the Editor has considered deflecting by changing 'justified' to 'self-justified'. This change, however, has been vetoed, he tells us, by his booksellers – as well as by Robert himself, rising from his grave with the threat of a curse (see Note 160) on textual meddlers.

2

The general tendency of the foregoing pages, by locating *Confessions* in the history, geography and controversies of the Scotland in which it is set, has been to foreground the novel's status as a historical novel, different from but comparable to Scott's work of the same period. However, when we begin to scrutinise *Confessions* closely, something about this doesn't quite work, and the final direction of the novel has recently been seen rather as attempting 'to deconstruct the great institution of the Romantic social-historical novel' (Kelly, p. 252) as practised by Scott.

The problems with the authority of 'history' begin in the detail. The Editor, during the very brief part of his narrative in paragraph one which is based on historical records rather than 'tradition', asserts that the Old Laird came into the Dalcastle estate in 1687: his marriage, we can take it, followed shortly after. Robert, the second son of Lady Dalcastle – although not necessarily of the marriage – is born a year after his elder brother (p. 14); but then Robert is positive in his memoirs that he meets Gil-Martin first on 25 March 1704 'when [he] had just entered into the eighteenth year of [his] age'. If Robert's seventeenth birthday is in early 1704, he must have been born in 1687 – two years before he can possibly have come into the world by the chronology of the Editor's narrative. There is then the matter of his being present with Gil-Martin at events in Edinburgh surrounding the parliamentary session of 1703, although the date given in court as the date of young George's death – 28 February 1705 – tends to chime with Robert's 1704 date.

We shouldn't rush into accusing Hogg of sloppy cross-checking here, although it's tempting. No author is so sloppy as to make eight plus five make twelve, as they do on p. 10. Hogg is being disruptive and disconcerting, as he is in the character he creates for himself when he appears in Thirlestane market in the Editor's resumed narrative (p. 171). That disruptiveness is deeply laid: Hogg went to the trouble of really publishing the year before *Confessions* the hoaxing letter in *Blackwood's Magazine* which stirs the Editor's interest and which he reprints in part (pp. 167–70). The Editor then, having been blanked by his creator's *alter ego*, Hogg the grumpy sheep-seller, at Thirlestane, finds what appears to be the grave described in Hogg's letter at a different site, containing a body which does not correspond to that described. The previous precise-ness of the novel's geography becomes blurred as well; reports clash;

witnesses disagree; the written record leaves us destabilised and uncertain.[3] Authorship itself, as in some of the work of Edgar Allen Poe, is a shadowy game of masking and hoaxing.

We can see both the elusiveness of the novel's chronology and the doubtful provenance of the exhumation that provides Robert's memoirs as reinforcements of the darker spiritual disruptions that lie at the novel's heart. At first glance the appearance of the devil (if it is he) to 'claim' Robert at the very moment of his assurance of election belongs to the narrative idiom of anti-Calvinist allegory. In the implied perversities of Christian teaching which are perpetuated in Wringhim's theology, what is proclaimed to be the assurance of salvation is in fact the assurance of its opposite – it betrays the 'justified' straight into the clutches of 'Auld Simmie' himself. While this idea underpins Hogg's novel, with its savage probing of Calvinist presumption, around it is conducted an extraordinary *tour de force*. Gil-Martin is not the cloven-hoofed intruder of Penpunt's Auchtermuchty story, with attendant talking corbies, who 'dart[s] into the air like a fiery dragon' (p. 140). That story itself serves to reinforce the difference between the 'de'il' of Scottish popular myth and the urbane, subtle, turbaned shape-shifter who stalks Robert across the townscapes and landscapes of southern Scotland in his own story. In popular story the de'il is known, spotted and sent packing by the shrewd, proletarian common-sense of Robin Ruthven and ever after guarded against in the folk-wisdom of the community, looking out always for 'the cloven foot peeping out frae aneath ilka sentence'. In Hogg's novel, however, the devil cannot be thus anticipated and known – although it is still the shrewd, vernacular, proletarian characters like Penpunt and Johnny Dods who are more likely to intuit his presence. Rather, he is Peter the Great; he is Mr Blanchard; he is Drummond; he *is* young George – 'Oh, it is he! It is he!' shriek Mrs Logan and the landlady in unison years after George's death (p. 60); he is anyone and everyone; he is Robert himself.

This has repercussions for the novel in two ways. One lies in the disruptions to normal narrative assumptions and procedures caused by Gil-Martin's play with appearance and identity. The other is in the way in which Hogg, by making the experience of the satanic

---

3 For further detailed discussion of the exhumation and its implications for the novel, see Michael York Mason, 'The Three Burials in Hogg's *Justified Sinner*', *Studies in Scottish Literature*, Vol.13, 1978, pp. 15-23.

excruciatingly solitary and subjective, takes his study into the blurred area between demonology and psychological disorder.

Both of these disruptions are rooted in the breakdown of everyday assumptions about the relationship between 'the self' and 'the other'. 'You think I am your brother, or that I am your second self,' are Gil-Martin's first words to Robert (p. 81), reading his thoughts. Both are true. Increasingly, after the death of George, it is as Robert's brother that Gil-Martin will appear to others – to Bell Calvert and Miss Logan, to Mrs Keeler and Lawyer Linkum (p. 123), to Robert himself (p. 130). Robert, meanwhile, appears to have lost conscious assurance of the coherence and stability of 'himself' – lending a sinister irony in the longer perspective to the appearance of the phrase 'written by himself' on his memoirs' and the novel's title-pages. For several weeks in Edinburgh, which the Editor has reported as a period during which George was perpetually and inexplicably haunted by Robert, Robert reports that he himself was bedridden, 'seized with a strange distemper':

> I generally conceived myself to be two people. When I lay in bed, I deemed there were two of us in it; when I sat up I always beheld another person, and always in the same position from the place where I sat or stood, which was about three paces off me towards my left side. It mattered not how many or how few were present: this my second self was sure to be present in his place . . . [O]ver the singular delusion that I was two persons my reasoning faculties had no power. The most perverse part of it was that I rarely conceived *myself* to be any of the two persons. I thought for the most part that my companion was one of them, and my brother the other; and I found that, to be obliged to speak and answer in the character of another man, was a most awkward business at the long run.   [p. 106]

Here recurs the phrase 'second self' which Gil-Martin first used: we also notice the problematic adjustment between 'self' and 'person' in the passage, and the pressure this places on the use of the first personal singular pronoun. Because the Editor has told us in his narrative of the dark drama of constant proximity between Robert's brother and the figure of Robert himself during this period, we are drawn to see here some mysterious coalescence between those events being acted out across the streets and closes of Edinburgh by Gil-Martin in the guise of Robert and Robert's interior experience in which he is and is not 'himself' acting an unstable part or parts in a haunting of his bedchamber. It is also, interestingly, the first of a number of instances in the novel of Robert 'sharing' a bed with another – always male – presence, episodes almost always marked by disturbance and disorientation.[4]

Subsequently the 'second self' theory will be revived by Robert as he becomes increasingly prone to long periods of memory blackout during which he is reported as having committed various atrocities. The first instance occurs when, flanked by Mrs Keeler and his companion, both confirming his rape of the former's daughter, he exclaims, 'It is impossible that I can have been doing a thing and not doing it at the same time,' but admits that earlier incidents 'persuade me I have a second self; or that there is some other being who appears in my likeness' (p. 122). Later, after a longer period during which he is reported to have murdered Mrs Keeler's daughter and his own mother – deeds again confirmed by the gravely reproachful Gil-Martin – Robert voices the conclusion that he has 'two souls, which take possession of my bodily frame by turns, the one being all unconscious of what the other performs' (p. 132).

Modern clinical psychology has, of course, its own frameworks within which to account for such disorders of the self, and David Punter, among others, is prepared to describe the novel as 'a detailed . . . account of schizophrenia' (Punter, p. 149). Certainly, as readers brought up in a culture in part shaped by the secularisation and clinicisation of mental disorder, we find ourselves disturbingly torn between the compelling, almost 'modern' authenticity of Robert's psychological testimony on the one hand, and on the other the actualisation of the demonic in the novel through Gil-Martin and, in the novel's final stages, the cacophony of unearthly manifestations that dog Robert's last, ghastly wanderings towards the site of his suicide. *Confessions* does not offer us a 'modern' case-study in which the mind contains in itself all of its own demons. Gil-Martin can stroll coolly into Mr Watson's printing house in green hunting coat and turban, and crimson-pawed fiends can bicker and clamour all night across the roof of Tam Douglas's Ancrum cottage about possession of Robert's soul.

Also, as the basis of identity is queried and conventional notions of similarity and difference uprooted, narrative itself begins to fall apart and lose its ability to construct accounts of events. Multiple identity is at the disrupted centre of Robert's spiritual experiences and also at the disrupted centre of Hogg's multi-narrated novel. In

4 This is discussed further in relation to the sexual and misogynistic themes of the novel by Eve Kosovsky Sedwick. See Select Bibliography.

this process of shape-changing, Hogg is the author; he is the Editor; he is Robert; he is a contributor of letters to *Blackwood's*; he is a rustic market-trader preoccupied with 'paulies' and 'yowes'. This contending plurality of authorial identities frames Gil-Martin's and is similarly elusive.

It can be seen how, in the passage from Robert's memoirs which was quoted above on p. XVIX, narrative language itself begins to falter as relationships between self and other, and self and self, dip below the horizon of what passes for 'normality'. We hear in the novel also how Calvinist discourse, feeding always on the Old Testament prophets and the Epistles of Paul, deploys biblical metaphor to relocate statements about the self and individual action, instantly recycling the present into a kind of Third Testament validated by the vast mechanism of biblical foreshadowing. In passages of Robert's memoirs metaphor and actuality can blur: the idiom of his reporting constructs a myth of his life which takes precedence over 'reality' – or what passes for reality in the Editor's 1820s mindset. Hogg uses the various testimonies about the night of George's murder to exemplify some of these perplexities. Different 'witnesses' coming forward at various times in the novel demonstrate some of the subjectivity and some of the self-interest that attend upon witnessing. Last to testify is Robert himself:

> The duel was fierce, but the might of Heaven prevailed, and not my might. The ungodly and reprobate young man fell covered with wounds, and with curses and blasphemy in his mouth, while I escaped uninjured. Thereto his power extended not.   [p. 118]

Then he adds:

> I will not deny that my own immediate impressions of this affair in some degree differed from this statement. But this is precisely as my illustrious friend described it to me afterwards, and I can rely implicitly on his information, as he was at that time a looker-on, and my senses all in a state of agitation . . .

Apart from the grim comedy of Robert's naïvety and self-delusion, this moment reminds us trenchantly of the extent to which uncertainties and competing agendas intrude themselves between the moment of experience and the moment of narration, placing the narrating self in a negotiable, unsteady relationship with the experiencing self. In less bizarre ways, the testimonies of Bell Calvert and her erstwhile partner concerning the events of that night have also been hijacked, delayed and coloured by preoccupation and self-interest.

Hogg thus dramatises the elusiveness of 'the truth' in the world of the novel in a number of ways. One is simply through exposing the editorial efforts of 1820s man, seeking to explicate and endeavouring to sustain a sort of commonsensical, pragmatic approach to writing history. Happy to let tradition and hearsay substitute for historical records, and equally happy to construct detailed conversations at which no one but the long-dead interlocutors could possibly have been present, the Editor colours his narrative with his own agendas. He is entrenchedly hostile to Calvinism, being, as he is, in favour of what he calls 'nature, utility, and common sense' (p. 10). He is also in favour of what one might today call 'guy stuff' (male clubbishness, drinking, sexual licence and sports) and so views with hostility and incomprehension Robert's determined disruptions of these activities. He is against all modes of irrationality; he in favour of 'modernity' and wary of all kinds of intellectual rigour. In all of this, perhaps because of his lack of intellectual rigour, the Editor appears strangely, perhaps culpably innocent of the problems that his own methods raise.

It is, however, through the attempts to establish legal certainty in the world of *Confessions* that Hogg most trenchantly exposes the gulf between the assumptions on which narrative and even civil order are predicated and the more swirling, disturbing world that individuals in the novel occupy. Here especially the devilish play with similarity, difference and identity exposes the fragile nature of those assumptions. Establishing 'the truth' is hard enough for the authorities amid the volatile factionalism of Scotland's capital in the autumn of 1703. Whigs accuse Cavaliers; Cavaliers accuse Whigs; windows are broken; gangs surge up and down the High Street and adjacent closes, forming and reforming, until the political identities of the mobs become muddled and merge (like Robert's and Gil-Martin's). Lord Queensbury convenes a hurried court which is 'completely puzzled' until it manages to work out that 'a few gentlemen, two-thirds of whom were strenuous Whigs themselves, had joined in mauling the whole Whig population of Edinburgh' (p. 23).

A more grave example of judicial bamboozlement occurs, however, when Drummond is falsely convicted of George's murder in a case of mistaken identity conjured up by Gil-Martin, although not so perfectly conjured that Bell Calvert's testimony might not have saved Drummond had it not been suppressed. Identity in the world of the novel is an especially uncertain proof; but on what else can legal process found its own narratives? Bell is then herself the beneficiary of a courtroom dispute which brilliantly reinforces the disruptive force of interrupted identity. The identity in question, however, is not now that of an individual but that of a set of inanimate objects.

Bessy Gillies is called to the bar to identify the goods stolen from Arabella Logan by (it is alleged) Bell Calvert and her male accomplice (p. 47). There are silver spoons and clothes. These are laid out as exhibits in the courtroom, having been found in possession of the accused. If they can be identified as the same goods as were removed by theft from Bell Calvert's house, then the narrative link can be completed whereby it can be stated beyond reasonable doubt that the accused carried out the robbery. They are, Bessy agrees, spoons 'very like' those that were stolen, and a dress is 'very like' her mistress's. But they are also 'very like' other spoons and other dresses. To the frustration of the (anglophone) questioner, the (vernacular) Bessy declines, therefore, to state that they are the same items as were previously in her mistress's possession. Similarity of appearance, she says, is not a signifier of continuity of identity: 'Like is an ill mark' (p. 49). The case collapses.

Perhaps Bessy Gillies is wasted in service and ought to be doing a degree in philosophy. Although her stubborn, counter-intuitive stance is in one sense a 'fix' designed to exonerate Bell Calvert on a legal technicality, on the other it is strikingly apt in a novel where like is indeed 'an ill mark'. Wringhim thinks he is 'like' Melchisedec, but Barnet thinks he is more 'like' the Pharisee in the Temple (p. 72) – biblical comparisons can point to contested likenesses too. More strangely, Gil-Martin can be 'like' anyone he chooses, but is not those persons, nor they he, a fact unacknowledged in the construction of legal narrative of the kind that determines judicial conviction. The law, like Hogg's Editor, and like historiography itself, needs to occupy a space where 'common-sense' assumptions are not so radically undermined: otherwise law's and history's attempts to make sense of – to 'edit' – the world are destined to collapse. Bessy's scepticism is in this context obstructive and perverse, like, in its different way, Robert's behaviour at the tennis-match: tennis and legal fiction are both kinds of play. In this context too Robert's memoirs tell of events that appear inexplicable: such things cannot happen, and so cannot have happened. The Editor's eagerness to embrace modern comforts and textual strategies – his 'hand-me-down Enlightenment rationalism' (Kelly, p. 272) – leaves him none the less exposed and uncertain. He acknowledges that Robert's memoirs must seem like an allegory or parable, but admits that he 'cannot tell' (p. 167). The Editor will never end up like Robert, half-mad and hanging strangled on a hayrick; but nor will he – or, it is to be hoped, we – ever test the limits of experience as Robert has. Historical distance and cultural progress – if that is what has happened in the intervening century – will not themselves guarantee this, however; and the recognisable landscapes and townscapes of the Scotland of the novel meanwhile remind us of the continuity of place that naggingly connects the present to the past. At the heart of Robert's confession lies a set of possibilities that, like his corpse, will not moulder away conventionally because they have been more than a hundred years buried in the landscape. The Scottish soil curiously preserves both body and text, and both decline to make themselves amenable to editorial or any other kind of 'authority'.

DAVID BLAIR
University of Kent at Canterbury

SELECT BIBLIOGRAPHY

David Groves, *James Hogg: The Growth of a Writer*, Edinburgh University Press, 1988

Gary Kelly, *English Fiction of the Romantic Period 1789–1830*, Longman, 1989 (Chapter 7)

Robert Kiely, *The Romantic Novel in England*, Harvard University Press, 1972 (Chapter xi)

Emma Letley, *From Galt to Douglas Brown: Nineteenth-Century Fiction and Scots Language*, Scottish Academic Press, 1988 (Chapter 1)

Susan M. Levin, *The Romantic Art of Confession*, Camden House, 1998 (Chapter 6)

David Punter, *The Literature of Terror: A History of Gothic Fictions from 1765 to the Present Day*, Longman, 1980; revised 1996 as Vol. I (of two volumes) of *The Literature of Terror: The Gothic Tradition* (Chapter 5)

Eve Kosovsky Sedgwick, *Between Men: English Literature and Male Homosocial Desire*, Columbia University Press, 1985 (Chapter 6); reprinted as 'Murder Incorporated: *Confessions of a Justified Sinner*', in Duncan Wu (ed.), *Romanticism: A Critical Reader*, Blackwell, 1995, pp. 359–78

Louis Simpson, *James Hogg: A Critical Study*, Oliver & Boyd, 1962

Jeremy Tambling: *Confession: Sexuality, Sin , the Subject*, Manchester University Press, 1990 (Chapter 5)

Nicola Watson, *Revolution and the Form of the British Novel 1790–1825: Intercepted Letters, Interrupted Seductions*, Oxford University Press, 1994 (Chapter 4)

THE PRIVATE MEMOIRS
AND CONFESSIONS OF A
JUSTIFIED SINNER

The Editor's Narrative

It APPEARS from tradition, as well as some parish registers still extant, that the lands of Dalcastle (or Dalchastel, as it is often spelled) were possessed by a family of the name of Colwan, about one hundred and fifty years ago, and for at least a century previous to that period. That family was supposed to have been a branch of the ancient family of Colquhoun, and it is certain that from it spring the Cowans that spread towards the Border. I find that, in the year 1687, George Colwan succeeded his uncle of the same name, in the lands of Dalchastel and Balgrennan; and, this being all I can gather of the family from history, to tradition I must appeal for the remainder of the motley adventures of that house. But, of the matter furnished by the latter of these powerful monitors, I have no reason to complain: it has been handed down to the world in unlimited abundance; and I am certain that, in recording the hideous events which follow, I am only relating to the greater part of the inhabitants of at least four counties of Scotland matters of which they were before perfectly well informed.

This George was a rich man, or supposed to be so, and was married, when considerably advanced in life, to the sole heiress and reputed[1] daughter of a Baillie[2] Orde, of Glasgow. This proved a conjunction anything but agreeable to the parties contracting. It is well known that the Reformation principles had long before that time taken a powerful hold of the hearts and affections of the people of Scotland, although the feeling was by no means general, or in equal degrees; and it so happened that this married couple felt completely at variance on the subject. Granting it to have been so, one would have thought that the laird, owing to his retiring situation, would have been the one that inclined to the stern doctrines of the reformers; and that the young and gay dame from the city would have adhered to the free principles cherished by the court party, and indulged in rather to extremity, in opposition to their severe and carping contemporaries.

The contrary, however, happened to be the case. The laird was what his country neighbours called 'a droll, careless chap', with a very limited proportion of the fear of God in his heart, and very nearly as little of the fear of man. The laird had not intentionally wronged or offended either of the parties,[3] and perceived not the necessity of deprecating their vengeance. He had hitherto believed that he was living in most cordial terms with the greater part of the inhabitants of the earth, and with the powers above in particular: but woe be unto him if he was not soon convinced of the fallacy of such damning security! for his lady was the most severe and gloomy of all bigots to the principles of the Reformation. Hers were not the tenets of the great reformers, but theirs mightily overstrained and deformed. Theirs was an unguent hard to be swallowed; but hers was that unguent embittered and overheated until nature could not longer bear it. She had imbibed her ideas from the doctrines of one flaming predestinarian divine alone; and these were so rigid that they became a stumbling block to many of his brethren, and a mighty handle for the enemies of his party to turn the machine of the state against them.

The wedding festivities at Dalcastle partook of all the gaiety, not of that stern age, but of one previous to it. There was feasting, dancing, piping, and singing: the liquors were handed around in great fullness, the ale in large wooden bickers,[4] and the brandy in capacious horns of oxen. The laird gave full scope to his homely glee. He danced – he snapped his fingers to the music – clapped his hands and shouted at the turn of the tune. He saluted[5] every girl in the hall whose appearance was anything tolerable, and requested of their sweethearts to take the same freedom with his bride, by way of retaliation. But there she sat at the head of the hall in still and blooming beauty, absolutely refusing to tread a single measure with any gentleman there. The only enjoyment in which she appeared to partake was in now and then stealing a word of sweet conversation with her favourite pastor about divine things; for he had accompanied her home after marrying her to her husband, to see her fairly settled in her new dwelling. He addressed her several times by her new name, Mrs Colwan; but she turned away her head disgusted, and looked with pity and contempt towards the old inadvertent sinner, capering away in the height of his unregenerated mirth. The minister perceived the workings of her pious mind, and thence forward addressed her by the courteous title of Lady Dalcastle, which sounded somewhat better, as not coupling her name with one of the wicked: and there is too great reason to believe that, for all the solemn vows she had come under, and these were of no ordinary binding, particularly on the laird's part, she at that time despised, if not abhorred him, in her heart.

The good parson again blessed her, and went away. She took leave of him with tears in her eyes, entreating him often to visit her in that heathen land of the Amorite, the Hittite, and the Girgashite:[6] to which he assented, on many solemn and qualifying conditions – and then the comely bride retired to her chamber to pray.

It was customary, in those days, for the bride's-man and maiden, and a few select friends, to visit the new-married couple after they had retired to rest, and drink a cup to their healths, their happiness, and a numerous posterity. But the laird delighted not in this: he wished to have his jewel to himself; and, slipping away quietly from his jovial party, he retired to his chamber to his beloved, and bolted the door. He found her engaged with the writings of the Evangelists,[7] and terribly demure. The laird went up to caress her; but she turned away her head, and spoke of the follies of aged men, and something of the broad way that leadeth to destruction.[8] The laird did not thoroughly comprehend this allusion; but being considerably flustered by drinking, and disposed to take all in good part, he only remarked, as he took off his shoes and stockings, that, 'whether the way was broad or narrow, it was time that they were in their bed.'

'Sure, Mr Colwan, you won't go to bed tonight, at such an important period of your life, without first saying prayers for yourself and me.'

When she said this, the laird had his head down almost to the ground, loosing his shoe-buckle; but when he heard of *prayers*, on such a night, he raised his face suddenly up, which was all over as flushed and red as a rose, and answered: 'Prayers, mistress! Lord help your crazed head, is this a night for prayers?'

He had better have held his peace. There was such a torrent of profound divinity poured out upon him that the laird became ashamed, both of himself and his new-made spouse, and wist not what to say: but the brandy helped him out.

'It strikes me, my dear, that religious devotion would be somewhat out of place tonight,' said he. 'Allowing that it is ever so beautiful, and ever so beneficial, were we to ride on the rigging of it at all times, would we not be constantly making a farce of it: it would be like reading the Bible and the jest-book, verse about, and would render the life of man a medley of absurdity and confusion.'

But, against the cant of the bigot or the hypocrite, no reasoning can aught avail. If you would argue until the end of life, the infallible creature must alone be right. So it proved with the laird. One Scripture text followed another, not in the least connected, and one sentence of the profound Mr Wringhim's sermons after another, proving the duty of family worship, till the laird lost patience, and, tossing himself into bed, said carelessly that he would leave that duty upon her shoulders for one night.

The meek mind of Lady Dalcastle was somewhat disarranged by this sudden evolution. She felt that she was left rather in an awkward situation. However, to show her unconscionable spouse that she was resolved to hold fast her integrity, she kneeled down and prayed in terms so potent that she deemed she was sure of making an impression on him. She did so; for in a short time the laird began to utter a response so fervent that she was utterly astounded, and fairly driven from the chain of her orisons. He began, in truth, to sound a nasal bugle[9] of no ordinary calibre – the notes being little inferior to those of a military trumpet. The lady tried to proceed, but every returning note from the bed burst on her ear with a louder twang, and a longer peal, till the concord of sweet sounds became so truly pathetic that the meek spirit of the dame was quite overcome; and, after shedding a flood of tears, she arose from her knees, and retired to the chimney-corner with her Bible in her lap, there to spend the hours in holy meditation till such time as the inebriated trumpeter should awaken to a sense of propriety.

The laird did not awake in any reasonable time; for, he being overcome with fatigue and wassail, his sleep became sounder, and his Morphean measures[10] more intense. These varied a little in their structure; but the general run of the bars sounded something in this way: 'Hic-hoc-wheew!' It was most profoundly ludicrous; and could not have missed exciting risibility in anyone save a pious, a disappointed, and humbled bride.

The good dame wept bitterly. She could not for her life go and awaken the monster, and request him to make room for her: but she retired somewhere, for the laird, on awaking next morning, found that he was still lying alone. His sleep had been of the deepest and most genuine sort; and, all the time that it lasted, he had never once thought of either wives, children, or sweethearts, save in the way of dreaming about them; but, as his spirit began again by slow degrees to verge towards the boundaries of reason, it became lighter and more buoyant from the effects of deep repose, and his dreams partook of that buoyancy, yea, to a degree hardly expressible. He dreamed of the reel, the jig, the strathspey, and the corant;[11] and the elasticity of his frame was such that he was bounding over the heads of maidens, and making his feet skimmer[12] against the ceiling, enjoying, the while, the most ecstatic emotions. These grew too fervent for the shackles of the drowsy god[13] to restrain. The nasal bugle ceased its prolonged sounds in one moment, and a sort of hectic laugh took its place. 'Keep it going – play up, you devils!' cried the laird,[14] without changing his position on the pillow. But this exertion to hold the fiddlers at their work fairly awakened the delighted dreamer, and, though he could not refrain from continuing his laugh, he at length, by tracing out a regular chain of facts, came to be sensible of his real situation. 'Rabina, where are you? What's become of you, my dear?' cried the laird. But there was no voice nor anyone that answered or regarded. He flung open the curtains, thinking to find her still on her knees, as he had seen her, but she was not there, either sleeping or waking. 'Rabina! Mrs Colwan!' shouted he, as loud as he could call, and then added in the same breath, 'God save the king – I have lost my wife!'

He sprung up and opened the casement: the daylight was beginning to streak the east, for it was spring, and the nights were short, and the mornings very long. The laird half dressed himself in an instant, and strode through every room in the house, opening the windows as he went, and scrutinising every bed and every corner. He came into the hall where the wedding festival had been held; and as he opened the various window-boards, loving couples flew off like hares surprised too late in the morning among the early braird.[15] 'Hoo-boo! Fie, be frightened!' cried the laird. 'Fie, rin like fools, as if ye were caught in an ill-turn!' His bride was not among them; so he was obliged to betake himself to further search. 'She will be praying in some corner, poor woman,' said he to himself. 'It is an unlucky thing this praying. But, for my part, I fear I have behaved very ill; and I must endeavour to make amends.' The laird continued his search, and at length found his beloved in the same bed with her Glasgow cousin who had acted as bridesmaid. 'You sly and malevolent imp,' said the laird; 'you have played me such a trick when I was fast asleep! I have not known a frolic so clever, and, at the same time, so severe. Come along, you baggage you!'

'Sir, I will let you know that I detest your principles and your person alike,' said she. 'It shall never be said, sir, that my person was at the control of a heathenish man of Belial[16] – a dangler among the daughters of women – a promiscuous dancer – and a player of unlawful games. Forgo your rudeness, sir, I say, and depart away from my presence and that of my kinswoman.'

'Come along, I say, my charming Rab. If you were the pink of all puritans, and the saint of all saints, you are my wife, and must do as I command you.'

'Sir, I will sooner lay down my life than be subjected to your godless will; therefore I say, desist, and begone with you.'

But the laird regarded none of these testy sayings: he rolled her in a blanket, and bore her triumphantly away to his chamber, taking care to keep a fold or two of the blanket always rather near to her mouth, in case of any outrageous forthcoming of noise.

The next day at breakfast the bride was long in making her appearance. Her maid asked to see her; but George did not choose that anybody should see her but himself: he paid her several visits, and always turned the key as he came out. At length breakfast was served; and during the time of refreshment the laird tried to break several jokes; but it was remarked that they wanted their accustomed brilliancy, and that his nose was particularly red at the top.

Matters, without all doubt, had been very bad between the newmarried couple; for in the course of the day the lady deserted her quarters, and returned to her father's house in Glasgow, after having been a night on the road; stage-coaches and steamboats having then no existence in that quarter. Though Baillie Orde had acquiesced in his wife's asseveration regarding the likeness of their only daughter to her father, he never loved or admired her greatly; therefore this behaviour nothing astounded him. He questioned her strictly as to the grievous offence committed against her, and could discover nothing that warranted a procedure so fraught with disagreeable consequences. So, after mature deliberation, the baillie addressed her as follows:

'Aye, aye, Raby! An' sae I find that Dalcastle has actually refused to say prayers with you when you ordered him; an' has guidit[17] you in a rude indelicate manner, outstepping the respect due to my daughter – as my daughter. But, wi' regard to what is due to his own wife, of that he's a better judge nor me. However, since he has behaved in that manner to *my daughter*, I shall be revenged on him for aince; for I shall return the obligation to ane nearer to him: that is, I shall take pennyworths of[18] his wife – an' let him lick at that.'

'What do you mean, sir?' said the astonished damsel.

'I mean to be revenged on that villain Dalcastle,' said he, 'for what he has done to my daughter. Come hither, Mrs Colwan, you shall pay for this.'

So saying, the baillie began to inflict corporal punishment on the runaway wife. His strokes were not indeed very deadly, but he made a mighty flourish in the infliction, pretending to be in a great rage only at the Laird of Dalcastle. 'Villain that he is!' exclaimed he, 'I shall teach him to behave in such a manner to a child of mine, be she as she may; since I cannot get at himself, I shall lounder[19] her that is nearest to him in life. Take you that and that, Mrs Colwan, for your husband's impertinence!'

The poor afflicted woman wept and prayed, but the baillie would not abate aught of his severity. After fuming, and beating her with many stripes, far drawn, and lightly laid down, he took her up to her chamber, five stories high, locked her in, and there he fed her on bread and water, all to be revenged on the presumptuous Laird of Dalcastle; but ever and anon, as the baillie came down the stair from carrying his daughter's meal, he said to himself: 'I shall make the sight of the laird the blithest she ever saw in her life.'

Lady Dalcastle got plenty of time to read, and pray, and meditate; but she was at a great loss for one to dispute with about religious tenets; for she found that, without this advantage, about which there was a perfect rage at that time, the reading and learning of Scripture texts, and sentences of intricate doctrine, availed her naught; so she was often driven to sit at her casement and look out for the approach of the heathenish Laird of Dalcastle.

That hero, after a considerable lapse of time, at length made his appearance. Matters were not hard to adjust; for his lady found that there was no refuge for her in her father's house; and so, after some sighs and tears, she accompanied her husband home. For all that had passed, things went on no better. She *would* convert the laird in spite of his teeth: the laird would not be converted. She *would* have the laird to say family prayers, both morning and evening: the laird would neither pray morning nor evening. He would not even sing psalms, and kneel beside her while she performed the exercise; neither would he converse at all times, and in all places, about the sacred mysteries of religion, although his lady took occasion to contradict flatly every assertion that he made, in order that she might spiritualize him by drawing him into argument.

The laird kept his temper a long while, but at length his patience wore out; he cut her short in all her futile attempts at spiritualisation, and mocked at her wire-drawn[20] degrees of faith, hope, and repentance. He also dared to doubt of the great standard doctrine of absolute predestination, which put the crown on the lady's Christian resentment. She declared her helpmate to be a limb of Antichrist,[21] and one with whom no regenerated person could associate. She therefore bespoke a separate establishment, and, before the expiry of the first six months, the arrangements of the separation were amicably adjusted. The upper, or third, storey of the old mansion- house was awarded to the lady for her residence.

She had a separate door, a separate stair, a separate garden, and walks that in no instance intersected the laird's; so that one would have thought the separation complete. They had each their own parties, selected from their own sort of people; and, though the laird never once chafed himself about the lady's companies, it was not long before she began to intermeddle about some of his.

'Who is that fat bouncing dame that visits the laird so often and always by herself?' said she to her maid Martha one day.

'Oh dear, mem, how can I ken? We're banished frae our acquaintances here, as weel as frae the sweet gospel ordinances.'

'Find me out who that jolly dame is, Martha. You, who hold communion with the household of this ungodly man, can be at no loss to attain this information. I observe that she always casts her eye up toward our windows, both in coming and going; and I suspect that she seldom departs from the house empty-handed.'

That same evening Martha came with the information that this august visitor was a Miss Logan, an old an intimate acquaintance of the laird's, and a very worthy respectable lady, of good connections, whose parents had lost their patrimony in the civil wars.

'Ha! very well!' said the lady; 'very well, Martha! But, nevertheless, go thou and watch this respectable lady's motions and behaviour the next time she comes to visit the laird – and the next after that. You will not, I see, lack opportunities.'

Martha's information turned out of that nature that prayers were said in the uppermost story of Dalcastle house against the Canaanitish woman,[22] every night and every morning; and great discontent prevailed there, even to anathemas[23] and tears. Letter after letter was dispatched to Glasgow; and at length, to the lady's great consolation, the Revd Mr Wringhim arrived safely and devoutly in her elevated sanctuary. Marvellous was the conversation between these gifted people. Wringhim had held in his doctrines that there were eight different kinds of FAITH, all perfectly distinct in their operations and effects. But the lady, in her secluded state, had discovered another five, making twelve [sic] in all: the adjusting of the existence or fallacy of these five faiths served for a most enlightened discussion of nearly seventeen hours; in the course of which the two got warm in their arguments, always in proportion as they receded from nature, utility, and common sense. Wringhim at length got into unwonted fervour about some disputed point between one of these faiths and TRUST: when the lady, fearing that zeal was getting beyond its wonted barrier, broke in on his vehement asseverations with the following abrupt discomfiture: 'But, sir, as long as I remember, what is to be done with this case of open and avowed inquity?'

The minister was struck dumb. He leaned him back on his chair, stroked his beard, hemmed – considered, and hemmed again, and then said, in an altered and softened tone: 'Why, that is a secondary consideration; you mean the case between your husband and Miss Logan?'

'The same, sir. I am scandalised at such intimacies going on under my nose. The sufferance of it is a great and crying evil.'

'Evil, madam, may be either operative, or passive. To them it is an evil, but to us none. We have no more to do with the sins of the wicked and unconverted here than with those of an infidel Turk; for all earthly bonds and fellowships are absorbed and swallowed up in the holy community of the Reformed Church. However, if it is your wish, I shall take him to task, and reprimand and humble him in such a manner that *he* shall be ashamed of his doings, and renounce such deeds for ever, out of mere self-respect, though all unsanctified the heart, as well as the deed, may be. To the wicked, all things are wicked; but to the just, all things are just and right.'

'Ah, that is a sweet and comfortable saying, Mr Wringhim! How delightful to think that a justified person can do no wrong! Who would not envy the liberty wherewith we are made free? Go to my husband, that poor unfortunate, blindfolded person, and open his eyes to his degenerate and sinful state; for well are you fitted to the task.'

'Yea, I will go in unto him, and confound him. I will lay the strong holds of sin and Satan as flat before my face as the dung that is spread out to fatten the land.'

'Master, there's a gentleman at the fore-door wants a private word o' ye.'

'Tell him I'm engaged: I can't see any gentleman tonight. But I shall attend on him tomorrow as soon as he pleases.'

'He's coming straight in, sir. Stop a wee bit, sir, my master is engaged. He cannot see you at present, sir.'

'Stand aside, thou Moabite![24] My mission admits of no delay. I come to save him from the jaws of destruction!'

'An that be the case, sir, it maks a wide difference; an', as the danger may threaten us a', I fancy I may as weel let ye gang by as fight wi' ye, sin' ye seem sae intent on 't. – The man says he's comin' to save ye, an' canna stop, sir. Here he is.'[25]

The laird was going to break out into a volley of wrath against Waters, his servant; but, before he got a word pronounced, the Revd

Mr Wringhim had stepped inside the room, and Waters had retired, shutting the door behind him.

No introduction could be more malapropos: it was impossible; for at that very moment the laird and Arabella Logan were both sitting on one seat, and both looking on one book, when the door opened. 'What is it, sir?' said the laird fiercely.

'A message of the greatest importance, sir,' said the divine, striding unceremoniously up to the chimney, turning his back to the fire, and his face to the culprits. 'I think you should know me, sir?' continued he, looking displeasedly at the laird, with his face half turned round.

'I think I should,' returned the laird. 'You are a Mr How's-teyca'-him, of Glasgow, who did me the worst turn ever I got done to me in my life. You gentry are always ready to do a man such a turn. Pray, sir, did you ever do a good job for anyone to counterbalance that? For, if you have not, you ought to be – '

'Hold, sir, I say! None of your profanity before me. If I do evil to anyone on such occasions, it is because he will have it so; therefore, the evil is not of my doing. I ask you, sir, before God and this witness, I ask you, have you kept solemnly and inviolate the vows which I laid upon you that day? Answer me!'

'Has the partner whom you bound me to kept hers inviolate? Answer me that, sir! None can better do so than you, Mr How'steyca'-you.'

'So, then, you confess your backslidings, and avow the profligacy of your life. And this person here is, I suppose, the partner of your iniquity – she whose beauty hath caused you to err! Stand up, both of you, till I rebuke you, and show you what you are in the eyes of God and man.'

'In the first place, stand you still there, till I tell you what you are in the eyes of God and man. You are, sir, a presumptuous, selfconceited pedagogue, a stirrer up of strife and commotion in church, in state, in families, and communities. You are one, sir, whose righteousness consists in splitting the doctrines of Calvin into thousands of undistinguishable films,[26] and in setting up a system of justifying-grace against all breaches of all laws, moral or divine. In short, sir, you are a mildew – a canker-worm in the bosom of the Reformed Church, generating a disease of which she will never be purged, but by the shedding of blood. Go thou in peace, and do these abominations no more; but humble thyself, lest a worse reproof come upon thee.'

Wringhim heard all this without flinching. He now and then

twisted his mouth in disdain, treasuring up, meantime, his vengeance against the two aggressors; for he felt that he had them on the
hip,[27] and resolved to pour out his vengeance and indignation upon
them. Sorry am I that the shackles of modern decorum restrain me
from penning that famous rebuke; fragments of which have been
attributed to every divine of old notoriety throughout Scotland. But
I have it by heart; and a glorious morsel it is to put into the hands of
certain incendiaries. The metaphors are so strong and so appalling
that Miss Logan could only stand them a very short time; she was
obliged to withdraw in confusion. The laird stood his ground with
much ado, though his face was often crimsoned over with the hues
of shame and anger. Several times he was on the point of turning the
officious sycophant to the door; but good manners, and an inherent
respect that he entertained for the clergy, as the immediate servants
of the Supreme Being, restrained him.

Wringhim, perceiving these symptoms of resentment, took them
for marks of shame and contrition, and pushed his reproaches
farther than ever divine ventured to do in a similar case. When he
had finished, to prevent further discussion, he walked slowly and
majestically out of the apartment, making his robes to swing behind
him in a most magisterial manner; he being, without doubt, elated
with his high conquest. He went to the upper storey, and related to
his metaphysical associate his wonderful success; how he had driven
the dame from the house in tears and deep confusion, and left the
backsliding laird in such a quandary of shame and repentance that
he could neither articulate a word nor lift up his countenance. The
dame thanked him most cordially, lauding his friendly zeal and
powerful eloquence; and then the two again set keenly to the
splitting of hairs, and making distinctions in religion where none
existed.

They being both children of adoption, and secured from falling
into snares, or anyway under the power of the wicked one, it was
their custom, on each visit, to sit up a night in the same apartment,
for the sake of sweet spiritual converse; but that time, in the course
of the night, they differed so materially on a small point somewhere
between justification and final election that the minister, in the heat
of his zeal, sprung from his seat, paced the floor, and maintained his
point with such ardour that Martha was alarmed, and, thinking they
were going to fight, and that the minister would be a hard match for
her mistress, she put on some clothes, and twice left her bed and
stood listening at the back of the door, ready to burst in should need
require it. Should anyone think this picture over-strained, I can

assure him that it is taken from nature and from truth; but I will not likewise aver that the theologist was neither crazed nor inebriated. If the listener's words were to be relied on, there was no love, no accommodating principle manifested between the two, but a fiery burning zeal, relating to points of such minor importance that a true Christian would blush to hear them mentioned, and the infidel and profane make a handle of them to turn our religion to scorn.

Great was the dame's exultation at the triumph of her beloved pastor over her sinful neighbours in the lower parts of the house; and she boasted of it to Martha in high-sounding terms. But it was of short duration; for, in five weeks after that, Arabella Logan came to reside with the laird as his housekeeper, sitting at his table and carrying the keys as mistress-substitute of the mansion. The lady's grief and indignation were now raised to a higher pitch than ever; and she set every agent to work, with whom she had any power, to effect a separation between these two suspected ones. Remonstrance was of no avail: George laughed at them who tried such a course, and retained his housekeeper, while the lady gave herself up to utter despair; for, though she would not consort with her husband herself, she could not endure that any other should do so.

But, to countervail this grievous offence, our saintly and afflicted dame, in due time, was safely delivered of a fine boy, whom the laird acknowledged as his son and heir, and had him christened by his own name, and nursed in his own premises. He gave the nurse permission to take the boy to his mother's presence if ever she should desire to see him; but, strange as it may appear, she never once desired to see him from the day that he was born. The boy grew up, and was a healthful and happy child; and, in the course of another year, the lady presented him with a brother. A brother he certainly was, in the eye of the law, and it is more than probable that he was his brother in reality. But the laird thought otherwise; and, though he knew and acknowledged that he was obliged to support and provide for him, he refused to acknowledge him in other respects. He neither would countenance the banquet nor take the baptismal vows on him in the child's name; of course, the poor boy had to live and remain an alien from the visible church for a year and a day;[28] at which time, Mr Wringhim, out of pity and kindness, took the lady herself as sponsor for the boy, and baptised him by the name of Robert Wringhim – that being the noted divine's own name.

George was brought up with his father, and educated partly at the parish school, and partly at home, by a tutor hired for the purpose.

He was a generous and kind-hearted youth; always ready to oblige, and hardly ever dissatisfied with anybody. Robert was brought up with Mr Wringhim, the laird paying a certain allowance for him yearly; and there the boy was early inured to all the sternness and severity of his pastor's arbitrary and unyielding creed. He was taught to pray twice every day, and seven times on Sabbath days; but he was only to pray for the elect, and, like David of old, doom all that were aliens from God to destruction. He had never, in that family into which he had been as it were adopted, heard aught but evil spoken of his reputed father and brother; consequently he held them in utter abhorrence, and prayed against them every day, often 'that the old hoary sinner might be cut off in the full flush of his iniquity, and be carried quick into hell; and that the young stem of the corrupt trunk might also be taken from a world that he disgraced, but that his sins might be pardoned, because he knew no better'.

Such were the tenets in which it would appear young Robert was bred. He was an acute boy, an excellent learner, had ardent and ungovernable passions, and, withal, a sternness of demeanour from which other boys shrunk. He was the best grammarian, the best reader, writer, and accountant in the various classes that he attended, and was fond of writing essays on controverted points of theology, for which he got prizes, and great praise from his guardian and mother. George was much behind him in scholastic acquirements, but greatly his superior in personal prowess, form, feature, and all that constitutes gentility in the deportment and appearance. The laird had often manifested to Miss Logan an earnest wish that the two young men should never meet, or at all events that they should be as little conversant as possible; and Miss Logan, who was as much attached to George as if he had been her own son, took every precaution, while he was a boy, that he should never meet with his brother; but, as they advanced towards manhood, this became impracticable. The lady was removed from her apartments in her husband's house to Glasgow, to her great content; and all to prevent the young laird being tainted with the company of her and her second son; for the laird had felt the effects of the principles they professed, and dreaded them more than persecution, fire, and sword. During all the dreadful times that had overpast, though the laird had been a moderate man, he had still leaned to the side of kingly prerogative, and had escaped confiscation and fines, without ever taking any active hand in suppressing the Covenanters. But, after experiencing a specimen of their tenets and manner in his wife, from a secret favourer of them and their doctrines, he grew alarmed at the prevalence of such stern and factious principles, now that there was no check or restraint upon them; and from that time he began to set himself against them, joining with the Cavalier party of that day in all their proceedings.

It so happened that, under the influence of the Earls of Seafield and Tullibardine, he was returned for a Member of Parliament in the famous session that sat at Edinburgh when the Duke of Queensberry was commissioner, and in which party spirit ran to such an extremity. The young laird went with his father to the court, and remained in town all the time that the session lasted; and, as all interested people of both factions flocked to the town at that period, so the important Mr Wringhim was there among the rest, during the greater part of the time, blowing the coal of revolutionary principles with all his might, in every society to which he could obtain admission. He was a great favourite with some of the west country gentlemen of that faction, by reason of his unbending impudence. No opposition could for a moment cause him either to blush, or retract one item that he had advanced. Therefore the Duke of Argyle and his friends made such use of him as sportsmen often do of terriers, to start the game,[29] and make a great yelping noise to let them know whither the chase is proceeding. They often did this out of sport, in order to tease their opponent; for of all pesterers that ever fastened on man he was the most insufferable: knowing that his coat protected him from manual chastisement, he spared no acrimony and delighted in the chagrin and anger of those with whom he contended. But he was sometimes likewise *of real use* to the heads of the Presbyterian faction, and therefore was admitted to their tables, and of course conceived himself a very great man.

His ward accompanied him; and, very shortly after their arrival in Edinburgh, Robert, for the first time, met with the young laird his brother, in a match at tennis. The prowess and agility of the young squire drew forth the loudest plaudits of approval from his associates, and his own exertion alone carried the game every time on the one side, and that so far as all along to count three for their one. The hero's name soon ran round the circle, and when his brother Robert, who was an onlooker, learned who it was that was gaining so much applause, he came and stood close beside him all the time that the game lasted, always now and then putting in a cutting remark by way of mockery.

George could not help perceiving him, not only on account of his impertinent remarks, but he, moreover, stood so near him that he several times impeded him in his rapid evolutions, and of course got himself shoved aside in no very ceremonious way. Instead of making him keep his distance, these rude shocks and pushes, accompanied sometimes with hasty curses, only made him cling the closer to this king of the game. He seemed determined to maintain his right to his place as an onlooker, as well as any of those engaged in the game, and, if they had tried him at an argument, he would have carried his point; or perhaps he wished to quarrel with this spark of his jealousy and aversion, and draw the attention of the gay crowd to himself by these means; for, like his guardian, he knew no other pleasure but what consisted in opposition. George took him for some impertinent student of divinity, rather set upon a joke than anything else. He perceived a lad with black clothes, and a methodistical face, whose countenance and eye he disliked exceedingly, several times in his way, and that was all the notice he took of him the first time they two met. But the next day, and every succeeding one, the same devilish-looking youth attended him as constantly as his shadow; was always in his way as with intention to impede him, and ever and anon his deep and malignant eye met those of his elder brother with a glance so fierce that it sometimes startled him.

The very next time that George was engaged at tennis, he had not struck the ball above twice till the same intrusive being was again in his way. The party played for considerable stakes that day, namely, a dinner and wine at the Black Bull tavern; and George, as the hero and head of his party, was much interested in its honour; consequently the sight of this moody and hellish-looking student affected him in no very pleasant manner. 'Pray, sir, be so good as keep without the range of the ball,' said he.

'Is there any law or enactment that can compel me to do so?' said the other, biting his lip with scorn.

'If there is not, they are here that shall compel you,' returned George. 'So, friend, I rede you to be on your guard.'

As he said this, a flush of anger glowed in his handsome face and flashed from his sparkling blue eye; but it was a stranger to both, and momently took its departure. The black-coated youth set up his cap before, brought his heavy brows over his deep dark eyes, put his hands in the pockets of his black plush breeches, and stepped a little farther into the semicircle, immediately on his brother's right hand, than he had ever ventured to do before. There he set himself firm on his legs, and, with a face as demure as death, seemed determined to keep his ground. He pretended to be following the ball with his eyes; but every moment they were glancing aside at George. One of the competitors chanced to say rashly, in the moment of exultation, 'That's a damned fine blow, George!' On which the intruder took up the word, as characteristic of the competitors, and repeated it every stroke that was given, making such a ludicrous use of it that several of the onlookers were compelled to laugh immoderately; but the players were terribly nettled at it, as he really contrived, by dint of sliding in some canonical terms, to render the competitors and their game ridiculous.

But matters at length came to a crisis that put them beyond sport. George, in flying backward to gain the point at which the ball was going to light, came inadvertently so rudely in contact with this obstreperous interloper that he not only overthrew him, but also got a grievous fall over his legs; and, as he arose, the other made a spurn at him with his foot, which, if it had hit to its aim, would undoubtedly have finished the course of the young laird of Dalcastle and Balgrennan. George, being irritated beyond measure, as may well be conceived, especially at the deadly stroke aimed at him, struck the assailant with his racket, rather slightly, but so that his mouth and nose gushed out blood; and, at the same time, he said, turning to his cronies: 'Does any of you know who the infernal puppy is?'

'Do you not know, sir?' said one of the onlookers, a stranger, 'the gentleman is your own brother, sir – Mr Robert Wringhim Colwan!'

'No, not Colwan, sir,' said Robert, putting his hands in his pockets, and setting himself still farther forward than before, 'not a Colwan, sir; henceforth I disclaim the name.'

'No, certainly not,' repeated George. 'My mother's son you may be – but *not a Colwan*! There you are right.' Then, turning around to his informer, he said: 'Mercy be about us, sir! Is this the crazy minister's son from Glasgow?'

This question was put in the irritation of the moment, but it was too rude, and far too out of place, and no one deigned any answer to it. He felt the reproof, and felt it deeply; seeming anxious for some opportunity to make an acknowledgment, or some reparation.

In the meantime, young Wringhim was an object to all of the uttermost disgust. The blood flowing from his mouth and nose he took no pains to stem, neither did he so much as wipe it away; so that it spread over all his cheeks, and breast, even off at his toes. In that state did he take up his station in the middle of the competitors; and he did not now keep his place, but ran about, impeding everyone who attempted to make at the ball. They loaded him with execrations, but it availed nothing; he seemed courting persecution and buffetings, keeping steadfastly to his old joke of damnation, and marring the game so completely that, in spite of every effort on the part of the players, he forced them to stop their game and give it up. He was such a rueful-looking object, covered with blood, that none of them had the heart to kick him, although it appeared the only thing he wanted; and, as for George, he said not another word to him, either in anger or reproof.

When the game was fairly given up, and the party were washing their hands in the stone fount, some of them besought Robert Wringhim to wash himself; but he mocked at them, and said he was much better as he was. George, at length, came forward abashedly towards him, and said: 'I have been greatly to blame, Robert, and am very sorry for what I have done. But, in the first instance, I erred through ignorance, not knowing you were my brother, which you certainly are; and, in the second, through a momentary irritation, for which I am ashamed. I pray you, therefore, to pardon me, and give me your hand.'

As he said this, he held out his hand towards his polluted brother; but the froward predestinarian took not his from his breeches pocket, but lifting his foot, he gave his brother's hand a kick. 'I'll give you what will suit such a hand better than mine,' said he, with a sneer. And then, turning lightly about, he added: 'Are there to be no more of these damned fine blows, gentlemen? For shame, to give up such a profitable and edifying game!'

'This is too bad,' said George. 'But, since it is thus, I have the less to regret.' And, having made this general remark, he took no more note of the uncouth aggressor. But the persecution of the latter terminated not on the play-ground: he ranked up among them, bloody and disgusting as he was, and, keeping close by his brother's side, he marched along with the party all the way to the Black Bull. Before they got there, a great number of boys and idle people had surrounded them, hooting and incommoding them exceedingly, so that they were glad to get into the inn; and the unaccountable monster actually tried to get in alongst with them, to make one of the party at dinner. But the innkeeper and his men, getting the hint, by force prevented him from entering, although he attempted it again and again, both by telling lies and offering a bribe. Finding he could not prevail, he set to exciting the mob at the door to acts of violence; in which he had like to have succeeded. The landlord had no other shift, at last, but to send privately for two officers, and have him carried to the guard-house; and the hilarity and joy of the party of young gentlemen, for the evening, was quite spoiled by the inauspicious termination of their game.

The Revd Robert Wringhim was now to send for, to release his beloved ward. The messenger found him at table, with a number of the leaders of the Whig faction, the Marquis of Annandale being in the chair; and, the prisoner's note being produced, Wringhim read it aloud, accompanying it with some explanatory remarks. The circumstances of the case being thus magnified and distorted, it excited the utmost abhorrence, both of the deed and the perpetrators, among the assembled faction. They declaimed against the act as an unnatural attempt on the character, and even the life, of an unfortunate brother, who had been expelled from his father's house. And, as party spirit was the order of the day, an attempt was made to lay the burden of it to that account. In short, the young culprit got some of the best blood of the land to enter as his securities, and was set at liberty. But, when Wringhim perceived the plight that he was in, he took him, as he was, and presented him to his honourable patrons. This raised the indignation against the young laird and his associates a thousand-fold, which actually roused the party to temporary madness. They were, perhaps, a little excited by the wine and spirits they had swallowed; else a casual quarrel between two young men, at tennis, could not have driven them to such extremes. But certain it is that, from one at first arising to address the party on the atrocity of the offence, both in a moral and political point of view, on a sudden there were six on their feet, at the same time, expatiating on it; and, in a very short time thereafter, everyone in the room was up talking with the utmost vociferation, all on the same subject, and all taking the same side in the debate.

In the midst of this confusion, someone or other issued from the house, which was at the back of the Canongate,[30] calling out: 'A plot, a plot! Treason, treason! Down with the bloody incendiaries at the Black Bull!'

The concourse of people that were assembled in Edinburgh at that time was prodigious; and, as they were all actuated by political motives, they wanted only a ready-blown coal to set the mountain on fire. The evening being fine, and the streets thronged, the cry ran from mouth to mouth through the whole city. More than that, the mob that had of late been gathered to the door of the Black Bull had, by degrees, dispersed; but, they being young men, and idle vagrants, they had only spread themselves over the rest of the street to lounge in search of further amusement: consequently, a word was sufficient to send them back to their late rendezvous, where they had previously witnessed something they did not much approve of.

The master of the tavern was astonished at seeing the mob again assembling; and that with such hurry and noise. But, his inmates being all of the highest respectability, he judged himself sure of protection, or at least of indemnity. He had two large parties in his house at the time; the largest of which was of the Revolutionist faction. The other consisted of our young tennis-players, and their associates, who were all of the Jacobite order; or, at all events, leaned to the Episcopal side. The largest party were in a front room; and the attack of the mob fell first on their windows, though rather with fear and caution. Jingle went one pane; then a loud hurrah; and that again was followed by a number of voices, endeavouring to restrain the indignation from venting itself in destroying the windows, and to turn it on the inmates. The Whigs, calling the landlord, inquired what the assault meant: he cunningly answered that he suspected it was some of the youths of the Cavalier, or High-Church party, exciting the mob against them. The party consisted mostly of young gentlemen, by that time in a key to engage in any row: and, at all events, to suffer nothing from the other party, against whom their passions were mightily inflamed.

The landlord, therefore, had no sooner given them the spiritrousing intelligence than everyone, as by instinct, swore his own natural oath, and grasped his own natural weapon. A few of those of the highest rank were armed with swords, which they boldly drew; those of the subordinate orders immediately flew to such weapons as the room, kitchen, and scullery afforded – such as tongs, pokers, spits, racks, and shovels; and breathing vengeance on the prelatic party, the children of Antichrist and the heirs of damnation! the barterers of the liberties of their country, and betrayers of the most sacred trust – thus elevated, and thus armed, in the cause of right, justice, and liberty, our heroes rushed to the street, and attacked the mob with such violence that they broke the mass in a moment, and dispersed their thousands like chaff before the wind. The other party of young Jacobites, who sat in a room farther from the front, and were those against whom the fury of the mob was meant to have been directed, knew nothing of this second uproar, till the noise of the sally made by the Whigs assailed their ears; being then informed that the mob had attacked the house on account of the treatment they themselves had given to a young gentleman of the adverse faction, and that another jovial party had issued from the house in their defence, and was now engaged in an unequal combat, the sparks likewise flew to the field to back their defenders with all their prowess, without troubling their heads about who they were.

A mob is like a spring tide in an eastern storm, that retires only to return with more overwhelming fury. The crowd was taken by surprise when such a strong and well-armed party issued from the house with so great fury, laying all prostrate that came in their way. Those who were next to the door, and were, of course, the first whom the imminent danger assailed, rushed backwards among the crowd with their whole force. The Black Bull standing in a small square half-way between the High Street and the Cowgate,[31] and the entrance to it being by two closes, into these the pressure outwards was simultaneous, and thousands were moved to an involuntary flight, they knew not why.

But the High Street of Edinburgh, which they soon reached, is a dangerous place in which to make an open attack upon a mob. And it appears that the entrances to the tavern had been somewhere near to the Cross, on the south side of the street; for the crowd fled with great expedition, both to the east and west, and the conquerors, separating themselves as chance directed, pursued impetuously, wounding and maiming as they flew. But it so chanced that, before either of the wings had followed the flying squadrons of their enemies for the space of a hundred yards each way, – the devil an enemy they had to pursue! – the multitude had vanished like so many thousands of phantoms! What could our heroes do? Why, they faced about to return towards their citadel, the Black Bull. But that feat was not so easily, nor so readily accomplished as they divined. The unnumbered alleys on each side of the street had swallowed up the multitude in a few seconds; but from these they were busy reconnoitring; and, perceiving the deficiency in the number of their assailants, the rush from both sides of the street was as rapid, and as wonderful, as the disappearance of the crowd had been a few minutes before. Each close vomited out its levies, and these better armed with missiles than when they sought it for a temporary retreat. Woe then to our two columns of victorious Whigs! The mob actually closed around them as they would have swallowed them up; and, in the meanwhile, shower after shower of the most abominable weapons of offence[32] were rained in upon them. If the gentlemen were irritated before, this inflamed them still further; but their danger was now so apparent they could not shut their eyes on it; therefore, both parties, as if actuated by the same spirit, made a desperate effort to join, and the greater part effected it; but some were knocked down, and others were separated from their friends, and blithe to become silent members of the mob.

The battle now raged immediately in front of the closes leading to the Black Bull; the small body of Whig gentlemen was hardly bested, and it is likely would have been overcome and trampled down every man, had they not been then and there joined by the young Cavaliers; who, fresh to arms, broke from the wynd,[33] opened the head of the passage, laid about them manfully, and thus kept up the spirits of the exasperated Whigs, who were the men in fact that wrought the most deray among the populace.

The town-guard was now on the alert; and two companies of the Cameronian Regiment, with the Hon. Captain Douglas, rushed down from the Castle[34] to the scene of action; but, for all the noise and hubbub that these caused in the street, the combat had become so close and inveterate that numbers of both sides were taken prisoners fighting hand to hand, and could scarcely be separated when the guardsmen and soldiers had them by the necks.

Great was the alarm and confusion that night in Edinburgh; for everyone concluded that it was a party scuffle, and, the two parties being so equal in power, the most serious consequences were anticipated. The agitation was so prevailing that every party in town, great and small, was broken up; and the lord-commissioner thought proper to go to the Council Chamber himself, even at that late hour, accompanied by the sheriffs of Edinburgh and Linlithgow,[35] with sundry noblemen besides, in order to learn something of the origin of the affray.

For a long time the court was completely puzzled. Every gentleman brought in exclaimed against the treatment he had received, in most bitter terms, blaming a mob set on him and his friends by the adverse party, and matters looked extremely ill until at length they began to perceive that they were examining gentlemen of both parties, and that they had been doing so from the beginning, almost alternately, so equally had the prisoners been taken from both parties. Finally, it turned out that a few gentlemen, two-thirds of whom were strenuous Whigs themselves, had joined in mauling the whole Whig population of Edinburgh. The investigation disclosed nothing the effect of which was not ludicrous; and the Duke of Queensberry, whose aim was at that time to conciliate the two factions, tried all that he could to turn the whole fracas into a joke – an unlucky frolic where no ill was meant on either side, and which yet had been productive of a great deal.

The greater part of the people went home satisfied; but not so the

Revd Robert Wringhim. He did all that he could to inflame both judges and populace against the young Cavaliers, especially against the young Laird of Dalcastle, whom he represented as an incendiary, set on by an unnatural parent to slander his mother, and make away with a hapless and only brother; and, in truth that declaimer against all human merit had that sort of powerful, homely, and bitter eloquence which seldom missed affecting his hearers: the consequence at that time was that he made the unfortunate affair between the two brothers appear in extremely bad colours, and the populace retired to their homes impressed with no very favourable opinion of either the Laird of Dalcastle or his son George, neither of whom were there present to speak for themselves.

As for Wringhim himself, he went home to his lodgings, filled with gall and with spite against the young laird, whom he was made to believe the aggressor, and that intentionally. But most of all he was filled with indignation against the father, whom he held in abhorrence at all times, and blamed solely for this unmannerly attack made on his favourite ward, namesake, and adopted son; and for the public imputation of a crime to his own reverence in calling the lad *his* son, and thus charging him with a sin against which he was well known to have levelled all the arrows of church censure with unsparing might.

But, filled as his heart was with some portion of these bad feelings, to which all flesh is subject, he kept, nevertheless, the fear of the Lord always before his eyes so far as never to omit any of the external duties of religion, and farther than that man hath no power to pry. He lodged with the family of a Mr Miller, whose lady was originally from Glasgow, and had been a hearer and, of course, a great admirer of Mr Wringhim. In that family he made public worship every evening; and that night, in his petitions at a throne of grace, he prayed for so many vials of wrath to be poured on the head of some particular sinner that the hearers trembled, and stopped their ears. But that he might not proceed with so violent a measure, amounting to excommunication, without due scripture warrant, he began the exercise of the evening by singing the following verses, which it is a pity should ever have been admitted into a Christian psalmody, being so adverse to all its mild and benevolent principles:

> Set thou the wicked over him,
> *And upon his right hand*
> *Give thou his greatest enemy,*
> *Even Satan, leave to stand.*

And, when by thee he shall be judged,
  Let him remembered be;
And let his prayer be turned to sin
  When he shall call on thee.

Few be his days; and in his room
  His charge another take;
His children let be fatherless;
  His wife a widow make:

Let God his father's wickedness
  Still to remembrance call;
And never let his mother's sin
  Be blotted out at all.

As he in cursing pleasure took
  So let it to him fall;
As he delighted not to bless,
  So bless him not at all.

As cursing he like clothes put on,
  Into his bowels so,
Like water, and into his bones
  Like oil, down let it go.[36]

Young Wringhim only knew the full purport of this spiritual song; and went to his bed better satisfied than ever that his father and brother were castaways, reprobates, aliens from the Church and the true faith, and cursed in time and eternity.

The next day George and his companions met as usual – all who were not seriously wounded of them. But, as they strolled about the city, the rancorous eye and the finger of scorn was pointed against them. None of them was at first aware of the reason; but it threw a damp over their spirits and enjoyments, which they could not master. They went to take a forenoon game at their old play of tennis, not on a match, but by way of improving themselves; but they had not well taken their places till young Wringhim appeared in his old station, at his brother's right hand, with looks more demure and determined than ever. His lips were primmed so close that his mouth was hardly discernible, and his dark deep eye flashed gleams of holy indignation on the godless set, but particularly on his brother. His presence acted as a mildew on all social intercourse or enjoyment; the game was marred, and ended ere ever it was well begun. There were whisperings apart – the party separated, and, in order to shake off the blighting influence of this dogged persecutor, they entered sundry houses of their acquaintances, with an understanding that they were to meet on the Links[37] for a game at cricket.

They did so; and, stripping off part of their clothes, they began that violent and spirited game. They had not played five minutes till Wringhim was stalking in the midst of them, and totally impeding the play. A cry arose from all corners of: 'Oh, this will never do. Kick him out of the play-ground! Knock down the scoundrel; or bind him, and let him lie in peace.'

'By no means,' cried George. 'It is evident he wants nothing else. Pray do not humour him so much as to touch him with either foot or finger.' Then, turning to a friend, he said in a whisper: 'Speak to him, Gordon; he surely will not refuse to let us have the ground to ourselves, if you request it of him.'

Gordon went up to him, and requested of him, civilly, but ardently, 'to retire to a certain distance, else none of them could or would be answerable, however sore he might be hurt.'

He turned disdainfully on his heel, uttered a kind of pulpit hem! and then added, 'I will take my chance of that; hurt me, any of you, at your peril.'

The young gentlemen smiled, through spite and disdain of the dogged animal. Gordon followed him up, and tried to remonstrate with him; but he let him know that 'it was his pleasure to be there at that time; and, unless he could demonstrate to him what superior right he and his party had to that ground, in preference to him, and to the exclusion of all others, he was determined to assert his right, and the rights of his fellow-citizens, by keeping possession of whatsoever part of that common field he chose.'

'You are no gentleman, sir,' said Gordon.

'Are you one, sir?' said the other.

'Yes, sir. I will let you know that I am, by God!'

'Then, thanks be to Him whose name you have profaned, I am none. If *one* of the party be a gentleman, *I do hope in God I am not!*'

It was now apparent to them all that he was courting obloquy and manual chastisement from their hands, if by any means he could provoke them to the deed; and, apprehensive that he had some sinister and deep-laid design in hunting after such a singular favour, they wisely restrained one another from inflicting the punishment that each of them yearned to bestow, personally, and which he so well deserved.

But the unpopularity of the younger George Colwan could no longer be concealed from his associates. It was manifested wherever the populace were assembled; and his young and intimate friend, Adam Gordon, was obliged to warn him of the circumstance that he might not be surprised at the gentlemen of their acquaintance withdrawing themselves from his society, as they could not be seen with him without being insulted. George thanked him; and it was agreed between them that the former should keep himself retired during the daytime while he remained in Edinburgh, and that at night they should meet together, along with such of their companions as were disengaged.

George found it every day more and more necessary to adhere to this system of seclusion; for it was not alone the hisses of the boys and populace that pursued him – a fiend of more malignant aspect was ever at his elbow, in the form of his brother. To whatever place of amusement he betook himself, and however well he concealed his intentions of going there from all flesh living, there was his brother Wringhim also, and always within a few yards of him, generally about the same distance, and ever and anon darting looks at him that chilled his very soul. They were looks that cannot be described; but they were felt piercing to the bosom's deepest core. They affected even the onlookers in a very particular manner, for all whose eyes caught a glimpse of these hideous glances followed them to the object towards which they were darted: the gentlemanly and mild demeanour of that object generally calmed their startled apprehensions; for no one ever yet noted the glances of the young man's eye, in the black coat, at the face of his brother, who did not at first manifest strong symptoms of alarm.

George became utterly confounded; not only at the import of this persecution, but how in the world it came to pass that this unaccountable being knew all his motions, and every intention of his heart, as it were intuitively. On consulting his own previous feelings and resolutions, he found that the circumstances of his going to such and such a place were often the most casual incidents in nature – the caprice of a moment had carried him there, and yet he had never sat or stood many minutes till there was the selfsame being, always in the same position with regard to himself, as regularly as the shadow is cast from the substance, or the ray of light from the opposing denser medium.

For instance, he remembered one day of setting out with the intention of going to attend divine worship in the High Church,[38] and when, within a short space of its door, he was overtaken by young Kilpatrick of Closeburn, who was bound to the Grey-Friars[39] to see his sweetheart, as he said: 'and if you will go with me,

Colwan,' said he, 'I will let you see her too, and then you will be just as far forward as I am.'

George assented at once, and went; and, after taking his seat, he leaned his head forwards on the pew to repeat over to himself a short ejaculatory prayer, as had always been his custom on entering the house of God. When he had done, he lifted his eye naturally towards that point on his right hand where the fierce apparition of his brother had been wont to meet his view: there he was, in the same habit, form, demeanour, and precise point of distance, as usual! George again laid down his head, and his mind was so astounded that he had nearly fallen into a swoon. He tried shortly after to muster up courage to look at the speaker, at the congregation, and at Captain Kilpatrick's sweetheart in particular; but the fiendish glances of the young man in the black clothes were too appalling to be withstood – his eye caught them whether he was looking that way or not: at length his courage was fairly mastered, and he was obliged to look down during the remainder of the service.

By night or by day it was the same. In the gallery of the Parliament House,[40] in the boxes of the playhouse, in the church, in the assembly, in the streets, suburbs, and the fields; and every day, and every hour, from the first encounter of the two, the attendance became more and more constant, more inexplicable, and altogether more alarming and insufferable, until at last George was fairly driven from society, and forced to spend his days in his and his father's lodgings with closed doors. Even there, he was constantly harassed with the idea that, the next time he lifted his eyes, he would to a certainty see that face, the most repulsive to all his feelings of aught the earth contained. The attendance of that brother was now become like the attendance of a demon on some devoted being that had sold himself to destruction; his approaches as undiscerned, and his looks as fraught with hideous malignity. It was seldom that he saw him either following him in the streets, or entering any house or church after him; he only appeared in his place, George wist not how, or whence; and, having sped so ill in his first friendly approaches, he had never spoken to his equivocal attendant a second time.

It came at length into George's head, as he was pondering, by himself, on the circumstances of this extraordinary attendance, that perhaps his brother had relented, and, though of so sullen and unaccommodating a temper that he would not acknowledge it, or beg a reconciliation, it might be for that very purpose that he followed his steps night and day in that extraordinary manner. 'I cannot for my life see for what other purpose it can be,' thought he. 'He never offers to attempt my life; nor dares he, if he had the inclination; therefore, although his manner is peculiarly repulsive to me, I shall not have my mind burdened with the reflection that my own mother's son yearned for a reconciliation with me and was repulsed by my haughty and insolent behaviour. The next time he comes to my hand, I am resolved that I will accost him as one brother ought to address another, whatever it may cost me; and, if I am still flouted with disdain, then shall the blame rest with him.'

After this generous resolution, it was a good while before his gratuitous attendant appeared at his side again; and George began to think that his visits were discontinued. The hope was a relief that could not be calculated; but still George had a feeling that it was too supreme to last. His enemy had been too pertinacious to abandon his design, whatever it was. He, however, began to indulge in a little more liberty, and for several days he enjoyed it with impunity.

George was, from infancy, of a stirring active disposition and could not endure confinement; and, having been of late much restrained in his youthful exercises by this singular persecutor, he grew uneasy under such restraint, and, one morning, chancing to awaken very early, he arose to make an excursion to the top of Arthur's Seat,[41] to breathe the breeze of the dawning, and see the sun arise out of the eastern ocean. The morning was calm and serene; and as he walked down the south back of the Canongate, towards the Palace, the haze was so close around him that he could not see the houses on the opposite side of the way. As he passed the Lord-Commissioner's house, the guards were in attendance, who cautioned him not to go by the Palace, as all the gates would be shut and guarded for an hour to come, on which he went by the back of St Anthony's gardens, and found his way into that little romantic glade adjoining to the saint's chapel and well. He was still involved in a blue haze, like a dense smoke, but yet in the midst of it the respiration was the most refreshing and delicious. The grass and the flowers were loaden with dew; and, on taking off his hat to wipe his forehead, he perceived that the black glossy fur of which his chaperon was wrought was all covered with a tissue of the most delicate silver – a fairy web, composed of little spheres, so minute that no eye could discern any of them; yet there they were shining in lovely millions. Afraid of defacing so beautiful and so delicate a garnish, he replaced his hat with the greatest caution, and went on his way light of heart.

As he approached the swire[42] at the head of the dell – that little delightful verge from which in one moment the eastern limits and shores of Lothian[43] arise on the view – as he approached it, I say, and a little space from the height, he beheld, to his astonishment, a bright halo in the cloud of haze, that rose in a semicircle over his head like a pale rainbow. He was struck motionless at the view of the lovely vision; for it so chanced that he had never seen the same appearance before, though common at early morn. But he soon perceived the cause of the phenomenon, and that it proceeded from the rays of the sun from a pure unclouded morning sky striking upon this dense vapour which refracted them. But, the better all the works of nature are understood, the more they will be ever admired. That was a scene that would have entranced the man of science with delight, but which the uninitiated and sordid man would have regarded less than the mole rearing up his hill in silence and in darkness.

George did admire this halo of glory, which still grew wider, and less defined, as he approached the surface of the cloud. But, to his utter amazement and supreme delight, he found, on reaching the top of Arthur's Seat, that this sublunary rainbow, this terrestrial glory, was spread in its most vivid hues beneath his feet. Still he could not perceive the body of the sun, although the light behind him was dazzling; but the cloud of haze lying dense in that deep dell that separates the hill from the rocks of Salisbury, and the dull shadow of the hill mingling with that cloud made the dell a pit of darkness. On that shadowy cloud was the lovely rainbow formed, spreading itself on a horizontal plain, and having a slight and brilliant shade of all the colours of the heavenly bow, but all of them paler and less defined. But this terrestrial phenomenon of the early morn cannot be better delineated than by the name given of it by the shepherd boys, 'The little wee ghost of the rainbow.'

Such was the description of the morning, and the wild shades of the hill, that George gave to his father and Mr Adam Gordon that same day on which he had witnessed them; and it is necessary that the reader should comprehend something of their nature to under-stand what follows.

He seated himself on the pinnacle of the rocky precipice, a little within the top of the hill to the westward, and, with a light and buoyant heart, viewed the beauties of the morning, and inhaled its salubrious breeze. 'Here,' thought he, 'I can converse with nature without disturbance, and without being intruded on by any appalling or obnoxious visitor.' The idea of his brother's dark and malevolent looks coming at that moment across his mind, he turned his eyes instinctively to the right, to the point where that unwelcome guest was wont to make his appearance. Gracious Heaven! What an apparition was there presented to his view! He saw, delineated in the cloud, the shoulders, arms, and features of a human being of the most dreadful aspect. The face was the face of his brother, but dilated to twenty times the natural size. Its dark eyes gleamed on him through the mist, while every furrow of its hideous brow frowned deep as the ravines on the brow of the hill. George started, and his hair stood up in bristles as he gazed on this horrible monster. He saw every feature and every line of the face distinctly as it gazed on him with an intensity that was hardly brookable. Its eyes were fixed on him, in the same manner as those of some carnivorous animal fixed on its prey; and yet there was fear and trembling in these unearthly features, as plainly depicted as murderous malice. The giant apparition seemed sometimes to be cowering down as in terror, so that nothing but his brow and eyes were seen; still these never turned one moment from their object – again it rose imperceptively up, and began to approach with great caution; and, as it neared, the dimensions of its form lessened, still continuing, however, far above the natural size.

George conceived it to be a spirit. He could conceive it to be nothing else; and he took it for some horrid demon by which he was haunted, that had assumed the features of his brother in every lineament, but, in taking on itself the human form, had miscalculated dreadfully on the size, and presented itself thus to him in a blownup, dilated frame of embodied air, exhaled from the caverns of death or the regions of devouring fire. He was further confirmed in the belief that it was a malignant spirit on perceiving that it approached him across the front of a precipice, where there was not footing for thing of mortal frame. Still, what with terror and astonishment, he continued riveted to the spot, till it approached, as he deemed, to within two yards of him; and then, perceiving that it was setting itself to make a violent spring on him, he started to his feet and fled distractedly in the opposite direction, keeping his eye cast behind him lest he had been seized in that dangerous place. But the very first bolt that he made in his flight he came in contact with a real body of flesh and blood, and that with such violence that both went down among some scragged rocks, and George rolled over the other. The being called out 'Murder'; and, rising, fled precipitately. George then perceived that it was his brother; and being confounded between the shadow and the substance, he knew not what he was doing or what he had done; and, there being only one natural way of retreat from the brink of the rock, he likewise arose and pursued the affrighted culprit with all his speed towards the top of the hill. Wringhim was braying out, 'Murder! murder!' at which George, being disgusted, and his spirits all in a ferment from some hurried idea of intended harm, the moment he came up with the craven he seized him rudely by the shoulder, and clapped his hand on his mouth. 'Murder, you beast!' said he; 'what do you mean by roaring out murder in that way? Who the devil is murdering you, or offering to murder you?'

Wringhim forced his mouth from under his brother's hand and roared with redoubled energy 'Eh! Egh! Murder! murder!' etc. George had felt resolute to put down this shocking alarm, lest someone might hear it and fly to the spot, or draw inferences widely different from the truth; and, perceiving the terror of this elect youth to be so great that expostulation was vain, he seized him by the mouth and nose with his left hand so strenuously that he sank his fingers into his cheeks. But, the poltroon[44] still attempting to bray out, George gave him such a stunning blow with his fist on the left temple that he crumbled, as it were, to the ground, but more from the effects of terror than those of the blow. His nose, however, again gushed out blood, a system of defence which seemed as natural to him as that resorted to by the race of stinkards.[45] He then raised himself on his knees and hams, and raising up his ghastly face, while the blood streamed over both ears, he besought his life of his brother, in the most abject whining manner, gaping and blubbering most piteously.

'Tell me then, sir,' said George, resolved to make the most of the wretch's terror – 'tell me for what purpose it is that you haunt my steps? Tell me plainly, and instantly, else I will throw you from the verge of that precipice.'

'Oh, I will never do it again! I will never do it again! Spare my life, dear, good brother! Spare my life! Sure I never did you any hurt.'

'Swear to me, then, by the God that made you, that you will never henceforth follow after me to torment me with your hellish threatening looks; swear that you will never again come into my presence without being invited. Will you take an oath to this effect?'

'Oh yes! I will, I will!'

'But this is not all: you must tell me for what purpose you sought me out here this morning?'

'Oh, brother! For nothing but your good. I had nothing at heart but your unspeakable profit, and great and endless good.'

'So, then, you indeed knew that I was here?'

'I was told so by a friend, but I did not believe him; a–a–at least I did not know that it was true till I saw you.'

'Tell me this one thing, then, Robert, and all shall be forgotten and forgiven. Who was that friend?'

'You do not know him.'

'How then does he know me?'

'I cannot tell.'

'Was he here present with you today?'

'Yes; he was not far distant. He came to this hill with me.'

'Where then is he now?'

'I cannot tell.'

'Then, wretch, confess that the devil was that friend who told you I was here, and who came here with you. None else could possibly know of my being here.'

'Ah! how little you know of him! Would you argue that there is neither man nor spirit endowed with so much foresight as to deduce natural conclusions from previous actions and incidents but the devil? Alas, brother! But why should I wonder at such abandoned notions and principles? It was fore-ordained that you should cherish them, and that they should be the ruin of your soul and body, before the world was framed. Be assured of this, however, that I had no aim of seeking you but your good!'

'Well, Robert, I will believe it. I am disposed to be hasty and passionate: it is a fault in my nature; but I never meant, or wished you evil; and God is my witness that I would as soon stretch out my hand to my own life, or my father's, as to yours.' At these words, Wringhim uttered a hollow exulting laugh, put his hands in his pockets, and withdrew a space to his accustomed distance. George continued: 'And now, once for all, I request that we may exchange forgiveness, and that we may part and remain friends.'

'Would such a thing be expedient, think you? Or consistent with the glory of God? I doubt it.' 'I can think of nothing that would be more so. Is it not consistent with every precept of the Gospel? Come, brother, say that our reconciliation is complete.'

'Oh yes, certainly! I tell you, brother, according to the flesh: it is just as complete as the lark's is with the adder, no more so, nor ever can. Reconciled, forsooth! To what would I be reconciled?'

As he said this, he strode indignantly away. From the moment that he heard his life was safe, he assumed his former insolence and revengeful looks – and never were they more dreadful than on parting with his brother that morning on the top of the hill. 'Well, go thy way,' said George; 'some would despise, but I pity thee. If thou art not a limb of Satan, I never saw one.'

The sun had now dispelled the vapours; and, the morning being lovely beyond description, George sat himself down on the top of the hill, and pondered deeply on the unaccountable incident that had befallen to him that morning. He could in nowise comprehend it; but, taking it with other previous circumstances, he could not get quit of a conviction that he was haunted by some evil genius in the shape of his brother, as well as by that dark and mysterious wretch himself. In no other way could he account for the apparition he saw that morning on the face of the rock, nor for several sudden appearances of the same being, in places where there was no possibility of any foreknowledge that he himself was to be there, and as little that the same being, if he were flesh and blood like other men, could always start up in the same position with regard to him. He determined, therefore, on reaching home, to relate all that had happened, from beginning to end, to his father, asking his counsel and his assistance, although he knew full well that his father was not the fittest man in the world to solve such a problem. He was now involved in party politics, over head and ears; and, moreover, he could never hear the names of either of the Wringhims mentioned without getting into a quandary of disgust and anger; and all that he would deign to say of them was, to call them by all the opprobrious names he could invent.

It turned out as the young man from the first suggested: old Dalcastle would listen to nothing concerning them with any patience. George complained that his brother harassed him with his presence at all times, and in all places. Old Dal asked why he did not kick the dog out of his presence whenever he felt him disagreeable? George said he seemed to have some demon for a familiar. Dal answered that he did not wonder a bit at that, for the young spark was the third in a direct line who had all been children of adultery; and it was well known that all such were born half-deils themselves, and nothing was more likely than that they should hold intercourse with their fellows. In the same style did he sympathise with all his son's late sufferings and perplexities.

In Mr Adam Gordon, however, George found a friend who entered into all his feelings, and had seen and known everything about the matter. He tried to convince him that at all events there could be nothing supernatural in the circumstances; and that the vision he had seen on the rock, among the thick mist, was the shadow of his brother approaching behind him. George could not swallow this, for he had seen his own shadow on the cloud, and, instead of approaching to aught like his own figure, he perceived nothing but a halo of glory round a point of the cloud that was whiter and purer than the rest. Gordon said, if he would go with him to a mountain of his father's, which he named, in Aberdeen-shire, he would show him a giant spirit of the same dimensions, any morning at the rising of the sun, provided he shone on that spot. This statement excited George's curiosity exceedingly; and, being disgusted with some things about Edinburgh, and glad to get out of the way, he consented to go with Gordon to the Highlands for a space. The day was accordingly set for their departure, the old laird's assent obtained, and the two young sparks parted in a state of great impatience for their excursion.

One of them found out another engagement, however, the instant after this last was determined on. Young Wringhim went off the hill that morning, and home to his upright guardian again, without washing the blood from his face and neck; and there he told a most woeful story indeed: how he had gone out to take a morning's walk on the hill, where he had encountered with his reprobate brother among the mist, who had knocked him down and very near murdered him; threatening dreadfully, and with horrid oaths, to throw him from the top of the cliff.

· The wrath of the great divine was kindled beyond measure. He cursed the aggressor in the name of the Most High; and bound himself, by an oath, to cause that wicked one's transgressions return upon his own head sevenfold. But, before he engaged further in the business of vengeance, he kneeled with his adopted son, and committed the whole cause unto the Lord, whom he addressed as one coming breathing burning coals of juniper,[46] and casting his lightnings before him, to destroy and root out all who had moved hand or tongue against the children of the promise. Thus did he arise confirmed, and go forth to certain conquest.

We cannot enter into the detail of the events that now occurred without forestalling a part of the narrative of one who knew all the circumstances – was deeply interested in them, and whose relation is of higher value than anything that can be retailed out of the stores of tradition and old registers; but, his narrative being different from these, it was judged expedient to give the account as thus publicly handed down to us. Suffice it that, before evening, George was apprehended, and lodged in jail, on a criminal charge of an assault and battery, to the shedding of blood, with the intent of committing fratricide. Then was the old laird in great consternation, and blamed himself for treating the thing so lightly, which seemed to have been gone about, from the beginning, so systematically, and with an intent which the villains were now going to realise, namely, to get the young laird disposed of; and then his brother, in spite of the old gentleman's teeth, would be laird himself.

Old Dal now set his whole interest to work among the noblemen and lawyers of his party. His son's case looked exceedingly ill, owing to the former assault before witnesses, and the unbecoming expressions made use of by him on that occasion, as well as from the present assault, which George did not deny, and for which no moving cause or motive could be made to appear.

On his first declaration before the sheriff, matters looked no better: but then the sheriff was a Whig. It is well known how differently the people of the present day, in Scotland, view the cases of their own party-men and those of opposite political principles. But this day is nothing to that in such matters, although, God knows, they are still sometimes barefaced enough. It appeared, from all the witnesses in the first case, that the complainant was the first aggressor – that he refused to stand out of the way, though apprised of his danger; and, when his brother came against him inadvertently, he had aimed a blow at him with his foot, which, if it had taken effect, would have killed him. But as to the story of the apparition in fair daylight – the flying from the face of it – the running foul of his brother – pursuing him, and knocking him down, why the judge smiled at the relation, and saying: 'It was a very extraordinary story,' he remanded George to prison, leaving the matter to the High Court of Justiciary.

When the case came before that court, matters took a different turn. The constant and sullen attendance of the one brother upon the other excited suspicions; and these were in some manner confirmed when the guards at Queensberry House deponed that the prisoner went by them on his way to the hill that morning, about twenty minutes before the complainant, and, when the latter passed, he asked if such a young man had passed before him, describing the prisoner's appearance to them; and that, on being answered in the affirmative, he mended his pace and fell a-running.

The Lord Justice, on hearing this, asked the prisoner if he had any suspicions that his brother had a design on his life.

He answered that all along, from the time of their first unfortunate meeting, his brother had dogged his steps so constantly, and so unaccountably, that he was convinced it was with some intent out of the ordinary course of events; and that if, as his lordship supposed, it was indeed his shadow that he had seen approaching him through the mist, then, from the cowering and cautious manner that it advanced, there was no little doubt that his brother's design had been to push him headlong from the cliff that morning.

A conversation then took place between the Judge and the Lord Advocate; and, in the meantime, a bustle was seen in the hall; on which the doors were ordered to be guarded, and, behold, the precious Mr R. Wringhim was taken into custody, trying to make his escape out of court. Finally it turned out that George was honourably acquitted, and young Wringhim bound over to keep the peace, with heavy penalties and securities.

That was a day of high exultation to George and his youthful associates, all of whom abhorred Wringhim; and, the evening being spent in great glee, it was agreed between Mr Adam Gordon and George that their visit to the Highlands, though thus long delayed, was not to be abandoned; and though they had, through the machinations of an incendiary, lost the season of delight, they would still find plenty of sport in deer-shooting. Accordingly, the day was set a second time for their departure; and, on the day preceding that, all the party were invited by George to dine with him once more at the sign of the Black Bull of Norway. Everyone promised to attend, anticipating nothing but festivity and joy. Alas, what short-sighted improvident creatures we are, all of us; and how often does the evening cup of joy lead to sorrow in the morning!

The day arrived – the party of young noblemen and gentlemen met, and were as happy and jovial as men could be. George was never seen so brilliant, or so full of spirits; and exulting to see so many gallant young chiefs and gentlemen about him, who all gloried in the same principles of loyalty (perhaps this word should have been written *disloyalty*), he made speeches, gave toasts, and sung songs, all leaning slyly to the same side,[47] until a very late hour. By that time he had pushed the bottle so long and so freely that its fumes had taken possession of every brain to such a degree that they held Dame Reason rather at the staff's end, overbearing all her counsels and expostulations; and it was imprudently proposed by a wild inebriated spark, and carried by a majority of voices, that the whole party should adjourn to a bagnio[48] for the remainder of the night.

They did so; and it appears from what follows that the house to which they retired must have been somewhere on the opposite side of the street to the Black Bull Inn, a little farther to the eastward. They had not been an hour in that house till some altercation chanced to arise between George Colwan and a Mr Drummond, the younger son of a nobleman of distinction. It was perfectly casual, and no one thenceforward, to this day, could ever tell what it was about, if it was not about the misunderstanding of some word or term that the one had uttered. However it was, some high words passed between them; these were followed by threats, and, in less than two minutes from the commencement of the quarrel, Drummond left the house in apparent displeasure, hinting to the other that they two should settle that in a more convenient place.

The company looked at one another, for all was over before any of them knew such a thing was begun. 'What the devil is the matter?' cried one. 'What ails Drummond?' cried another. 'Who has he quarrelled with?' asked a third.

'Don't know.' – 'Can't tell, on my life.' – 'He has quarrelled with his wine, I suppose, and is going to send it a challenge.'

Such were the questions, and such the answers that passed in the jovial party, and the matter was no more thought of.

But in the course of a very short space, about the length of which the ideas of the company were the next day at great variance, a sharp rap came to the door. It was opened by a female; but, there being a chain inside, she only saw one side of the person at the door. He appeared to be a young gentleman, in appearance like him who had lately left the house, and asked, in a low whispering voice, 'if young Dalcastle was still in the house?' The woman did not know. 'If he is,' added he, 'pray tell him to speak with me for a few minutes.' The woman delivered the message before all the party, among whom there were then sundry courteous ladies of notable distinction, and George, on receiving it, instantly rose from the side of one of them, and said, in the hearing of them all, 'I will bet a hundred merks[49] that is Drummond.' – 'Don't go to quarrel with him, George,' said one. – 'Bring him in with you,' said another. George stepped out; the door was again bolted, the chain drawn across, and the inadvertent party, left within, thought no more of the circumstance till the morning, that the report had spread over the city that a young gentleman had been slain, on a little washinggreen at the side of the North Loch,[50] and at the very bottom of the close where this thoughtless party had been assembled.

Several of them, on first hearing the report, hasted to the deadroom in the Guard-house, where the corpse had been deposited, and soon discovered the body to be that of their friend and late entertainer, George Colwan. Great were the consternation and grief of all concerned, and, in particular, of his old father and Miss Logan; for George had always been the sole hope and darling of both, and the news of the event paralysed them so as to render them incapable of all thought or exertion. The spirit of the old laird was broken by the blow, and he descended at once from a jolly, goodnatured and active man to a mere driveller, weeping over the body of his son, kissing his wound, his lips, and his cold brow alternately; denouncing vengeance on his murderers, and lamenting that he himself had not met the cruel doom, so that the hope of his race might have been preserved. In short, finding that all further motive of action and object of concern or of love, here below, were for ever removed from him, he abandoned himself to despair, and threatened to go down to the grave with his son.

But, although he made no attempt to discover the murderers, the arm of justice was not idle; and, it being evident to all that the crime must infallibly be brought home to young Drummond, some of his friends sought him out, and compelled him, sorely against his will, to retire into concealment till the issue of the proof that should be led was made known. At the same time, he denied all knowledge of the incident with a resolution that astonished his intimate friends and relations, who to a man suspected him guilty. His father was not in Scotland, for I think it was said to me that this young man was second son to a John, Duke of Melfort,[51] who lived abroad with the royal family of the Stuarts; but this young gentleman lived with the relations of his mother, one of whom, an uncle, was a Lord of Session:[52] these, having thoroughly effected his concealment, went away, and listened to the evidence; and the examination of every new witness convinced them that their noble young relative was the slayer of his friend.

All the young gentlemen of the party were examined, save Drummond, who, when sent for, could not be found, which circumstance sorely confirmed the suspicions against him in the minds of judges and jurors, friends and enemies; and there is little doubt that the care of his relations in concealing him injured his character and his cause. The young gentlemen of whom the party was composed varied considerably with respect to the quarrel between him and the deceased. Some of them had neither heard nor noted it; others had, but not one of them could tell how it began. Some of them had heard the threat uttered by Drummond on leaving the house, and one only had noted him lay his hand on his sword. Not one of them could swear that it was Drummond who came to the door and desired to speak with the deceased, but the general impression on the minds of them all was to that effect; and one of the women swore that she heard the voice distinctly at the door, and every word that voice pronounced, and at the same time heard the deceased say that it was Drummond's.

On the other hand, there were some evidences on Drummond's

part, which Lord Craigie, his uncle, had taken care to collect. He produced the sword which his nephew had worn that night, on which there was neither blood nor blemish; and, above all, he insisted on the evidence of a number of surgeons, who declared that both the wounds which the deceased had received had been given behind. One of these was below the left arm, and a slight one; the other was quite through the body, and both evidently inflicted with the same weapon, a two-edged sword, of the same dimensions as that worn by Drummond.

Upon the whole, there was a division in the court, but a majority decided it. Drummond was pronounced guilty of the murder; outlawed for not appearing, and a high reward offered for his apprehension. It was with the greatest difficulty that he escaped on board of a small trading vessel, which landed him in Holland, and from thence, flying into Germany, he entered into the service of the Emperor Charles VI.[53] Many regretted that he was not taken, and made to suffer the penalty due for such a crime, and the melancholy incident became a pulpit theme over a great part of Scotland, being held up as a proper warning to youth to beware of such haunts of vice and depravity, the nurses of all that is precipitate, immoral, and base, among mankind.

After the funeral of this promising and excellent young man, his father never more held up his head. Miss Logan, with all her art, could not get him to attend to any worldly thing, or to make any settlement whatsoever of his affairs, save making her over a present of what disposable funds he had about him. As to his estates, when they were mentioned to him, he wished them all in the bottom of the sea, and himself along with them. But, whenever she mentioned the circumstance of Thomas Drummond having been the murderer of his son, he shook his head, and once made the remark that 'It was all a mistake, a gross and fatal error; but that God, who had permitted such a flagrant deed, would bring it to light in his own time and way.' In a few weeks he followed his son to the grave, and the notorious Robert Wringhim took possession of his estates as the lawful son of the late laird, born in wedlock, and under his father's roof. The investiture was celebrated by prayer, singing of psalms, and religious disputation. The late guardian and adopted father, and the mother of the new laird, presided on the grand occasion, making a conspicuous figure in all the work of the day; and, though the youth himself indulged rather more freely in the bottle than he had ever been seen to do before, it was agreed by all present that there had never been a festivity so sanctified within the great hall of Dalcastle. Then, after due thanks returned, they parted rejoicing in spirit; which thanks, by the by, consisted wholly in telling the Almighty what he was; and informing, with very particular precision, what they were who addressed him; for Wringhim's whole system of popular declamation consisted, it seems, in this – to denounce all men and women to destruction, and then hold out hopes to his adherents that they were the chosen few, included in the promises, and who could never fall away. It would appear that this pharisaical[54] doctrine is a very delicious one, and the most grateful of all others to the worst characters.

But the ways of heaven are altogether inscrutable, and soar as far above and beyond the works and the comprehensions of man as the sun, flaming in majesty, is above the tiny boy's evening rocket. It is the controller of Nature alone that can bring light out of darkness, and order out of confusion. Who is he that causeth the mole, from his secret path of darkness, to throw up the gem, the gold, and the precious ore? The same that from the mouths of babes and sucklings[55] can extract the perfection of praise, and who can make the most abject of his creatures instrumental in bringing the most hidden truths to light.

Miss Logan had never lost the thought of her late master's prediction that Heaven would bring to light the truth concerning the untimely death of his son. She perceived that some strange conviction, too horrible for expression, preyed on his mind from the moment that the fatal news reached him to the last of his existence; and, in his last ravings, he uttered some incoherent words about justification by faith alone and absolute and eternal predestination having been the ruin of his house. These, to be sure, were the words of superannuation, and of the last and severest kind of it; but, for all that, they sunk deep into Miss Logan's soul, and at last she began to think with herself: 'Is it possible the Wringhims, and the sophisticating wretch who is in conjunction with them, the mother of my late beautiful and amiable young master, can have effected his destruction? If so, I will spend my days, and my little patrimony, in endeavours to rake up and expose the unnatural deed.'

In all her outgoings and incomings Mrs Logan (as she was now styled) never lost sight of this one object. Every new disappointment only whetted her desire to fish up some particulars concerning it; for she thought so long and so ardently upon it that by degrees it became settled in her mind as a sealed truth. And, as woman is always most jealous of her own sex in such matters, her suspicions were fixed on her greatest enemy, Mrs Colwan, now the Lady Dowager of Dalcastle. All was wrapt in a chaos of confusion and darkness; but at last, by dint of a thousand sly and secret inquiries, Mr Logan found out where Lady Dalcastle had been on the night that the murder happened, and likewise what company she had kept, as well as some of the comers and goers; and she had hopes of having discovered a clue, which, if she could keep hold of the thread, would lead her through darkness to the light of truth.

Returning very late one evening from a convocation of family servants, which she had drawn together in order to fish something out of them, her maid having been in attendance on her all the evening, they found, on going home, that the house had been broken and a number of valuable articles stolen therefrom. Mrs Logan had grown quite heartless before this stroke, having been altogether unsuccessful in her inquiries, and now she began to entertain some resolutions of giving up the fruitless search.

In a few days thereafter, she received intelligence that her clothes and plate were mostly recovered, and that she for one was bound over to prosecute the depredator, provided the articles turned out to be hers, as libelled in the indictment, and as a king's evidence had given out. She was likewise summoned, or requested, I know not which, being ignorant of these matters, to go as far as the town of Peebles in Tweedside, in order to survey these articles on such a day, and make affidavit to their identity before the Sheriff. She went accordingly; but, on entering the town by the North Gate, she was accosted by a poor girl in tattered apparel, who with great earnestness inquired if her name was not Mrs Logan? On being answered in the affirmative, she said that the unfortunate prisoner in the Tolbooth requested her, as she valued all that was dear to her in life, to go and see her before she appeared in court at the hour of cause, as she (the prisoner) had something of the greatest moment to impart to her. Mrs Logan's curiosity was excited, and she followed the girl straight to the Tolbooth, who by the way said to her that she would find in the prisoner a woman of superior mind, who had gone through all the vicissitudes of life. 'She has been very unfortunate, and I fear very wicked,' added the poor thing, 'but she is my mother, and God knows, with all her faults and failings, she has never been unkind to me. You, madam, have it in your power to save her; but she has wronged you, and therefore, if you will not do it for her sake, do it for mine, and the God of the fatherless will reward you.'

Mrs Logan answered her with a cast of the head, and a hem! and only remarked, that 'the guilty must not always be suffered to escape, or what a world must we be doomed to live in!'

She was admitted to the prison, and found a tall emaciated figure, who appeared to have once possessed a sort of masculine beauty in no ordinary degree, but was now considerably advanced in years. She viewed Mrs Logan with a stern, steady gaze, as if reading her features as a margin to her intellect; and when she addressed her it was not with that humility, and agonised fervour, which are natural for one in such circumstances to address to another who has the power of her life and death in her hands.

'I am deeply indebted to you for this timely visit, Mrs Logan,' said she. 'It is not that I value life, or because I fear death, that I have sent for you so expressly. But the manner of the death that awaits me has something peculiarly revolting in it to a female mind. Good God! when I think of being hung up, a spectacle to a gazing, gaping multitude, with numbers of which I have had intimacies and connections, that would render the moment of parting so hideous, that, believe me, it rends to flinders a soul born for another sphere than that in which it has moved, had not the vile selfishness of a lordly fiend ruined all my prospects and all my hopes. Hear me then; for I do not ask your pity: I only ask of you to look to yourself, and behave with womanly prudence. If you deny this day that these goods are yours, there is no other evidence whatever against my life, and it is safe for the present. For, as for the word of the wretch who has betrayed me, it is of no avail; he has prevaricated so notoriously to save himself. If you deny them, you shall have them all again to the value of a mite, and more to the bargain. If you swear to the identity of them, the process will, one way and another, cost you the half of what they are worth.' 'And what security have I for that?' said Mrs Logan.

'You have none but *my word*,' said the other proudly, 'and that never yet was violated. If you cannot take that, I know the worst you can do. But I had forgot – I have a poor helpless child without, waiting and starving about the prison door. Surely it was of her that I wished to speak. This shameful death of mine will leave her in a deplorable state.'

'The girl seems to have candour and strong affections,' said Mrs Logan. 'I grievously mistake if such a child would not be a thousand times better without such a guardian and director.'

'Then will you be so kind as to come to the Grass Market[56] and see me put down?' said the prisoner. 'I thought a woman would estimate a woman's and a mother's feelings, when such a dreadful throw was at stake, at least in part. But you are callous, and have never known any feelings but those of subordination to your old unnatural master. Alas, I have no cause of offence! I have wronged you; and justice must take its course. Will you forgive me before we part?'

Mrs Logan hesitated, for her mind ran on something else. On which the other subjoined: 'No, you will not forgive me, I see. But you will pray to God to forgive me? I know you will do that.'

Mrs Logan heard not this jeer, but, looking at the prisoner with an absent and stupid stare, she said: 'Did you know my late master?'

'Ay, that I did, and never for any good,' said she. 'I knew the old and the young spark both, and was by when the latter was slain.'

This careless sentence affected Mrs Logan in a most peculiar manner. A shower of tears burst from her eyes ere it was done, and, when it was, she appeared like one bereaved of her mind. She first turned one way and then another, as if looking for something she had dropped. She seemed to think she had lost her eyes, instead of her tears, and at length, as by instinct, she tottered close up to the prisoner's face, and, looking wistfully and joyfully in it, said, with breathless earnestness: 'Pray, mistress, what is your name?'

'My name is Arabella Calvert,' said the other. 'Miss, mistress, or widow, as you choose, for I have been all the three, and that not once nor twice only. Ay, and something beyond all these. But, as for you, you have never been anything!'

'Ay, ay! and so you are Bell Calvert? Well, I thought so – I thought so,' said Mrs Logan; and, helping herself to a seat, she came and sat down close by the prisoner's knee. 'So you are indeed Bell Calvert, so called once. Well, of all the world you are the woman whom I have longed and travailed the most to see. But you were invisible; a being to be heard of, not seen.'

'There have been days, madam,' returned she, 'when I was to be seen, and when there were few to be seen like me. But since that time there have indeed been days on which I was not to be seen. My crimes have been great, but my sufferings have been greater. So great that neither you nor the world can ever either know or conceive them. I hope they will be taken into account by the Most High. Mine have been crimes of utter desperation. But whom am I speaking to? You had better leave me to myself, mistress.'

'Leave you to yourself? That I will be loth to do till you tell me where you were that night my young master was murdered.' 'Where the devil would, I was! Will that suffice you? Ah, it was a vile action! A night to be remembered that was! Won't you be going? I want to trust my daughter with a commission.'

'No, Mrs Calvert, you and I part not till you have divulged that mystery to me.'

'You must accompany me to the other world, then, for you shall not have it in this.'

'If you refuse to answer me, I can have you before a tribunal, where you shall be sifted to the soul.'

'Such miserable inanity! What care I for your threatenings of a tribunal? I who must soon stand before my last earthly one? What could the word of such a culprit avail? Or, if it could, where is the judge that could enforce it?'

'Did you not say that there was some mode of accommodating matters on that score?'

'Yes, I prayed you to grant me my life, which is in your power. The saving of it would not have cost you a plack,[57] yet you refused to do it. The taking of it will cost you a great deal, and yet to that purpose you adhere. I can have no parley with such a spirit. I would not have my life in a present from its motions, nor would I exchange courtesies with its possessor.'

'Indeed, Mrs Calvert, since ever we met, I have been so busy thinking about who you might be that I know not what you have been proposing. I believe I meant to do what I could to save you. But, once for all, tell me everything that you know concerning that amiable young gentleman's death, and here is my hand there shall be nothing wanting that I can effect for you.'

'No, I despise all barter with such mean and selfish curiosity; and, as I believe *that* passion is stronger with you, than fear with me, we part on equal terms. Do your worst; and my secret shall go to the gallows and the grave with me.'

Mrs Logan was now greatly confounded, and after proffering in vain to concede everything she could ask in exchange, for the particulars relating to the murder, she became the suppliant in her turn. But the unaccountable culprit, exulting in her advantage, laughed her to scorn; and finally, in a paroxysm of pride and impatience, called in the jailor and had her expelled, ordering him in her hearing not to grant her admittance a second time, on any pretence.

Mrs Logan was now hard put to it, and again driven almost to despair. She might have succeeded in the attainment of that she thirsted for most in life so easily had she known the character with which she had to deal. Had she known to have soothed her high and afflicted spirit: but that opportunity was past, and the hour of examination at hand. She once thought of going and claiming her articles, as she at first intended; but then, when she thought again of the Wringhims swaying it at Dalcastle, where she had been wont to hear them held in such contempt, if not abhorrence, and perhaps of holding it by the most diabolical means, she was withheld from marring the only chance that remained of having a glimpse into that mysterious affair.

Finally, she resolved not to answer to her name in the court, rather than to appear and assert a falsehood, which she might be called on to certify by oath. She did so; and heard the Sheriff give orders to the officers to make inquiry for Miss Logan from Edinburgh, at the various places of entertainment in town, and to expedite her arrival in court, as things of great value were in dependence. She also heard the man who had turned king's evidence against the prisoner examined for the second time, and sifted most cunningly. His answers gave anything but satisfaction to the Sheriff, though Mrs Logan believed them to be mainly truth. But there were a few questions and answers that struck her above all others.

'How long is it since Mrs Calvert and you became acquainted?'

'About a year and a half.'

'State the precise time, if you please; the day, or night, according to your remembrance.'

'It was on the morning of the 28th of February, 1705.'

'What time of the morning?'

'Perhaps about one.'

'So early as that? At what place did you meet then?'

'It was at the foot of one of the north wynds of Edinburgh.'

'Was it by appointment that you met?'

'No, it was not.'

'For what purpose was it then?'

'For no purpose.'

'How is it that you chance to remember the day and hour so minutely, if you met that woman, whom you have accused, merely by chance, and for no manner of purpose, as you must have met others that night, perhaps to the amount of hundreds, in the same way?'

'I have good cause to remember it, my lord.'

'What was that cause? – No answer? – You don't choose to say what that cause was?'

'I am not at liberty to tell.'

The Sheriff then descended to other particulars, all of which tended to prove that the fellow was an accomplished villain, and that the principal share of the atrocities had been committed by him.

Indeed the Sheriff hinted that he suspected the only share Mrs Calvert had in them was in being too much in his company, and too true to him. The case was remitted to the Court of Justiciary; but Mrs Logan had heard enough to convince her that the culprits first met at the very spot, and the very hour, on which George Colwan was slain; and she had no doubt that they were incendiaries set on by his mother, to forward her own and her darling son's way to opulence. Mrs Logan was wrong, as will appear in the sequel; but her antipathy to Mrs Colwan made her watch the event with all care. She never quitted Peebles as long as Bell Calvert remained there, and, when she was removed to Edinburgh, the other followed. When the trial came on, Mrs Logan and her maid were again summoned as witnesses before the jury, and compelled by the prosecutor for the Crown to appear.

The maid was first called; and, when she came into the witness box, the anxious and hopeless looks of the prisoner were manifest to all. But the girl, whose name, she said, was Bessy Gillies, answered in so flippant and fearless a way that the auditors were much amused. After a number of routine questions, the depute-advocate asked her if she was at home on the morning of the fifth of September last, when her mistress's house was robbed.

'Was I at hame, say ye? Na, faith-ye, lad! An' I had been at hame, there had been mair to dee. I wad hae raised sic a yelloch!'

'Where were you that morning?'

'Where was I, say you? I was in the house where my mistress was, sitting dozing an' half sleeping in the kitchen. I thought aye she would be setting out every minute, for twa hours.'

'And, when you went home, what did you find?'

'What found we? Be my sooth, we found a broken lock, an' toom kists.'

'Relate some of the particulars, if you please.'

'O, sir, the thieves didna stand upon particulars: they were halesale dealers in a' our best wares.'

'I mean, what passed between your mistress and you on the occasion?'

'What passed, say ye? O, there wasna muckle: I was in a great passion, but she was dung doitrified a wee. When she gaed to put the key i' the door, up it flew to the fer wa'. "Bless ye, jaud, what's the meaning o' this?" quo she. "Ye hae left the door open, ye tawpie!" quo she. "The ne'er o' that I did," quo I, "or may my shakel bane never turn another key." When we got the candle lightit, a' the house was in a hoad-road. "Bessy, my woman," quo she, "we are baith ruined and undone creatures." "The deil a bit," quo I; "that I deny positively. H'mh! to speak o' a lass o' my age being ruined and undone! I never had muckle except what was within a good jerkin,[58] an' let the thief ruin me there wha can."'

'Do you remember aught else that your mistress said on the occasion? Did you hear her blame any person?'

'O, she made a gread deal o' grumphing an' groaning about the *misfortune*, as she ca'd it, an' I think she said it was a part o' the ruin wrought by the Ringans, or some sic name. "They'll hae't a'! They'll hae't a'!" cried she, wringing her hands; "a'! they'll hae' a', an' hell wi't, an' they'll get them baith." "Aweel, that's aye some satisfaction," quo I.'

'Whom did she mean by the Ringans, do you know?'

'I fancy they are some creatures that she has dreamed about, for I think there canna be as ill folks living as she ca's them.'

'Did you never hear say that the prisoner at the bar there, Mrs Calvert, or Bell Calvert, was the robber of her house; or that she was one of the Ringans?'

'Never. Somebody tauld her lately that ane Bell Calvert robbed her house, but she disna believe it. Neither do I.'

'What reasons have you for doubting it?'

'Because it was nae woman's fingers that broke up the bolts an' the locks that were torn open that night.'

'Very pertinent, Bessy. Come then within the bar, and look at these articles on the table. Did you ever see these silver spoons before?'

'I hae seen some very like them, and whaever has seen siller spoons has done the same.'

'Can you swear you never saw them before?'

'Na, na, I wadna swear to ony siller spoons that ever war made, unless I had put a private mark on them wi' my ain hand, an' that's what I never did to ane.'

'See, they are all marked with a C.'

'Sae are a' the spoons in Argyle,[59] an' the half o' them in Edinburgh I think. A C is a very common letter, an' so are a' the names that begin wi't. Lay them by, lay them by, an' gie the poor woman her spoons again. They are marked wi' her ain name, an' I hae little doubt they are hers, an' that she has seen better days.'

'Ah, God bless her heart!' sighed the prisoner; and that blessing was echoed in the breathings of many a feeling breast.

'Did you ever see this gown before, think you?'

'I hae seen ane very like it.'

'Could you not swear that gown was your mistress's once?'

'No, unless I saw her hae't on, an' kend that she had paid for't. I am very scrupulous about an oath. *Like* is an ill mark. Sae ill indeed that I wad hardly swear to anything.'

'But you say that gown is *very like* one your mistress used to wear.'

'I never said sic a thing. It is like one I hae seen her hae out airing on the hay raip i' the back green. It is very like ane I hae seen Mrs Butler in the Grass Market wearing too: I rather think it is the same. Bless you, sir, I wadna swear to my ain forefinger, if it had been as lang out o' my sight an' brought in an' laid on that table.'

'Perhaps you are not aware, girl, that this scrupulousness of yours is likely to thwart the purposes of justice, and bereave your mistress of property to the amount of a thousand merks.' (*From the Judge.*)

'I canna help that, my lord: that's her look-out. For my part, I am resolved to keep a clear conscience, till I be married, at any rate.'

'Look over these things and see if there is any one article among them which you can fix on as the property of your mistress.'

'No ane o' them, sir, no ane o' them. An oath is an awfu' thing, especially when it is for life or death. Gie the poor woman her things again, an' let my mistress pick up the next she finds: that's my advice.'[60]

When Mrs Logan came into the box, the prisoner groaned and laid down her head. But how she was astonished when she heard her deliver herself something to the following purport! – That, whatever penalties she was doomed to abide, she was determined she would not bear witness against a woman's life, from a certain conviction that it could not be a woman who broke her house. 'I have no doubt that I may find some of my own things there,' added she, 'but, if they were found in her possession, she has been made a tool, or the dupe, of an infernal set, who shall be nameless here. I believe she *did not* rob me, and for that reason I will have no hand in her condemnation.'

The Judge: 'This is the most singular perversion I have ever witnessed. Mrs Logan, I entertain strong suspicions that the prisoner, or her agents, have made some agreement with you on this matter to prevent the course of justice.'

'So far from that, my lord, I went into the jail at Peebles to this woman, whom I had never seen before, and proffered to withdraw my part in the prosecution, as well as my evidence, provided she would tell me a few simple facts; but she spurned at my offer, and had me turned insolently out of the prison, with orders to the jailor never to admit me again on any pretence.'

The prisoner's counsel, taking hold of this evidence, addressed the jury with great fluency; and, finally, the prosecution was withdrawn, and the prisoner dismissed from the bar, with a severe reprimand for her past conduct, and an exhortation to keep better company.

It was not many days till a caddy[61] came with a large parcel to Mrs Logan's house, which parcel he delivered into her hands, accompanied with a sealed note, containing an inventory of the articles, and a request to know if the unfortunate Arabella Calvert would be admitted to converse with Mrs Logan.

Never was there a woman so much overjoyed as Mrs Logan was at this message. She returned compliments. Would be most happy to see her; and no article of the parcel should be looked at, or touched, till her arrival. It was not long till she made her appearance, dressed in somewhat better style than she had yet seen her; delivered her over the greater part of the stolen property, besides many things that either never had belonged to Mrs Logan or that she thought proper to deny in order that the other might retain them.

The tale that she told of her misfortunes was of the most distressing nature, and was enough to stir up all the tender, as well as abhorrent feelings in the bosom of humanity. She had suffered every deprivation in fame, fortune, and person. She had been imprisoned; she had been scourged, and branded as an impostor; and all on account of her resolute and unmoving fidelity and truth to several of the very worst of men, every one of whom had abandoned her to utter destitution and shame. But this story we cannot enter on at present, as it would perhaps mar the thread of our story, as much as it did the anxious anticipations of Mrs Logan, who sat pining and longing for the relation that follows.

'Now I know, Mrs Logan, that you are expecting a detail of the circumstances relating to the death of Mr George Colwan; and, in gratitude for your unbounded generosity and disinterestedness, I will tell you all that I know, although, for causes that will appear obvious to you, I had determined never in life to divulge one circumstance of it. I can tell you, however, that you will be disappointed, for it was not the gentleman who was accused, found guilty, and would have suffered the utmost penalty of the law had he not made his escape. *It was not he*, I say, who slew your young master, nor had he any hand in it.'

'I never thought he had. But, pray, how do you come to know this?'

'You shall hear. I had been abandoned in York by an artful and consummate fiend; and found guilty of being art and part concerned in the most heinous atrocities, and, in his place, suffered what I yet shudder to think of. I was banished the county, begged my way with my poor outcast child up to Edinburgh, and was there obliged, for the second time in my life, to betake myself to the most degrading of all means to support two wretched lives. I hired a dress, and betook me, shivering, to the High Street, too well aware that my form and appearance would soon draw me suitors enow at that throng and intemperate time of the Parliament. On my very first stepping out to the street, a party of young gentlemen was passing. I heard by the noise they made, and the tenor of their speech, that they were more then mellow, and so I resolved to keep near them, in order, if possible, to make some of them my prey. But, just as one of them began to eye me, I was rudely thrust into a narrow close by one of the guardsmen. I had heard to what house the party was bound, for the men were talking exceedingly loud, and making no secret of it: so I hasted down the close, and round below to the one where their rendezvous was to be; but I was too late, they were all housed and the door bolted. I resolved to wait, thinking they could not all stay long; but I was perishing with famine, and was like to fall down. The moon shone as bright as day, and I perceived, by a sign at the bottom of the close, that there was a small tavern of a certain description up two stairs there. I went up and called, telling the mistress of the house my plan. She approved of it mainly, and offered me her best apartment, provided I could get one of these noble mates to accompany me. She abused Lucky Sudds, as she called her, at the inn where the party was, envying her huge profits, no doubt, and giving me afterwards something to drink, for which I really felt exceedingly grateful in my need. I stepped downstairs in order to be on the alert. The moment that I reached the ground, the door of Lucky Sudds' house opened and shut, and down came the Honourable Thomas Drummond, with hasty and impassioned strides, his sword rattling at his heel. I accosted him in a soft and soothing tone. He was taken with my address; for he instantly stood still and gazed intently at me, then at the place, and then at me again. I beckoned him to follow me, which he did without further ceremony, and we soon found ourselves together in the best room of a house where everything was wretched. He still looked about him, and at me; but all this while he had never spoken a word. At length, I asked if he would take any refreshment? "If you please," said he. I asked what he would have, but he only answered, "Whatever you choose, madam." If he was taken with my address, I was much more taken with his; for he was a complete gentleman, and a gentleman will ever act as one.

'At length, he began as follows: "I am utterly at a loss to account for this adventure, madam. It seems to me like enchantment, and I can hardly believe my senses. An English lady, I judge, and one, who from her manner and address should belong to the first class of society, in such a place as this, is indeed matter of wonder to me. At the foot of a close in Edinburgh! And at this time of the night! Surely it must have been no common reverse of fortune that reduced you to this?" I wept, or pretended to do so; on which he added, "Pray, madam, take heart. Tell me what has befallen you; and if I can do anything for you, in restoring you to your country or your friends, you shall command my interest."

'I had great need of a friend then, and I thought now was the time to secure one. So I began and told him the moving tale I have told you. But I soon perceived that I had kept by the naked truth too unvarnishedly, and thereby quite overshot my mark. When he learned that he was sitting in a wretched corner of an irregular house, with a felon, who had so lately been scourged and banished as a swindler and impostor, his modest nature took the alarm, and he was shocked, instead of being moved with pity. His eye fixed on some of the casual stripes[62] on my arm, and from that moment he became restless and impatient to be gone. I tried some gentle arts to retain him, but in vain; so, after paying both the landlady and me for pleasures he had neither tasted nor asked, he took his leave.

'I showed him downstairs; and, just as he turned the corner of the next land,[63] a man came rushing violently by him; exchanged looks with him, and came running up to me. He appeared in great agitation, and was quite out of breath; and, taking my hand in his, we ran upstairs together without speaking, and were instantly in the apartment I had left, where a stoup of wine still stood untasted. "Ah, this is fortunate!" said my new spark, and helped himself. In the meanwhile, as our apartment was a corner one, and looked both east and north, I ran to the eastern casement to look after Drummond. Now, note me well: I saw him going eastward in his tartans and bonnet, and the gilded hilt of his claymore[64] glittering in the moon; and, at the very same time, I saw two men, the one in black, and the other likewise in tartans, coming towards the steps from the opposite bank, by the foot of the loch; and I saw Drummond and they eyeing each other as they passed. I kept view of *him* till he vanished towards Leith Wynd, and by that time the two strangers had come close up under our window. This is what I wish you to pay particular attention to. I had only lost sight of Drummond (who had given me his name and address) for the short space of time that we took in running up one pair of short stairs; and during that space he had halted a moment, for, when I got my eye on him again, he had not crossed the mouth of the next entry, nor proceeded above ten or twelve paces, and, *at the same time*, I saw the two men coming down the bank on the opposite side of the loch, at about three hundred paces' distance. Both he and they were distinctly in my view, and never within speech of each other, until he vanished into one of the wynds leading towards the bottom of the High Street, at which precise time the two strangers came below my window; so that it was quite clear he neither could be one of them nor have any communication with them.

'Yet, mark me again; for, of all things I have ever seen, this was the most singular. When I looked down at the two strangers, *one of them was extremely like Drummond*. So like was he that there was not one item in dress, form, feature, nor voice, by which I could distinguish the one from the other. I was certain it was not he, because I had seen the one going and the other approaching at the same time, and my impression at the moment was that I looked upon some spirit, or demon, in his likeness. I felt a chillness creep all round my heart, my knees tottered, and, withdrawing my head from the open casement that lay in the dark shade, I said to the man who was with me, "Good God, what is this?"

"What is it, my dear?" said he, as much alarmed as I was.

"As I live, there stands an apparition!" said I.

'He was not so much afraid when he heard me say so, and, peeping cautiously out, he looked and listened awhile, and then, drawing back, he said in a whisper, "They are both living men, and one of them is he I passed at the corner."

' "That he is not," said I, emphatically. "To that I will make oath."

'He smiled and shook his head, and then added, "I never then saw a man before, whom I could not know again, particularly if he was the very last I had seen. But what matters it whether it be or not? As it is no concern of ours, let us sit down and enjoy ourselves."

' "But it *does* matter a very great deal with me, sir," said I. "Bless me, my head is giddy – my breath quite gone, and I feel as if I were surrounded with fiends. Who are you, sir?"

' "You shall know that ere we two part, my love," said he. "I cannot conceive why the return of this young gentleman to the spot he so lately left should discompose you. I suppose he got a glance of you as he passed, and has returned to look after you, and that is the whole secret of the matter."

' "If you will be so civil as to walk out and join him then, it will oblige me hugely," said I, "for I never in my life experienced such boding apprehensions of evil company. I cannot conceive how you should come up here without asking my permission. Will it please you to be gone, sir?" I was within an ace of prevailing. He took out his purse – I need not say more – I was bribed to let him remain. Ah, had I kept my frail resolution of dismissing him at that moment, what a world of shame and misery had been evited! But that, though uppermost still in my mind, has nothing ado here.

'When I peeped over again, the two men were disputing in a whisper, the one of them in violent agitation and terror, and the other upbraiding him, and urging him on to some desperate act. At length I heard the young man in the Highland garb say indignantly, "Hush, recreant! It is God's work which you are commissioned to execute, and it must be done. But, if you positively decline it, I will do it myself, and do you beware of the consequences."

' "Oh, I will, I will!" cried the other in black clothes, in a wretched beseeching tone. "You shall instruct me in this, as in all things else."

'I thought all this while I was closely concealed from them, and wondered not a little when he in tartans gave me a sly nod, as much as to say, "What do you think of this?" or, "Take note of what you see," or something to that effect; from which I perceived that, whatever he was about, he did not wish it to be kept a secret. For all that, I was impressed with a terror and anxiety that I could not overcome, but it only made me mark every event with the more intense curiosity. The Highlander, whom I still could not help regarding as the evil genius of Thomas Drummond, performed every action as with the quickness of thought. He concealed the youth in black in a narrow entry, a little to the westward of my windows, and, as he was leading him across the moonlight green by the shoulder, I perceived, for the first time, that both of them were armed with rapiers. He pushed him without resistance into the dark shaded close, made another signal to me, and hasted up the close to Lucky Sudds' door. The city and the morning were so still that I heard every word that was uttered, on putting my head out a little. He knocked at the door sharply, and, after waiting a considerable space, the bolt was drawn, and the door, as I conceived, edged up as far as the massy chain would let it. "Is young Dalcastle still in the house?" said he sharply.

'I did not hear the answer, but I heard him say, shortly after, "If he is, pray tell him to speak with me for a few minutes." He then withdrew from the door, and came slowly down the close, in a lingering manner, looking oft behind him. Dalcastle came out; advanced a few steps after him, and then stood still, as if hesitating whether or not he should call out a friend to accompany him; and that instant the door behind him was closed, chained, and the iron bolt drawn; on hearing of which, he followed his adversary without further hesitation. As he passed below my window, I heard him say, "I beseech you, Tom, let us do nothing in this matter rashly"; but I could not hear the answer of the other, who had turned the corner.

'I roused up my drowsy companion, who was leaning on the bed, and we both looked together from the north window. We were in the shade, but the moon shone full on the two young gentlemen. Young Dalcastle was visibly the worse of liquor, and, his back being turned towards us, he said something to the other which I could not make out, although he spoke a considerable time, and, from his tones and gestures, appeared to be reasoning. When he had done, the tall young man in the tartans drew his sword, and, his face being straight to us, we heard him say distinctly, "No more words about it, George, if you please; but if you be a man, as I take you to be, draw your sword, and let us settle it here."

'Dalcastle drew his sword, without changing his attitude; but he spoke with more warmth, for we heard his words, "Think you that I fear you, Tom? Be assured, sir, I would not fear ten of the best of your name, at each other's backs: all that I want is to have friends with us to see fair play, for, if you close with me, you are a dead man."

'The other stormed at these words. "You are a braggart, sir,"cried he, "a wretch – a blot on the cheek of nature – a blight on the Christian world – a reprobate – I'll have your soul, sir. You must play at tennis, and put down elect brethren in another world tomorrow." As he said this, he brandished his rapier, exciting Dalcastle to offence. He gained his point. The latter, who had previously drawn, advanced upon his vapouring and licentious antagonist, and a fierce combat ensued. My companion was delighted beyond measure, and I could not keep him from exclaiming, loud enough to have been heard, "That's grand! That's excellent!" For me, my heart quaked like an aspen. Young Dalcastle either had a decided advantage over his adversary, or else the other thought proper to let him have it; for he shifted, and swore, and flitted from Dalcastle's thrusts like a shadow, uttering oft-times a sarcastic laugh, that seemed to provoke the other beyond all bearing. At one time, he would spring away to a great distance, then advance again on young Dalcastle with the swiftness of lightning. But that young

hero always stood his ground, and repelled the attack: he never gave
way, although they fought nearly twice round the bleaching green,
which you know is not a very small one. At length they fought close
up to the mouth of the dark entry, where the fellow in black stood
all this while concealed, and then the combatant in tartans closed
with his antagonist, or pretended to do so; but, the moment they
began to grapple, he wheeled about, turning Colwan's back towards
the entry, and then cried out, "Ah, hell has it! My friend, my friend!"

'That moment the fellow in black rushed from his cover with his
drawn rapier, and gave the brave young Dalcastle two deadly
wounds in the back, as quick as arm could thrust, both of which I
thought pierced through his body. He fell, and, rolling himself on
his back, he perceived who it was that had slain him thus foully, and
said, with a dying emphasis, which I never heard equalled, "Oh, dog
of hell, it is you who has done this!"

'He articulated some more, which I could not hear for other
sounds; for, the moment that the man in black inflicted the deadly
wound, my companion called out, "That's unfair, you rip! That's
damnable! To strike a brave fellow behind! One at a time, you
cowards!" etc., to all which the unnatural fiend in the tartans
answered with a loud exulting laugh; and then, taking the poor
paralysed murderer by the bow of the arm, he hurried him in the
dark entry once more, where I lost sight of them for ever.'

Before this time Mrs Logan had risen up; and, when the narrator
had finished, she was standing with her arms stretched upwards at
their full length, and her visage turned down, on which were
portrayed the lines of the most absolute horror. 'The dark suspicions
of my late benefactor have been just, and his last prediction is
fulfilled,' cried she. 'The murderer of the accomplished George
Colwan has been his own brother, set on, there is little doubt, by her
who bare them both, and her directing angel, the self-justified bigot.
Aye, and yonder they sit, enjoying the luxuries so dearly purchased,
with perfect impunity! If the Almighty do not hurl them down,
blasted with shame and confusion, there is no hope of retribution in
this life. And, by His might, I will be the agent to accomplish it! Why
did the man not pursue the foul murderers? Why did he not raise the
alarm, and call the watch?'

'He? The wretch! He durst not move from the shelter he had
obtained. No, not for the soul of him. He was pursued for his life, at
the moment when he first flew into my arms. But I did not know it;
no, I did not *then* know him. May the curse of heaven and the blight
of hell, settle on the detestable wretch, he pursue for the sake of

justice! No; his efforts have all been for evil, but never for good. But *I* raised the alarm; miserable and degraded as I was, I pursued and raised the watch myself. Have you not heard the name of Bell Calvert coupled with that hideous and mysterious affair?'

'Yes, I have. In secret often I have heard it. But how came it that you could never be found? How came it that you never appeared in defence of the Honourable Thomas Drummond; you, the only person who could have justified him?'

'I could not, for I then fell under the power and guidance of a wretch who durst not for the soul of him be brought forward in the affair. And, what was worse, his evidence would have overborne mine, for he would have sworn that the man who called out and fought Colwan was the same he met leaving my apartment, and there was an end of it. And, moreover, it is well known that this same man – this wretch of whom I speak, never mistook one man for another in his life, which makes the mystery of the likeness between this incendiary and Drummond the more extraordinary.'

'If it was Drummond, after all that you have asserted, then are my surmises still wrong.'

'There is nothing of which I can be more certain than that it was not Drummond. We have nothing on earth but our senses to depend upon: if these deceive us, what are we to do? I own I cannot account for it; nor ever shall be able to account for it as long as I live.'

'Could you know the man in black, if you saw him again?'

'I think I could, if I saw him walk or run: his gait was very particular. He walked as if he had been flat-soled, and his legs made of steel, without any joints in his feet or ankles.'

'The very same! The very same! The very same! Pray will you take a few days' journey into the country with me, to look at such a man?'

'You have preserved my life, and for you I will do anything. I will accompany you with pleasure: and I think I can say that I will know him, for his form left an impression on my heart not soon to be effaced. But of this I am sure that my unworthy companion will recognise him, and that he will be able to swear to his identity every day as long as he lives.'

'Where is he? Where is he? Oh! Mrs Calvert, where is he?'

'Where is he? He is the wretch whom you heard giving me up to the death; who, after experiencing every mark of affection that a poor ruined being could confer, and after committing a thousand atrocities of which she was ignorant, became an informer to save his diabolical life, and attempted to offer up mine as a sacrifice for all.

We will go by ourselves first, and I will tell you if it is necessary to send any farther.'

The two dames, the very next morning, dressed themselves like country goodwives, and, hiring two stout ponies furnished with pillions,[65] they took their journey westward, and the second evening after leaving Edinburgh they arrived at the village about two miles below Dalcastle, where they alighted. But Mrs Logan, being anxious to have Mrs Calvert's judgment, without either hint or preparation, took care not to mention that they were so near to the end of their journey. In conformity with this plan, she said, after they had sat a while: 'Heigh-ho, but I am weary! What, suppose we should rest a day here before we proceed farther on our journey?'

Mrs Calvert was leaning on the casement and looking out when her companion addressed these words to her, and by far too much engaged to return any answer, for her eyes were riveted on two young men who approached from the farther end of the village; and at length, turning round her head, she said, with the most intense interest, 'Proceed farther on our journey, did you say? That we need not do; for, as I live, here comes the very man!'

Mrs Logan ran to the window, and, behold, there was indeed Robert Wringhim Colwan (now the Laird of Dalcastle) coming forward almost below their window, walking arm in arm with another young man, and, as the two passed, the latter looked up and made a sly signal to the two dames, biting his lip, winking with his left eye, and nodding his head. Mrs Calvert was astonished at this recognisance, the young man's former companion having made exactly such another signal on the night of the duel, by the light of the moon; and it struck her, moreover, that she had somewhere seen this young man's face before. She looked after him, and he winked over his shoulder to her; but she was prevented from returning his salute by her companion, who uttered a loud cry, between a groan and shriek, and fell down on the floor with a rumble like a wall that had suddenly been undermined. She had fainted quite away, and required all her companion's attention during the remainder of the evening, for she had scarcely ever well recovered out of one fit before she fell into another, and in the short intervals she raved like one distracted or in a dream. After falling into a sound sleep by night, she recovered her equanimity, and the two began to converse seriously on what they had seen. Mrs Calvert averred that the young man who passed next to the window *was* the very man who stabbed George Colwan in the back, and she said she was willing to take her oath on it at any time when required, and was certain, if the wretch Ridsley saw him, that he would make oath to the same purport, for that his walk was so peculiar no one of common discernment could mistake it.

Mrs Logan was in great agitation, and said: 'It is what I have suspected all along, and what I am sure my late master and benefactor was persuaded of, and the horror of such an idea cut short his days. That wretch, Mrs Calvert, is the born brother of him he murdered, sons of the same mother they were, whether or not of the same father, the Lord only knows. But, oh, Mrs Calvert, that is not the main thing that has discomposed me, and shaken my nerves to pieces at this time. Who do you think the young man was who walked in his company tonight?'

'I cannot for my life recollect, but am convinced I have seen the same fine form and face before.'

'And did not he seem to know us, Mrs Calvert? You who are able to recollect things as they happened, did he not seem to recollect us, and make signs to that effect?'

'He did, indeed, and apparently with great good humour.'

'Oh, Mrs Calvert, hold me, else I shall fall into hysterics again! Who is he? Who is he? Tell me who you suppose he is, for I cannot say my own thought.'

'On my life, I cannot remember.'

'Did you note the appearance of the young gentleman you saw slain that night? Do you recollect aught of the appearance of my young master, George Colwan?'

Mrs Calvert sat silent, and stared the other mildly in the face. Their looks encountered, and there was an unearthly amazement that gleamed from each, which, meeting together, caught real fire, and returned the flame to their heated imaginations, till the two associates became like two statues, with their hands spread, their eyes fixed, and their chops fallen down upon their bosoms. An old woman who kept the lodging-house, having been called in before when Mrs Logan was faintish, chanced to enter at this crisis with some cordial; and, seeing the state of her lodgers, she caught the infection, and fell into the same rigid and statue-like appearance. No scene more striking was ever exhibited; and if Mrs Calvert had not resumed strength of mind to speak, and break the spell, it is impossible to say how long it might have continued. 'It is he, I believe,' said she, uttering the words as it were inwardly. 'It can be none other but he. But, no, it is impossible! I saw him stabbed through and through the heart; I saw him roll backward on the green in his own blood, utter his last words, and groan away his soul. Yet, if it is not he, who can it be?'

'It *is* he!' cried Mrs Logan, hysterically.

'Yes, yes, it *is* he!' cried the landlady, in unison.

'It is who?' said Mrs Calvert. 'Whom do you mean, mistress?'

'Oh, I don't know! I don't know! I was affrighted.'

'Hold your peace then till you recover your senses, and tell me, if you can, who that young gentleman is who keeps company with the new Laird of Dalcastle?'

'Oh, it is he! It is he!' screamed Mrs Logan, wringing her hands.

'Oh, it is he! It is he!' cried the landlady, wringing hers.

Mrs Calvert turned the latter gently and civilly out of the apartment, observing that there seemed to be some infection in the air of the room, and she would be wise for herself to keep out of it.

The two dames had a restless and hideous night. Sleep came not to their relief; for their conversation was wholly about the dead, who seemed to be alive, and their minds were wandering and groping in a chaos of mystery. 'Did you attend to his corpse, and know that he positively died and was buried?' said Mrs Calvert.

'Oh, yes, from the moment that his fair but mangled corpse was brought home, I attended it till that when it was screwed in the coffin. I washed the long stripes of blood from his lifeless form, on both sides of the body. I bathed the livid wound that passed through his generous and gentle heart. There was one through the flesh of his left side too, which had bled most outwardly of them all. I bathed them, and bandaged them up with wax and perfumed ointment, but still the blood oozed through all, so that when he was laid in the coffin he was like one newly murdered. My brave, my generous young master! He was always as a son to me, and no son was ever more kind or more respectful to a mother. But he was butchered – he was cut off from the earth ere he had well reached to manhood – most barbarously and unfairly slain. And how is it, how can it be, that we again see him here, walking arm in arm with his murderer?'

'The thing cannot be, Mrs Logan. It is a fantasy of our disturbed imaginations, therefore let us compose ourselves till we investigate this matter farther.'

'It cannot be in nature, that is quite clear,' said Mrs Logan. 'Yet how it should be that I should *think* so – I who knew and nursed him from his infancy – there lies the paradox. As you said once before, we have nothing but our senses to depend on, and, if you and I believe that we see a person, why, we do see him. Whose word, or whose reasoning can convince us against our own senses? We will disguise ourselves as poor women selling a few country wares, and we will go up to the Hall, and see what is to see, and hear what we can hear, for this is a weighty business in which we are engaged, namely, to turn the vengeance of the law upon an unnatural monster; and we will further learn, if we can, who this is that accompanies him.'

Mrs Calvert acquiesced, and the two dames took their way to Dalcastle, with baskets well furnished with trifles. They did not take the common path from the village, but went about, and approached the mansion by a different way. But it seemed as if some overruling power ordered it that they should miss no chance of attaining the information they wanted. For ere ever they came within half a mile of Dalcastle they perceived the two youths coming as to meet them, on the same path. The road leading from Dalcastle towards the north-east, as all the country knows, goes along a dark bank of brushwood called the Bogle-heuch.[66] It was by this track that the two women were going, and, when they perceived the two gentlemen meeting them, they turned back, and, the moment they were out of their sight, they concealed themselves in a thicket close by the road. They did this because Mrs Logan was terrified for being discovered, and because they wished to reconnoitre without being seen. Mrs Calvert now charged her, whatever she saw, or whatever she heard, to put on a resolution, and support it, for if she fainted there and was discovered, what was to become of her!

The two young men came on, in earnest and vehement conversation; but the subject they were on was a terrible one, and hardly fit to be repeated in the face of a Christian community. Wringhim was disputing the boundlessness of the true Christian's freedom, and expressing doubts that, chosen as he knew he was from all eternity, still it might be possible for him to commit acts that would exclude him from the limits of the covenant. The other argued, with mighty fluency, that the thing was utterly impossible, and altogether inconsistent with eternal predestination. The arguments of the latter prevailed, and the laird was driven to sullen silence. But, to the women's utter surprise, as the conquering disputant passed, he made a signal of recognisance through the brambles to them, as formerly, and, that he might expose his associate fully, and in his true colours, he led him backwards and forwards by the women more than twenty times, making him to confess both the crimes that he had done and those he had in contemplation. At length he said to him: 'Assuredly I saw some strolling vagrant women on this walk, my dear friend: I wish we could find them, for there is little doubt that they are concealed here in your woods.'

'I wish we *could* find them,' answered Wringhim. 'We would have fine sport maltreating and abusing them.'

'That we should, that we should! Now tell me, Robert, if you found a malevolent woman, the latent enemy of your prosperity, lurking in these woods to betray you, what would you inflict on her?'

'I would tear her to pieces with my dogs, and feed them with her flesh. Oh, my dear friend, there is an old strumpet who lived with my unnatural father, whom I hold in such utter detestation that I stand constantly in dread of her, and would sacrifice the half of my estate to shed her blood!'

'What will you give me if I will put her in your power, and give you a fair and genuine excuse for making away with her; one for which you shall answer at any bar, here or hereafter?'

'I should like to see the vile hag put down. She is in possession of the family plate, that is mine by right, as well as a thousand valuable relics, and great riches besides, all of which the old profligate gifted shamefully away. And it is said, besides all these that she has sworn my destruction.'

'She has, she has. But I see not how she can accomplish that, seeing the deed was done so suddenly, and in the silence of the night.'

'It was said there were some onlookers. But where shall we find that disgraceful Miss Logan?'

'I will show you her by and by. But will you then consent to the other meritorious deed? Come, be a man, and throw away scruples.'

'If you can convince me that the promise is binding I will.'

'Then step this way, till I give you a piece of information.'

They walked a little way out of hearing, but went not out of sight; therefore, though the women were in a terrible quandary, they durst not stir, for they had some hopes that this extraordinary person was on a mission of the same sort with themselves, knew of them, and was going to make use of their testimony. Mrs Logan was several times on the point of falling into a swoon, so much did the appearance of the young man impress her, until her associate covered her face that she might listen without embarrassment. But this latter dialogue roused different feelings within them; namely, those arising from imminent personal danger. They saw his waggish associate point out the place of their concealment to Wringhim, who came towards them, out of curiosity to see what his friend meant by what he believed to be a joke, manifestly without crediting it in the least degree. When he came running away, the other called after him: 'If she is too hard for you, call to me.' As he said this, he hasted out of sight in the contrary direction, apparently much delighted with the joke.

Wringhim came rushing through the thicket impetuously, to the very spot where Mrs Logan lay squatted. She held the wrapping close about her head, but he tore it off and discovered her. 'The curse of God be on thee!' said he. 'What fiend has brought thee here, and for what purpose art thou come? But, whatever has brought thee, *I have thee*!' and with that he seized her by the throat. The two women, when they heard what jeopardy they were in from such a wretch, had squatted among the underwood at a small distance from each other, so that he had never observed Mrs Calvert; but, no sooner had he seized her benefactor, than, like a wildcat, she sprung out of the thicket, and had both hands fixed at his throat, one of them twisted in his stock,[67] in a twinkling. She brought him back-over among the brushwood, and the two fixing on him like two harpies, mastered him with ease. Then indeed was he woefully beset. He deemed for a while that his friend was at his back, and, turning his bloodshot eyes towards the path, he attempted to call; but there was no friend there, and the women cut short his cries by another twist of his stock. 'Now, gallant and rightful Laird of Dalcastle,' said Mrs Logan, 'what hast thou to say for thyself? Lay thy account to dree the weird[68] thou hast so well earned. Now shalt thou suffer due penance for murdering thy brave and only brother.'

'Thou liest, thou hag of the pit! I touched not my brother's life.'

'I saw thee do it with these eyes that now look thee in the face; ay, when his back was to thee, too, and while he was hotly engaged with thy friend,' said Mrs Calvert.

'I heard thee confess it again and again this same hour,' said Mrs Logan.

'Ay, and so did I,' said her companion. 'Murder will out, though the Almighty should lend hearing to the ears of the willow, and speech to the seven tongues of the woodriff.'[69]

'You are liars and witches!' said he, foaming with rage, 'and creatures fitted from the beginning for eternal destruction. I'll have your bones and your blood sacrificed on your cursed altars! O Gil-Martin! Gil-Martin! Where art thou now? Here, here is the proper food for blessed vengeance! Hilloa!'

There was no friend, no Gil-Martin there to hear or assist him: he was in the two women's mercy, but they used it with moderation. They mocked, they tormented, and they threatened him; but, finally, after putting him in great terror, they bound his hands behind his back, and his feet fast with long straps of garters which they chanced to have in their baskets, to prevent him from pursuing them till they were out of his reach. As they left him, which they did in the middle of the path, Mrs Calvert said: 'We could easily put an end to thy sinful life, but our hands shall be free of thy blood. Nevertheless thou art still in our power, and the vengeance of thy country shall overtake thee, thou mean and cowardly murderer, ay, and that more suddenly than thou art aware!'

The women posted to Edinburgh; and as they put themselves under the protection of an English merchant, who was journeying thither with twenty horses laden, and armed servants, so they had scarcely any conversation on the road. When they arrived at Mrs Logan's house, then they spoke of what they had seen and heard, and agreed that they had sufficient proof to condemn young Wringhim, who they thought richly deserved the severest doom of the law.

'I never in my life saw any human being,' said Mrs Calvert, whom I thought so like a fiend. If a demon could inherit flesh and blood, that youth is precisely such a being as I could conceive that demon to be. The depth and the malignity of his eye is hideous. His breath is like the airs from a charnel house, and his flesh seems fading from his bones, as if the worm that never dies were gnawing it away already.'

'He was always repulsive, and every way repulsive,' said the other, 'but he is now indeed altered greatly to the worse. While we were hand-fasting him, I felt his body to be feeble and emaciated; but yet I know him to be so puffed up with spiritual pride that I believe he weens every one of his actions justified before God, and, instead of having stings of conscience for these, he takes great merit to himself in having effected them. Still my thoughts are less about him than the extraordinary being who accompanies him. He does everything with so much ease and indifference, so much velocity and effect, that all bespeak him an adept in wickedness. The likeness to my late hapless young master is so striking that I can hardly believe it to be a chance model; and I think he imitates him in everything, for some purpose or some effect on his sinful associate. Do you know that he is so like in every lineament, look, and gesture, that, against the clearest light of reason, I cannot in my mind separate the one from the other, and have a certain indefinable expression on my mind that they are one and the same being, or that the one was a prototype of the other.'

'If there is an earthly crime,' said Mrs Calvert, 'for the due punishment of which the Almighty may be supposed to subvert the order of nature, it is fratricide. But tell me, dear friend, did you remark to what the subtle and hellish villain was endeavouring to prompt the assassin?'

'No, I could not comprehend it. My senses were altogether so bewildered that I thought they had combined to deceive me, and I gave them no credit.'

'Then hear me: I am almost certain he was using every persuasion to induce him to make away with his mother; and I likewise conceive that I heard the incendiary give his consent!'

'This is dreadful. Let us speak and think no more about it, till we see the issue. In the meantime, let us do that which is our bounden duty – go and divulge all that we know relating to this foul murder.'

Accordingly the two women went to Sir Thomas Wallace of Craigie, the Lord Justice Clerk (who was, I think, either uncle or grandfather to young Drummond, who was outlawed and obliged to fly his country on account of Colwan's death), and to that gentleman they related every circumstance of what they had seen and heard. He examined Calvert very minutely, and seemed deeply interested in her evidence – said he knew she was relating the truth, and, in testimony of it, brought a letter of young Drummond's from his desk, wherein that young gentleman, after protesting his innocence in the most forcible terms, confessed having been with such a woman in such a house, after leaving the company of his friends; and that, on going home, Sir Thomas's servant had let him in, in the dark, and from these circumstances he found it impossible to prove an alibi. He begged of his relative, if ever an opportunity offered, to do his endeavour to clear up that mystery, and remove the horrid stigma from his name in his country, and among his kin, of having stabbed a friend behind his back.

Lord Craigie, therefore, directed the two women to the proper authorities, and, after hearing their evidence there, it was judged proper to apprehend the present Laird of Dalcastle, and bring him to his trial. But, before that, they sent the prisoner in the Tolbooth,[70] he who had seen the whole transaction along with Mrs Calvert, to take a view of Wringhim privately; and, his discrimination being so well known as to be proverbial all over the land, they determined secretly to be ruled by his report. They accordingly sent him on a pretended mission of legality to Dalcastle, with orders to see and speak with the proprietor, without giving him a hint what was wanted. On his return, they examined him, and he told them that he found all things at the place in utter confusion and dismay;

that the lady of the place was missing, and could not be found, dead or alive. On being asked if he had ever seen the proprietor before, he looked astounded and unwilling to answer. But it came out that he had; and that he had once seen him kill a man on such a spot at such an hour.

Officers were then dispatched, without delay, to apprehend the monster, and bring him to justice. On these going to the mansion, and inquiring for him, they were told he was at home; on which they stationed guards, and searched all the premises, but he was not to be found. It was in vain that they overturned beds, raised floors, and broke open closets: Robert Wringhim Colwan was lost once and for ever. His mother also was lost; and strong suspicions attached to some of the farmers and house servants to whom she was obnoxious, relating to her disappearance.

The Honourable Thomas Drummond became a distinguished officer in the Austrian service, and died in the memorable year for Scotland, 1715;[71] and this is all with which history, justiciary records, and tradition, furnish me relating to these matters.

I have now the pleasure of presenting my readers with an original document of a most singular nature, and preserved for their perusal in a still more singular manner. I offer no remarks on it, and make as few additions to it, leaving everyone to judge for himself. We have heard much of the rage of fanaticism in former days, but nothing to this.

The Private Memoirs and Confessions
of a Sinner written by Himself

MY LIFE has been a life of trouble and turmoil; of change and vicissitude; of anger and exultation; of sorrow and of vengeance. My sorrows have all been for a slighted gospel, and my vengeance has been wreaked on its adversaries. Therefore, in the might of Heaven, I will sit down and write: I will let the wicked of this world know what I have done in the faith of the promises, and justification by grace, that they may read and tremble, and bless their gods of silver and gold that the minister of Heaven was removed from their sphere before their blood was mingled with their sacrifices.

I was born an outcast in the world, in which I was destined to act so conspicuous a part. My mother was a burning and a shining light, in the community of Scottish worthies, and in the days of her virginity had suffered much in the persecution of the saints. But it so pleased Heaven that, as a trial of her faith, she was married to one of the wicked; a man all over spotted with the leprosy of sin. As well might they have conjoined fire and water together, in hopes that they would consort and amalgamate, as purity and corruption. She fled from his embraces the first night after their marriage, and from that time forth his iniquities so galled her upright heart that she quitted his society altogether, keeping her own apartments in the same house with him.

I was the second son of this unhappy marriage, and, ere ever I was born, my father according to the flesh disclaimed all relation or connection with me, and all interest in me, save what the law compelled him to take, which was to grant me a scanty maintenance; and had it not been for a faithful minister of the gospel; my mother's early instructor, I should have remained an outcast from the church visible. He took pity on me, admitting me not only into that, but into the bosom of his own household and ministry also, and to him am I indebted, under Heaven, for the high conceptions and glorious discernment between good and evil, right and wrong, which I attained even at an early age. It was he who directed my studies aright, both in the learning of the ancient fathers and the doctrines of the reformed church, and designed me for his assistant and successor in the holy office. I missed no opportunity of perfecting myself particularly in all the minute points of theology in which my reverend father and mother took great delight; but at length I acquired so much skill that I astonished my teachers, and made them gaze at one another. I remember that it was the custom, in my patron's house, to ask questions of the Single Catechism round every Sabbath night. He asked the first, my mother the second, and so on, everyone saying the question asked and then asking the next. It fell to my mother to ask Effectual Calling[72] at me. I said the answer with propriety and emphasis. 'Now, madam,' added I, my question to you is: What is *In*effectual Calling?'

'Ineffectual Calling? There is no such thing, Robert,' said she.

'But there is, madam,' said I, 'and that answer proves how much you say these fundamental precepts by rote, and without any consideration. Ineffectual Calling is *the outward call of the gospel* without any effect on the hearts of unregenerated and impenitent sinners. Have not all these the same calls, warnings, doctrines, and reproofs, that we have? And is not this Ineffectual Calling? Has not Ardinferry the same? Has not Patrick M'Lure the same? *Has not the Laird of Dalcastle and his reprobate heir* the same? And will any tell me that *this is not In*effectual Calling?'

'What a wonderful boy he is!' said my mother.

'I'm feared he turn out to be a conceited gowk,'[73] said old Barnet, the minister's man.

'No,' said my pastor, and *father* (as I shall henceforth denominate him). 'No, Barnet, he *is* a wonderful boy; and no marvel, for I have prayed for these talents to be bestowed on him from his infancy: and do you think that Heaven would refuse a prayer so disinterested? No, it is impossible. But my dread is, madam,' continued he, turning to my mother, 'that he is yet in the bond of iniquity.'

'God forbid!' said my mother.

'I have struggled with the Almighty long and hard,' continued he; 'but have as yet no certain token of acceptance in his behalf. I have indeed fought a hard fight, but have been repulsed by him who hath seldom refused my request; although I cited his own words against him, and endeavoured to hold him at his promise, he hath so many turnings in the supremacy of his power, that I have been rejected. How dreadful is it to think of our darling being still without the pale of the covenant![74] But I have vowed a vow, and in that there is hope.'

My heart quaked with terror when I thought of being still living in a state of reprobation, subjected to the awful issues of death, judgment, and eternal misery, by the slightest accident or casualty;

and I set about the duty of prayer myself with the utmost earnestness. I prayed three times every day, and seven times on the Sabbath; but, the more frequently and fervently that I prayed, I sinned still the more. About this time, and for a long period afterwards, amounting to several years, I lived in a hopeless and deplorable state of mind; for I said to myself, 'If my name is not written in the book of life from all eternity, it is in vain for me to presume that either vows or prayers of mine, or those of all mankind combined, can ever procure its insertion now.' I had come under many vows, most solemnly taken, every one of which I had broken; and I saw with the intensity of juvenile grief that there was no hope for me. I went on sinning every hour, and all the while most strenuously warring against sin, and repenting of every one transgression as soon after the commission of it as I got leisure to think. But, oh, what a wretched state this unregenerated state is, in which every effort after righteousness only aggravates our offences! I found it vanity to contend; for, after communing with my heart, the conclusion was as follows: 'If I could repent me of all my sins, and shed tears of blood for them, still have I not a load of original transgression pressing on me that is enough to crush me to the lowest hell. I may be angry with my first parents for having sinned but how I shall repent me of their sin is beyond what I am able to comprehend.'

Still, in those days of depravity and corruption, I had some of those principles implanted in my mind which were afterwards to spring up with such amazing fertility among the heroes of the faith and the promises. In particular, I felt great indignation against all the wicked of this world, and often wished for the means of ridding it of such a noxious burden. I liked John Barnet, my reverend father's serving-man, extremely ill; but, from a supposition that he might be one of the justified, I refrained from doing him any injury. He gave always his word against me, and when we were by ourselves, in the barn or the fields, he rated me with such severity for my faults that my heart could brook it no longer. He discovered some notorious lies that I had framed, and taxed me with them in such a manner that I could in no wise get off. My cheek burnt with offence, rather than shame; and he, thinking he had got the mastery of me, exulted over me most unmercifully, telling me I was a selfish and conceited blackguard, who made great pretences towards religious devotion to cloak a disposition tainted with deceit, and that it would not much astonish him if I brought myself to the gallows.

I gathered some courage from his over-severity, and answered him as follows: 'Who made thee a judge of the actions or dispositions of the Almighty's creatures – thou who art a worm and no man in his sight? How it befits thee to deal out judgments and anathemas! Hath he not made one vessel to honour, and another to dishonour,[75] as in the case with myself and thee? Hath he not builded his stories in the heavens, and laid the foundations thereof in the earth, and how can a being like thee judge between good and evil, that are both subjected to the workings of his hand; or of the opposing principles in the soul of man, correcting, modifying, and refining one another?'

I said this with that strong display of fervour for which I was remarkable at my years, and expected old Barnet to be utterly confounded; but he only shook his head, and, with the most provoking grin, said: 'There he goes! Sickan sublime and ridiculous sophistry I never heard come out of another mouth but ane. There needs nae aiths to be sworn afore the session wha is your father, young goodman. I ne'er, for my part, saw a son sae like a dad, sin' my een first opened.' With that he went away, saying with an ill-natured wince: 'You made to honour and me to dishonour! Dirty bow-kail thing that thou be'st!'[76]

'I will have the old rascal on the hip for this, if I live,' thought I. So I went and asked my mother if John was a righteous man. She could not tell, but supposed he was, and therefore I got no encouragement from her. I went next to my reverend father, and inquired his opinion, expecting as little from that quarter. He knew the elect as it were by instinct, and could have told you of all those in his own, and some neighbouring parishes, who were born within the boundaries of the covenant of promise, and who were not.

'I keep a good deal in company with your servant, old Barnet, father,' said I.

'You do, boy, you do, I see,' said he.

'I wish I may not keep too much in his company,' said I, 'not knowing what kind of society I am in. Is John a good man, father?'

'Why, boy, he is but so so. A morally good man John is, but very little of the leaven of true righteousness, which is faith, within. I am afraid old Barnet, with all his stock of morality, will be a castaway.'

My heart was greatly cheered by this remark; and I sighed very deeply, and hung my head to one side. The worthy father observed me, and inquired the cause, when I answered as follows: 'How dreadful the thought, that I have been going daily in company and fellowship with one whose name is written on the red-letter side of the book of life; whose body and soul have been, from all eternity, consigned over to everlasting destruction, and to whom the blood of the atonement can never, never reach! Father, this is an awful thing, and beyond my comprehension.'

'While we are in the world, we must mix with the inhabitants thereof,' said he; 'and the stains which adhere to us by reason of this mixture, which is unavoidable, shall all be washed away. It is our duty, however, to shun the society of wicked men as much as possible, lest we partake of their sins, and become sharers with them in punishment. John, however, is morally a good man, and may yet get a cast of grace.'

'I always thought him a good man till today,' said I, 'when he threw out some reflections on your character, so horrible that I quake to think of the wickedness and malevolence of his heart. He was rating me very impertinently for some supposed fault, which had no being save in his own jealous brain, when I attempted to reason him out of his belief in the spirit of calm Christian argument. But how do you think he answered me? He did so, sir, by twisting his mouth at me, and remarking that such sublime and ridiculous sophistry never came out of another mouth but one (meaning yours) and that no oath before a kirk session was necessary to prove who was my dad, for that he had never seen a son so like a father as I was like mine.'

'He durst not for his soul's salvation, and for his daily bread, which he values much more, say such a word, boy; therefore, take care what you assert,' said my reverend father.

'He said these very words, and will not deny them, sir,' said I.

My reverend father turned about in great wrath and indignation, and went away in search of John, but I kept out of the way, and listened at a back window; for John was dressing the plot of ground behind the house; and I hope it was no sin in me that I did rejoice in the dialogue which took place, it being the victory of righteousness over error.

'Well, John, this is a fine day for your delving work.'

'Ay, it's a tolerable day, sir.'

'Are you thankful in heart, John, for such temporal mercies as these?'

'Aw doubt we're a' ower little thankfu', sir, baith for temporal an' speeritual mercies; but it isna aye the maist thankfu' heart that maks the greatest fraze wi' the tongue.'

'I hope there is nothing personal under that remark, John?'

'Gin the bannet fits ony body's head, they're unco welcome to it, sir, for me.'

'John, I do not approve of these innuendoes. You have an arch malicious manner of vending your aphorisms, which the men of the world are too apt to read the wrong way, for your dark hints are sure to have *one* very bad meaning.'

'Hout na, sir, it's only bad folks that think sae. They find ma bits o' gibes come hame to their hearts wi' a kind o' yerk, an' that gars them wince.'

'That saying is ten times worse than the other, John; it is a manifest insult: it is just telling me to my face that you think me a bad man.'

'A body canna help his thoughts, sir.'

'No, but a man's thoughts are generally formed from observation. Now I should like to know, even from the mouth of a misbeliever, what part of my conduct warrants such a conclusion.'

'Nae particular pairt, sir; I draw a' my conclusions frae the haill o' a man's character, an' I'm no that aften far wrong.'

'Well, John, and what sort of general character do you suppose mine to be?'

'Yours is a Scripture character, sir, an' I'll prove it.'

'I hope so, John. Well, which of the Scripture characters do you think approximates nearest to my own?'

'Guess, sir, guess; I wish to lead a proof.'

'Why, if it be an Old Testament character, I hope it is Melchisedec,[77] for at all events you cannot deny there is one point of resemblance: I, like him, am a preacher of righteousness. If it be a New Testament character, I suppose you mean the Apostle of the Gentiles,[78] of whom I am an unworthy representative.'

'Na, na, sir, better nor that still, an' fer closer is the resemblance. When ye bring me to the point, I maun speak. Ye are the just Pharisee, sir, that gaed up wi' the poor publican to pray in the Temple;[79] an' ye're acting the very same pairt at this time, an' saying i' your heart, "God, I thank thee that I am not as other men are, an' in nae way like this poor misbelieving unregenerate sinner, John Barnet.'

'I hope I may say so indeed.'

'There now! I tauld you how it was! But, d'ye hear, maister. Here stands the poor sinner, John Barnet, your beadle an' servantman, wha wadna change chances wi' you in the neist world, nor consciences in this, for ten times a' that you possess – your justification by faith an' awthegither.'

'You are extremely audacious and impertinent, John; but the language of reprobation cannot affect me: I came only to ask you one question, which I desire you to answer candidly. Did you ever say to anyone that I was the boy Robert's natural father?'

'Hout na, sir! Ha-ha-ha! Aih, fie, na, sir! I durst-na say that for my life. I doubt the black stool,[80] an' the sack gown, or maybe the juggs wad hae been my portion had I said sic a thing as that. Hout, hout! Fie, fie! Unco-like doings thae for a Melchizedek or a Saint Paul!'

'John, you are a profane old man, and I desire that you will not presume to break your jests on me. Tell me, dare you say, or dare you think, that I am the natural father of that boy?'

'Ye canna hinder me to think whatever I like, sir, nor can I hinder mysel.'

'But did you ever *say* to anyone that he resembled me, and fathered himself well enough?'

'I hae said mony a time that he resembled you, sir. Naebody can mistake that.'

'But, John, there are many natural reasons for such likenesses, besides that of consanguinity. They depend much on the thoughts and affections of the mother; and it is probable that the mother of this boy, being deserted by her worthless husband, having turned her thoughts on me, as likely to be her protector, may have caused this striking resemblance.'

'Ay, it may be, sir. I coudna say.'

'I have known a lady, John, who was delivered of a blackamoor child, merely from the circumstance of having got a start by the sudden entrance of her negro servant, and not being able to forget him for several hours.'

'It may be, sir; but I ken this – an' I had been the laird, I wadna hae ta'en that story in.'

'So, then, John, you positively think, from a casual likeness, that this boy is my son?'

'Man's thoughts are vanity, sir; they come unasked, an' gang away without a dismissal, an' he canna' help them. I'm neither gaun to say that I *think* he's your son, nor that I think he's *no* your son: sae ye needna pose me nae mair about it.'

'Hear then my determination, John. If you do not promise to me, in faith and honour, that you never will say, or insinuate such a thing again in your life, as that that boy is my natural son, I will take the keys of the church from you, and dismiss you from my service.'

John pulled out the keys, and dashed them on the gravel at the reverend minister's feet. 'There are the keys o' your kirk, sir! I hae never had muckle mense o' them sin' ye entered the door o't. I hae carried them this three and thretty year, but they have aye been like to burn a hole i' my pouch sin' ever they were turned for your admittance. Tak them again, an' gie them to wha you will, and muckle gude may he get o' them. Auld John may dee a beggar in a hay barn, or at the back of a dike, but he sall aye be master o' his ain thoughts an' gie them vent or no, as he likes.'[81]

He left the manse[82] that day, and I rejoiced in the riddance; for I disdained to be kept so much under by one who was in bond of iniquity, and of whom there seemed no hope, as he rejoiced in his frowardness, and refused to submit to that faithful teacher, his master.

It was about this time that my reverend father preached a sermon, one sentence of which affected me most disagreeably. It was to the purport that every unrepented sin was productive of a new sin with each breath that a man drew; and every one of these new sins added to the catalogue in the same manner. I was utterly confounded at the multitude of my transgressions; for I was sensible that there were great numbers of sins of which I had never been able thoroughly to repent, and these momentary ones, by moderate calculation, had, I saw, long ago, amounted to a hundred and fifty thousand in the minute, and I saw no end to the series of repentances to which I had subjected myself. A lifetime was nothing to enable me to accomplish the sum, and then being, for anything I was certain of, in my state of nature, and the grace of repentance withheld from me – what was I to do, or what was to become of me? In the meantime, I went on sinning without measure; but I was still more troubled about the multitude than the magnitude of my transgressions, and the small minute ones puzzled me more than those that were more heinous, as the latter had generally some good effects in the way of punishing wicked men, froward boys, and deceitful women; and I rejoiced, even then in my early youth, at being used as a scourge in the hand of the Lord; another Jehu, a Cyrus, or a Nebuchadnezzar.[83]

On the whole, I remember that I got into great confusion relating to my sins and repentances, and knew neither where to begin nor how to proceed, and often had great fears that I was wholly without Christ, and that I would find God a consuming fire to me.[84] I could not help running into new sins continually; but then I was mercifully dealt with, for I was often made to repent of them most heartily, by reason of bodily chastisements received on these delinquencies being discovered. I was particularly prone to lying, and I cannot but admire the mercy that has freely forgiven me all these juvenile sins. Now that I know them all to be blotted out, and that I am an accepted person, I may the more freely confess them: the truth is, that one lie always paved the way for another, from hour to hour, from day to day, and from year to year; so that I found myself constantly involved in a labyrinth of deceit, from which it was impossible to extricate myself. If I knew a person to be a godly one, I could almost have kissed his feet; but, against the carnal portion of mankind, I set my face continually. I esteemed the true ministers of the gospel; but the prelatic party, and the preachers up of good works I abhorred, and to this hour I account them the worst and most heinous of all transgressors.

There was only one boy at Mr Wilson's class who kept always the upper hand of me in every part of education. I strove against him from year to year, but it was all in vain; for he was a very wicked boy, and I was convinced he had dealings with the Devil. Indeed, it was believed all over the country that his mother was a witch; and I was at length convinced that it was no human ingenuity that beat me with so much ease in the Latin, after I had often sat up a whole night with my reverend father, studying my lesson in all its bearings. I often read as well and sometimes better than he; but, the moment Mr Wilson began to examine us, my opponent popped up above me. I determined (as I knew him for a wicked person, and one of the Devil's handfasted children) to be revenged on him, and to humble him by some means or other. Accordingly I lost no opportunity of setting the master against him, and succeeded several times in getting him severely beaten for faults of which he was innocent. I can hardly describe the joy that it gave to my heart to see a wicked creature suffering, for, though he deserved it not for one thing, he richly deserved it for others. This may be by some people accounted a great sin in me; but I deny it, for I did it as a duty, and what a man or boy does for the right will never be put into the sum of his transgressions.

This boy, whose name was M'Gill, was, at all his leisure hours engaged in drawing profane pictures of beasts, men, women, houses, and trees, and, in short, of all things that his eye encountered. These profane things the master often smiled at, and admired; therefore I began privately to try my hand likewise. I had scarcely tried above once to draw the figure of a man, ere I conceived that I had hit the very features of Mr Wilson. They were so particular that they could not be easily mistaken, and I was so tickled and pleased with the droll likeness that I had drawn, that I laughed immoderately at it. I tried no other figure but this; and I tried it in every situation in which a man and a schoolmaster could be placed. I often wrought for hours together at this likeness, nor was it long before I made myself so much master of the outline that I could have drawn it in any situation whatever, almost offhand. I then took M'Gill's account book of algebra home with me, and at my leisure put down a number of gross caricatures of Mr Wilson here and there, several of them in situations notoriously ludicrous. I waited the discovery of this treasure with great impatience; but the book, chancing to be one that M'Gill was not using, I saw it might be long enough before I enjoyed the consummation of my grand scheme: therefore with all the ingenuity I was master of, I brought it before our dominie's[85] eye. But never shall I forget the rage that gleamed in the tyrant's phiz![86] I was actually terrified to look at him, and trembled at his voice. M'Gill was called upon, and examined relating to the obnoxious figures. He denied flatly that any of them were of his doing. But the master inquiring at him whose they were, he could not tell, but affirmed it to be some trick. Mr Wilson at one time began, as I thought, to hesitate; but the evidence was so strong against M'Gill that at length his solemn asseverations of innocence only proved an aggravation of his crime. There was not one in the school who had ever been known to draw a figure but himself, and on him fell the whole weight of the tyrant's vengeance. It was dreadful; and I was once in hopes that he would not leave life in the culprit. He, however, left the school for several months, refusing to return to be subjected to punishment for the faults of others, and I stood king of the class.

Matters were at last made up between M'Gill's parents and the schoolmaster, but by that time I had got the start of him, and never in my life did I exert myself so much as to keep the mastery. It was in vain; the powers of enchantment prevailed, and I was again turned down with the tear in my eye. I could think of no amends but one, and, being driven to desperation, I put it in practice. I told a lie of him. I came boldly up to the master, and told him that M'Gill had in my hearing cursed him in a most shocking manner, and called him vile names. He called M'Gill, and charged him with the crime, and the proud young coxcomb was so stunned at the atrocity of the charge that his face grew as red as crimson, and the words stuck in his throat as he feebly denied it. His guilt was manifest, and he was again flogged most nobly and dismissed the school for ever in disgrace, as a most incorrigible vagabond.

This was a great victory gained, and I rejoiced and exulted exceedingly in it. It had, however, very nigh cost me my life; for not long thereafter I encountered M'Gill in the fields, on which he came up and challenged me for a liar, daring me to fight him. I refused, and said that I looked on him as quite below my notice; but he would not quit me, and finally told me that he should either *lick me*, or I should *lick him*, as he had no other means of being revenged on such a scoundrel. I tried to intimidate him, but it would not do; and I believe I would have given all that I had in the world to be quit of him. He at length went so far as first to kick me, and then strike me on the face; and, being both older and stronger than he, I thought it scarcely became me to take such insults patiently. I was, nevertheless, well aware that the devilish powers of his mother would finally prevail; and either the dread of this, or the inward consciousness of having wronged him, certainly unnerved my arm, for I fought wretchedly, and was soon wholly overcome. I was so sore defeated that I kneeled and was going to beg his pardon; but another thought struck me momentarily, and I threw myself on my face, and inwardly begged aid from heaven; at the same time I felt as if assured that my prayer was heard, and would be answered. While I was in this humble attitude, the villain kicked me with his foot and cursed me; and I, being newly encouraged, arose and encountered him once more. We had not fought long at this second turn before I saw a man hastening towards us; on which I uttered a shout of joy, and laid on valiantly; but my very next look assured me that the man was old John Barnet, whom I had likewise wronged all that was in my power, and between these two wicked persons I expected anything but justice. My arm was again enfeebled, and that of my adversary prevailed, I was knocked down and mauled most grievously, and, while the ruffian was kicking and cuffing me at his will and pleasure, up came old John Barnet, breathless with running, and, at one blow with his open hand, levelled my opponent with the earth. 'Tak ye that, maister!' said John, 'to learn ye better breeding. Hout awa, man! An ye will fight, fight fair. Gude sauf us, ir ye a gentleman's brood, that ye will kick an' cuff a lad when he's down?'

When I heard this kind and unexpected interference, I began once more to value myself on my courage, and, springing up, I made at my adversary; but John, without saying a word, bit his lip, and seizing me by the neck threw me down. M'Gill begged of him to stand and see fair play, and suffer us to finish the battle; for, added he, 'he is a liar, and a scoundrel, and deserves ten times more than I can give him.'

'I ken he's a' that ye say, an' mair, my man,' quoth John. 'But am I sure that ye're no as bad, an' waur? It says nae muckle for ony o' ye to be tearing like tikes[87] at one anither here.'

John cocked his cudgel and stood between us, threatening to

knock the one dead who first offered to lift his hand against the other; but, perceiving no disposition in any of us to separate, he drove me home before him like a bullock, and keeping close guard behind me, lest M'Gill had followed. I felt greatly indebted to John, yet I complained of his interference to my mother, and the old officious sinner got no thanks for his pains.

As I am writing only from recollection, so I remember of nothing farther in these early days, in the least worthy of being recorded. That I was a great, a transcendent sinner, I confess. But still I had hopes of forgiveness, because I never sinned from principle, but accident; and then I always *tried* to repent of these sins by the slump,[88] for individually it was impossible; and, though not always successful in my endeavours, I could not help that; the grace of repentance being withheld from me, I regarded myself as in no degree accountable for the failure. Moreover, there were many of the most deadly sins into which I never fell, for I dreaded those mentioned in the Revelations as excluding sins,[89] so that I guarded against them continually. In particular, I brought myself to despise, if not to abhor, the beauty of women, looking on it as the greatest snare to which mankind was subjected, and though young men and maidens, and even old women (my mother among the rest), taxed me with being an unnatural wretch, I gloried in my acquisition; and, to this day, am thankful for having escaped the most dangerous of all snares.

I kept myself also free of the sins of idolatry and misbelief, both of a deadly nature; and, upon the whole, I think I had not then broken, that is, absolutely broken, above four out of the ten commandments; but, for all that, I had more sense than to regard either my good works, or my evil deeds, as in the smallest degree influencing the eternal decrees of God concerning me, either with regard to my acceptance or reprobation. I depended entirely on the bounty of free grace, holding all the righteousness of man as filthy rags,[90] and believing in the momentous and magnificent truth that, the more heavily loaden with transgressions, the more welcome was the believer at the throne of grace. And I have reason to believe that it was this dependence and this belief that at last ensured my acceptance there.

I come now to the most important period of my existence – the period that has modelled my character, and influenced every action of my life – without which, this detail of my actions would have been as a tale that hath been told – a monotonous farrago – an uninteresting harangue – in short, a thing of nothing. Whereas, lo!

it must now be a relation of great and terrible actions, done in the might, and by the commission of heaven. Amen.

Like the sinful king of Israel, I had been walking softly before the Lord for a season.[91] I had been humbled for my transgressions, and, as far as I recollect, sorry on account of their numbers and heinousness. My reverend father had been, moreover, examining me every day regarding the state of my soul, and my answers sometimes appeared to give him satisfaction, and sometimes not. As for my mother, she would harp on the subject of my faith for ever; yet, though I knew her to be a Christian, I confess that I always despised her motley instructions, nor had I any great regard for her person. If this was a crime in me, I never could help it. I confess it freely, and believe it was a judgment from heaven inflicted on her for some sin of former days, and that I had no power to have acted otherwise towards her than I did.

In this frame of mind was I when my reverend father one morning arose from his seat, and, meeting me as I entered the room, he embraced me, and welcomed me into the community of the just upon earth. I was struck speechless, and could make no answer save by looks of surprise. My mother also came to me, kissed, and wept over me; and, after showering unnumbered blessings on my head, she also welcomed me into the society of *the just made perfect*.[92] Then each of them took me by a hand, and my reverend father explained to me how he had wrestled with God, as the patriarch of old had done,[93] not for a night, but for days and years, and that in bitterness and anguish of spirit, on my account; but that *he* had at last prevailed, and had now gained the long and earnestly desired assurance of my acceptance with the Almighty, in and through the merits and sufferings of his Son. That I was now a justified person, adopted among the number of God's children – my name written in the Lamb's book of life,[94] and that no by-past transgression, nor any future act of my own, or of other men, could be instrumental in altering the decree. 'All the powers of darkness,' added he, 'shall never be able to pluck you again out of your Redeemer's hand. And now, my son, be strong and steadfast in the truth. Set your face against sin, and sinful men, and resist even to blood, as many of the faithful of this land have done, and your reward shall be double. I am assured of your acceptance by the word and spirit of Him who cannot err, and your sanctification and repentance unto life will follow in due course. Rejoice and be thankful, for you are plucked as a brand out of the burning,[95] and now your redemption is sealed and sure.'

I wept for joy to be thus assured of my freedom from all sin, and of the impossibility of my ever again falling away from my new state. I bounded away into the fields and the woods, to pour out my spirit in prayer before the Almighty for his kindness to me: my whole frame seemed to be renewed; every nerve was buoyant with new life; I felt as if I could have flown in the air, or leaped over the tops of the trees. An exaltation of spirit lifted me, as it were, far above the earth and the sinful creatures crawling on its surface; and I deemed myself as an eagle among the children of men, soaring on high, and looking down with pity and contempt on the grovelling creatures below.

As I thus wended my way, I beheld a young man of a mysterious appearance coming towards me. I tried to shun him, being bent on my own contemplations; but he cast himself in my way, so that I could not well avoid him; and, more than that, I felt a sort of invisible power that drew me towards him, something like the force of enchantment, which I could not resist. As we approached each other, our eyes met and I can never describe the strange sensations that thrilled through my whole frame at that impressive moment; a moment to me fraught with the most tremendous consequences; the beginning of a series of adventures which has puzzled myself, and will puzzle the world when I am no more in it. That time will now soon arrive, sooner than anyone can devise who knows not the tumult of my thoughts and the labour of my spirit; and when it hath come and passed over, when my flesh and my bones are decayed, and my soul has passed to its everlasting home, then shall the sons of men ponder on the events of my life; wonder and tremble, and tremble and wonder how such things should be.

That strange youth and I approached each other in silence, and slowly, with our eyes fixed on each other's eyes. We approached till not more than a yard intervened between us, and then stood still and gazed, measuring each other from head to foot. What was my astonishment on perceiving that he was the same being as myself! The clothes were the same to the smallest item. The form was the same; the apparent age; the colour of the hair; the eyes; and, as far as recollection could serve me from viewing my own features in a glass, the features too were the very same. I conceived at first that I saw a vision, and that my guardian angel had appeared to me at this important era of my life; but this singular being read my thoughts in my looks, anticipating the very words that I was going to utter.

'You think I am your brother,' said he; 'or that I am your second self. I am indeed your brother, not according to the flesh, but in my belief of the same truths, and my assurance in the same mode of redemption, than which I hold nothing so great or so glorious on earth.'

'Then you are an associate well adapted to my present state,' said I. 'For this time is a time of great rejoicing in spirit to me. I am on my way to return thanks to the Most High for my redemption from the bonds of sin and misery. If you will join with me heart and hand in youthful thanksgiving, then shall we two go and worship together; but, if not, go your way, and I shall go mine.'

'Ah, you little know with how much pleasure I will accompany you, and join with you in your elevated devotions,' said he fervently. 'Your state is a state to be envied indeed; but I have been advised of it, and am come to be a humble disciple of yours; to be initiated into the true way of salvation by conversing with you, and perhaps of being assisted by your prayers.'

My spiritual pride being greatly elevated by this address, I began to assume the preceptor, and questioned this extraordinary youth with regard to his religious principles, telling him plainly, if he was one who expected acceptance with God at all, on account of good works, that I would hold no communion with him. He renounced these at once, with the greatest vehemence, and declared his acquiescence in my faith. I asked if he believed in the eternal and irrevocable decrees of God, regarding the salvation and condemnation of all mankind? He answered that he did so: aye, what would signify all things else that he believed, if he did not believe in that? We then went on to commune about all our points of belief; and in everything that I suggested he acquiesced, and, as I thought that day, often carried them to extremes, so that I had a secret dread he was advancing blasphemies. He had such a way with him, and paid such a deference to all my opinions, that I was quite captivated, and, at the same time, I stood in a sort of awe of him, which I could not account for, and several times was seized with an involuntary inclination to escape from his presence by making a sudden retreat. But he seemed constantly to anticipate my thoughts, and was sure to divert my purpose by some turn in the conversation that particularly interested me. He took care to dwell much on the theme of the impossibility of those ever falling away who were once accepted and received into covenant with God, for he seemed to know that in that confidence, and that trust, my whole hopes were centred.

We moved about from one place to another, until the day was wholly spent. My mind had all the while been kept in a state of agitation resembling the motion of a whirlpool, and, when we came to separate, I then discovered that the purpose for which I had sought the fields had been neglected, and that I had been diverted from the worship of God by attending to the quibbles and dogmas of this singular and unaccountable being, who seemed to have more knowledge and information than all the persons I had ever known put together.

We parted with expressions of mutual regret, and when I left him I felt a deliverance, but at the same time a certain consciousness that I was not thus to get free of him, but that he was like to be an acquaintance that was to stick to me for good or for evil. I was astonished at his acuteness and knowledge about everything; but, as for his likeness to me, that was quite unaccountable. He was the same person in every respect, but yet he was not always so; for I observed several times, when we were speaking of certain divines and their tenets, that his face assumed something of the appearance of theirs; and it struck me that, by setting his features to the mould of other people's, he entered at once into their conceptions and feelings. I had been greatly flattered, and greatly interested by his conversation; whether I had been the better for it or the worse, I could not tell. I had been diverted from returning thanks to my gracious Maker for his great kindness to me, and came home as I went away, but not with the same buoyancy and lightness of heart. Well may I remember the day in which I was first received into the number, and made an heir to all the privileges of the children of God, and on which I first met this mysterious associate, who from that day forth contrived to wind himself into all my affairs, both spiritual and temporal, to this day on which I am writing the account of it. It was on the 25th day of March, 1704, when I had just entered the eighteenth year of my age. Whether it behoves me to bless God for the events of that day, or to deplore them, has been hid from my discernment, though I have inquired into it with fear and trembling; and I have now lost all hopes of ever discovering the true import of these events until that day when my accounts are to make up and reckon for in another world.

When I came home, I went straight into the parlour, where my mother was sitting by herself. She started to her feet, and uttered a smothered scream. 'What ails you, Robert?' cried she. 'My dear son, what is the matter with you?'

'Do you see anything the matter with me?' said I. 'It appears that the ailment is with yourself, and either in your crazed head or your dim eyes, for there is nothing the matter with me.'

'Ah, Robert, you are ill!' cried she. 'You are very ill, my dear boy;

you are quite changed; your very voice and manner are changed. Ah, Jane, haste you up to the study, and tell Mr Wringhim to come here on the instant and speak to Robert.'

'I beseech you, woman, to restrain yourself,' said I. 'If you suffer your frenzy to run away with your judgment in this manner, I will leave the house. What do you mean? I tell you, there is nothing ails me: I never was better.'

She screamed, and ran between me and the door, to bar my retreat: in the meantime my reverend father entered, and I have not forgot how he gazed, through his glasses, first at my mother, and then at me. I imagined that his eyes burnt like candles, and was afraid of him, which I suppose made my looks more unstable than they would otherwise have been.

'What is all this for?' said he. 'Mistress! Robert! What is the matter here?'

'Oh, sir, our boy!' cried my mother; 'our dear boy, Mr Wringhim! Look at him, and speak to him: he is either dying or translated, sir!'

He looked at me with a countenance of great alarm; mumbling some sentences to himself, and then taking me by the arm, as if to feel my pulse, he said, with a faltering voice: 'Something has indeed befallen you, either in body or mind, boy, for you are transformed, since the morning, that I could not have known you for the same person. Have you met with any accident?'

'No.'

'Have you seen anything out of the ordinary course of nature?'

'No.'

'Then, Satan, I fear, has been busy with you, tempting you in no ordinary degree at this momentous crisis of your life?'

My mind turned on my associate for the day, and the idea that he might be an agent of the Devil had such an effect on me that I could make no answer.

'I see how it is,' said he; 'you are troubled in spirit, and I have no doubt that the enemy of our salvation has been busy with you. Tell me this, has he overcome you, or has he not?'

'He has not, my dear father,' said I. 'In the strength of the Lord, I hope I have withstood him. But indeed, if he has been busy with me, I knew it not. I have been conversant this day with one stranger only, whom I took rather for an angel of light.'

'It is one of the Devil's most profound wiles to appear like one,' said my mother.

'Woman, hold thy peace!' said my reverend father. 'Thou pretendest to teach what thou knowest not. Tell me this, boy: did this stranger, with whom you met, adhere to the religious principles in which I have educated you?'

'Yes, to every one of them in their fullest latitude,' said I.

'Then he was no agent of the Wicked One with whom you held converse,' said he: 'for that is the doctrine that was made to overturn the principalities and powers, the might and dominion of the kingdom of darkness. Let us pray.'

After spending about a quarter of an hour in solemn and sublime thanksgiving, this saintly man and minister of Christ Jesus, gave out that the day following should be kept by the family as a day of solemn thanksgiving, and spent in prayer and praise, on account of the calling and election of one of its members; or rather for the election of that individual being revealed on earth, as well as confirmed in Heaven.

The next day was with me a day of holy exultation. It was begun by my reverend father laying his hands upon my head and blessing me, and then dedicating me to the Lord in the most awful and impressive manner. It was in no common way that he exercised this profound rite, for it was done with all the zeal and enthusiasm of a devotee to the true cause, and a champion on the side he had espoused. He used these remarkable words, which I have still treasured up in my heart: 'I give him unto Thee only, to Thee wholly and to Thee for ever. I dedicate him unto Thee, soul, body, and spirit. Not as the wicked of this world, or the hirelings of a Church profanely called by Thy name, do I dedicate this Thy servant to Thee: Not in words and form, learned by rote, and dictated by the limbs of Antichrist, but, Lord, I give him into Thy hand, as a captain putteth a sword into the hand of his sovereign, wherewith to lay waste his enemies. May he be a two-edged weapon in Thy hand and a spear coming out of Thy mouth, to destroy, and overcome, and pass over; and may the enemies of Thy Church fall down before him, and be as dung to fat the land!'[96]

From the moment, I conceived it decreed, not that I should be a minister of the gospel, but a champion of it, to cut off the enemies of the Lord from the face of the earth; and I rejoiced in the commission, finding it more congenial to my nature to be cutting sinners off with the sword than to be haranguing them from the pulpit, striving to produce an effect which God, by his act of absolute predestination, had for ever rendered impracticable. The more I pondered on these things the more I saw of the folly and inconsistency of ministers in spending their lives striving and remonstrating with sinners in order to induce them to do that which they had it not in their power to do. Seeing that God had from all eternity decided the fate of every individual that was to be born of woman, how vain was it in man to endeavour to save those whom their Maker had, by an unchangeable decree, doomed to destruction. I could not disbelieve the doctrine which the best of men had taught me, and towards which he made the whole of the Scriptures to bear, and yet it made the economy of the Christian world appear to me as an absolute contradiction. How much more wise would it be, thought I, to begin and cut sinners off with the sword! For till that is effected, the saints can never inherit the earth in peace. Should I be honoured as an instrument to begin this great work of purification, I should rejoice in it. But, then, where had I the means, or under what direction was I to begin? There was one thing clear, I was now the Lord's and it behoved me to bestir myself in His service. Oh that I had an host at my command, then would I be as a devouring fire among the workers of iniquity!

Full of these great ideas, I hurried through the city, and sought again the private path through the field and wood of Finnieston,[97] in which my reverend preceptor had the privilege of walking for study, and to which he had a key that was always at my command. Near one of the stiles, I perceived a young man sitting in a devout posture, reading a Bible. He rose, lifted his hat, and made an obeisance to me, which I returned and walked on. I had not well crossed the stile till it struck me I knew the face of the youth and that he was some intimate acquaintance, to whom I ought to have spoken. I walked on, and returned, and walked on again, trying to recollect who he was; but for my life I could not. There was, however, a fascination in his look and manner that drew me back towards him in spite of myself, and I resolved to go to him, if it were merely to speak and see who he was.

I came up to him and addressed him, but he was so intent on his book that, though I spoke, he lifted not his eyes. I looked on the book also, and still it seemed a Bible, having columns, chapters, and verses; but it was in a language of which I was wholly ignorant, and all intersected with red lines and verses. A sensation resembling a stroke of electricity came over me, on first casting my eyes on that mysterious book, and I stood motionless. He looked up, smiled, closed his book, and put it in his bosom. 'You seem strangely affected, dear sir, by looking at my book,' said he mildly.

'In the name of God, what book is that?' said I. 'Is it a Bible?'

'It is *my* Bible, sir,' said he, 'but I will cease reading it, for I am glad to see you. Pray, is not this a day for holy festivity with you?' I stared in his face, but made no answer, for my senses were bewildered.

'Do you not know me?' said he. 'You appear to be somehow at a loss. Had not you and I some sweet communion and fellowship yesterday?'

'I beg your pardon, sir,' said I. 'But, surely, if you are the young gentleman with whom I spent the hours yesterday, you have the chameleon art of changing your appearance; I never could have recognised you.'

'My countenance changes with my studies and sensations,' said he. 'It is a natural peculiarity in me, over which I have not full control. If I contemplate a man's features seriously, mine own gradually assume the very same appearance and character. And what is more, by contemplating a face minutely, I not only attain the same likeness but, with the likeness, I attain the very same ideas as well as the same mode of arranging them, so that, you see, by looking at a person attentively, I by degrees assume his likeness, and by assuming his likeness I attain to the possession of his most secret thoughts. This, I say, is a peculiarity in my nature, a gift of the God that made me; but, whether or not given me for a blessing, He knows Himself, and so do I. At all events, I have this privilege, I can never be mistaken of a character in whom I am interested.'

'It is a rare qualification,' replied I, 'and I would give worlds to possess it. Then, it appears that it is needless to dissemble with you, since you can at any time extract our most secret thoughts from our bosoms. You already know my natural character?'

'Yes,' said he, 'and it is that which attaches me to you. By assuming your likeness yesterday, I became acquainted with your character, and was no less astonished at the profundity and range of your thoughts than at the heroic magnanimity[98] with which these were combined. And now, in addition to these, you are dedicated to the great work of the Lord; for which reasons I have resolved to attach myself as closely to you as possible, and to render you all the service of which my poor abilities are capable.'

I confess that I was greatly flattered by these compliments paid to my abilities by a youth of such superior qualifications; by one who, with a modesty and affability rare at his age, combined a height of genius and knowledge almost above human comprehension. Nevertheless, I began to assume a certain superiority of demeanour towards him, as judging it incumbent on me to do so, in order to keep up his idea of my exalted character. We conversed again till the day was near a close; and the things that he strove most to inculcate on my mind were the infallibility of the elect, and the preordination of all things that come to pass. I pretended to controvert the first of these, for the purpose of showing him the extent of my argumentative powers, and said that 'indubitably there were degrees of sinning which would induce the Almighty to throw off the very elect'. But behold my hitherto humble and modest companion took up the argument with such warmth that he put me not only to silence but to absolute shame.

'Why, sir,' said he, 'by vending such an insinuation, you put discredit on the great atonement, in which you trust. Is there not enough of merit in the blood of Jesus to save thousands of worlds, if it was for these worlds that he died? Now, when you know, as you do (and as every one of the elect may know of himself) that this Saviour died for you, namely and particularly, dare you say that there is not enough of merit in His great atonement to annihilate all your sins, let them be as heinous and atrocious as they may? And, moreover, do you not acknowledge that God hath pre-ordained and decreed whatsoever comes to pass? Then, how is it that you should deem it in your power to eschew one action of your life, whether good or evil? Depend on it, the advice of the great preacher[99] is genuine: "What thine hand findeth to do, do it with all thy might, for none of us knows what a day may bring forth." That is, none of us knows what is pre-ordained, but whatever it is pre-ordained we *must* do, and none of these things will be laid to our charge.'

I could hardly believe that these sayings were genuine or orthodox; but I soon felt that, instead of being a humble disciple of mine, this new acquaintance was to be my guide and director, and all under the humble guise of one stooping at my feet to learn the right. He said that he saw I was ordained to perform some great action for the cause of Jesus and His Church, and he earnestly coveted being a partaker with me; but he besought of me never to think it possible for me to fall from the truth, or the favour of Him who had chosen me, else that misbelief would baulk every good work to which I set my face.

There was something so flattering in all this that I could not resist it. Still, when he took leave of me, I felt it as a great relief; and yet, before the morrow, I wearied and was impatient to see him again. We carried on our fellowship from day to day, and all the while I knew not who he was, and still my mother and reverend father kept insisting that I was an altered youth, changed in my appearance, my manners, and my whole conduct; yet something always prevented me from telling them more about my new acquaintance than I had done on the first day we met. I rejoiced in him, was proud of him, and soon could not live without him; yet, though resolved every day to disclose the whole story of my connection with him, I had it not in my power. Something always prevented me, till at length I thought no more of it, but resolved to enjoy his fascinating company in private, and by all means to keep my own with him. The resolution was vain: I set a bold face to it, but my powers were inadequate to the task; my adherent, with all the suavity imaginable, was sure to carry his point. I sometimes fumed, and sometimes shed tears at being obliged to yield to proposals against which I had at first felt every reasoning power of my soul rise in opposition; but for all that he never failed in carrying conviction along with him in effect, for he either forced me to acquiesce in his measures, and assent to the truth of his positions, or he put me so completely down that I had not a word left to advance against them.

After weeks, and I may say months of intimacy, I observed, somewhat to my amazement, that we had never once prayed together; and, more than that, that he had constantly led my attentions away from that duty, causing me to neglect it wholly. I thought this a bad mark of a man seemingly so much set on inculcating certain important points of religion, and resolved next day to put him to the test, and request him to perform that sacred duty in name of us both. He objected boldly; saying there were very few people indeed with whom he could join in prayer, and he made a point of never doing it, as he was sure they were to ask many things of which he disapproved, and that, if he were to officiate himself, he was as certain to allude to many things that came not within the range of their faith. He disapproved of prayer altogether in the manner it was generally gone about, he said. Man made it merely a selfish concern, and was constantly employed asking, asking, for everything. Whereas it became all God's creatures to be content with their lot, and only to kneel before him in order to thank him for such benefits as he saw meet to bestow. In short, he argued with such energy that before we parted I acquiesced, as usual, in his position, and never mentioned prayer to him any more.

Having been so frequently seen in his company, several people happened to mention the circumstance to my mother and reverend father; but at the same time had all described him differently. At length, they began to examine me with respect to the company I kept, as I absented myself from home day after day. I told them I kept company only with one young gentleman, whose whole manner of thinking on religious subjects I found so congenial with my own that I could not live out of his society. My mother began to lay down some of her old hackneyed rules of faith, but I turned from hearing her with disgust; for, after the energy of my new friend's reasoning, hers appeared so tame I could not endure it. And I confess with shame that my reverend preceptor's religious dissertations began, about this time, to lose their relish very much, and by degrees became exceedingly tiresome to my ear. They were so inferior, in strength and sublimity, to the most common observations of my young friend, that in drawing a comparison the former appeared as nothing. He, however, examined me about many things relating to my companion, in all of which I satisfied him, save in one: I could neither tell him who my friend was, what was his name, nor of whom he was descended; and I wondered at myself how I had never once adverted to such a thing for all the time we had been intimate.

I inquired the next day what his name was; as I said I was often at a loss for it, when talking with him. He replied that there was no occasion for any one friend ever naming another, when their society was held in private, as ours was; for his part he had never once named me since we first met, and never intended to do so, unless by my own request. 'But if you cannot converse without naming me, you may call me Gil for the present,' added he, 'and if I think proper to take another name at any future period, it shall be with your approbation.'

'Gil!' said I. 'Have you no name but Gil? Or which of your names is it? Your Christian or surname?'

'Oh, you must have a surname too, must you!' replied he. 'Very well, you may call me Gil-Martin. It is not my *Christian* name; but it *is* a name which may serve your turn.'

'This is very strange!' said I. 'Are you ashamed of your parents that you refuse to give your real name?'

'I have no parents save one, whom I do not acknowledge,' said he proudly. 'Therefore, pray drop that subject, for it is a disagreeable one. I am a being of a very peculiar temper, for, though I have servants and subjects more than I can number, yet, to gratify a certain whim, I have left them, and retired to this city, and, for all the society it contains, you see I have attached myself only to you. This is a secret, and I tell you only in friendship, therefore pray let it remain one, and say not another word about the matter.'

I assented, and said no more concerning it; for it instantly struck me that this was no other than the Czar Peter of Russia,[100] having heard that he had been travelling through Europe in disguise, and I cannot say that I had not thenceforward great and mighty hopes of high preferment, as a defender and avenger of the oppressed Christian Church, under the influence of this great potentate. He had hinted as much already, as that it was more honourable, and of more avail to put down the wicked with the sword than try to reform them, and I thought myself quite justified in supposing that he intended me for some great employment, that he had thus selected me for his companion out of all the rest in Scotland, and even pretended to learn the great truths of religion from my mouth. From that time I felt disposed to yield to such a great prince's suggestions without hesitation.

Nothing ever astonished me so much as the uncommon powers with which he seemed invested. In our walk one day, we met with a Mr Blanchard, who was reckoned a worthy, pious divine, but quite of the moral cast,[101] who joined us; and we three walked on, and rested together in the fields. My companion did not seem to like him, but, nevertheless, regarded him frequently with deep attention, and there were several times, while he seemed contemplating him, and trying to find out his thoughts, that his face became so like Mr Blanchard's that it was impossible to have distinguished the one from the other. The antipathy between the two was mutual, and discovered itself quite palpably in a short time. When my companion the prince was gone, Mr Blanchard asked me anent him, and I told him that he was a stranger in the city, but a very uncommon and great personage. Mr Blanchard's answer to me was as follows: 'I never saw anybody I disliked so much in my life, Mr Robert; and if it be true that he is a stranger here, which I doubt, believe me he is come for no good.'

'Do you not perceive what mighty powers of mind he is possessed of?' said I, 'and also how clear and unhesitating he is on some of the most interesting points of divinity?'

'It is for his great mental faculties that I dread him,' said he. 'It is incalculable what evil such a person as he may do, if so disposed. There is a sublimity in his ideas, with which there is to me a mixture of terror; and, when he talks of religion, he does it as one that rather dreads its truths than reverences them. He, indeed, pretends great strictness of orthodoxy regarding some of the points of doctrine embraced by the reformed church; but you do not seem to perceive that both you and he are carrying these points to a dangerous extremity. Religion is a sublime and glorious thing, the bonds of society on earth, and the connector of humanity with the Divine nature; but there is nothing so dangerous to man as the wresting of any of its principles, or forcing them beyond their due bounds: this is of all others the readiest way to destruction. Neither is there anything so easily done. There is not an error into which a man can fall which he may not press Scripture into his service as proof of the probity of, and though your boasted theologian shunned the full discussion of the subject before me, while you pressed it, I can easily see that both you and he are carrying your ideas of absolute predestination, and its concomitant appendages, to an extent that overthrows all religion and revelation together; or, at least, jumbles them into a chaos, out of which human capacity can never select what is good. Believe me, Mr Robert, the less you associate with that illustrious stranger the better, for it appears to me that your creed and his carries damnation on the very front of it.'

I was rather stunned at this; but pretended to smile with disdain, and said it did not become youth to control age; and, as I knew our principles differed fundamentally, it behoved us to drop the subject. He, however, would not drop it, but took both my principles and me fearfully to task, for Blanchard was an eloquent and powerfulminded old man; and, before we parted, I believe I promised to drop my new acquaintance, and was *all but* resolved to do it.

As well might I have laid my account with shunning the light of day. He was constant to me as my shadow, and by degrees he acquired such an ascendency over me that I never was happy out of his company, nor greatly so in it. When I repeated to him all that Mr Blanchard had said, his countenance kindled with indignation and rage; and then by degrees his eyes sunk inward, his brow lowered, so that I was awed, and withdrew my eyes from looking at him. A while afterwards as I was addressing him, I chanced to look him again in the face, and the sight of him made me start violently. He had made himself so like Mr Blanchard that I actually believed I had been addressing that gentleman, and that I had done so in some absence of mind that I could not account for. Instead of being amused at the quandary I was in, he seemed offended: indeed, he never was truly amused with anything. And he then asked me sullenly, if I conceived such personages as he to have no other endowments than common mortals?

I said I never conceived that princes or potentates had any greater share of endowments than other men, and frequently not so much. He shook his head, and bade me think over the subject again; and there was an end of it. I certainly felt every day the more disposed to acknowledge such a superiority in him; and, from all that I could gather, I had now no doubt that he was Peter of Russia. Everything combined to warrant the supposition, and, of course, I resolved to act in conformity with the discovery I had made.

For several days the subject of Mr Blanchard's doubts and doctrines formed the theme of our discourse. My friend deprecated them most devoutly; and then again he would deplore them, and lament the great evil that such a man might do among the human race. I joined with him in allowing the evil in its fullest latitude; and, at length, after he thought he had fully prepared my nature for such a trial of its powers and abilities, he proposed calmly that we two should make away with Mr Blanchard. I was so shocked that my bosom became as it were a void, and the beatings of my heart sounded loud and hollow in it; my breath cut, and my tongue and palate became dry and speechless. He mocked at my cowardice, and began a-reasoning on the matter with such powerful eloquence that, before we parted, I felt fully convinced that it was my bounden duty to slay Mr Blanchard; but my will was far, very far from consenting to the deed.

I spent the following night without sleep, or nearly so; and the next morning, by the time the sun arose, I was again abroad, and in the company of my illustrious friend. The same subject was resumed, and again he reasoned to the following purport: That supposing me placed at the head of any army of Christian soldiers, all bent on putting down the enemies of the Church, would I have any hesitation in destroying and rooting out these enemies? None, surely. Well then, when I saw and was convinced that here was an individual who was doing more detriment to the Church of Christ on earth than tens of thousands of such warriors were capable of doing, was it not my duty to cut him off, and save the elect? 'He who would be a champion in the cause of Christ and His Church, my brave young friend,' added he, 'must begin early, and no man can calculate to what an illustrious eminence small beginnings may lead. If the man Blanchard is worthy, he is only changing his situation for a better one; and, if unworthy, it is better that one fall than that a thousand souls perish. Let us be up and doing in our vocations. For me, my resolution is taken; I have but one great aim in this world, and I never for a moment lose sight of it.'

I was obliged to admit the force of his reasoning; for, though I cannot from memory repeat his words, his eloquence was of that overpowering nature that the subtlety of other men sunk before it; and there is also little doubt that the assurance I had that these words were spoken by a great potentate who could raise me to the highest eminence (provided that I entered into his extensive and decisive measures) assisted mightily in dispelling my youthful scruples and qualms of conscience; and I thought moreover that, having such a powerful back friend to support me, I hardly needed to be afraid of the consequences. I consented! But begged a little time to think of it. He said the less one thought of a duty the better; and we parted.

But the most singular instance of this wonderful man's power over my mind was that he had as complete influence over me by night as by day. All my dreams corresponded exactly with his suggestions; and, when he was absent from me, still his arguments sunk deeper in my heart than even when he was present. I dreamed that night of a great triumph obtained, and, though the whole scene was but dimly and confusedly defined in my vision, yet the overthrow and death of Mr Blanchard was the first step by which I attained the eminent station I occupied. Thus, by dreaming of the event by night, and discoursing of it by day, it soon became so familiar to my mind that I almost conceived it as done. It was resolved on: which was the first and greatest victory gained; for there was no difficulty in finding opportunities enow of cutting off a man who, every good day, was to be found walking by himself in private grounds. I went and heard him preach for two days, and in fact I held his tenets scarcely short of blasphemy; they were such as I had never heard before, and his congregation, which was numerous, were turning up their ears and drinking in his doctrines with the utmost delight; for, Oh, they suited their carnal natures and self-sufficiency to a hair! He was actually holding it forth, as a fact, that 'it was every man's own blame if he was not saved!' What horrible misconstruction! And then he was alleging, and trying to prove from nature and reason, that no man ever was guilty of a sinful action who might not have declined it had he so chosen! 'Wretched controvertist!' thought I to myself an hundred times, 'shall not the sword of the Lord be moved from its place of peace for such presumptuous, absurd testimonies as these!'

When I began to tell the prince about these false doctrines, to my astonishment I found that he had been in the church himself, and had every argument that the old divine had used verbatim; and he remarked on them with great concern that these were not the tenets that corresponded with his views in society, and that he had agents in every city, and every land, exerting their powers to put them down. I asked, with great simplicity: 'Are all your subjects Christians, prince?'

'All my European subjects are, or deem themselves so,' returned he; 'and they are the most faithful and true subjects I have.'

Who could doubt, after this, that he was the Czar of Russia? I have nevertheless had reasons to doubt of his identity since that period, and which of my conjectures is right I believe the God of Heaven only knows, for I do not. I shall go on to write such things as I remember, and, if anyone shall ever take the trouble to read over these confessions, such a one will judge for himself. It will be observed that, since ever I fell in with this extraordinary person, I have written about him only, and I must continue to do so to the end of this memoir, as I have performed no great or interesting action in which he had not a principal share.

He came to me one day and said: 'We must not linger thus in executing what we have resolved on. We have much before our hands to perform for the benefit of mankind, both civil as well as religious. Let us do what we have to do here, and then we must wend our way to other cities, and perhaps to other countries. Mr Blanchard is to hold forth in the high church of Paisley[102] on Sunday next, on some particularly great occasion: this must be defeated; he must not go there. As he will be busy arranging his discourses, we may expect him to be walking by himself in Finnieston Dell the greater part of Friday and Saturday. Let us go and cut him off. What is the life of a man more than the life of a lamb, or any guiltless animal? It is not half so much, especially when we consider the immensity of the mischief this old fellow is working among our fellow-creatures. Can there be any doubt that it is the duty of one consecrated to God to cut off such a mildew?'

'I fear me, great sovereign,' said I, 'that your ideas of retribution are too sanguine, and too arbitrary for the laws of this country. I dispute not that your motives are great and high; but have you debated the consequences, and settled the result?'

'I have,' returned he, 'and hold myself amenable for the action to the laws of God and of equity; as to the enactments of men, I despise them. Fain would I see the weapon of the Lord of Hosts begin the work of vengeance that awaits it to do!'

I could not help thinking that I perceived a little derision of countenance on his face as he said this, nevertheless I sunk dumb before such a man, aroused myself to the task, seeing he would not have it deferred. I approved of it in theory, but my spirit stood aloof from the practice. I saw and was convinced that the elect of God would be happier, and purer, were the wicked and unbelievers all cut off from troubling and misleading them, but if it had not been the instigations of this illustrious stranger, I should never have presumed to begin so great a work myself. Yet, though he often aroused my zeal to the highest pitch, still my heart at times shrunk from the shedding of life-blood, and it was only at the earnest and unceasing instigations of my enlightened and voluntary patron that I at length put my hand to the conclusive work. After I said all that I could say, and all had been overborne (I remember my actions and words as well as it had been yesterday), I turned round hesitatingly, and looked up to Heaven for direction; but there was a dimness come over my eyes that I could not see. The appearance was as if there had been a veil drawn over me, so nigh that I put up my hand to feel it; and then Gil-Martin (as this great sovereign was pleased to have himself called) frowned, and asked me what I was grasping at. I knew not what to say, but answered, with fear and shame: 'I have no weapons, not one; nor know I where any are to be found.'

'The God whom thou servest will provide these,' said he, 'if thou provest worthy of the trust committed to thee.'

I looked again up into the cloudy veil that covered us and thought I beheld golden weapons of every description let down in it, but all with their points towards me. I kneeled, and was going to stretch out my hand to take one, when my patron seized me, as I thought, by the clothes, and dragged me away with as much ease as I had been a lamb, saying, with a joyful and elevated voice: 'Come, my friend, let us depart: thou art dreaming – thou art dreaming. Rouse up all the energies of thy exalted mind, for thou art an highly favoured one; and doubt thou not that He whom *thou* servest, will be ever at thy right and left hand, to direct and assist thee.'

These words, but particularly the vision I had seen, of the golden weapons descending out of Heaven, inflamed my zeal to that height that I was as one beside himself; which my parents perceived that night, and made some motions towards confining me to my room. I joined in the family prayers, and then I afterwards sung a psalm and prayed by myself; and I had good reasons for believing that that small oblation of praise and prayer was not turned to sin. But there are strange things, and unaccountable agencies in nature: He only who dwells between the Cherubim can unriddle them, and to Him the honour must redound for ever. Amen.

I felt greatly strengthened and encouraged that night, and the next morning I ran to meet my companion, out of whose eye I had now no life. He rejoiced at seeing me so forward in the great work of reformation by blood, and said many things to raise my hopes of future fame and glory; and then producing two pistols of pure beaten gold, he held them out and proffered me the choice of one, saying: 'See what thy master hath provided thee!' I took one of them eagerly, for I perceived at once that they were two of the very weapons that were let down from Heaven in the cloudy veil, the dim tapestry of the firmament; and I said to myself: 'Surely this is the will of the Lord.'

The little splendid and enchanting piece was so perfect, so complete, and so ready for executing the will of the donor, that I now longed to use it in his service. I loaded it with my own hand, as Gil- Martin did the other, and we took our stations behind a bush of hawthorn and bramble on the verge of the wood, and almost close to the walk. My patron was so acute in all his calculations that he never mistook an event. We had not taken our stand above a minute and a half till old Mr Blanchard appeared, coming slowly on the path. When we saw this, we cowered down, and leaned each of us a knee upon the ground, pointing the pistols through the bush, with an aim so steady that it was impossible to miss our victim.

He came deliberately on, pausing at times so long that we dreaded he was going to turn. Gil-Martin dreaded it, and I said I did, but wished in my heart that he might. He, however, came onward, and I will never forget the manner in which he came ! No, I don't believe I ever can forget it, either in the narrow bounds of time or the ages of eternity! He was a broadly, ill-shaped man, of a rude exterior, and a little bent with age; his hands were clasped behind his back and below his coat, and he walked with a slow swinging air that was very peculiar. When he paused and looked abroad on nature, the act was highly impressive: he seemed conscious of being all alone, and conversant only with God and the elements of his creation. Never was there such a picture of human inadvertency! a man approaching step by step to the one that was to hurl him out of one existence into another with as much ease and indifference as the ox goeth to the stall. Hideous vision, wilt thou not be gone from my mental sight! If not, let me bear with thee as I can!

When he came straight opposite to the muzzles of our pieces, Gil-Martin called out 'Eh!' with a short quick sound. The old man, without starting, turned his face and breast towards us, and looked into the wood, but looked over our heads.

'Now!' whispered my companion, and fired. But my hand refused the office, for I was not at that moment sure about becoming an assassin in the cause of Christ and His Church. I thought I heard a sweet voice behind me, whispering to me to beware, and I was going to look round, when my companion exclaimed: 'Coward, we are ruined!'

I had no time for an alternative: Gil-Martin's ball had not taken effect, which was altogether wonderful, as the old man's breast was within a few yards of him. 'Hilloa!' cried Blanchard, 'what is that for, you dog!' and with that he came forward to look over the bush. I hesitated, as I said, and attempted to look behind me; but there was no time: the next step discovered two assassins lying in covert, waiting for blood. 'Coward, we are ruined!' cried my indignant friend; and that moment my piece was discharged. The effect was as might have been expected: the old man first stumbled to one side, and then fell on his back. We kept our places, and I perceived my companion's eyes gleaming with an unnatural joy. The wounded man raised himself from the bank to a sitting posture, and I beheld his eyes swimming; he however appeared sensible, for we heard him saying in a low and rattling voice: 'Alas, alas! whom have I offended, that they should have been driven to an act like this! Come forth and show yourselves, that I may either forgive you before I die, or curse you in the name of the Lord.' He then fell a-groping with both hands on the ground, as if feeling for something he had lost manifestly in the agonies of death; and, with a solemn and interrupted prayer for forgiveness, he breathed his last.

I had become rigid as a statue, whereas my associate appeared to be elevated above measure. 'Arise, thou faint-hearted one, and let us be going,' said he. 'Thou hast done well for once; but wherefore hesitate in such a cause? This is but a small beginning of so great a work as that of purging the Christian world. But the first victim is a worthy one, and more of such lights must be extinguished immediately.'

We touched not our victim, nor anything pertaining to him, for fear of staining our hands with his blood; and the firing having brought three men within view, who were hasting towards the spot, my undaunted companion took both the pistols, and went forward as with intent to meet them, bidding me shift for myself I ran off in a contrary direction, till I came to the foot of the Pearman Sike,[103] and then, running up the hollow of that, I appeared on the top of the bank as if I had been another man brought in view by hearing the shots in such a place. I had a full view of a part of what passed, though not of all. I saw my companion going straight to meet the men, apparently with a pistol in every hand, waving in a careless manner. They seemed not quite clear of meeting with him, and so he went straight on, and passed between them. They looked after him, and came onwards; but, when they came to the old man lying stretched in his blood, then they turned and pursued my companion, though not so quickly as they might have done; and I understand that from the first they saw no more of him.

Great was the confusion that day in Glasgow. The most popular of all their preachers of morality was (what they called) murdered in cold blood, and a strict and extensive search was made for the assassin. Neither of the accomplices was found, however, that is certain, nor was either of them so much as suspected; but another man was apprehended under circumstances that warranted suspicion. This was one of the things that I witnessed in my life, which I never understood, and it surely was one of my patron's most dexterous tricks, for I must still say, what I have thought from the beginning, that like him there never was a man created. The young man who was taken up was a preacher; and it was proved that he had purchased firearms in town, and gone out with them that morning. But the far greatest mystery of the whole was that two of the men, out of the three who met my companion, swore that that unfortunate preacher was the man whom they met with a pistol in each hand, fresh from the death of the old divine. The poor fellow made a confused speech himself, which there is not the least doubt was quite true; but it was laughed to scorn, and an expression of horror ran through both the hearers and jury. I heard the whole trial, and so did Gil-Martin; but we left the journeyman preacher to his fate, and from that time forth I have had no faith in the justice of criminal trials. If once a man is prejudiced on one side, he will swear anything in support of such prejudice. I tried to expostulate with my mysterious friend on the horrid injustice of suffering this young man to die for our act, but the prince exulted in it more than the other, and said the latter was the most dangerous man of the two.

The alarm in and about Glasgow was prodigious. The country being divided into two political parties, the court and the country party, the former held meetings, issued proclamations, and offered rewards, ascribing all to the violence of party spirit, and deprecating the infernal measures of their opponents. I did not understand their political differences; but it was easy to see that the true Gospel preachers joined all on one side, and the upholders of pure morality and a blameless life on the other, so that this division proved a test to us, and it was forthwith resolved that we two should pick out some of the leading men of this unsaintly and heterodox cabal, and cut them off one by one, as occasion should suit.

Now, the ice being broke, I felt considerable zeal in our great work, but pretended much more; and we might soon have kidnapped them all through the ingenuity of my patron, had not our next attempt miscarried, by some awkwardness or mistake of mine. The consequence was that he was discovered fairly, and very nigh seized. I also was seen, and suspected so far that my reverend father, my mother, and myself were examined privately. I denied all knowledge of the matter; and they held it in such a ridiculous light, and their conviction of the complete groundlessness of the suspicion was so perfect, that their testimony prevailed, and the affair was hushed. I was obliged, however, to walk circumspectly, and saw my companion the prince very seldom, who was prowling about every day, quite unconcerned about his safety. He was every day a new man, however, and needed not to be alarmed at any danger; for such a facility had he in disguising himself that, if it had not been for a password which we had between us, for the purposes of recognition, I never could have known him myself.

It so happened that my reverend father was called to Edinburgh about this time, to assist with his counsel in settling the national affairs. At my earnest request I was permitted to accompany him, at which both my associate and I rejoiced, as we were now about to move in a new and extensive field. All this time I never knew where my illustrious friend resided. He never once invited me to call on him at his lodgings, nor did he ever come to our house, which made me sometimes to suspect that, if any of our great efforts in the cause of true religion were discovered, he intended leaving me in the lurch. Consequently, when we met in Edinburgh (for we travelled not in company), I proposed to go with him to look for lodgings, telling him at the same time what a blessed religious family my reverend instructor and I were settled in. He said he rejoiced at it, but he made a rule of never lodging in any particular house, but took these daily, or hourly, as he found it convenient, and that he never was at a loss in any circumstance.

'What a mighty trouble you put yourself to, great sovereign!' said I, 'and all, it would appear, for the purpose of seeing and knowing more and more of the human race.'

'I never go but where I have some great purpose to serve,' returned he, 'either in the advancement of my own power and dominion or in thwarting my enemies.'

'With all due deference to your great comprehension, my illustrious friend,' said I, 'it strikes me that you can accomplish very little either the one way or the other here, in the humble and private capacity you are pleased to occupy.'

'It is your own innate modesty that prompts such a remark,' said he. 'Do you think the gaining of *you* to my service is not an attainment worthy of being envied by the greatest potentate in Christendom? Before I had missed such a prize as the attainment of your services, I would have travelled over one half of the habitable globe.' – I bowed with great humility, but at the same time how could I but feel proud and highly flattered? He continued: 'Believe me, my dear friend, for such a prize I account no effort too high. For a man who is not only dedicated to the King of Heaven in the most solemn manner, soul, body, and spirit, but also chosen of him from the beginning, justified, sanctified, and received into a communion that never shall be broken, and from which no act of his shall ever remove him – the possession of such a man, I tell you, is worth kingdoms; because, every deed that he performs, he does it with perfect safety to himself and honour to me.'-I bowed again, lifting my hat, and he went on. – 'I am now going to put his courage in the cause he has espoused to a severe test - to a trial at which common nature would revolt, but he who is dedicated to be the sword of the Lord must raise himself above common humanity. You have a father and a brother according to the flesh: what do you know of them?'

'I am sorry to say I know nothing good,' said I. 'They are reprobates, castaways, beings devoted to the Wicked One, and, like him, workers of every species of iniquity with greediness.'

'They must both fall!' said he, with a sigh and melancholy look. 'It is decreed in the councils above that they must both fall by your hand.'

'The God of Heaven forbid it!' said I. 'They are enemies to Christ and His Church, that I know and believe; but they shall live and die in their iniquity for me, and reap their guerdon when their time cometh. There my hand shall not strike.'

'The feeling is natural, and amiable,' said he. 'But you *must* think again. Whether are the bonds of carnal nature or the bonds and vows of the Lord strongest?'

'I will not reason with you on this head, mighty potentate,' said I, 'for whenever I do so it is but to be put down. I shall only express my determination not to take vengeance out of the Lord's hand in this instance. It availeth not. These are men that have the mark of the beast in their foreheads and right hands; they are lost beings themselves, but have no influence over others. Let them perish in their sins; for they shall not be meddled with by me.'

'How preposterously you talk, my dear friend!' said he. 'These people are your greatest enemies; they would rejoice to see you annihilated. And, now that you have taken up the Lord's cause of being avenged on *His* enemies, wherefore spare those that are your own as well as His? Besides, you ought to consider what great advantages would be derived to the cause of righteousness and truth were the estate and riches of that opulent house in your possession, rather than in that of such as oppose the truth and all manner of holiness.'

This was a portion of the consequence of following my illustrious adviser's summary mode of procedure that had never entered into my calculation. I disclaimed all idea of being influenced by it; however, I cannot but say that the desire of being enabled to do so much good, by the possession of these bad men's riches, made some impression on my heart, and I said I would consider of the matter. I did consider it, and that right seriously as well as frequently; and there was scarcely an hour in the day on which my resolves were not animated by my great friend, till at length I began to have a longing desire to kill my brother, in particular. Should any man ever read this scroll, he will wonder at this confession, and deem it savage and unnatural. So it appeared to me at first, but a constant thinking of an event changes every one of its features. I have done all for the best, and as I was prompted, by one who knew right and wrong much better than I did. I *had* a desire to slay him, it is true, and such a desire too as a thirsty man has to drink; but, at the same time, this longing desire was mingled with a certain terror, as if I had dreaded that the drink for which I longed was mixed with deadly poison. My mind was so much weakened, or rather softened about this time, that my faith began a little to give way, and I doubted most presumptuously of the least tangible of all Christian tenets, namely, of the *infallibility of the elect*. I hardly comprehended the great work I had begun, and doubted of *my own* infallibility, or that of any created being. But I was brought over again by the unwearied diligence of my friend to repent of my backsliding, and view once more the superiority of the Almighty's counsels in its fullest latitude. Amen. I prayed very much in secret about this time, and that with great fervour of spirit, as well as humility; and my satisfaction at finding all my requests granted is not to be expressed.

My illustrious friend still continuing to sound in my ears the imperious duty to which I was called, of making away with my sinful relations, and quoting many parallel actions out of the Scriptures, and the writings of the holy fathers, of the pleasure the Lord took in such as executed his vengeance on the wicked, I was obliged to acquiesce in his measures, though with certain limitations. It was not easy to answer his arguments, and yet I was afraid that he soon perceived a leaning to his will on my part. 'If the acts of Jehu, in rooting out the whole house of his master, were ordered and approved of by the Lord,' said he, 'would it not have been more praiseworthy if one of Ahab's[104] own sons had stood up for the cause of the God of Israel, and rooted out the sinners and their idols out of the land?'

'It would certainly,' said I. 'To our duty to God all other duties must yield.'

'Go thou then and do likewise,' said he. 'Thou art called to a high vocation; to cleanse the sanctuary of thy God in this thy native land by the shedding of blood; go thou then like a ruling energy, a master spirit of desolation in the dwellings of the wicked, and high shall be your reward both here and hereafter.'

My heart now panted with eagerness to look my brother in the face. On which my companion, who was never out of the way, conducted me to a small square in the suburbs of the city, where there were a number of young noblemen and gentlemen playing at a vain, idle, and sinful game, at which there was much of the language of the accursed going on; and among these blasphemers he instantly pointed out my brother to me. I was fired with indignation at seeing him in such company, and so employed; and I placed myself close beside him to watch all his motions, listen to his words, and draw inferences from what I saw and heard. In what a sink of sin was he wallowing! I resolved to take him to task, and, if he refused to be admonished, to inflict on him some condign punishment; and, knowing that my illustrious friend and director was looking on, I resolved to show some spirit. Accordingly, I waited until I heard him profane his Maker's name three times, and then, my spiritual indignation being roused above all restraint, I went up and kicked him. Yes, I went boldly up and struck him with my foot, and meant to have given him a more severe blow than it was my fortune to inflict. It had, however, the effect of rousing up his corrupt nature to quarrelling and strife, instead of taking the chastisement of the Lord in humility and meekness. He ran furiously against me in the choler that is always inspired by the wicked one; but I overthrew him, by reason of impeding the natural and rapid progress of his unholy feet running to destruction. I also fell slightly; but his fall proved a severe one, he arose in wrath, and struck me with the mall which he held in his hand, until my blood flowed copiously; and from that moment I vowed his destruction in my heart. But I chanced to have no weapon at that time, nor any means of inflicting due punishment on the caitiff, which would not have been returned double on my head by him and his graceless associates. I mixed among them at the suggestion of my friend, and, following them to their den of voluptuousness and sin, I strove to be admitted among them, in hopes of finding some means of accomplishing my great purpose, while I found myself moved by the spirit within me so to do. But I was not only debarred, but, by the machinations of my wicked brother and his associates, cast into prison.

I was not sorry at being thus honoured to suffer in the cause of righteousness, and at the hands of sinful men; and, as soon as I was alone, I betook myself to prayer, deprecating the long-suffering of God towards such horrid sinners. My gaoler came to me, and insulted me. He was a rude unprincipled fellow, partaking of the loose and carnal manners of the age; but I remembered of having read, in the Cloud of Witnesses,[105] of such men formerly having been converted by the imprisoned saints; so I set myself, with all my heart, to bring about this man's repentance and reformation.

'Fat the deil are ye yoolling an' praying that gate for, man?' said he, coming angrily in. 'I thought the days o' praying prisoners had been a' ower. We had rowth o' them aince; an' they were the poorest an' the blackest bargains that ever poor gaolers saw. Gie up your crooning, or I'll pit you to an in-by place, where ye sall get plenty o't.'

'Friend,' said I, 'I am making my appeal at the bar where all human actions are seen and judged, and where you shall not be forgot, sinful as you are. Go in peace, and let me be.'

'Hae ye naebody nearer-hand hame to mak your appeal to, man?' said he. 'Because an ye hae-na, I dread you an' me may be unco weel acquaintit by an' by.'

I then opened up the mysteries of religion to him in a clear and perspicuous manner, but particularly the great doctrine of the election of grace; and then I added: 'Now, friend, you must tell me if you pertain to this chosen number. It is in every man's power to ascertain this, and it is every man's duty to do it.'

'An' fat the better wad you be for the kenning o' this, man?' said he.

'Because, if you are one of my brethren, I will take you into sweet communion and fellowship,' returned I. 'But, if you belong to the unregenerate, I have a commission to slay you.'

'The deil you hae, callant!' said he, gaping and laughing. 'An', pray now, fa was it that gae you siccan a braw commission?'

'My commission is sealed by the signet above,' said I, 'and that I will let you and all sinners know. I am dedicated to it by the most solemn vows and engagements. I am the sword of the Lord, and Famine and Pestilence are my sisters.[106] Woe then to the wicked of this land, for they must fall down dead together, that the Church may be purified!'

'Oo, foo, foo! I see how it is,' said he. 'Yours is a very braw commission, but you will have the small opportunity of carrying it through here. Take my advising, and write a bit of a letter to your friends, and I will send it, for this is no place for such a great man. If you cannot steady your hand to write, as I see you have been at your great work, a word of a mouth may do; for I do assure you this is not the place at all, of any in the world, for your operations.'[107]

The man apparently thought I was deranged in my intellect. He could not swallow such great truths at the first morsel. So I took his advice, and sent a line to my reverend father, who was not long in coming, and great was the gaoler's wonderment when he saw all the great Christian noblemen of the land sign my bond of freedom.

My reverend father took this matter greatly to heart, and bestirred himself in the good cause till the transgressors were ashamed to show their faces. My illustrious companion was not idle: I wondered that he came not to me in prison, nor at my release; but he was better employed, in stirring up the just to the execution of God's decrees; and he succeeded so well that my brother and all his associates had nearly fallen victims to their wrath. But many were wounded, bruised, and imprisoned, and much commotion prevailed in the city. For my part, I was greatly strengthened in my resolution by the anathemas of my reverend father, who, privately (that is in a family capacity) in his prayers, gave up my father and brother, according to the flesh, to Satan, making it plain to all my senses of perception that they were being given up of God, to be devoured by fiends of men, at their will and pleasure, and that *whosoever* should slay them would do God good service.

The next morning my illustrious friend met me at an early hour, and he was greatly overjoyed at hearing my sentiments now chime so much in unison with his own. I said: 'I longed for the day and the hour that I might look my brother in the face at Gilgal,[108] and visit on him the iniquity of his father and himself, for that I was now strengthened and prepared for the deed.'

'I have been watching the steps and movements of the profligate one,' said he, 'and, lo, I will take you straight to his presence. Let your heart be as the heart of the lion,[109] and your arms strong as the shekels of brass,[110] and swift to avenge as the bolt that descendeth from heaven, for the blood of the just and the good hath long flowed in Scotland. But already is the day of their avengement begun; the hero is at length arisen who shall send all such as bear enmity to the true Church, or trust in works of their own, to Tophet!'[111]

Thus encouraged, I followed my friend, who led me directly to the same court in which I had chastised the miscreant on the foregoing day; and, behold, there was the same group again assembled. They eyed me with terror in their looks, as I walked among them and eyed them with looks of disapprobation and rebuke; and I saw that the very eye of a chosen one lifted on these children of Belial was sufficient to dismay and put them to flight. I walked aside to my friend, who stood at a distance looking on, and he said to me: 'What thinkest thou now?' and I answered in the words of the venal prophet,[112] 'Lo, now, if I had a sword into mine hand I would even kill him.'

'Wherefore lackest thou it?' said he. 'Dost thou not see that they tremble at thy presence, knowing that the avenger of blood is among them.'

My heart was lifted up on hearing this, and again I strode into the midst of them, and, eyeing them with threatening looks, they were so much confounded that they abandoned their sinful pastime, and fled everyone to his house!

This was a palpable victory gained over the wicked, and I thereby knew that the hand of the Lord was with me. My companion also exulted, and said: 'Did not I tell thee? Behold thou dost not know one half of thy might, or of the great things thou art destined to do. Come with me and I will show thee more than this, for these young men cannot subsist without the exercises of sin. I listened to their councils, and I know where they will meet again.'

Accordingly he led me a little farther to the south, and we walked aside till by degrees we saw some people begin to assemble; and in a short time we perceived the same group stripping off their clothes to make them more expert in the practice of madness and folly. Their game was begun before we approached, and so also were the oaths and cursing. I put my hands in my pockets, and walked with dignity and energy into the midst of them. It was enough. Terror and astonishment seized them. A few of them cried out against me, but their voices were soon hushed amid the murmurs of fear. One of them, in the name of the rest, then came and besought of me to grant them liberty to amuse themselves; but I refused peremptorily, dared the whole multitude so much as to touch me with one of their fingers, and dismissed them in the name of the Lord.

Again they all fled and dispersed at my eye, and I went home in triumph, escorted by my friend, and some well-meaning young Christians, who, however, had not learned to deport themselves with soberness and humility. But my ascendancy over my enemies was great indeed; for wherever I appeared I was hailed with approbation, and, wherever my guilty brother made his appearance, he was hooted and held in derision, till he was forced to hide his disgraceful head, and appear no more in public.

Immediately after this I was seized with a strange distemper, which neither my friends nor physicians could comprehend, and it confined me to my chamber for many days; but I knew, myself, that I was bewitched, and suspected my father's reputed concubine of the deed. I told my fears to my reverend protector, who hesitated concerning them, but I knew by his words and looks that he was conscious I was right. I generally conceived myself to be two people. When I lay in bed, I deemed there were two of us in it; when I sat up I always beheld another person, and always in the same position from the place where I sat or stood, which was about three paces off me towards my left side. It mattered not how many or how few were present: this my second self was sure to be present in his place, and this occasioned a confusion in all my words and ideas that utterly astounded my friends, who all declared that, instead of being deranged in my intellect, they had never heard my conversation manifest so much energy or sublimity of conception; but, for all that, over the singular delusion that I was two persons my reasoning faculties had no power. The most perverse part of it was that I rarely conceived *myself* to be any of the two persons. I thought for the most part that my companion was one of them, and my brother the other; and I found that, to be obliged to speak and answer in the character of another man, was a most awkward business at the long run.

Who can doubt, from this statement, that I was bewitched, and that my relatives were at the ground of it? The constant and unnatural persuasion that I was my brother proved it to my own satisfaction, and must, I think, do so to every unprejudiced person. This victory of the Wicked One over me kept me confined in my chamber at Mr Millar's house for nearly a month, until the prayers of the faithful prevailed, and I was restored. I knew it was a chastisement for my pride, because my heart was lifted up at my superiority over the enemies of the Church; nevertheless I determined to make short work with the aggressor, that the righteous might not be subjected to the effect of his diabolical arts again.

I say I was confined a month. I beg he that readeth to take note of this, that he may estimate how much the word, or even the oath, of a wicked man is to depend on. For a month I saw no one but such as came into my room, and, for all that, it will be seen that there were plenty of the same set to attest upon oath that I saw my brother every day during this period; that I persecuted him with my presence day and night, while all the time I never saw his face save in a delusive dream. I cannot comprehend what manoeuvres my illustrious friend was playing off with them about this time; for he, having the art of personating whom he chose, had peradventure deceived them, else many of them had never all attested the same thing. I never saw any man so steady in his friendships and attentions as he; but as he made a rule of never calling at private houses, for fear of some discovery being made of his person, so I never saw him while my malady lasted; but, as soon as I grew better, I knew I had nothing ado but to attend at some of our places of meeting to see him again. He was punctual, as usual, and I had not to wait.

My reception was precisely as I apprehended. There was no flaring, no flummery,[113] nor bombastical pretensions, but a dignified return to my obeisance, and an immediate recurrence, in converse, to the important duties incumbent on us, in our stations, as reformers and purifiers of the Church.

'I have marked out a number of most dangerous characters in this city,' said he, 'all of whom must be cut off from cumbering the true vineyard before we leave this land. And, if you bestir not yourself in the work to which you are called, I must raise up others who shall have the honour of it.'

'I am, most illustrious prince, wholly at your service,' said I. 'Show but what ought to be done, and here is the heart to dare, and the hand to execute. You pointed out my relations, according to the flesh, as brands fitted to be thrown into the burning. I approve peremptorily of the award; nay, I thirst to accomplish it; for I myself have suffered severely from their diabolical arts. When once that trial of my devotion to the faith is accomplished, then be your future operations disclosed.'

'You are free of your words and promises,' said he.

'So will I be of my deeds in the service of my master, and that shalt thou see,' said I. 'I lack not the spirit, nor the will, but I lack experience woefully; and, because of that shortcoming, must bow to your suggestions.'

'Meet me here tomorrow be times,' said he, 'and perhaps you may hear of some opportunity of displaying your zeal in the cause of righteousness.'

I met him as he desired me; and he addressed me with a hurried and joyful expression, telling me that my brother was astir, and that a few minutes ago he had seen him pass on his way to the mountain. 'The hill is wrapped in a cloud,' added he, 'and never was there such an opportunity of executing divine justice on a guilty sinner. You may trace him in the dew, and shall infallibly find him on the top of some precipice; for it is only in secret that he dares show his debased head to the sun.'

'I have no arms, else assuredly I would pursue him and discomfit him,' said I.

'Here is a small dagger,' said he; 'I have nothing of weapon-kind about me save that, but it is a potent one; and, should you require it, there is nothing more ready or sure.'

'Will not you accompany me?' said I. 'Sure you will?'

'I will be with you, or near you,' said he. 'Go you on before.'

I hurried away as he directed me, and imprudently asked some of Queensberry's guards if such and such a young man passed by them going out from the city. I was answered in the affirmative, and till then had doubted of my friend's intelligence, it was so inconsistent with a profligate's life to be so early astir. When I got the certain intelligence that my brother was before me, I fell a-running, scarcely knowing what I did; and, looking several times behind me, I perceived nothing of my zealous and arbitrary friend. The consequence of this was that, by the time I reached St Anthony's well, my resolution began to give way. It was not my courage, for, now that I had once shed blood in the cause of the true faith, I was exceedingly bold and ardent, but, whenever I was left to myself, I was subject to sinful doubtings. These always hankered on one point. I doubted if the elect were infallible, and if the Scripture promises to them were binding in all situations and relations. I confess this, and that it was a sinful and shameful weakness in me, but my nature was subject to it, and I could not eschew it. I never doubted that I was one of the elect myself; for, besides the strong inward and spiritual conviction that I possessed, I had my kind father's assurance; and these had been revealed to him in that way and measure that they could not be doubted.

In this desponding state, I sat myself down on a stone, and bethought me of the rashness of my undertaking. I tried to ascertain, to my own satisfaction, whether or not I really had been commissioned of God to perpetrate these crimes in His behalf, for, in the eyes and by the laws of men, they were great and crying transgressions. While I sat pondering on these things, I was involved in a veil of white misty vapour, and, looking up to heaven, I was just about to ask direction from above, when I heard as it were a still small voice[114] close by me, which uttered some words of derision and chiding. I looked intensely in the direction whence it seemed to come, and perceived a lady robed in white, who hastened towards me. She regarded me with a severity of look and gesture that appalled me so much I could not address her; but she waited not for that, but coming close to my side said, without stopping: 'Preposterous wretch! How dare you lift your eyes to Heaven with such purposes in your heart? Escape homewards, and save your soul, or farewell for ever!'

These were all the words that she uttered, as far as I could ever recollect, but my spirits were kept in such a tumult that morning that something might have escaped me. I followed her eagerly with my eyes, but in a moment she glided over the rocks above the holy well, and vanished. I persuaded myself that I had seen a vision, and that the radiant being that had addressed me was one of the good angels, or guardian spirits, commissioned by the Almighty to watch over the steps of the just. My first impulse was to follow her advice, and make my escape home; for I thought to myself: 'How is this interested and mysterious foreigner a proper judge of the actions of a free Christian?'

The thought was hardly framed, nor had I moved in a retrograde direction six steps, when I saw my illustrious friend and great adviser descending the ridge towards me with hasty and impassioned strides. My heart fainted within me; and, when he came up and addressed me, I looked as one caught in a trespass. 'What hath detained thee, thou desponding trifler?' said he. 'Verily now shall the golden opportunity be lost which may never be recalled. I have traced the reprobate to his sanctuary in the cloud, and lo he is perched on the pinnacle of a precipice an hundred fathoms high. One ketch[115] with thy foot, or toss with thy finger, shall throw him from thy sight into the foldings of the cloud, and he shall be no more seen till found at the bottom of the cliff dashed to pieces. Make haste, therefore, thou loiterer, if thou wouldst ever prosper and rise to eminence in the work of thy Lord and Master.'

'I go no farther in this work,' said I, 'for I have seen a vision that has reprimanded the deed.'

'A vision?' said he. 'Was it that wench who descended from the hill?'

'The being that spake to me, and warned me of my danger, was indeed in the form of a lady,' said I.

'She also approached me and said a few words,' returned he, 'and I thought there was something mysterious in her manner. Pray, what did she say? For the words of such a singular message, and from such a messenger, ought to be attended to. If I understood her

aright, she was chiding us for our misbelief and preposterous delay.'
I recited her words, but he answered that I had been in a state of
sinful doubting at the time, and it was to these doubtings she had
adverted. In short, this wonderful and clear-sighted stranger soon
banished all my doubts and despondency, making me utterly
ashamed of them, and again I set out with him in the pursuit of my
brother. He showed me the traces of his footsteps in the dew, and
pointed out the spot where I should find him. 'You have nothing
more to do than go softly down behind him,' said he, 'which you can
do to within an ell of him, without being seen; then rush upon him,
and throw him from his seat, where there is neither footing nor
hold. I will go, meanwhile, and amuse his sight by some exhibition
in the contrary direction, and he shall neither know nor perceive
who had done him this *kind office*: for, exclusive of more weighty
concerns, be assured of this that, the sooner he falls, the fewer
crimes will he have to answer for, and his estate in the other world
will be proportionally more tolerable than if he spent a long
unregenerate life steeped in iniquity to the loathing of the soul.'

'Nothing can be more plain or more pertinent,' said I. 'Therefore,
I fly to perform that which is both a duty towards God and towards
man!'

'You shall yet rise to great honour and preferment,' said he.

'I value it not, provided I do honour and justice to the cause of my
master here,' said I.

'You shall be lord of your father's riches and demesnes,' added he.

'I disclaim and deride every selfish motive thereto relating,' said I,
'further than as it enables me to do good.'

'Aye, but that is a great and a heavenly consideration, that *longing
for ability to do good*,' said he – and, as he said so, I could not help
remarking a certain derisive exultation of expression which I could
not comprehend; and indeed I have noted this very often in my
illustrious friend, and sometimes mentioned it civilly to him, but he
has never failed to disclaim it. On this occasion I said nothing, but,
concealing his poniard in my clothes, I hasted up the mountain,
determined to execute my purpose before any misgivings should
again visit me; and I never had more ado than in keeping firm my
resolution. I could not help my thoughts, and there are certain
trains and classes of thoughts that have great power in enervating
the mind. I thought of the awful thing of plunging a fellow creature
from the top of a cliff into the dark and misty void below – of his
being dashed to pieces on the protruding rocks, and of hearing his
shrieks as he descended the cloud, and beheld the shagged points on

which he was to alight. Then I thought of plunging a soul so abruptly into Hell, or, at the best, sending it to hover on the confines of that burning abyss – of its appearance at the bar of the Almighty to receive its sentence. And then I thought: 'Will there not be a sentence pronounced against me there, by a jury of the just made perfect, and written down in the registers of Heaven?'

These thoughts, I say, came upon me unasked, and, instead of being able to dispel them, they mustered upon the summit of my imagination in thicker and stronger array: and there was another that impressed me in a very particular manner, though I have reason to believe not so strongly as those above written. It was this: 'What if I should fail in my first effort? Will the consequence not be that I am tumbled from the top of the rock myself?' and then all the feelings anticipated, with regard to both body and soul, must happen to me! This was a spine-breaking reflection; and yet, though the probability was rather on that side, my zeal in the cause of godliness was such that it carried me on, maugre all danger and dismay.

I soon came close upon my brother, sitting on the dizzy pinnacle, with his eyes fixed steadfastly in the direction opposite to me. I descended the little green ravine behind him with my feet foremost, and every now and then raised my head, and watched his motions. His posture continued the same, until at last I came so near him I could have heard him breathe if his face had been towards me. I laid my cap aside, and made me ready to spring upon him and push him over. I could not for my life accomplish it! I do not think it was that *I durst not*, I have always felt my courage equal to anything in a good cause. But I had not the heart, or something that I ought to have had. In short, it was not done in time, as it easily might have been. These THOUGHTS are hard enemies wherewith to combat! And I was so grieved that I could not effect my righteous purpose that I laid me down on my face and shed tears. Then, again, I thought of what my great enlightened friend and patron would say to me, and again my resolution rose indignant and indissoluble save by blood. I arose on my right knee and left foot, and had just begun to advance the latter forward: the next step my great purpose had been accomplished, and the culprit had suffered the punishment due to his crimes. But what moved him I knew not: in the critical moment he sprung to his feet, and, dashing himself furiously against me, he overthrew me, at the imminent peril of my life. I disencumbered myself by main force and fled, but he overhied me, knocked me down, and threatened, with dreadful oaths, to throw me from the cliff. After I was a little recovered from the stunning blow, I aroused myself to the combat; and, though I do not recollect the circumstances of that deadly scuffle very minutely, I know that I vanquished him so far as to force him to ask my pardon, and crave a reconciliation. I spurned at both and left him to the chastisements of his own wicked and corrupt heart.

My friend met me again on the hill and derided me in a haughty and stern manner for my imbecility and want of decision. I told him how nearly I had effected my purpose, and excused myself as well as I was able. On this, seeing me bleeding, he advised me to swear the peace against my brother, and have him punished in the meantime, he being the first aggressor. I promised compliance and we parted, for I was somewhat ashamed of my failure, and was glad to be quit for the present of one of whom I stood so much in awe.

When my reverend father beheld me bleeding a second time by the hand of a brother, he was moved to the highest point of displeasure; and, relying on his high interest and the justice of his cause, he brought the matter at once before the courts. My brother and I were first examined face to face. His declaration was a mere romance: mine was not the truth; but as it was by the advice of my reverend father, and that of my illustrious friend, both of whom I knew to be sincere Christians and true believers, that I gave it, I conceived myself completely justified on that score. I said I had gone up into the mountain early on the morning to pray, and had withdrawn myself, for entire privacy, into a little sequestered dell – had laid aside my cap, and was in the act of kneeling when I was rudely attacked by my brother, knocked over, and nearly slain. They asked my brother if this was true. He acknowledged that it was; that I was bare-headed, and in the act of kneeling when he ran foul of me without any intent of doing so. But the judge took him to task on the improbability of this, and put the profligate sore out of countenance. The rest of his tale told still worse, insomuch that he was laughed at by all present, for the judge remarked to him that, granting it was true that he had at first run against me on an open mountain and overthrown me by accident, how was it that, after I had extricated myself and fled, that he had pursued, overtaken, and knocked me down a second time? Would he pretend that all that was likewise by chance? The culprit had nothing to say for himself on this head, and I shall not forget my exultation and that of my reverend father when the sentence of the judge was delivered. It was that my wicked brother should be thrown into prison and tried on a criminal charge of assault and battery, with the intent of committing murder. This was a just and righteous judge, and saw things in their proper bearings, that is, he could discern between a righteous and a wicked man, and then there could be no doubt as to which of the two were acting right and which wrong.

Had I not been sensible that a justified person could do nothing wrong, I should not have been at my ease concerning the statement I had been induced to give on this occasion. I could easily perceive that, by rooting out the weeds from the garden of the Church, I heightened the growth of righteousness; but, as to the tardy way of giving false evidence on matters of such doubtful issue, I confess I saw no great propriety in it from the beginning. But I now only moved by the will and mandate of my illustrious friend. I had no peace or comfort when out of his sight, nor have I ever been able to boast of much in his presence; so true is it that a Christian's life is one of suffering.

My time was now much occupied, along with my reverend preceptor, in making ready for the approaching trial, as the prosecutors. Our counsel assured us of a complete victory, and that banishment would be the mildest award of the law on the offender. Mark how different was the result! From the shifts and ambiguities of a wicked Bench, who had a fellow-feeling of iniquity with the defenders, my suit was lost, the graceless libertine was absolved, and I was incarcerated, and bound over to keep the peace, with heavy penalties, before I was set at liberty.

I was exceedingly disgusted at this issue, and blamed the counsel of my friend to his face. He expressed great grief, and expatiated on the wickedness of our judicatories, adding: 'I see I cannot depend on you for quick and summary measures, but for your sake I shall be revenged on that wicked judge, and that you shall see in a few days.' The Lord Justice Clerk died that same week! But he died in his own house and his own bed, and by what means my friend effected it I do not know. He would not tell me a single word of the matter, but the judge's sudden death made a great noise, and I made so many curious inquiries regarding the particulars of it that some suspicions were like to attach to our family of some unfair means used. For my part I know nothing, and rather think he died by the visitation of Heaven, and that my friend had foreseen it, by symptoms, and soothed me by promises of complete revenge.

It was some days before he mentioned my brother's meditated death to me again, and certainly he then found me exasperated against him personally to the highest degree. But I told him that I could not now think any more of it owing to the late judgment of the court, by which, if my brother were missing or found dead, I would not only forfeit my life but my friends would be ruined by the penalties.

'I suppose you know and believe in the perfect safety of your soul,' said he, 'and that that is a matter settled from the beginning of time, and now sealed and ratified both in Heaven and earth?'

'I believe in it thoroughly and perfectly,' said I; 'and, whenever I entertain doubts of it, I am sensible of sin and weakness.'

'Very well, so then am I,' said he. 'I think I can now divine, with all manner of certainty, what will be the high and merited guerdon of your immortal part. Hear me then further: I give you my solemn assurance, and bond of blood, that no human hand shall ever henceforth be able to injure your life, or shed one drop of your precious blood; but it is on the condition that you walk always by my directions.'

'I will do so with cheerfulness,' said I, 'for, without your enlightened counsel, I feel that I can do nothing. But, as to your power of protecting my life, you must excuse me for doubting of it. Nay, were we in your proper dominions, you could not ensure that.'

'In whatever dominion or land I am, my power accompanies me,' said he, 'and it is only against human might and human weapon that I ensure your life; on that will I keep an eye, and on that you may depend. I have never broken word or promise with you. Do you credit me?'

'Yes, I do,' said I, 'for I see you are in earnest. I believe, though I do not comprehend you.'

'Then why do you not at once challenge your brother to the field of honour? Seeing you now act without danger, cannot you also act without fear?'

'It is not fear,' returned I, 'believe me, I hardly know what fear is. It is a doubt that, on all these emergencies, constantly haunts my mind that, in performing such and such actions, I may fall from my upright state. This makes fratricide a fearful task.'

'This is imbecility itself,' said he. 'We have settled and agreed on that point an hundred times. I would therefore advise that you challenge your brother to single combat. I shall ensure your safety, and he cannot refuse giving you satisfaction.'

'But then the penalties?' said I.

'We will try to evade these,' said he, 'and, supposing you should be caught, if once you are Laird of Dalcastle and Bagrennan, what are the penalties to you?'

'Might we not rather pop him off in private and quietness, as we did the deistical divine?' said I.

'The deed would be alike meritorious, either way,' said he. 'But may we not wait for years before we find an opportunity? My advice is to challenge him, as privately as you will, and there cut him off.'

'So be it then,' said I. 'When the moon is at the full, I will send for him forth to speak with one, and there will I smite him and slay him, and he shall trouble the righteous no more.'

'Then this is the very night,' said he. 'The moon is nigh to the full, and this night your brother and his sinful mates hold carousal; for there is an intended journey tomorrow. The exulting profligate leaves town, where we must remain till the time of my departure hence; and then is he safe, and must live to dishonour God, and not only destroy his own soul but those of many others. Alack, and woe is me! The sins that he and his friends will commit this very night will cry to Heaven against us for our shameful delay! When shall our great work of cleansing the sanctuary be finished, if we proceed at this puny rate?'

'I see the deed *must* be done, then,' said I, 'and, since it is so, it shall be done. I will arm myself forthwith, and from the midst of his wine and debauchery you shall call him forth to me, and there will I smite him with the edge of the sword,[116] that our great work be not retarded.'

'If thy execution were equal to thy intent, how great a man you soon might be!' said he. 'We shall make the attempt once more; and, if it fail again, why, I must use other means to bring about my high purposes relating to mankind. Home and make ready. I will go and procure what information I can regarding their motions, and will meet you in disguise twenty minutes hence, at the first turn of Hewie's Lane beyond the loch.'

'I have nothing to make ready,' said I, 'for I do not choose to go home. Bring me a sword, and we may consecrate it with prayer and vows, and, if I use it not to the bringing down of the wicked and profane, then may the Lord do so to me, and more also!'

We parted, and there was I left again to the multiplicity of my own thoughts for the space of twenty minutes, a thing my friend never failed in subjecting me to, and these were worse to contend with than hosts of sinful men. I prayed inwardly that these deeds of mine might never be brought to the knowledge of men who were incapable of appreciating the high motives that led to them; and then I sung part of the 10th Psalm,[117] likewise in spirit; but, for all these efforts, my sinful doubts returned, so that when my illustrious friend joined me, and proffered me the choice of two gilded rapiers, I declined accepting any of them, and began, in a very bold and energetic manner, to express my doubts regarding the justification of all the deeds of perfect men. He chided me severely and branded me with cowardice, a thing that my nature never was subject to; and then he branded me with falsehood and breach of the most solemn engagements both to God and man.

I was compelled to take the rapier, much against my inclination; but, for all the arguments, threats, and promises that he could use, I would not consent to send a challenge to my brother by his mouth. There was one argument only that he made use of which had some weight with me, but yet it would not preponderate. He told me my brother was gone to a notorious and scandalous habitation of women, and that, if I left him to himself for ever so short a space longer, it might embitter his state through ages to come. This was a trying concern to me; but I resisted it, and reverted to my doubts. On this he said that he had meant to do me honour, but, since I put it out of his power, he would do the deed, and take the responsibility on himself. 'I have with sore travail procured a guardship of your life,' added he. 'For my own, I have not; but, be that as it will, I shall not be baffled in my attempts to benefit my friends without a trial. You will at all events accompany me, and see that I get justice?'

'Certes, I will do thus much,' said I, 'and woe be to him if his arm prevail against my friend and patron!'

His lip curled with a smile of contempt, which I could hardly brook; and I began to be afraid that the eminence to which I had been destined by him was already fading from my view. And I thought what I should then do to ingratiate myself again with him, for without his countenance I had no life. 'I will be a man in act,' thought I, 'but in sentiment I will not yield, and for this he must surely admire me the more.'

As we emerged from the shadowy lane into the fair moonshine, I started so that my whole frame underwent the most chilling vibrations of surprise. I again thought I had been taken at unawares and was conversing with another person. My friend was equipped in the Highland garb, and so completely translated into another being that, save by his speech, all the senses of mankind could not have recognised him. I blessed myself, and asked whom it was his pleasure to personify tonight? He answered me carelessly that it was a spark whom he meant should bear the blame of whatever might fall out tonight; and that was all that passed on the subject.

We proceeded by some stone steps at the foot of the North Loch, in hot argument all the way. I was afraid that our conversation might be overheard, for the night was calm and almost as light as day, and we saw sundry people crossing us as we advanced. But the zeal of my friend was so high that he disregarded all danger, and continued to argue fiercely and loudly on my delinquency, as he was pleased to call it. I stood on one argument alone, which was that 'I did not think the Scripture promises to the elect, taken in their utmost latitude, warranted the assurance that they could do no wrong; and that, therefore, it behoved every man to look well to his steps.'

There was no religious scruple that irritated my enlightened friend and master so much as this. He could not endure it. And, the sentiments of our great covenanted reformers being on his side, there is not a doubt that I was wrong. He lost all patience on hearing what I advanced on this matter, and, taking hold of me, he led me into a darksome booth in a confined entry; and, after a friendly but cutting reproach, he bade me remain there in secret and watch the event. 'And, if I fall,' said he, 'you will not fail to avenge my death?'

I was so entirely overcome with vexation that I could make no answer, on which he left me abruptly, a prey to despair; and I saw or heard no more till he came down to the moonlight green followed by my brother. They had quarrelled before they came within my hearing, for the first words I heard were those of my brother, who was in a state of intoxication, and he was urging a reconciliation, as was his wont on such occasions. My friend spurned at the suggestion, and dared him to the combat; and after a good deal of boastful altercation, which the turmoil of my spirits prevented me from remembering, my brother was compelled to draw his sword and stand on the defensive. It was a desperate and terrible engagement. I at first thought that the royal stranger and great champion of the faith would overcome his opponent with ease, for I considered Heaven as on his side, and nothing but the arm of sinful flesh against him. But I was deceived. The sinner stood firm as a rock, while the assailant flitted about like a shadow, or rather like a spirit. I smiled inwardly, conceiving that these lightsome manoeuvres were all a sham to show off his art and mastership in the exercise, and that, whenever they came to close fairly, that instant my brother would be overcome. Still I was deceived. My brother's arm seemed invincible, so that the closer they fought the more palpably did it prevail. They fought round the green to the very edge of the water, and so round till they came close up to the covert where I stood. There being no more room to shift ground, my brother then forced him to come to close quarters, on which, the former still having the decided advantage, my friend quitted his sword and called out. I could resist no longer; so, springing from my concealment, I rushed between them with my sword drawn, and parted them as if they had been two schoolboys: then, turning to my brother, I addressed him as follows: 'Wretch! miscreant! knowest thou what thou art attempting? Wouldest thou lay thine hand on the Lord's anointed, or shed his precious blood? Turn thee to me, that I may chastise thee for all thy wickedness, and not for the many injuries thou hast done to me!' To it we went, with full thirst of vengeance on every side. The duel was fierce; but the might of Heaven prevailed, and not my might. The ungodly and reprobate young man fell covered with wounds, and with curses and blasphemy in his mouth, while I escaped uninjured. Thereto his power extended not.

I will not deny that my own immediate impressions of this affair in some degree differed from this statement. But this is precisely as my illustrious friend described it to me afterwards, and I can rely implicitly on his information, as he was at that time a looker-on, and my senses all in a state of agitation, and he could have no motive for saying what was not the positive truth.

Never till my brother was down did we perceive that there had been witnesses to the whole business. Our ears were then astounded by rude challenges of unfair play, which were quite appalling to me; but my friend laughed at them and conducted me off in perfect safety. As to the unfairness of the transaction, I can say thus much, that my royal friend's sword was down ere ever mine was presented. But if it still be accounted unfair to take up a conqueror, and punish him in his own way, I answer: That if a man is sent on a positive mission by his master, and hath laid himself under vows to do his work, he ought not to be too nice in the means of accomplishing it; and, further, I appeal to holy writ, wherein many instances are recorded of the pleasure the Lord takes in the final extinction of the wicked and profane; and this position I take to be unanswerable.

I was greatly disturbed in my mind for many days, knowing that the transaction had been witnessed, and sensible also of the perilous situation I occupied, owing to the late judgment of the court against me. But on the contrary, I never saw my enlightened friend in such high spirits. He assured me there was no danger; and again repeated that he warranted my life against the power of man. I thought proper, however, to remain in hiding for a week; but, as he said, to my utter amazement, the blame fell on another, who was not only accused but pronounced guilty by the general voice, and outlawed for non-appearance! How could I doubt, after this, that the hand of

Heaven was aiding and abetting me? The matter was beyond my comprehension; and, as for my friend, he never explained anything that was past, but his activity and art were without a parallel.

He enjoyed our success mightily; and for his sake I enjoyed it somewhat, but it was on account of his comfort only, for I could not for my life perceive in what degree the Church was better or purer than before these deeds were done. He continued to flatter me with great things, as to honours, fame and emolument; and above all, with the blessing and protection of Him to whom my body and soul were dedicated. But, after these high promises, I got no longer peace; for he began to urge the death of my father with such an unremitting earnestness that I found I had nothing for it but to comply. I did so; and cannot express his enthusiasm of approbation. So much did he hurry and press me in this that I was forced to devise some of the most openly violent measures, having no alternative. Heaven spared me the deed, taking, in that instance, the vengeance in its own hand; for, before my arm could effect the sanguine but meritorious act, the old man followed his son to the grave. My illustrious and zealous friend seemed to regret this somewhat; but he comforted himself with the reflection, that still I had the merit of it, having not only consented to it, but in fact effected it, for by doing the one action I had brought about both.

No sooner were the obsequies of the funeral over than my friend and I went to Dalcastle, and took undisputed possession of the houses, lands and effects that had been my father's; but his plate, and vast treasures of ready money, he had bestowed on a voluptuous and unworthy creature, who had lived long with him as a mistress. Fain would I have sent her after her lover, and gave my friend some hints on the occasion; but he only shook his head, and said that we must lay all selfish and interested motives out of the question.

For a long time, when I awaked in the morning, I could not believe my senses, that I was indeed the undisputed and sole proprietor of so much wealth and grandeur; and I felt so much gratified that I immediately set about doing all the good I was able, hoping to meet with all approbation and encouragement from my friend. I was mistaken. He checked the very first impulses towards such a procedure, questioned my motives, and uniformly made them out to be wrong. There was one morning that a servant said to me there was a lady in the back chamber who wanted to speak with me, but he could not tell me who it was, for all the old servants had left the mansion, every one on hearing of the death of the late laird, and those who had come knew none of the people in the neighbourhood. From several circumstances I had suspicions of private confabulations with women, and refused to go to her, but bid the servant inquire what she wanted. She would not tell, she could only state the circumstances to me; so I, being sensible that a little dignity of manner became me in my elevated situation, returned for answer that, if it was business that could not be transacted by my steward, it must remain untransacted. The answer which the servant brought back was of a threatening nature. She stated she *must* see me, and, if I refused her satisfaction there, she would compel it where I should not evite her.

My friend and director appeared pleased with my dilemma, and rather advised that I should hear what the woman had to say; on which I consented, provided she would deliver her mission in his presence. She came with manifest signs of anger and indignation, and began with a bold and direct charge against me of a shameful assault on one of her daughters; of having used the basest of means in order to lead her aside from the paths of rectitude; and, on the failure of these, of having resorted to the most unqualified measures.

I denied the charge in all its bearings, assuring the dame that I had never so much as seen either of her daughters to my knowledge, far less wronged them; on which she got into great wrath, and abused me to my face as an accomplished vagabond, hypocrite, and sensualist; and she went so far as to tell me roundly that if I did not *marry* her daughter, she would bring me to the gallows and that in a very short time.

'Marry your daughter, honest woman!' said I, 'on the faith of a Christian, I never saw your daughter; and you may rest assured in this, that I will neither marry you nor her. Do you consider how short a time I have been in this place? How much that time has been occupied? And how there was even a *possibility* that I could have accomplished such villainies?'

'And how long does your Christian reverence suppose you have remained in this place since the late laird's death?' said she.

'That is too well known to need recapitulation,' said I. 'Only a very few days, though I cannot at present specify the exact number; perhaps from thirty to forty, or so. But in all that time, certes, I have never seen either you or any of your two daughters that you talk of. You must be quite sensible of that.'

My friend shook his head three times during this short sentence, while the woman held up her hands in amazement and disgust, exclaiming: 'There goes the selfrighteous one! There goes the consecrated youth, who cannot err! You, sir, know, and the world shall know, of the faith that is in this most just, devout, and religious miscreant! Can you deny that you have already been in this place four months and seven days? Or that in that time you have been forbid my house twenty times? Or that you have persevered in your endeavours to effect the basest and most ungenerous of purposes? Or that you *have* attained them? Hypocrite and deceiver as you are! Yes, sir; I say, dare you deny that you have attained your vile, selfish, and degrading purposes towards a young, innocent, and unsuspecting creature, and thereby ruined a poor widow's only hope in this world? No, you cannot look in my face, and deny aught of this.'

'The woman is raving mad!' said I. 'You, illustrious sir, know that, in the first instance, I have not yet been in this place one month.' My friend shook his head again, and answered me: 'You are wrong, my dear friend; you are wrong. It is indeed the space of time that the lady hath stated, to a day, since you came here, and I came with you; and I am sorry that I know for certain that you have been frequently haunting her house, and have often had private correspondence with one of the young ladies, too. Of the nature of it I presume not to know.'

'You are mocking me,' said I. 'But as well may you try to reason me out of my existence as to convince me that I have been here even one month, or that any of those things you allege against me has the shadow of truth or evidence to support it. I will swear to you, by the great God that made me; and by – '

'Hold, thou most abandoned profligate!' cried she violently, 'and do not add perjury to your other detestable crimes. Do not, for mercy's sake, any more profane that name whose attributes you have wrested and disgraced. But tell me what reparation you propose offering to my injured child.'

'I again declare, before Heaven, woman, that, to the best of my knowledge and recollection, I never saw your daughter. I now think I have some faint recollection of having seen your face, but where, or in what place, puzzles me quite.'

'And, why?' said she. 'Because for months and days you have been in such a state of extreme inebriety, that your time has gone over like a dream that has been forgotten. I believe that, from the day you came first to my house, you have been in a state of utter delirium, and that principally from the fumes of wine and ardent spirits.'

'It is a manifest falsehood!' said I. 'I have never, since I entered on the possession of Dalcastle, tasted wine or spirits, saving once a few evenings ago; and, I confess to my shame, that I was led too far; but I have craved forgiveness and obtained it. I take my noble and distinguished friend there for a witness to the truth of what I assert; a man who has done more, and sacrificed more for the sake of genuine Christianity than any this world contains. Him you will believe.'

'I hope you have attained forgiveness,' said he, seriously. 'Indeed it would be next to blasphemy to doubt it. But, of late, you have been very much addicted to intemperance. I doubt if, from the first night you tasted the delights of drunkenness, that you have ever again been in your right mind until Monday last. Doubtless you have been for a good while most diligent in your addresses to this lady's daughter.'

'This is unaccountable,' said I. 'It is impossible that I can have been doing a thing and not doing it at the same time. But indeed, honest woman, there have several incidents occurred to me in the course of my life which persuade me I have a second self; or that there is some other being who appears in my likeness.'

Here my friend interrupted me with a sneer, and a hint that I was talking insanely; and then he added, turning to the lady: 'I know my friend Mr Colwan will do what is just and right. Go and bring the young lady to him, that he may see her, and he will then recollect all his former amours with her.'

'I humbly beg your pardon, sir,' said I. 'But the mention of such a thing as *amours* with any woman existing, to me, is really so absurd, so far from my principles, so from the purity of nature and frame to which I was born and consecrated, that I hold it as an insult, and regard it with contempt.'

I would have said more in reprobation of such an idea, had not my servant entered, and said that a gentleman wanted to see me on business. Being glad of an opportunity of getting quit of my lady visitor, I ordered the servant to show him in; and forthwith a little lean gentleman, with a long aquiline nose, and a bald head, daubed all over with powder and pomatum,[118] entered. I thought I recollected having seen him too, but could not remember his name, though he spoke to me with the greatest familiarity; at least, that sort of familiarity that an official person generally assumes. He bustled about and about, speaking to everyone, but declined listening for a single moment to any. The lady offered to withdraw, but he stopped her.

'No, no, Mrs Keeler, you need not go; you need not go; you *must* not go, madam. The business I came about concerns you – yes, that it does. Bad business yon of Walker's? Eh? Could not help it – did all I could, Mr Wringhim. Done your business. Have it all cut and dry here, sir. No, this is not it – Have it among them, though. – I'm at a little loss for your name, sir (addressing my friend) – seen you very often, though – exceedingly often – quite well acquainted with you.'

'No, sir, you are not,' said my friend, sternly. The intruder never regarded him; never so much as lifted his eyes from his bundle of law papers, among which he was bustling with great hurry and importance, but went on:

'*Im*possible! Have seen a face very like it, then – what did you say your name was, sir? – very like it indeed. Is it not the young laird who was murdered whom you resemble so much?'

Here Mrs Keeler uttered a scream, which so much startled me, that it seems I grew pale, and, on looking at my friend's face, there was something struck me so forcibly in the likeness between him and my late brother that I had very nearly fainted. The woman exclaimed that it was my brother's spirit that stood beside me.

'*Im*possible!' exclaimed the attorney. 'At least, I hope not, else his signature is not worth a pin. There is some balance due on yon business, madam. Do you wish your account? Because I have it here, ready discharged, and it does not suit letting such things lie over. This business of Mr Colwan's will be a severe one on you, madam – *ra*ther a severe one.'

'What business of mine, if it be your will, sir,' said I. 'For my part I never engaged you in business of any sort less or more.' He never regarded me, but went on: 'You may appeal, though. Yes, yes, there are such things as appeals for the refractory. Here it is, gentlemen. Here they are all together. Here is, in the first place, sir, your power of attorney, regularly warranted, sealed, and signed with your own hand.'

'I declare solemnly that I never signed that document,' said I.

'Aye, aye, the system of denial is not a bad one in general,' said my attorney. 'But at present there is no occasion for it. You do not deny your own hand?'

'I deny everything connected with the business,' cried I. 'I disclaim it *in toto*,[119] and declare that I know no more about it than the child unborn.'

'That is exceedingly good!' exclaimed he. 'I like your pertinacity vastly! I have three of your letters, and three of your signatures; that part is all settled, and I hope so is the whole affair; for here is the original grant to your father, which he has never thought proper to put in requisition.[120] Simple gentleman! But here have I, Lawyer Linkum, in one hundredth part of the time that any other notary, writer, attorney, or writer of the signet[121] in Britain would have done it, procured the signature of His Majesty's commissioner, and thereby confirmed the charter to you and your house, sir, for ever and ever – Begging your pardon, madam.' The lady, as well as myself, tried several times to interrupt the loquacity of Linkum, but in vain: he only raised his hand with a quick flourish, and went on: 'Here it is:

> JAMES, by the grace of God, King of Great Britain, France, and Ireland, to his right trusty cousin, sendeth greeting: And whereas his right leal and trust-worthy cousin, George Colwan, of Dalcastle and Balgrennan, hath suffered great losses, and undergone much hardship, on behalf of his Majesty's rights and titles; he therefore, for himself, and as prince and steward of Scotland, and by the consent of his right trusty cousins and councillors, hereby grants to the said George Colwan, his heirs and assignees whatsomever, heritably and irrevocably, all and haill the lands and others underwritten: *To wit*, All and haill, the five merk land of Kipplerig; the five poundland of Easter Knockward, with all the towers, fortalices, manor-places, houses, biggings, yards, orchards, tofts, crofts, mills, woods, fishings, mosses, muirs, meadows, commonties, pasturages, coals, coal-heughs, tennants, tenantries, services of free tenants, annexes, connexes, dependencies, parts, pendicles, and pertinents of the same whatsomever; to be peaceably brooked, joysed, set, used, and disposed of by him and his aboves, as specified, heritably and irrevocably, in all time coming: And, in testimony thereof, his Majesty, for himself, and as prince steward of Scotland, with the advice and consent of his foresaids, knowledge, proper motive, and kingly power, makes, erects, creates, unites, annexes, and incorporates, the whole lands above mentioned in a haill and free barony, by all the rights, miethes, and marches thereof, old and divided, as the same lies, in length and breadth, in houses, biggings, mills, multures, hawking, hunting, fishing; with court, plaint, herezeld, fock, fork, sack, sock, thole, thame, vert, wraik, waith, wair, venison, outfang thief, infang thief, pit and gallows, and all and sundry other commodities. Given at our Court of Whitehall, &c., &c. God save the King. *Compositio 5 lib*. 13.8. Registrate 26th September 1687[122]

'See, madam, here are ten signatures of privy councillors of that year, and here are other ten of the present year, with His Grace the Duke of Queensberry at the head. All right. See here it is, sir – all right – done your work. So you see, madam, this gentleman is the true and sole heritor of all the land that your father possesses, with all the rents thereof for the last twenty years, and upwards. Fine job for my employers! Sorry on your account, madam – can't help it.'

I was again going to disclaim all interest or connection in the matter but my friend stopped me; and the plaints and lamentations of the dame became so overpowering that they put an end to all further colloquy; but Lawyer Linkum followed me, and stated his great outlay, and the important services he had rendered me, until I was obliged to subscribe an order to him for £100 on my banker.

I was now glad to retire with my friend, and ask seriously for some explanation of all this. It was in the highest degree unsatisfactory. He confirmed all that had been stated to me; assuring me that I had not only been assiduous in my endeavours to seduce a young lady of great beauty, which it seemed I had effected, but that I had taken counsel, and got this supposed, old, false, and forged grant raked up and now signed, to ruin the young lady's family quite, so as to throw her entirely on myself for protection, and be wholly at my will.

This was to me wholly incomprehensible. I could have freely made oath to the contrary of every particular. Yet the evidences were against me, and of a nature not to be denied. Here I must confess that, highly as I disapproved of the love of women, and all intimacies and connections with the sex, I felt a sort of indefinite pleasure, an ungracious delight in having a beautiful woman solely at my disposal. But I thought of her spiritual good in the meantime. My friend spoke of my backslidings with concern; requesting me to make sure of my forgiveness, and to forsake them; and then he added some words of sweet comfort. But from this time forth I began to be sick at times of my existence. I had heart-burnings, longings, and yearnings that would not be satisfied; and I seemed hardly to be an accountable creature; being thus in the habit of executing transactions of the utmost moment without being sensible that I did them. I was a being incomprehensible to myself. Either I had a second self, who transacted business in my likeness, or else my body was at times possessed by a spirit over which it had no control, and of whose actions my own soul was wholly unconscious. This was an anomaly not to be accounted for by any philosophy of mine, and I was many times, in contemplating it, excited to terrors and mental torments hardly describable. To be in a state of consciousness and unconsciousness, at the same time, in the same body and same spirit, was impossible. I was under the greatest anxiety, dreading some change would take place momently in my nature; for of dates I could make nothing: one-half, or two-thirds of my time, seemed to me totally lost. I often, about this time, prayed with great fervour, and lamented my hopeless condition, especially in being liable to the commission of crimes which I was not sensible of and could not eschew. And I confess, notwithstanding the promises on which I had been taught to rely, I began to have secret terrors that the great enemy of man's salvation was exercising powers over me that might eventually lead to my ruin. These were but temporary and sinful fears, but they added greatly to my unhappiness.

The worst thing of all was, what hitherto I had never felt, and, as yet, durst not confess to myself, that the presence of my illustrious and devoted friend was becoming irksome to me. When I was by myself, I breathed freer, and my step was lighter; but, when he approached, a pang went to my heart, and, in his company, I moved and acted as if under a load that I could hardly endure. What a state to be in! And yet to shake him off was impossible – we were incorporated together – identified with one another, as it were, and the power was not in me to separate myself from him. I still knew nothing who he was, further than that he was a potentate of some foreign land, bent on establishing some pure and genuine doctrines of Christianity, hitherto only half understood, and less than half exercised. Of this I could have no doubts after all that he had said, done and suffered in the cause. But, alongst with this, I was also certain that he was possessed of some supernatural power, of the source of which I was wholly ignorant. That a man could be a Christian and at the same time a powerful necromancer, appeared inconsistent, and adverse to every principle taught in our Church and from this I was led to believe that he inherited his powers from on high, for I could not doubt either of the soundness of his principles or that he accomplished things impossible to account for. Thus was I sojourning in the midst of a chaos of confusion. I looked back on my bypast life with pain, as one looks back on a perilous journey, in which he has attained his end, without gaining any advantage either to himself or others; and I looked forward, as on a darksome waste, full of repulsive and terrific shapes, pitfalls, and precipices, to which there was no definite bourn, and from which I turned with disgust. With my riches, my unhappiness was increased tenfold; and here, with another great acquisition of property, for which I had pleaded, and which I had gained in a dream, my miseries and difficulties were increasing. My principal feeling, about this time, was an insatiable longing for something that I cannot describe or denominate properly, unless I say it was for *utter oblivion* that I longed. I desired to sleep; but it was for a deeper and longer sleep than that in which the senses were nightly steeped. I longed to be at rest and quiet, and close my eyes on the past and the future alike, as far as this frail life was concerned. But what had been formerly and finally settled in the councils above, I presumed not to call in question.

In this state of irritation and misery was I dragging on an existence, disgusted with all around me, and in particular with my mother, who, with all her love and anxiety, had such an insufferable mode of manifesting them that she had by this time rendered herself exceedingly obnoxious to me. The very sound of her voice at a distance went to my heart like an arrow, and made all my nerves to shrink; and, as for the beautiful young lady for whom they told me I had been so much enamoured, I shunned all intercourse with her or hers, as I would have done with the Devil. I read some of their letters and burnt them, but refused to see either the young lady or her mother on any account.

About this time it was that my worthy and reverend parent came with one of his elders to see my mother and myself. His presence always brought joy with it into our family, for my mother was uplifted, and I had so few who cared for me, or for whom I cared, that I felt rather gratified at seeing him. My illustrious friend was also much more attached to him than any other person, (except myself,) for their religious principles tallied in every point, and their conversation was interesting, serious, and sublime. Being anxious to entertain well and highly the man to whom I had been so much indebted, and knowing that, with all his integrity and righteousness, he disdained not the good things of this life, I brought from the late laird's well-stored cellars various fragrant and salubrious wines, and we drank, and became merry, and I found that my miseries and overpowering calamities passed away over my head like a shower that is driven by the wind. I became elevated and happy, and welcomed my guests an hundred times; and then I joined them in religious conversation, with a zeal and enthusiasm which I had not often experienced, and which made all their hearts rejoice, so that I said to myself: 'Surely every gift of God is a blessing, and ought to be used with liberality and thankfulness.'

The next day I waked from a profound and feverish sleep, and called for something to drink. There was a servant answered whom I had never seen before, and he was clad in my servant's clothes and livery. I asked for Andrew Handyside, the servant who had waited at table the night before; but the man answered with a stare and a smile:

'What do you mean, sirrah,' said I. 'Pray what do you here? Or what are you pleased to laugh at? I desire you to go about your business, and send me up Handyside. I want him to bring me something to drink.'

'Ye sanna want a drink, maister,' said the fellow. 'Tak a hearty ane, and see if it will wauken ye up something, sae that ye dinna ca' for ghaists through your sleep. Surely ye haena forgotten that Andrew Handyside has been in his grave these six months?'

This was a stunning blow to me. I could not answer further, but sunk back on my pillow as if I had been a lump of lead, refusing to take a drink or anything else at the fellow's hand, who seemed thus mocking me with so grave a face. The man seemed sorry, and grieved at my being offended, but I ordered him away, and continued sullen and thoughtful. Could I have again been for a season in utter oblivion to myself, and transacting business which I neither approved of nor had any connection with! I tried to recollect something in which I might have been engaged, but nothing was portrayed on my mind subsequent to the parting with my friends at a late hour the evening before. The evening before it certainly was: but, if so, how came it that Andrew Handyside, who served at table that evening, should have been in his grave six months! This was a circumstance somewhat equivocal; therefore, being afraid to arise lest accusations of I know not what might come against me, I was obliged to call once more in order to come at what intelligence I could. The same fellow appeared to receive my orders as before, and I set about examining him with regard to particulars. He told me his name was Scrape, that I hired him myself; of whom I hired him; and at whose recommendation. I smiled, and nodded so as to let the knave see I understood he was telling me a chain of falsehoods, but did not choose to begin with any violent asseverations to the contrary.

'And where is my noble friend and companion?' said I. 'How has he been engaged in the interim?'

'I dinna ken him, sir,' said Scrape, 'but have heard it said that the strange mysterious person that attended you, him that the maist part of folks countit uncanny, had gane awa wi' a Mr Ringan o'Glasko last year, and had never returned.'

I thanked the Lord in my heart for this intelligence, hoping that the illustrious stranger had returned to his own land and people, and that I should thenceforth be rid of his controlling and appalling presence. 'And where is my mother?' said I. – The man's breath cut short, and he looked at me without returning any answer. – 'I ask you where my mother is?' said I.

'God only knows, and not I, where she is,' returned he. 'He knows where her soul is, and, as for her body, if you dinna ken something o' it, I suppose nae man alive does.'

'What do you mean, you knave?' said I. 'What dark hints are these you are throwing out? Tell me precisely and distinctly what you know of my mother?'

'It is unco queer o' ye to forget, or pretend to forget everything that gate, the day, sir,' said he. 'I'm sure you heard enough about it yestreen; an' I can tell you there are some gayan ill-faurd stories gaun about that business. But, as the thing is to be tried afore the circuit lords, it wad be far wrang to say either this or that to influence the public mind; it is best just to let justice tak its swee. I hae naething to say, sir. Ye hae been a good enough maister to me, and paid my wages regularly, but ye hae muckle need to be innocent, for there are some heavy accusations rising against you.'[123]

'I fear no accusations of man,' said I, 'as long as I can justify my cause in the sight of Heaven; and that I can do this I am well aware. Go you and bring me some wine and water, and some other clothes than these gaudy and glaring ones.'

I took a cup of wine and water; put on my black clothes and walked out. For all the perplexity that surrounded me, I felt my spirits considerably buoyant. It appeared that I was rid of the two greatest bars to my happiness, by what agency I knew not. My mother, it seemed, was gone, who had become a grievous thorn in my side of late; and my great companion and counsellor, who tyrannised over every spontaneous movement of my heart, had likewise taken himself off. This last was an unspeakable relief; for I found that for a long season I had only been able to act by the motions of his mysterious mind and spirit. I therefore thanked God for my deliverance, and strode through my woods with a daring and heroic step; with independence in my eye, and freedom swinging in my right hand.

At the extremity of the Colwan wood, I perceived a figure approaching me with slow and dignified motion. The moment that I beheld it, my whole frame received a shock as if the ground on which I walked had sunk suddenly below me. Yet, at that moment, I knew not who it was; it was the air and motion of someone that I dreaded, and from whom I would gladly have escaped, but this I even had not power to attempt. It came slowly onward, and I advanced as slowly to meet it; yet, when we came within speech, I still knew not who it was. It bore the figure, air, and features of my late brother, I thought, exactly; yet in all these there were traits so forbidding, so mixed with an appearance of misery, chagrin and despair, that I still shrunk from the view, not knowing in whose face I looked. But, when the being spoke, both my mental and bodily frame received another shock more terrible than the first, for it was the voice of the great personage I had so long denominated my friend, of whom I had deemed myself for ever freed, and whose presence and counsels I now dreaded more than Hell. It was his voice, but so altered – I shall never forget it till my dying day. Nay, I can scarce conceive it possible that any earthly sounds could be so discordant, so repulsive to every feeling of a human soul, as the tones of the voice that grated on my ear at that moment. They were the sounds of the pit, wheezed through a grated cranny, or seemed so to my distempered imagination.

'So! Thou shudderest at my approach now, dost thou?' said he. 'Is this all the gratitude that you deign for an attachment of which the annals of the world furnish no parallel? An attachment which has caused me to forgo power and dominion, might, homage, conquest and adulation: all that I might gain one highly valued and sanctified spirit to my great and true principles of reformation among mankind. Wherein have I offended? What have I done for evil, or what have I not done for your good, that you would thus shun my presence?'

'Great and magnificent prince,' said I humbly, 'let me request of you to abandon a poor worthless wight to his own wayward fortune, and return to the dominion of your people. I am unworthy of the sacrifices you have made for my sake; and, after all your efforts, I do not feel that you have rendered me either more virtuous or more happy. For the sake of that which is estimable in human nature, depart from me to your own home, before you render me a being either altogether above or below the rest of my fellow creatures. Let me plod on towards Heaven and happiness in my own way, like those that have gone before me, and I promise to stick fast by the great principles which you have so strenuously inculcated, on condition that you depart and leave me for ever.'

'Sooner shall you make the mother abandon the child of her bosom; nay, sooner cause the shadow to relinquish the substance, than separate me from your side. Our beings are amalgamated, as it were, and consociated in one, and never shall I depart from this country until I can carry you in triumph with me.'

I can in nowise describe the effect this appalling speech had on me. It was like the announcement of death to one who had of late deemed himself free, if not of something worse than death, and of longer continuance. There was I doomed to remain in misery, subjugated, soul and body, to one whose presence was become more intolerable to me than aught on earth could compensate. And at that moment, when he beheld the anguish of my soul, he could not conceal that he enjoyed it. I was troubled for an answer, for which he was waiting: it became incumbent on me to say something after such a protestation of attachment; and, in some degree to shake the validity of it, I asked, with great simplicity, where he had been all this while?

'Your crimes and your extravagances forced me from your side for a season,' said he, 'but now that I hope the day of grace is returned, I am again drawn towards you by an affection that has neither bounds nor interest;[124] an affection for which I receive not even the poor return of gratitude, and which seems to have its radical sources in fascination. I have been far, far abroad, and have seen much, and transacted much, since I last spoke with you. During that space, I grievously suspect that you have been guilty of great crimes and misdemeanours, crimes that would have sunk an unregenerated person to perdition; but as I knew it to be only a temporary falling off, a specimen of that liberty by which the chosen and elected ones are made free, I closed my eyes on the wilful debasement of our principles, knowing that the transgressions could never be accounted to your charge, and that in good time you would come to your senses, and throw the whole weight of your crimes on the shoulders that had voluntarily stooped to receive the load.'

'Certainly I will,' said I, 'as I and all the justified have a good right to do. But what crimes? What misdemeanours and transgressions do you talk about? For my part, I am conscious of none, and am utterly amazed at insinuations which I do not comprehend.'

'You have certainly been left to yourself for a season,' returned he, 'having gone on rather like a person in a delirium than a Christian in his sober sense. You are accused of having made away with your mother privately; as also of the death of a beautiful young lady, whose affections you had seduced.'

'It is an intolerable and monstrous falsehood!' cried I, interrupting him. 'I never laid a hand on a woman to take away her life, and have even shunned their society from my childhood. I know nothing of my mother's exit, nor of that young lady's whom you mention. Nothing whatever.'

'I hope it is so,' said he. 'But it seems there are some strong presumptuous proofs against you, and I came to warn you this day that a precognition is in progress, and that unless you are perfectly convinced, not only of your innocence but of your ability to prove it, it will be the safest course for you to abscond, and let the trial go on without you.'

'Never shall it be said that I shrunk from such a trial as this,' said I. 'It would give grounds for suspicions of guilt that never had existence, even in thought. I will go and show myself in every public place, that no slanderous tongue may wag against me. I have shed the blood of sinners, but of these deaths I am guiltless; therefore I will face every tribunal, and put all my accusers down.'

'Asseveration will avail you but little,' answered he, composedly. 'It is, however, justifiable in its place, although to me it signifies nothing, who know too well that you *did* commit both crimes, in your own person, and with your own hands. Far be it from me to betray you; indeed, I would rather endeavour to palliate the offences; for, though adverse to nature, I can prove them not to be so to the cause of pure Christianity, by the mode of which we have approved of it, and which we wish to promulgate.'

'If this that you tell me be true,' said I, 'then is it as true that I have two souls, which take possession of my bodily frame by turns, the one being all unconscious of what the other performs; for as sure as I have at this moment a spirit within me, fashioned and destined to eternal felicity, as sure am I utterly ignorant of the crimes you now lay to my charge.'

'Your supposition may be true in effect,' said he. 'We are all subjected to two distinct natures in the same person. I myself have suffered grievously in that way. The spirit that now directs my energies is not that with which I was endowed at my creation. It is changed within me, and so is my whole nature. My former days were those of grandeur and felicity. But, would you believe it? *I was not then a Christian*. Now I am. I have been converted to its truths by passing through the fire, and, since my final conversion, my misery has been extreme. You complain that I have not been able to render you more happy than you were. Alas! do you expect it in the difficult and exterminating career which you have begun? I, however, promise you this – a portion of the only happiness which I enjoy, sublime in its motions, and splendid in its attainments – I will place you on the right hand of my throne, and show you the grandeur of my domains, and the felicity of my millions of true professors.'

I was once more humbled before this mighty potentate, and

promised to be ruled wholly by his directions, although at that moment my nature shrunk from the concessions, and my soul longed rather to be enclosed in the deeps of the sea, or involved once more in utter oblivion. I was like Daniel in the den of lions,[125] without his faith in Divine support, and wholly at their mercy. I felt as one round whose body a deadly snake is twisted, which continues to hold him in its fangs, without injuring him, further than in moving its scaly infernal folds with exulting delight, to let its victim feel to whose power he has subjected himself; and thus did I for a space drag an existence from day to day, in utter weariness and helplessness; at one time worshipping with great fervour of spirit, and at other times so wholly left to myself as to work all manner of vices and follies with greediness. In these my enlightened friend never accompanied me, but I always observed that he was the first to lead me to every one of them, and then leave me in the lurch. The next day, after these my fallings off, he never failed to reprove me gently, blaming me for my venial transgressions; but then he had the art of reconciling all, by reverting to my justified and infallible state, which I found to prove a delightful healing salve for every sore.

But, of all my troubles, this was the chief: I was every day and every hour assailed with accusations of deeds of which I was wholly ignorant; of acts of cruelty, injustice, defamation, and deceit; of pieces of business which I could not be made to comprehend; with lawsuits, details, arrestments of judgment, and a thousand interminable quibbles from the mouth of my loquacious and conceited attorney. So miserable was my life rendered by these continued attacks that I was often obliged to lock myself up for days together, never seeing any person save my man Samuel Scrape, who was a very honest blunt fellow, a staunch Cameronian,[126] but withal very little conversant in religious matters. He said he came from a place called Penpunt, which I thought a name so ludicrous that I called him by the name of his native village, an appellation of which he was very proud, and answered everything with more civility and perspicuity when I denominated him Penpunt, than Samuel, his own Christian name. Of this peasant was I obliged to make a companion on sundry occasions, and strange indeed were the details which he gave me concerning myself, and the ideas of the country people concerning me. I took down a few of these in writing, to put off the time, and here leave them on record to show how the best and greatest actions are misconstrued among sinful and ignorant men: 'You say, Samuel, that I hired you myself – that I have been a good enough master to you, and have paid you your weekly wages punctually. Now, how is it that you say this, knowing, as you do, that I never hired you, and never paid you a sixpence of wages in the whole course of my life, excepting this last month?'

'Ye may as weel say, master, that water's no water, or that stanes are no stanes. But that's just your gate, an' it's a great pity aye to do a thing an' profess the clean contrair. Weel then, since you havena paid me ony wages, an' I can prove day and date when I was hired, an' came hame to your service, will you be sae kind as to pay me now? That's the best way o' curing a man o' the mortal disease o' leasing-making that I ken o'.'

'I should think that Penpunt and Cameronian principles would not admit of a man taking twice payment for the same article.'

'In sic a case as this, sir, it disna hinge upon principles, but a piece o' good manners; an' I can tell you that, at sic a crisis, a Cameronian is a gayan weel-bred man. He's driven to this, and he maun either make a breach in his friend's good name, or in his purse; an' Oh, sir, whilk o' thae, think you, is the most precious? For instance, an a Galloway drover[127] had comed to the town o' Penpunt, an' said to a Cameronian (the folk's a' Cameronians there), "Sir, I want to buy your cow," "Vera weel," says the Cameronian, "I just want to sell the cow, sae gie me twenty punds Scots, an' take her w' ye." It's a bargain. The drover takes away the cow, an' gies the Cameronian his twenty pund Scots. But after that, he meets him again on the white sands, amang a' the drovers an' dealers o' the land, an' the Gallowayman, he says to the Cameronian, afore a' thae witnesses, "Come, Master Whiggam, I hae never paid you for yon bit useless cow that I bought. I'll pay her the day, but you maun mind the luckpenny; there's muckle need for 't" – or something to that purpose. The Cameronian then turns out to be a civil man, an' canna bide to make the man baith a feele an' liar at the same time, afore a' his associates; an' therefore he pits his principles aff at the side, to be a kind o' sleepin' partner, as it war, an' brings up his good breeding to stand at the counter: he pockets the money, gies the Galloway drover time o' day, an' comes his way. An' wha's to blame? *Man mind yoursel* is the first commandment. A Cameronian's principles never came atween him an' his purse, nor sanna in the present case; for, as I canna bide to make you out a leear, I'll thank you for my wages.'

'Well, you shall have them, Samuel, if you declare to me that I hired you myself in this same person, and bargained with you with this same tongue and voice with which I speak to you just now.'

'That I do declare, unless ye hae twa persons o' the same

appearance, and twa tongues to the same voice. But, 'od saif us, sir, do you ken what the auld wives o' the clachan say about you?'

'How should I, when no one repeats it to me?'

'Oo, I trow it's a' stuff – folk shouldna heed what's said by auld crazy kimmers. But there are some o' them weel ken'd for witches, too; an' they say, "Lord have a care o' us!" They say the deil's often seen gaun sidie for sidie w' ye, whiles in ae shape, an' whiles in another. An' they say that he whiles takes your ain shape, or else enters into you, and then you turn a deil yoursel.'

I was so astounded at this terrible idea that had gone abroad, regarding my fellowship with the Prince of Darkness, that I could make no answer to the fellow's information, but sat like one in a stupor; and if it had not been for my well-founded faith, and conviction that I was a chosen and elected one before the world was made, I should at that moment have given in to the popular belief, and fallen into the sin of despondency; but I was preserved from such a fatal error by an inward and unseen supporter. Still the insinuation was so like what I felt myself that I was greatly awed and confounded.

The poor fellow observed this, and tried to do away the impression by some further sage remarks of his own.

'Hout, dear sir, it is balderdash, there's nae doubt o't. It is the crownhead o' absurdity to tak in the havers o' auld wives for gospel. I told them that my master was a peeous man, an' a sensible man; an', for praying, that he could ding auld Macmillan[128] himsel. "Sae could the deil," they said, "when he liket, either at preaching or praying, if these war to answer his ain ends." "Na, na," says I, "but he's a strick believer in a' the truths o' Christianity, my master." They said, sae was Satan, for that he was the firmest believer in a' the truths of Christianity that was out o' Heaven; an' that, sin' the Revolution that the Gospel had turned sae rife, he had been often driven to the shift o' preaching it himsel, for the purpose o' getting some wrang tenets introduced into it, and thereby turning it into blasphemy and ridicule.'[129]

I confess, to my shame, that I was so overcome by this jumble of nonsense that a chillness came over me, and, in spite of all my efforts to shake off the impression it had made, I fell into a faint. Samuel soon brought me to myself, and, after a deep draught of wine and water, I was greatly revived, and felt my spirit rise above the sphere of vulgar conceptions and the restrained views of unregenerate men. The shrewd but loquacious fellow, perceiving this, tried to make some amends for the pain he had occasioned to me by the following story, which I noted down, and which was brought on by a conversation to the following purport:

'Now, Penpunt, you may tell me all that passed between you and the wives of the clachan. I am better of that stomach qualm with which I am sometimes seized, and shall be much amused by hearing the sentiments of noted witches regarding myself and my connections.'

'Weel, you see, sir, I says to them, "It will be lang afore the deil intermeddle wi' as serious a professor, and as fervent a prayer as my master, for, gin he gets the upper hand o' sickan men, wha's to be safe?" An', what think ye they said, sir? There was ane Lucky Shaw set up her lang lantern chafts, an' answered me, an' a' the rest shanned and noddit in assent an' approbation: "Ye silly, sauchless, Cameronian cuif!" quo she, "is that a' that ye ken about the wiles and doings o' the Prince o' the Air, that rules an' works in the bairns of disobedience? Gin ever he observes a proud professor, wha has mae than ordinary pretensions to a divine calling, and that reards and prays till the very howlets learn his preambles, *that's* the man Auld Simmie fixes on to mak a dishclout o'. He canna get rest in Hell, if he sees a man, or a set of men o' this stamp, an, when he sets fairly to work, it is seldom that he disna bring them round till his ain measures by hook or by crook. Then, Oh! it is a grand prize for him, an' a proud Deil he is, when he gangs hame to his ain ha', wi' a batch o' the souls o' sic strenuous professors on his back. Aye, I trow, auld Ingleby, the Liverpool packman, never came up Glasco street wi' prouder pomp when he had ten horselaids afore him o' Flanders lace, an' Hollin lawn, an' silks an' satins frae the eastern Indians, than Satan wad strodge into Hell with a packlaid o' the souls o' proud professors on his braid shoulders. Ha, ha, ha! I think I see how the auld thief wad be gaun through his gizened dominions, crying his wares, in derision, 'Wha will buy a fresh, cauler divine, a bouzy bishop, a fasting zealot, or a piping priest?' For a' their prayers an' their praises, their aumuses, an' their penances, their whinings, their howlings, their rantings, an' their ravings, here they come at last! Behold the end! Here go the rare and precious wares! A fat professor for a bodle, an' a lean ane for half a merk!" I declare I trembled at the auld hag's ravings, but the lave o' the kimmers applauded the sayings as sacred truths. An' then Lucky went on: "There are many wolves in sheep's claithing, among us, my man, mony deils aneath the masks o' zealous professors, roaming about in kirks and meeting-houses o' the land. It was but the year afore the last that the people o' the town o' Auchtermuchty[130] grew so rigidly righteous that the meanest hind among them became a shining light in ither towns an' parishes. There was naught to be heard, neither night nor day, but preaching, praying, argumentation, an' catechising in a' the famous town o' Auchtermuchty. The young men wooed their sweethearts out o' the Song o' Solomon,[131] an' the girls returned answers in strings o' verses out o' the Psalms. At the lintswinglings, they said questions round; and read chapters, and sang hymns at bridals; auld and young prayed in their dreams, an' prophesied in their sleep, till the deils in the farrest nooks o' Hell were alarmed, and moved to commotion. Gin it hadna been an auld carl, Robin Ruthven, Auchtermuchty wad at that time hae been ruined and lost for ever. But Robin was a cunning man, an' had rather mae wits than his ain, for he had been in the hands o' the fairies when he was young, an' a' kinds o' spirits were visible to his een, an' their language as familiar to him as his ain mother tongue. Robin was sitting on the side o' the West Lomond, ae still gloomy night in September, when he saw a bridal o' corbie craws coming east the lift, just on the edge o' the gloaming. The moment that Robin saw them, he kenned, by their movements, that they were craws o' some ither warld than this; so he signed himself, and crap into the middle o' his bourock. The corbie craws came a' an' sat down round about him, an' they poukit their black sooty wings, an' spread them out to the breeze to cool; and Robin heard ae corbie speaking, an' another answering him; and the tane said to the tither: 'Where will the ravens find a prey the night?' 'On the lean crazy souls o' Auchtermuchty,' quo the tither. 'I fear they will be o'er weel wrappit up in the warm flannens o' faith, an clouted wi' the dirty duds o' repentance, for us to mak a meal o',' quo the first. 'Whaten vile sounds are these that I hear coming bumming up the hill?' 'Oh, these are the hymns and praises o' the auld wives and creeshy louns o' Auchtermuchty, wha are gaun crooning their way to Heaven; an', gin it warna for the shame o' being beat, we might let our great enemy tak them. For sic a prize as he will hae! Heaven, forsooth! What shall we think o' Heaven, if it is to be filled wi' vermin like thae, amang whom there is mair poverty and pollution than I can name.' 'No matter for that,' said the first, 'we cannot have our power set at defiance; though we should put them on the thief's hole, we must catch them, and catch them with their own bait, too. Come all to church tomorrow, and I'll let you hear how I'll gull the saints of Auchtermuchty. In the meantime, there is a feast on the Sidlaw hills[132] tonight, below the hill of Macbeth – Mount, Diabolus, and fly.' Then, with loud croaking and crowing, the bridal of corbies again scaled the dusky air, and left Robin Ruthven in the middle of his cairn.

' "The next day the congregation met in the kirk of Auchtermuchty, but the minister made not his appearance. The elder ran out and in making inquiries; but they could learn nothing, save that the minister was missing. They ordered the clerk to sing a part of the 119th Psalm,[133] until they saw if the minister would cast up. The clerk did as he was ordered, and, by the time he reached the 77th verse, a strange divine entered the church, by the *western* door, and advanced solemnly up to the pulpit. The eyes of all the congregation were riveted on the sublime stranger, who was clothed in a robe of black sackcloth, that flowed all around him, and trailed far behind, and they weened him an angel, come to exhort them, in disguise. He read out his text from the Prophecies of Ezekiel, which consisted of these singular words: 'I will overturn, overturn, overturn it; and it shall be no more, until he come, whose right it is, and I will give it him.'[134]

' "From these words he preached such a sermon as never was heard by human ears, at least never by ears of Auchtermuchty. It was a true, sterling, gospel sermon – it was striking, sublime, and awful in the extreme. He finally made out the IT, mentioned in the text, to mean, properly and positively, the notable town of Auchtermuchty. He proved all the people in it, to their perfect satisfaction, to be in the gall of bitterness and bond of iniquity, and he assured them that God would overturn them, their principles, and professions; and that they should be no more, until the Devil, the town's greatest enemy, came, and then it should be given unto him for a prey, for it was his right, and to him it belonged, if there was not forthwith a radical change made in all their opinions and modes of worship.

' "The inhabitants of Auchtermuchty were electrified – they were charmed; they were actually raving mad about the grand and sublime truths delivered to them by this eloquent and impressive preacher of Christianity. 'He is a prophet of the Lord,' said one, 'sent to warn us, as Jonah was sent to the Ninevites.'[135] 'Oh, he is an angel sent from Heaven, to instruct this great city,' said another, 'for no man ever uttered truths so sublime before.' The good people of Auchtermuchty were in perfect raptures with the preacher, who had thus sent them to Hell by the slump, tag-rag, and bobtail! Nothing in the world delights a truly religious people so much as consigning them to eternal damnation. They wandered after the preacher – they crowded together, and spoke of his sermon with admiration, and still, as they conversed, the wonder and the admiration increased; so that honest Robin Ruthven's words would not be listened to. It was in vain that he told them he heard a raven speaking, and another raven answering him: the people laughed him to scorn, and kicked him out of their assemblies, as a one who spoke evil of dignities; and they called him a warlock, an' a daft body, to think to mak language out o' the crouping o' craws.

' "The sublime preacher could not be heard of, although all the country was sought for him, even to the minutest corner of St Johnston[136] and Dundee; but as he had announced another sermon on the same text, on a certain day, all the inhabitants of that populous country, far and near, flocked to Auchtermuchty. Cupar, Newburgh, and Strathmiglo, turned out men, women and children. Perth and Dundee gave their thousands; and, from the East Nook of Fife to the foot of the Grampian hills, there was nothing but running and riding that morning to Auchtermuchty. The kirk would not hold the thousandth part of them. A splendid tent was erected on the brae north of the town, and round that the countless congregation assembled. When they were all waiting anxiously for the great preacher, behold, Robin Ruthven set up his head in the tent, and warned his countrymen to beware of the doctrines they were about to hear, for he could prove, to their satisfaction, that they were all false, and tended to their destruction!

' "The whole multitude raised a cry of indignation against Robin, and dragged him from the tent, the elders rebuking him, and the multitude threatening to resort to stronger measures; and, though he told them a plain and unsophisticated tale of the black corbies, he was only derided. The great preacher appeared once more, and went through his two discourses with increased energy and approbation. All who heard him were amazed, and many of them went into fits, writhing and foaming in a state of the most horrid agitation. Robin Ruthven sat on the outskirts of the great assembly, listening with the rest, and perceived what they, in the height of their enthusiasm, perceived not – the ruinous tendency of the tenets so sublimely inculcated. Robin kenned the voice of his friend the corby-craw again, and was sure he could not be wrong: sae, when public worship was finished, a' the elders an' a' the gentry flocked about the great preacher, as he stood on the green brae in the sight of the hale congregation, an' a' war alike anxious to pay him some mark o' respect. Robin Ruthven came in amang the thrang, to try to effect what he had promised; and, with the greatest readiness and simplic-ity, just took haud o' the side o' the wide gown, an', in sight of a' present, held it aside as high as the preacher's knee, and, behold, there was a pair o' cloven feet! The auld thief was fairly catched in the very height o' his proud conquest, an' put down by an auld carl. He could feign nae mair, but, gnashing on Robin wi' his teeth, he dartit into the air like a fiery dragon, an' keust a reid rainbow o'er the taps o' the Lomonds.

' "A' the auld wives an weavers o' Auchtermuchty fell down flat wi' affright, an' betook them to their prayers aince again, for they saw the dreadfu' danger they had escapit, an' frae that day to this it is a hard matter to gar an Auchtermuchty man listen to a sermon at a', an' a harder ane still to gar him applaud ane, for he thinks aye that he sees the cloven foot peeping out frae aneath ilka sentence.

' "Now, this is a true story, my man," quo the auld wife, "an', whenever you are doubtfu' of a man, take auld Robin Ruthven's plan, an' look for the cloven foot, for it's a thing that winna weel hide; an' it appears whiles where ane wadna think o't. It will keek out frae aneath the parson's gown, the lawyer's wig, and the Cameronian's blue bannet; but still there is a gouden rule whereby to detect it, an' that never, never fails." The auld witch didna gie me the rule, an' though I hae heard tell o't often an' often, shame fa' me an I ken what it is! But ye will ken it well, an' it wad be nae the waur of a trial on some o' your friends, maybe; for they say there's a certain gentleman seen walking wi' you whiles, that, wherever he sets his foot, the grass withers as gin it war scoudered wi' a het ern. His presence be about us! What's the matter wi' you, master? Are ye gaun to take the calm o' the stamock again?'[137]

The truth is, that the clown's absurd story, with the still more ridiculous application, made me sick at heart a second time. It was not because I thought my illustrious friend was the Devil, or that I took a fool's idle tale as a counterbalance to Divine revelation that had assured me of my justification in the sight of God before the existence of time. But, in short, it gave me a view of my own state, at which I shuddered, as indeed I now always did when the image of my devoted friend and ruler presented itself to my mind. I often communed with my heart on this, and wondered how a connection, that had the well-being of mankind solely in view, could be productive of fruits so bitter. I then went to try my works by the Saviour's golden rule,[138] as my servant had put it into my head to do; and, behold, not one of them could stand the test. I had shed blood on a ground on which I could not admit that any man had a right to shed mine; and I began to doubt the motives of my adviser once more, not that they were intentionally bad, but that his was some great mind led astray by enthusiasm or some overpowering passion.

He seemed to comprehend every one of these motions of my heart, for his manner towards me altered every day. It first became anything but agreeable, then supercilious, and, finally, intolerable; so that I resolved to shake him off, cost what it would, even though I should be reduced to beg my bread in a foreign land. To do it at home was impossible, as he held my life in his hands, to sell it whenever he had a mind; and, besides, his ascendancy over me was as complete as that of a huntsman over his dogs. I was even so weak as, the next time I met with him, to look steadfastly at his foot, to see if it was not cloven into two hoofs. It was the foot of a gentleman in every respect, so far as appearances went, but the form of his counsels was somewhat equivocal, and, if not double, they were amazingly crooked.

But, if I had taken my measures to abscond and fly from my native place, in order to free myself of this tormenting, intolerant, and bloody reformer, he had likewise taken his to expel me, or throw me into the hands of justice. It seems that, about this time, I was haunted by some spies connected with my late father and brother, of whom the mistress of the former was one. My brother's death had been witnessed by two individuals; indeed, I always had an impression that it was witnessed by more than one, having some faint recollection of hearing voices and challenges close beside me; and this woman had searched about until she found these people; but, as I shrewdly suspected, not without the assistance of the only person in my secret – my own warm and devoted friend. I say this, because I found that he had them concealed in the neighbourhood, and then took me again and again where I was fully exposed to their view, without being aware. One time in particular, on pretence of gratifying my revenge on that base woman, he knew so well where she lay concealed that he led me to her, and left me to the mercy of two viragos who had very nigh taken my life. My time of residence at Dalcastle was wearing to a crisis. I could no longer live with my tyrant, who haunted me like my shadow; and, besides, it seems there were proofs of murder leading against me from all quarters. Of part of these I deemed myself quite free, but the world deemed otherwise; and how the matter would have gone God only knows, for, the case never having undergone a judicial trial, I do not. It perhaps, however, behoves me here to relate all that I know of it, and it is simply this:

On the first of June, 1712 (well may I remember the day), I was sitting locked in my secret chamber, in a state of the utmost despondency, revolving in my mind what I ought to do to be free of my persecutors, and wishing myself a worm, or a moth, that I might be crushed and at rest, when behold Samuel entered, with eyes like to start out of his head, exclaiming: 'For God's sake, master, fly and hide yourself, for your mother's found, an' as sure as you're a living soul, the blame is gaun to fa' on you!'

'My mother found!' said I. 'And, pray, where has she been all this while?' In the meantime, I was terribly discomposed at the thoughts of her return.

'Been, sir! Been? Why, she has been where ye pat her, it seems – lying buried in the sands o' the linn.[139] I can tell you, ye will see her a frightsome figure, sic as I never wish to see again. An' the young lady is found too, sir: an' it is said the Devil – I beg pardon, sir, *your friend*, I mean – it is said your *friend* has made the discovery, an' the folk are away to raise officers, an' they will be here in an hour or two at the farthest, sir; an' sae you hae not a minute to lose, for there's proof, sir, strong proof, an' sworn proof, that ye were last seen wi' them baith; sae, unless ye can gie a' the better an account o' baith yoursel an' them either hide or flee for your bare life.'

'I will neither hide nor fly,' said I, 'for I am as guiltless of the blood of these women as the child unborn.'

'The country disna think sae, master; an' I can assure you that, should evidence fail, you run a risk o' being torn limb frae limb. They are bringing the corpse here, to gar ye touch them baith afore witnesses, an' plenty o' witnesses there will be!'

'They shall not bring them here,' cried I, shocked beyond measure at the experiment about to be made. 'Go, instantly and debar them from entering my gate with their bloated and mangled carcases.'

'The body of your own mother, sir!' said the fellow emphatically. I was in terrible agitation; and, being driven to my wits' end, I got up and strode furiously round and round the room. Samuel wist not what to do, but I saw by his staring he deemed me doubly guilty. A tap came to the chamber door: we both started like guilty creatures; and as for Samuel, his hairs stood all on end with alarm, so that, when I motioned to him, he could scarcely advance to open the door. He did so at length, and who should enter but my illustrious friend, manifestly in the utmost state of alarm. The moment that Samuel admitted him, the former made his escape by the prince's side as he entered, seemingly in a state of distraction. I was little better, when I saw this dreaded personage enter my chamber, which he had never before attempted; and, being unable to ask his errand, I suppose I stood and gazed on him like a statue.

'I come with sad and tormenting tidings to you, my beloved and ungrateful friend,' said he, 'but, having only a minute left to save your life, I have come to attempt it. There is a mob coming towards you with two dead bodies, which will place you in circumstances disagreeable enough: but that is not the worst, for of that you may be able to clear yourself. At this moment there is a party of officers, with a Justiciary warrant from Edinburgh, surrounding the house, and about to begin the search of it for you. If you fall into their hands, you are inevitably lost; for I have been making earnest inquiries, and find that everything is in train for your ruin.'

'Aye, and who has been the cause of all this?' said I, with great bitterness. But he stopped me short, adding, 'There is no time for such reflections at present; I gave my word of honour that your life should be safe from the hand of man. So it shall, if the power remain with me to save it. I am come to redeem my pledge, and to save your life by the sacrifice of my own. Here – not one word of expostulation, change habits with me, and you may then pass by the officers, and guards, and even through the approaching mob, with the most perfect temerity. There is a virtue in this garb, and, instead of offering to detain you, they shall pay you obeisance. Make haste, and leave this place for the present, flying where you best may, and, if I escape from these dangers that surround me, I will endeavour to find you out, and bring you what intelligence I am able.'

I put on his green frock coat,[140] buff belt, and a sort of a turban that he always wore on his head, somewhat resembling a bishop's mitre: he drew his hand thrice across my face, and I withdrew as he continued to urge me. My hall door and postern gate were both strongly guarded, and there were sundry armed people within, searching the closets; but all of them made way for me, and lifted their caps as I passed by them. Only one superior officer accosted me, asking if I had seen the culprit. I knew not what answer to make, but chanced to say, with great truth and propriety: 'He is safe enough.' The man beckoned with a smile, as much as to say: 'Thank you, sir, that is quite sufficient,' and I walked deliberately away.

I had not well left the gate till, hearing a great noise coming from the deep glen towards the east, I turned that way, deeming myself quite secure in this my new disguise, to see what it was, and if matters were as had been described to me. There I met a great mob, sure enough, coming with two dead bodies stretched on boards, and decently covered with white sheets. I would fain have examined their appearance, had I not perceived the apparent fury in the looks of the men, and judged from that how much more safe it was for me not to intermeddle in the affray. I cannot tell how it was, but I felt a strange and unwonted delight in viewing this scene, and a certain pride of heart in being supposed the perpetrator of the unnatural crimes laid to my charge. This was a feeling quite new to me; and if there were virtues in the robes of the illustrious foreigner, who had without all dispute preserved my life at this time: I say, if there was any inherent virtue in these robes of his, as he had suggested, this was one of their effects, that they turned my heart towards that which was evil, horrible, and disgustful.

I mixed with the mob to hear what they were saying. Every tongue was engaged in loading me with the most opprobrious epithets! One called me a monster of nature; another an incarnate devil; and another a creature made to be cursed in time and eternity. I retired from them and, winded my way southwards, comforting myself with the assurance that so mankind had used and persecuted the greatest fathers and apostles of the Christian Church, and that their vile opprobrium could not alter the counsels of Heaven concerning me.

On going over that rising ground called Dorington Moor, I could not help turning round and taking a look of Dalcastle. I had little doubt that it would be my last look, and nearly as little ambition that it should not. I thought how high my hopes of happiness and advancement had been on entering that mansion, and taking possession of its rich and extensive domains, and how miserably I had been disappointed. On the contrary, I had experienced nothing but chagrin, disgust, and terror; and I now consoled myself with the hope that I should henceforth shake myself free of the chains of my great tormentor, and for that privilege was I willing to encounter any earthly distress. I could not help perceiving that I was now on a path which was likely to lead me into a species of distress hitherto unknown, and hardly dreamed of by me, and that was total destitution. For all the riches I had been possessed of a few hours previous to this, I found that here I was turned out of my lordly possessions without a single merk, or the power of lifting and commanding the smallest sum, without being thereby discovered and seized. Had it been possible for me to have escaped in my own clothes, I had a considerable sum secreted in these, but, by the sudden change, I was left without a coin for present necessity. But I had hope in Heaven, knowing that the just man would not be left destitute; and that, though many troubles surrounded him, he would at last be set free from them all. I was possessed of strong and brilliant parts, and a liberal education; and, though I had somehow unaccountably suffered my theological qualifications to fall into desuetude, since my acquaintance with the ablest and most rigid of all theologians, I had nevertheless hopes that, by preaching up redemption by grace, preordination, and eternal purpose, I should yet be enabled to benefit mankind in some country, and rise to high distinction.

These were some of the thoughts by which I consoled myself as I posted on my way southwards, avoiding the towns and villages, and falling into the crossways that led from each of the great roads passing east and west to another. I lodged the first night in the house of a country weaver, into which I stepped at a late hour, quite overcome with hunger and fatigue, having travelled not less than thirty miles from my late home. The man received me ungraciously, telling me of a gentleman's house at no great distance, and of an inn a little farther away; but I said I delighted more in the society of a man like him than that of any gentleman of the land, for my concerns were with the poor of this world, it being easier for a camel to go through the eye of a needle than for a rich man to enter into the kingdom of heaven.[141]

The weaver's wife, who sat with a child on her knee, and had not hitherto opened her mouth, hearing me speak in that serious and religious style, stirred up the fire with her one hand; then, drawing a chair near it, she said: 'Come awa, honest lad, in by here; sin' it be sae that you belang to Him wha gies us a' that we hae, it is but right that you should share a part. You are a stranger, it is true, but *them* that winna entertain a stranger will never entertain an angel unawares.'

I never was apt to be taken with the simplicity of nature; in general I despised it; but, owing to my circumstances at the time, I was deeply affected by the manner of this poor woman's welcome. The weaver continued in a churlish mood throughout the evening, apparently dissatisfied with what his wife had done in entertaining me, and spoke to her in a manner so crusty that I thought proper to rebuke him, for the woman was comely in her person, and virtuous in her conversation; but the weaver, her husband, was large of make, illfavoured, and pestilent; therefore did I take him severely to task for the tenor of his conduct; but the man was froward, and answered me rudely with sneering and derision and, in the height of his caprice, he said to his wife: 'Whan focks are sae keen of a chance o' entertaining angels, gude-wife, it wad maybe be worth their while to tak tent what kind o' angels they are. It wadna wonder me vera muckle an ye had entertained your friend the Deil the night, for aw thought aw fand a saur o' reek an' brimstane about him. *He's* nane o' the best o' angels, an' focks winna hae muckle credit by entertaining him.'

Certainly, in the assured state I was in, I had as little reason to be alarmed at mention being made of the Devil as any person on earth: of late, however, I felt that the reverse was the case, and that any allusion to my great enemy moved me exceedingly. The weaver's speech had such an effect on me that both he and his wife were alarmed at my looks. The latter thought I was angry, and chided her husband gently for his rudeness; but the weaver himself rather seemed to be confirmed in his opinion that I was the Devil, for he looked round like a startled roebuck, and immediately betook him to the family Bible.

I know not whether it was on purpose to prove my identity or not, but I think he was going to desire me either to read a certain portion of Scripture that he had sought out, or to make family worship, had not the conversation at that instant taken another turn; for the weaver, not knowing how to address me, abruptly asked my name, as he was about to put the Bible into my hands. Never having considered myself in the light of a malefactor, but rather as a champion in the cause of truth, and finding myself perfectly safe under my disguise, I had never once thought of the utility of changing my name, and, when the man asked me, I hesitated; but, being compelled to say something, I said my name was Cowan. The man stared at me, and then at his wife, with a look that spoke a knowledge of something alarming or mysterious.

'Ha! Cowan?' said he. 'That's most extraordinar! Not Colwan, I hope?'

'No: Cowan is my surname,' said I. 'But why not Colwan, there being so little difference in the sound?'

'I was feared ye might be that waratch that the Deil has taen the possession o', an' eggit him on to kill baith his father an' his mother, his only brother, an' his sweetheart,' said he; 'an', to say the truth, I'm no that sure about you yet, for I see you're gaun wi' arms on ye.'

'Not I, honest man,' said I. 'I carry no arms; a man conscious of his innocence and uprightness of heart needs not to carry arms in his defence now.'

'Aye, aye, maister,' said he; 'an' pray what div ye ca' this bit windlestrae that's appearing here?' With that he pointed to something on the inside of the breast of my frock-coat. I looked at it, and there certainly was the gilded haft of a poniard, the same weapon I had seen and handled before, and which I knew my illustrious companion carried about with him; but till that moment I knew not that I was in possession of it. I drew it out: a more dangerous or insidious- looking weapon could not be conceived. The weaver and his wife were both frightened, the latter in particular; and she being my friend, and I dependent on their hospitality for that night, I said: 'I declare I knew not that I carried this small rapier, which has been in my coat by chance, and not by any design of mine. But, lest you should think that I meditate any mischief to any under this roof, I give it into your hands, requesting of you to lock it by till tomorrow, or when I shall next want it.'

The woman seemed rather glad to get hold of it; and taking it from me, she went into a kind of pantry out of my sight, and locked the weapon up; and then the discourse went on.

'There cannot be such a thing in reality,' said I, 'as the story you were mentioning just now, of a man whose name resembles mine.'

'It's likely that you ken a wee better about the story than I do, maister,' said he, 'suppose you do leave the 'L' out of your name. An' yet I think sic a waratch, an' a murderer, wad hae taen a name wi' some gritter difference in the sound. But the story is just that true that there were twa o' the Queen's officers here nae mair than an hour ago, in pursuit o' the vagabond, for they gat some intelligence that he had fled this gate; yet they said he had been last seen wi' black claes on, an' they supposed he was clad in black. His ain servant is wi' them, for the purpose o' kennin the scoundrel, an' they're galloping through the country like madmen. I hope in God they'll get him, an' rack his neck for him!'

I could not say 'Amen' to the weaver's prayer, and therefore tried to compose myself as well as I could, and made some religious comment on the causes of the nation's depravity. But suspecting that my potent friend had betrayed my flight and disguise, to save his life, I was very uneasy, and gave myself up for lost. I said prayers in the family, with the tenor of which the wife was delighted, but the weaver still dissatisfied; and, after a supper of the most homely fare, he tried to start an argument with me, proving that everything for which I had interceded in my prayer was irrelevant to man's present state. But I, being weary and distressed in mind, shunned the contest, and requested a couch whereon to repose.

I was conducted into the other end of the house, among looms, treadles, pirns,[142] and confusion without end; and there, in a sort of box, was I shut up for my night's repose, for the weaver, as he left me, cautiously turned the key of my apartment, and left me to shift for myself among the looms, determined that I should escape from the house with nothing. After he and his wife and children were crowded into their den, I heard the two mates contending furiously about me in suppressed voices, the one maintaining the probability that I was the murderer, and the other proving the impossibility of it. The husband, however, said as much as let me understand that he had locked me up on purpose to bring the military, or officers of justice, to seize me. I was in the utmost perplexity, yet for all that, and the imminent danger I was in, I fell asleep, and a more troubled and tormenting sleep never enchained a mortal frame. I had such dreams that they will not bear repetition, and early in the morning I awaked, feverish, and parched with thirst.

I went to call mine host, that he might let me out to the open air, but, before doing so, I thought it necessary to put on some clothes. In attempting to do this, a circumstance arrested my attention (for which I could in nowise account, which to this day I cannot unriddle, nor shall I ever be able to comprehend it while I live): the frock and turban, which had furnished my disguise on the preceding day, were both removed, and my own black coat and cocked hat laid down in their place. At first I thought I was in a dream, and felt the weaver's beam, web, and treadle-strings with my hands, to convince myself that I was awake. I was certainly awake; and there was the door locked firm and fast as it was the evening before. I carried my own black coat to the small window and examined it. It was my own in verity; and the sums of money that I had concealed in case of any emergency, remained untouched. I trembled with astonishment; and on my return from the small window went doiting in amongst the weaver's looms, till I entangled myself, and could not get out again without working great deray amongst the coarse linen threads that stood in warp from one end of the apartment unto the other. I had no knife whereby to cut the cords of this wicked man, and therefore was obliged to call out lustily for assistance. The weaver came half naked, unlocked the door, and, setting in his head and long neck, accosted me thus:

'What now, Mr Satan? What for are ye roaring that gate? Are you fawn inna little hell, instead o' the big muckil ane? Deil be in your reistit trams! What for have ye abscondit yoursel into ma leddy's wab for?'

'Friend, I beg your pardon,' said I. 'I wanted to be at the light, and have somehow unfortunately involved myself in the intricacies of your web, from which I cannot get clear without doing you a great injury. Pray do lend your experienced hand to extricate me.'

'May aw the pearls o' damnation light on your silly snout, an I dinna estricat ye weel enough! Ye ditit, donnart, deil's burd that ye be! What made ye gang howkin in there to be a poor man's ruin? Come out, ye vile rag-of-a-muffin, or I gar ye come out wi' mair shame and disgrace, an' fewer haill banes in your body.'

My feet had slipped down through the double warpings of a web, and not being able to reach the ground with them (there being a small pit below) I rode upon a number of yielding threads, and, there being nothing else that I could reach, to extricate myself was impossible. I was utterly powerless; and, besides, the yarn and cords hurt me very much. For all that, the destructive weaver seized a loom-spoke, and began a-beating me most unmercifully, while, entangled as I was, I could do nothing but shout aloud for mercy, or assistance, whichever chanced to be within hearing.

The latter at length made its appearance in the form of the weaver's wife, in the same state of dishabille with himself, who instantly interfered, and that most strenuously, on my behalf. Before her arrival, however, I had made a desperate effort to throw myself out of the entanglement I was in; for the weaver continued repeating his blows and cursing me so that I determined to get out of his meshes at any risk. The effect made my case worse; for, my feet being wrapt among the nether threads, as I threw myself from my saddle on the upper ones, my feet brought the others up through these, and I hung with my head down and my feet as firm as they had been in a vice. The predicament of the web being thereby increased, the weaver's wrath was doubled in proportion, and he laid on without mercy.

At this critical juncture the wife arrived, and without hesitation rushed before her offended lord, withholding his hand from injuring me further, although then it was uplifted along with the loomspoke in overbearing ire. 'Dear Johnny! I think ye be gaen dementit this morning. Be quiet, my dear, an' dinna begin a Boddel Brigg[143] business in your ain house. What for ir ye persecutin' a servant o' the Lord's that gate, an' pitting the life out o' him wi' his head down an' his heels up?'

'Had ye said a servant o' the Deil's, Nans, ye wad hae been nearer the nail, for gin he binna the Auld Ane himsel, he's gayan sib till him. There, didna I lock him in on purpose to bring the military on him; an' in the place o' that, hasna he keepit me in a sleep a' this while as deep as death? An' here do I find him abscondit like a speeder i' the mids o' my leddy's wab, an' me dreamin' a' the night that I had the Deil i' my house, an' that he was clapper-clawin me ayont the loom. Have at you, ye brunstane thief!' and, in spite of the good woman's struggles, he lent me another severe blow.

'Now, Johnny Dods, my man! Oh, Johnny Dods, think if that be like a Christian, and ane o' the heroes o' Boddel Brigg, to entertain a stranger, an' then bind him in a web wi' his head down, an' mell him to death! Oh, Johnny Dods, think what you are about! Slack a pin, an' let the good honest religious lad out.'

The weaver was rather overcome, but still stood to his point that I was the Deil, though in better temper; and, as he slackened the web to release me, he remarked, half laughing: 'Wha wad hae thought that John Dods should hae escapit a' the snares an' dangers that circumfauldit him, an' at last should hae weaved a net to catch the Deil.'

The wife released me soon, and carefully whispered me, at the same time, that it would be as well for me to dress and be going. I was not long in obeying, and dressed myself in my black clothes, hardly knowing what I did, what to think, or whither to betake myself. I was sore hurt by the blows of the desperate ruffian; and, what was worse, my ankle was so much strained that I could hardly set my foot to the ground. I was obliged to apply to the weaver once more, to see if I could learn anything about my clothes, or how the change was effected. 'Sir,' said I, 'how comes it that you have robbed me of my clothes, and put these down in their place over night?'

'Ha! thae claes? Me pit down the claes!' said he, gaping with astonishment, and touching the clothes with the point of his forefinger. 'I never saw them afore, as I have death to meet wi': so help me God!'

He strode into the work-house where I slept, to satisfy himself that my clothes were not there, and returned perfectly aghast with consternation. 'The doors were baith fast lockit,' said he. 'I could hae defied a rat either to hae gotten out or in. My dream has been true! My dream has been true! The Lord judge between thee and me; but in His name, I charge you to depart out o' this house; an', gin it be your will, dinna tak the braidside o't w'ye, but gang quietly out at the door wi' your face foremost. Wife, let naught o' this enchanter's remain i' the house, to be a curse, an' a snare to us; gang an' bring him his gildit weapon, an' may the Lord protect a' his ain against its hellish an' deadly point!'[144]

The wife went to seek my poniard, trembling so excessively that she could hardly walk, and, shortly after, we heard a feeble scream from the pantry. The weapon had disappeared with the clothes, though under double lock and key; and, the terror of the good people having now reached a disgusting extremity, I thought proper to make a sudden retreat, followed by the weaver's anathemas.

My state both of body and mind was now truly deplorable. I was hungry, wounded, and lame, an outcast and a vagabond in society; my life sought after with avidity, and all for doing that to which I was predestined by Him who fore-ordains whatever comes to pass. I knew not whither to betake me. I had purposed going into England and there making some use of the classical education I had received, but my lameness rendered this impracticable for the present. I was therefore obliged to turn my face towards Edinburgh, where I was little known – where concealment was more practicable than by skulking in the country, and where I might turn my mind to something that was great and good. I had a little money, both Scotch and English, now in my possession, but not one friend in the whole world on whom I could rely. One devoted friend, it is true, I had, but he was become my greatest terror. To escape from him, I now felt that I would willingly travel to the farthest corners of the world, and be subjected to every deprivation; but after the certainty of what had taken place last night, after I had travelled thirty miles by secret and by-ways, I saw not how escape from him was possible.

Miserable, forlorn, and dreading every person that I saw, either behind or before me, I hasted on towards Edinburgh, taking all the by and unfrequented paths; and, the third night after I left the weaver's house, I reached the West Port,[145] without meeting with anything remarkable. Being exceedingly fatigued and lame, I took lodgings in the first house I entered, and for these I was to pay two groats a week, and to board and sleep with a young man who wanted a companion to make his rent easier. I liked this; having found from experience that the great personage who had attached himself to me, and was now become my greatest terror among many surrounding evils, generally haunted me when I was alone, keeping aloof from all other society.

My fellow lodger came home in the evening, and was glad at my coming. His name was Linton, and I changed mine to Elliot. He was a flippant unstable being, one on whom nothing appeared a difficulty, in his own estimation, but who could effect very little after all. He was what is called by some a compositor, in the Queen's printing house, then conducted by a Mr James Watson.[146] In the course of our conversation that night, I told him I was a first-rate classical scholar, and would gladly turn my attention to some business wherein my education might avail me something; and that there was nothing would delight me so much as an engagement in the Queen's printing office. Linton made no difficulty in bringing about that arrangement. His answer was: 'Oo, gud sir, you are the very man we want. Gud bless your breast and your buttons, sir! Aye, that's neither here nor there. That's all very well. Ha, ha, ha. A byword in the house, sir. But, as I was saying, you are the very *man* we want. You will get any money you like to ask, sir. *Any* money you like, sir. God bless your buttons! – That's settled – All done – Settled, settled – I'll do it, I'll do it – No more about it; no more about it. Settled, settled.'

The next day I went with him to the office, and he presented me to Mr Watson as the most wonderful genius and scholar ever known. His recommendation had little sway with Mr Watson, who only smiled at Linton's extravagances, as one does at the prattle of an infant. I sauntered about the printing office for the space of two or three hours, during which time Watson bustled about with green spectacles on his nose, and took no heed of me. But, seeing that I still lingered, he addressed me at length, in a civil gentlemanly way, and inquired concerning my views. I satisfied him, with all my answers, in particular those to his questions about the Latin and Greek languages; but when he came to ask testimonials of my character and acquirements, and found that I could produce none, he viewed me with a jealous eye, and said he dreaded I was some n'erdo- weel, run from my parents or guardians, and he did not choose to employ any such. I said my parents were both dead; and that, being thereby deprived of the means of following out my education, it behoved me to apply to some business in which my education might be of some use to me. He said he would take me into the office, and pay me according to the business I performed and the manner in which I deported myself; but he could take no man into Her Majesty's printing office upon a regular engagement who could not produce the most respectable references with regard to morals.

I could not but despise the man in my heart who laid such a stress upon morals, leaving grace out of the question; and viewed it as a deplorable instance of human depravity and self-conceit; but, for all that, I was obliged to accept of his terms, for I had an inward thirst and longing to distinguish myself in the great cause of religion, and I thought, if once I could print my own works, how I would astonish mankind, and confound their self-wisdom and their esteemed morality – blow up the idea of any dependence on good works, and *morality*, forsooth! And I weened that I might thus get me a name even higher than if I had been made a general of the Czar Peter's troops against the infidels.

I attended the office some hours every day, but got not much encouragement, though I was eager to learn everything, and could soon have set types considerably well. It was here that I first conceived the idea of writing this journal, and having it printed, and applied to Mr Watson to print it for me, telling him it was a religious parable such as *The Pilgrim's Progress*.[147] He advised me to print it close, and make it a pamphlet, and then, if it did not sell, it would not cost me much; but that religious pamphlets, especially if they had a shade of allegory in them, were the very rage of the day. I put my work to the press, and wrote early and late; and encouraging my companion to work at odd hours and on Sundays, before the press-work of the second sheet was begun, we had the work all in types, corrected, and a clean copy thrown off for further revisal. The first sheet was wrought off; and I never shall forget how my heart exulted when at the printing house this day I saw what numbers of my works were to go abroad among mankind, and I determined with myself that I would not put the Border name of Elliot, which I had assumed, to the work.

Thus far have my History and Confessions been carried. I must now furnish my Christian readers with a key to the process, management, and winding up of the whole matter; which I propose, by the assistance of God, to limit to a very few pages.

Chesters,[148] *July 27, 1712.* My hopes and prospects are a wreck. My precious journal is lost! Consigned to the flames! My enemy hath found me out, and there is no hope of peace or rest for me on this side the grave.

In the beginning of last week, my fellow lodger came home, running in a great panic, and told me a story of the Devil having appeared twice in the printing house, assisting the workmen at the printing of my book, and that some of them had been frightened out of their wits. That the story was told to Mr Watson, who till that time had never paid any attention to the treatise, but who, out of curiosity, began and read a part of it, and thereupon flew into a great rage, called my work a medley of lies and blasphemy, and ordered the whole to be consigned to the flames, blaming his foreman, and all connected with the press, for letting a work go so far that was enough to bring down the vengeance of Heaven on the concern.

If ever I shed tears through perfect bitterness of spirit it was at that time, but I hope it was more for the ignorance and folly of my countrymen than the overthrow of my own hopes. But my attention was suddenly aroused to other matters, by Linton mentioning that it was said by some in the office the Devil had inquired for me.

'Surely you are not such a fool,' said I, 'as to believe that the Devil really was in the printing office?'

'Oo, Gud bless you, sir! Saw him myself; gave him a nod, and good-day. Rather a gentlemanly personage – Green Circassian[149] hunting coat and turban – Like a foreigner – Has the power of vanishing in one moment though – Rather a suspicious circumstance that. Otherwise, his appearance not much against him.'

If the former intelligence thrilled me with grief, this did so with terror. I perceived who the personage was that had visited the printing house in order to further the progress of my work; and, at the approach of every person to our lodgings, I from that instant trembled every bone, lest it should be my elevated and dreaded friend. I could not say I had ever received an office at his hand that was not friendly, yet these offices had been of a strange tendency; and the horror with which I now regarded him was unaccountable to myself. It was beyond description, conception, or the soul of man to bear. I took my printed sheets, the only copy of my unfinished work existing; and, on pretence of going straight to Mr Watson's office, decamped from my lodgings at Portsburgh[150] a little before the fall of evening, and took the road towards England.

As soon as I got clear of the city, I ran with a velocity I knew not before I had been capable of. I flew out the way towards Dalkeith so swiftly that I often lost sight of the ground, and I said to myself, 'Oh, that I had the wings of a dove, that I might fly to the farthest corners of the earth, to hide me from those against whom I have no power to stand!'[151]

I travelled all that night and the next morning, exerting myself beyond my power; and about noon the following day I went into a yeoman's house, the name of which was Ellanshaws, and requested of the people a couch of any sort to lie down on, for I was ill, and could not proceed on my journey. They showed me to a stable loft where there were two beds, on one of which I laid me down; and, falling into a sound sleep, I did not awake till the evening, that other three men came from the fields to sleep in the same place, one of whom lay down beside me, at which I was exceedingly glad. They fell all sound asleep, and I was terribly alarmed at a conversation I overheard somewhere outside the stable. I could not make out a sentence, but trembled to think I knew one of the voices at least, and, rather than not be mistaken, I would that any man had run me through with a sword. I fell into a cold sweat, and once thought of instantly putting hand to my own life, as my only means of relief (may the rash and sinful thought be in mercy forgiven!) when I heard as it were two persons at the door, contending, as I thought, about their right and interest in me. That the one was forcibly preventing the admission of the other, I could hear distinctly, and their language was mixed with something dreadful and mysterious. In an agony of terror, I awakened my snoring companion with great difficulty, and asked him, in a low whisper, who these were at the door. The man lay silent and listening till fairly awake, and then asked if I heard anything. I said I had heard strange voices contending at the door.

'Then I can tell you, lad, it has been something neither good nor canny,'[152] said he. 'It's no for naething that our horses are snorking that gate.'

For the first time, I remarked that the animals were snorting and rearing as if they wished to break through the house. The man called to them by their names, and ordered them to be quiet; but they raged still the more furiously. He then roused his drowsy companions, who were alike alarmed at the panic of the horses, all of them declaring that they had never seen either Mause or Jolly start in their lives before. My bedfellow and another then ventured down the ladder, and I heard one of them then saying: 'Lord be wi' us! What can be i' the house? The sweat's rinning off the poor beasts like water.'

They agreed to sally out together, and if possible to reach the kitchen and bring a light. I was glad at this, but not so much so when I heard the one man saying to the other, in a whisper: 'I wish that stranger man may be canny enough.'

'God kens!' said the other. 'It does nae look unco weel.'

The lad in the other bed, hearing this, set up his head in manifest affright as the other two departed for the kitchen; and, I believe, he would have been glad to have been in their company. This lad was next the ladder, at which I was extremely glad, for had he not been there, the world should not have induced me to wait the return of these two men. They were not well gone before I heard another distinctly enter the stable, and come towards the ladder. The lad who was sitting up in his bed, intent on the watch, called out: 'Wha's that there? Walker, is that you? Purdie, I say is it you?'

The darkling intruder paused for a few moments, and then came towards the foot of the ladder. The horses broke loose, and, snorting and neighing for terror, raged through the house. In all my life I never heard so frightful a commotion. The being that occasioned it all now began to mount the ladder towards our loft, on which the lad in the bed next the ladder sprung from his couch, crying out: 'The Lord Almighty preserve us! What can it be?' With that he sped across the loft and by my bed, praying lustily all the way; and, throwing himself from the other end of the loft into a manger, he darted, naked as he was, through among the furious horses, and, making the door that stood open, in a moment he vanished and left me in the lurch. Powerless with terror, and calling out fearfully, I tried to follow his example; but, not knowing the situation of the places with regard to one another, I missed the manger, and fell on the pavement in one of the stalls. I was both stunned and lamed on the knee; but, terror prevailing, I got up and tried to escape. It was out of my power; for there were divisions and cross-divisions in the house, and mad horses smashing everything before them, so that I knew not so much as on what side of the house the door was. Two or three times was I knocked down by the animals, but all the while I never stinted crying out with all my power. At length, I was seized by the throat and hair of the head, and dragged away, I wist not whither. My voice was now laid, and all my powers, both mental and bodily, totally overcome; and I remember no more till I found myself lying naked on the kitchen table of the farmhouse, and something like a horse's rug thrown over me. The only hint that I got from the people of the house on coming to myself was that my absence would be good company; and that they had got me in a woeful state, one which they did not choose to describe, or hear described.

As soon as daylight appeared, I was packed about my business, with the hisses and execrations of the yeoman's family, who viewed me as a being to be shunned, ascribing to me the visitations of that unholy night. Again was I on my way southwards, as lonely, hopeless, and degraded a being as was to be found on life's weary round. As I limped out the way, I wept, thinking of what I might have been, and what I really had become: of my high and flourishing hopes when I set out as the avenger of God on the sinful children of men; of all that I had dared for the exaltation and progress of the truth; and it was with great difficulty that my faith remained unshaken, yet was I preserved from that sin, and comforted myself with the certainty that the believer's progress through life is one of warfare and suffering.

My case was indeed a pitiable one. I was lame, hungry, fatigued, and my resources on the very eve of being exhausted. Yet these were but secondary miseries, and hardly worthy of a thought compared with those I suffered inwardly. I not only looked around me with terror at everyone that approached, but I was become a terror to myself; or, rather, my body and soul were become terrors to each other; and, had it been possible, I felt as if they would have gone to war. I dared not look at my face in a glass, for I shuddered at my own image and likeness. I dreaded the dawning, and trembled at the approach of night, nor was there one thing in nature that afforded me the least delight.

In this deplorable state of body and mind, was I jogging on towards the Tweed, by the side of the small river called Ellan,[153] when, just at the narrowest part of the glen, whom should I meet full in the face but the very being in all the universe of God I would the most gladly have shunned. I had no power to fly from him, neither durst I, for the spirit within me, accuse him of falsehood and renounce his fellowship. I stood before him like a condemned criminal, staring him in the face, ready to be winded, twisted, and tormented as he pleased. He regarded me with a sad and solemn look. How changed was now that majestic countenance to one of haggard despair – changed in all save the extraordinary likeness to my late brother, a resemblance which misfortune and despair tended only to heighten. There were no kind greetings passed between us at meeting, like those which pass between the men of the world; he looked on me with eyes that froze the currents of my blood, but spoke not till I assumed as much courage as to articulate: 'You here! I hope you have brought me tidings of comfort?'

'Tidings of despair!' said he. 'But such tidings as the timid and the ungrateful deserve, and have reason to expect. You are an outlaw, and a vagabond in your country, and a high reward is offered for your apprehension. The enraged populace have burnt your house, and all that is within it; and the farmers on the land bless themselves at being rid of you. So fare it with everyone who puts his hand to the great work of man's restoration to freedom, and draweth back, contemning the light that is within him! Your enormities caused me to leave you to yourself for a season, and you see what the issue has been. You have given some evil ones power over you, who long to devour you, both soul and body, and it has required all my power and influence to save you. Had it not been for my hand, you had been torn in pieces last night; but for once I prevailed. We must leave this land forthwith, for here there is neither peace, safety, nor comfort for us. Do you now and here pledge yourself to one who has so often saved your life and has put his own at stake to do so? Do you pledge yourself that you will henceforth be guided by my counsel, and follow me whithersoever I choose to lead?' 'I have always been swayed by your counsel,' said I, 'and for your sake, principally, am I sorry that all our measures have proved abortive. But I hope still to be useful in my native isle, therefore let me plead that your highness will abandon a poor despised and outcast wretch to his fate, and betake you to your realms, where your presence cannot but be greatly wanted.'

'Would that I could do so!' said he woefully. 'But to talk of that is to talk of an impossibility. I am wedded to you so closely that I feel as if I were the same person. Our essences are one, our bodies and spirits being united, so that I am drawn towards you as by magnetism, and, wherever you are, there must my presence be with you.'

Perceiving how this assurance affected me, he began to chide me most bitterly for my ingratitude; and then he assumed such looks that it was impossible for me longer to bear them; therefore I staggered out of the way, begging and beseeching of him to give me up to my fate, and hardly knowing what I said; for it struck me that, with all his assumed appearance of misery and wretchedness, there were traits of exultation in his hideous countenance manifesting a secret and inward joy at my utter despair.

It was long before I durst look over my shoulder, but, when I did so, I perceived this ruined and debased potentate coming slowly on the same path, and I prayed that the Lord would hide me in the bowels of the earth or depths of the sea. When I crossed the Tweed, I perceived him still a little behind me; and, my despair being then at its height, I cursed the time I first met with such a tormentor; though on a little recollection it occurred that it was at that blessed time when I was solemnly dedicated to the Lord, and assured of my final election, and confirmation, by an eternal decree never to be annulled. This being my sole and only comfort, I recalled my curse upon the time, and repented me of my rashness.

After crossing the Tweed, I saw no more of my persecutor that day, and had hopes that he had left me for a season; but, alas, what hope was there of my relief after the declaration I had so lately heard! I took up my lodgings that night in a small miserable inn in the village of Ancrum,[154] of which the people seemed alike poor and ignorant. Before going to bed, I asked if it was customary with them to have family worship of evenings. The man answered that they were so hard set with the world they often could not get time, but if I would be so kind as to officiate they would be much obliged to me. I accepted the invitation, being afraid to go to rest lest the commotions of the foregoing night might be renewed, and continued the worship as long as in decency I could. The poor people thanked me, hoped my prayers would be heard both on their account and my own, seemed much taken with my abilities, and wondered how a man of my powerful eloquence chanced to be wandering about in a condition so forlorn. I said I was a poor student of theology, on my way to Oxford. They stared at one another with expressions of wonder, disappointment, and fear. I afterwards came to learn, that the term *theology* was by them quite misunderstood, and that they had some crude conceptions that nothing was taught at Oxford but the *black arts*, which ridiculous idea prevailed over all the south of Scotland. For the present I could not understand what the people meant, and less so when the man asked me, with deep concern 'if I was serious in my intentions of going to Oxford? He hoped not, and that I would be better guided.

I said my education wanted finishing; but he remarked that the Oxford arts were a bad finish for a religious man's education. Finally, I requested him to sleep with me, or in my room all the night, as I wanted some serious and religious conversation with him, and likewise to convince him that the study of the fine arts, though not absolutely necessary, were not incompatible with the character of a Christian divine. He shook his head, and wondered how I could call them *fine arts* – hoped I did not mean to convince him by any ocular demonstration, and at length reluctantly condescended to sleep with me, and let the lass and wife sleep together for one night. I believe he would have declined it had it not been some hints from his wife, stating that it was a good arrangement, by which I understood there were only two beds in the house, and that when I was preferred to the lass's bed, she had one to shift for.

The landlord and I accordingly retired to our homely bed, and conversed for some time about indifferent matters, till he fell sound asleep. Not so with me: I had that within which would not suffer me to close my eyes; and, about the dead of night, I again heard the same noises and contention begin outside the house as I had heard the night before; and again I heard it was about a sovereign and peculiar right in me. At one time the noise was on the top of the house, straight above our bed, as if the one party were breaking through the roof, and the other forcibly preventing it; at another it was at the door, and at a third time at the window; but still mine host lay sound by my side, and did not waken. I was seized with terrors indefinable, and prayed fervently, but did not attempt rousing my sleeping companion until I saw if no better could be done. The women, however, were alarmed, and, rushing into our apartment, exclaimed that all the devils in hell were besieging the house. Then, indeed, the landlord awoke, and it was time for him,

for the tumult had increased to such a degree that it shook the house
to its foundations, being louder and more furious than I could have
conceived the heat of battle to be when the volleys of artillery are
mixed with groans, shouts, and blasphemous cursing. It thundered
and lightened; and there were screams, groans, laughter, and
execrations, all intermingled.

I lay trembling and bathed in a cold perspiration, but was soon
obliged to bestir myself, the inmates attacking me one after the
other.

'Oh, Tam Douglas! Tam Douglas! Haste ye an' rise out fra-yont
that incarnal devil!' cried the wife. 'Ye are in ayont the auld ane
himsel, for our lass Tibbie saw his cloven cloots last night.'

'Lord forbid!' roared Tam Douglas, and darted over the bed like a
flying fish. Then, hearing the unearthly tumult with which he was
surrounded, he turned to the side of the bed, and addressed me thus,
with long and fearful intervals:

'If ye be the Deil, rise up, an' depart in peace out o' this house –
afore the bedstrae take kindling about ye, an' than it 'll maybe be
the waur for ye. Get up – an' gang awa out amang your cronies,
like a good lad. There's nae body here wishes you ony ill. D'ye
hear me?'

'Friend,' said I, 'no Christian would turn out a fellow creature on
such a night as this and in the midst of such a commotion of the
villagers.'

'Na, if ye be a mortal man,' said he, 'which I rather think, from the
use you made of the holy book. Nane o' your practical jokes on
strangers an' honest foks. These are some o' your Oxford tricks, an'
I'll thank you to be ower wi' them. Gracious heaven, they are
brikkin through the house at a' the four corners at the same time!'

The lass Tibby, seeing the innkeeper was not going to prevail
with me to rise, flew towards the bed in desperation, and, seizing me
by the waist, soon landed me on the floor, saying: 'Be ye deil, be ye
chiel, ye's no lie there till baith the house an' us be swallowed up!'[155]

Her master and mistress applauding the deed, I was obliged to
attempt dressing myself, a task to which my powers were quite
inadequate in the state I was in, but I was readily assisted by every
one of the three; and, as soon as they got my clothes thrust on in a
loose way, they shut their eyes lest they should see what might drive
them distracted, and thrust me out to the street, cursing me, and
calling on the fiends to take their prey and be gone.

The scene that ensued is neither to be described nor believed if it
were. I was momently surrounded by a number of hideous fiends,

who gnashed on me with their teeth, and clenched their crimson paws in my face; and at the same instant I was seized by the collar of my coat behind, by my dreaded and devoted friend, who pushed me on and, with his gilded rapier waving and brandishing around me, defended me against all their united attacks. Horrible as my assailants were in appearance (and they all had monstrous shapes) I felt that I would rather have fallen into their hands than be thus led away captive by my defender at his will and pleasure without having the right or power to say my life, or any part of my will, was my own. I could not even thank him for his potent guardianship, but hung down my head, and moved on I knew not whither, like a criminal led to execution, and still the infernal combat continued till about the dawning, at which time I looked up, and all the fiends were expelled but one, who kept at a distance; and still my persecutor and defender pushed me by the neck before him.

At length he desired me to sit down and take some rest, with which I complied, for I had great need of it, and wanted the power to withstand what he desired. There, for a whole morning did he detain me, tormenting me with reflections on the past, and pointing out the horrors of the future, until a thousand times I wished myself non-existent. 'I have attached myself to your wayward fortune,' said he, 'and it has been my ruin as well as thine. Ungrateful as you are, I cannot give you up to be devoured; but this is a life that it is impossible to brook longer. Since our hopes are blasted in this world, and all our schemes of grandeur overthrown; and since our everlasting destiny is settled by a decree which no act of ours can invalidate, let us fall by our own hands, or by the hands of each other; die like heroes; and, throwing off this frame of dross and corruption, mingle with the pure ethereal essence of existence, from which we derived our being.'

I shuddered at a view of the dreadful alternative, yet was obliged to confess that in my present circumstances existence was not to be borne. It was in vain that I reasoned on the sinfulness of the deed, and on its damning nature; he made me condemn myself out of my own mouth, by allowing the absolute nature of justifying grace and the impossibility of the elect ever falling from the faith, or the glorious end to which they were called; and then he said, this granted, self-destruction was the act of a hero, and none but a coward would shrink from it, to suffer a hundred times more every day and night that passed over his head.

I said I was still contented to be that coward; and all that I begged of him was to leave me to my fortune for a season, and to the just judgement of my Creator; but he said his word and honour were engaged on my behalf, and these, in such a case, were not to be violated. 'If you will not pity yourself, have pity on me,' added he. 'Turn your eyes on me, and behold to what I am reduced.'

Involuntarily did I turn at the request, and caught a half glance of his features. May no eye destined to reflect the beauties of the New Jerusalem[156] inward upon the beatific soul behold such a sight as mine then beheld! My immortal spirit, blood and bones, were all withered at the blasting sight; and I arose and withdrew, with groanings which the pangs of death shall never wring from me.

Not daring to look behind me, I crept on my way, and that night reached this hamlet on the Scottish border; and being grown reckless of danger, and hardened to scenes of horror, I took up my lodging with a poor hind, who is a widower, and who could only accommodate me with a bed of rushes at his fireside. At midnight I heard some strange sounds, too much resembling those to which I had of late been inured; but they kept at a distance, and I was soon persuaded that there was a power protected that house superior to those that contended for or had the mastery over me. Overjoyed at finding such an asylum, I remained in the humble cot. This is the third day I have lived under the roof, freed of my hellish assailants, spending my time in prayer, and writing out this my journal, which I have fashioned to stick in with my printed work, and to which I intend to add portions while I remain in this pilgrimage state, which, I find too well, cannot be long.

August 3, 1712. This morning the hind has brought me word from Redesdale,[157] whither he had been for coals, that a stranger gentleman had been traversing that country, making the most earnest inquiries after me, or one of the same appearance; and, from the description that he brought of this stranger, I could easily perceive who it was. Rejoicing that my tormentor has lost traces of me for once, I am making haste to leave my asylum, on pretence of following this stranger, but in reality to conceal myself still more completely from his search. Perhaps this may be the last sentence ever I am destined to write. If so, farewell, Christian reader! May God grant to thee a happier destiny than has been allotted to me here on earth, and the same assurance of acceptance above! Amen.

Ault-Righ,[158] *August 24, 1712.* Here am I, set down on the open moor to add one sentence more to my woeful journal; and, then, farewell, all beneath the sun!

On leaving the hind's cottage on the Border, I hasted to the north-west, because in that quarter I perceived the highest and wildest hills before me. As I crossed the mountains above Hawick, I exchanged clothes with a poor homely shepherd, whom I found lying on a hillside, singing to himself some woeful love ditty. He was glad of the change, and proud of his saintly apparel; and I was no less delighted with mine, by which I now supposed myself completely disguised; and I found moreover that in this garb of a common shepherd I was made welcome in every house.

I slept the first night in a farmhouse nigh to the church of Roberton, without hearing or seeing aught extraordinary; yet I observed next morning that all the servants kept aloof from me, and regarded me with looks of aversion. The next night I came to this house, where the farmer engaged me as a shepherd; and, finding him a kind, worthy, and religious man, I accepted of his terms with great gladness. I had not, however, gone many times to the sheep, before all the rest of the shepherds told my master that I knew nothing about herding, and begged of him to dismiss me. He perceived too well the truth of their intelligence but, being much taken with my learning and religious conversation, he would not put me away, but set me to herd his cattle.

It was lucky for me that before I came here a report had prevailed, perhaps for an age, that this farmhouse was haunted at certain seasons by a ghost. I say it was lucky for me for I had not been in it many days before the same appalling noises began to prevail around me about midnight, often continuing till near the dawning. Still they kept aloof, and without doors; for this gentleman's house, like the cottage I was in formerly, seemed to be a sanctuary from all demoniacal power. He appears to be a good man and a just, and mocks at the idea of supernatural agency, and he either does not hear these persecuting spirits or will not acknowledge it, though of late he appears much perturbed.

The consternation of the menials has been extreme. They ascribe all to the ghost, and tell frightful stories of murders having been committed there long ago. Of late, however, they are beginning to suspect that it is I that am haunted; and, as I have never given them any satisfactory account of myself, they are whispering that I am a murderer, and haunted by the spirits of those I have slain.

August 30. This day I have been informed that I am to be banished the dwelling-house by night, and to sleep in an outhouse by myself, to try if the family can get any rest when freed of my presence. I have peremptorily refused acquiescence, on which my master's brother struck me, and kicked me with his foot. My body being quite exhausted by suffering, I am grown weak and feeble both in mind and bodily frame, and actually unable to resent any insult or injury. I am the child of earthly misery and despair, if ever there was one existent. My master is still my friend; but there are so many masters here, and everyone of them alike harsh to me, that I wish myself in my grave every hour of the day. If I am driven from the family sanctuary by night, I know I shall be torn in pieces before morning; and then who will deign or dare to gather up my mangled limbs, and give me honoured burial?

My last hour is arrived: I see my tormentor once more approaching me in this wild. Oh, that the earth would swallow me up, or the hill fall and cover me! Farewell for ever!

September 7, *1712.* My devoted, princely, but sanguine friend has been with me again and again. My time is expired and I find a relief beyond measure, for he has fully convinced me that no act of mine can mar the eternal counsel, or in the smallest degree alter or extenuate one event which was decreed before the foundations of the world were laid. He said he had watched over me with the greatest anxiety, but, perceiving my rooted aversion towards him, he had forborne troubling me with his presence. But now, seeing that I was certainly to be driven from my sanctuary that night, and that there would be a number of infernals watching to make a prey of my body, he came to caution me not to despair, for that he would protect me at all risks, if the power remained with him. He then repeated an ejaculatory prayer, which I was to pronounce, if in great extremity. I objected to the words as equivocal, and susceptible of being rendered in a meaning perfectly dreadful; but he reasoned against this, and all reasoning with him is to no purpose. He said he did not ask me to repeat the words unless greatly straitened; and that I saw his strength and power giving way, and when perhaps nothing else could save me.

The dreaded hour of night arrived; and, as he said, I was expelled from the family residence, and ordered to a byre, or cowhouse, that stood parallel with the dwelling-house behind, where, on a divot loft,[159] my humble bedstead stood, and the cattle grunted and puffed below me. How unlike the splendid halls of Dalcastle! And to what I am now reduced, let the reflecting reader judge. Lord, thou knowest all that I have done for Thy cause on earth! Why then art Thou laying Thy hand so sore upon me? Why hast Thou set me as a butt of Thy malice? But Thy will must be done! Thou wilt repay me in a better world. Amen.

September 8. My first night of trial in this place is overpast! Would that it were the last that I should ever see in this detested world! If the horrors of hell are equal to those I have suffered, eternity will be of short duration there, for no created energy can support them for one single month, or week. I have been buffeted as never living creature was. My vitals have all been torn, and every faculty and feeling of my soul racked, and tormented into callous insensibility. I was even hung by the locks over a yawning chasm, to which I could perceive no bottom, and then – not till then, did I repeat the tremendous prayer! – I was instantly at liberty; and what I now am, the Almighty knows! Amen.

September 18, 1712. Still am I living, though liker to a vision than a human being; but this is my last day of mortal existence. Unable to resist any longer, I pledged myself to my devoted friend that on this day we should die together, and trust to the charity of the children of men for a grave. I am solemnly pledged; and, though I dared to repent, I am aware he will not be gainsaid, for he is raging with despair at his fallen and decayed majesty, and there is some miserable comfort in the idea that my tormentor shall fall with me. Farewell, world, with all thy miseries; for comforts or enjoyments hast thou none! Farewell, woman, whom I have despised and shunned; and man, whom I have hated; whom, nevertheless, I desire to leave in charity! And thou, sun, bright emblem of a far brighter effulgence, I bid farewell to thee also! I do not now take my last look of thee, for to thy glorious orb shall a poor suicide's last earthly look be raised. But, ah! who is yon that I see approaching furiously, his stern face blackened with horrid despair! My hour is at hand. Almighty God, what is this that I am about to do! The hour of repentance is past, and now my fate is inevitable. Amen, for ever! I will now seal up my little book, and conceal it; and cursed be he who trieth to alter or amend.[160]

END OF THE MEMOIRS

[*The Editor's Narrative Concluded*]

WHAT CAN THIS WORK BE? Sure, you will say, it must be an allegory; or (as the writer calls it) a religious PARABLE, showing the dreadful danger of self-righteousness? I cannot tell. Attend to the sequel: which is a thing so extraordinary, so unprecedented, and so far out of the common course of human events that, if there were not hundreds of living witnesses to attest the truth of it, I would not bid any rational being believe it.

In the first place, take the following extract from an authentic letter, published in *Blackwood's Magazine* for August, 1823.

On the top of a wild height called Cowan's-Croft, where the lands of three proprietors meet all at one point, there has been for long and many years the grave of a suicide marked out by a stone standing at the head and another at the feet. Often have I stood musing over it myself, when a shepherd on one of the farms, of which it formed the extreme boundary, and thinking what could induce a young man, who had scarcely reached the prime of life, to brave his Maker, and rush into His presence by an act of his own erring hand, and one so unnatural and preposterous. But it never once occurred to me, as an object of curiosity, to dig up the mouldering bones of the culprit, which I considered as the most revolting of all objects. The thing was, however, done last month, and a discovery made of one of the greatest natural phenomena that I have heard of in this country.

The little traditionary history that remains of this unfortunate youth is altogether a singular one. He was not a native of the place, nor would he ever tell from what place he came; but he was remarkable for a deep, thoughtful, and sullen disposition. There was nothing against his character that anybody knew of here, and he had been a considerable time in the place. The last service he was in was with a Mr Anderson, of Eltrive (Ault-Righ, the King's Burn), who died about 100 years ago, and who had hired him during the summer to herd a stock of young cattle in Eltrive Hope. It happened one day in the month of September that James Anderson, his master's son, went with this young man to the Hope to divert himself. The herd had his dinner along with him, and about one o'clock, when the boy proposed going home, the former pressed him very hard to stay and take share of his dinner; but the boy refused for fear his parents might be alarmed about him, and said he *would* go home: on which the herd said to him, 'Then, if ye winna stay with me, James, ye may depend on't I'll cut my throat afore ye come back again.'

I have heard it likewise reported, but only by one person, that there had been some things stolen out of his master's house a good while before, and that the boy had discovered a silver knife and fork that was a part of the stolen property, in the herd's possession that day, and that it was this discovery that drove him to despair.

The boy did not return to the Hope that afternoon; and, before evening, a man coming in at the pass called The Hart Loup, with a drove of lambs, on the way for Edinburgh, perceived something like a man standing in a strange frightful position at the side of one of Eldinhope hayricks. The driver's attention was riveted on this strange uncouth figure, and, as the drove-road passed at no great distance from the spot, he first called, but, receiving no answer, he went up to the spot, and behold it was the above-mentioned young man, who had hung himself in the hay-rope that was tying down the rick.

This was accounted a great wonder; and everyone said, if the Devil had not assisted him, it was impossible the thing could have been done; for, in general, these ropes are so brittle, being made of green hay, that they will scarcely bear to be bound over the rick. And, the more to horrify the good people of this neighbourhood, the driver said, when he first came in view, *he could almost give his oath* that he saw two people busily engaged at the hayrick going round it and round it, and he thought they were dressing it.

If this asseveration approximated at all to truth, it makes this evident at least, that the unfortunate young man had hanged himself after the man with the lambs came in view. He was, however, quite dead when he cut him down. He had fastened two of the old hayropes at the bottom of the rick on one side (indeed, they are all fastened so when first laid on) so that he had nothing to do but to loosen two of the ends on the other side. These he had tied in a knot round his neck, and then slackening his knees, and letting himself down gradually, till the hay-rope bore all his weight, he had contrived to put an end to his existence in that way. Now the fact is, that, if you try all the ropes that are thrown over all the outfield hayricks in Scotland, there is not one among a thousand of them will hang a collie dog; so that the manner of this wretch's death was rather a singular circumstance.

Early next morning, Mr Anderson's servants went reluctantly away, and, taking an old blanket with them for a winding sheet, they rolled up the body of the deceased, first in his own plaid,[161] letting the hay-rope still remain about his neck, and then, rolling the old blanket over all, they bore the loathed remains away to the distance of three miles or so, on spokes, to the top of Cowan's-Croft, at the very point where the Duke of Buccleuch's land, the Laird of Drummelzier's, and Lord Napier's meet, and there they buried him, with all that he had on and about him, silver knife and fork and altogether. Thus far went tradition, and no one ever disputed one jot of the disgusting oral tale.

A nephew of that Mr Anderson's who was with the hapless youth that day he died says that, as far as he can gather from the relations of friends that he remembers, and of that same uncle in particular, it is one hundred and five years next month (that is September 1823) since that event happened; and I think it likely that this gentleman's information is correct. But sundry other people, much older than he, whom I have consulted, pretend that it is six or seven years more. They say they have heard that Mr James Anderson was then a boy ten years of age; that he lived to an old age, upwards of fourscore, and it is two and forty years since he died. Whichever way it may be, it was about that period some way: of that there is no doubt.

It so happened that two young men, William Shiel and W. Sword, were out on an adjoining height this summer, casting peats, and it came into their heads to open this grave in the wilderness, and see if there were any of the bones of the suicide of former ages and centuries remaining. They did so, but opened only one half of the grave, beginning at the head and about the middle at the same time. It was not long till they came upon the old blanket – I think they said not much more than a foot from the surface. They tore that open, and there was the hay-rope lying stretched down alongst his breast, so fresh that they saw at first sight that it was made of *risp*, a sort of long sword-grass that grows about marshes and the sides of lakes. One of the young men seized the rope and pulled by it, but the old enchantment of the Devil remained – it would not break; and so he pulled and pulled at it, till behold the body came up into a sitting posture, with a broad blue bonnet on its head, and its plaid around it, all as fresh as that day it was laid in! I never heard of a preservation so wonderful, if it be true as was related to me, for still I have not had the curiosity to go and view the body myself. The features were all so plain that an acquaintance might easily have known him. One of the lads gripped the face of the corpse with his finger and thumb, and the cheeks felt quite soft and fleshy, but the dimples remained and did not spring out again. He had fine yellow hair, about nine inches long; but not a hair of it could they pull out till they cut part of it off with a knife. They also cut off some portions of his clothes, which were all quite fresh, and distributed them among their acquaintances, sending a portion to me, among the rest, to keep as natural curiosities. Several gentlemen have in a manner forced me to give them fragments of these enchanted garments: I have, however, retained a small portion for you, which I send along with this, being a piece of his plaid, and another of his waistcoat breast, which you will see are still as fresh as that day they were laid in the grave.

His broad blue bonnet was sent to Edinburgh several weeks ago, to the great regret of some gentlemen connected with the land, who wished to have it for a keepsake. For my part, fond as I am of blue bonnets, and broad ones in particular, I declare I durst not have worn that one. There was nothing of the silver knife and fork discovered, that I heard of, nor was it very likely it should; but it would appear he had been very near run out of cash, which I daresay had been the cause of his utter despair; for, on searching his pockets, nothing was found but three old Scotch halfpennies. These young men meeting with another shepherd afterwards, his curiosity was so much excited that they went and digged up the curious remains a second time, which was a pity, as it is likely that by these exposures to the air, and the impossibility of burying it up again as closely as it was before, the flesh will now fall to dust.

The letter from which the above is an extract, is signed James Hogg, and dated from Altrive Lake, August 1st, 1823. It bears the stamp of authenticity in every line; yet so often had I been hoaxed by the ingenious fancies displayed in that magazine, that when this relation met my eye I did not believe it; but, from the moment that I perused it, I half formed the resolution of investigating these wonderful remains personally, if any such existed; for, in the immediate vicinity of the scene, as I supposed, I knew of more attractive metal[162] than the dilapidated remains of mouldering suicides.

Accordingly, having some business in Edinburgh in September last, and being obliged to wait a few days for the arrival of a friend from London, I took that opportunity to pay a visit to my townsman and fellow collegian, Mr L—t of C—d,[163] advocate. I mentioned to him Hogg's letter, asking him if the statement was founded at all on truth. His answer was: 'I suppose so. For my part I never doubted the thing, having been told that there has been a deal of talking about it up in the Forest for some time past. But God knows! Hogg has imposed as ingenious lies on the public ere now.'

I said, if it was within reach, I should like exceedingly to visit both the Shepherd and the Scotch mummy he had described. Mr L—t assented on the first proposal, saying he had no objections to take a ride that length with me, and make the fellow produce his credentials. That we would have a delightful jaunt through a romantic and now classical country, and some good sport into the bargain, provided he could procure a horse for me, from his father-in-law,[164] next day. He sent up to a Mr L—w[165] to inquire, who returned for answer that there was an excellent pony at my service, and that he himself would accompany us, being obliged to attend a great sheepfair at Thirlestane; and that he was certain the Shepherd would be there likewise.

Mr L—t said that was the very man we wanted to make our party complete; and at an early hour next morning we started for the ewefair of Thirlestane,[166] taking *Blackwood's Magazine* for August along with us. We rode through the ancient royal burgh of Selkirk, halted and corned our horses at a romantic village, nigh to some deep linns on the Ettrick, and reached the market ground at Thirlestanegreen a little before midday. We soon found Hogg, standing near the foot of the market, as he called it, beside a great drove of *paulies*, a species of stock that I never heard of before. They were small sheep, striped on the backs with red chalk. Mr L—t introduced me to him as a great wool-stapler, come to raise the price of that article; but he eyed me with distrust, and, turning his back on us, answered: 'I hae sell'd mine.'

I followed, and, showing him the above-quoted letter, said I was exceedingly curious to have a look of these singular remains he had so ingeniously described; but he only answered me with the remark that 'It was a queer fancy for a wool-stapler to tak.'

His two friends then requested him to accompany us to the spot, and to take some of his shepherds with us to assist in raising the body; but he spurned at the idea, saying: ' 'Od bless ye, lad! I hae ither matters to mind. I hae a' thae paulies to sell, an' a' yon

Highland stotts down on the green, every ane; an' then I hae ten scores o' yowes to buy after, an', if I canna first sell my ain stock, I canna buy nae ither body's. I hae mair ado than I can manage the day, foreby ganging to houk up hunder-year-auld banes.'[167]

Finding that we could make nothing of him, we left him with his *paulies*, Highland stotts, grey jacket, and broad blue bonnet, to go in search of some other guide. L—w soon found one, for he seemed acquainted with every person in the fair. We got a fine old shepherd, named W—m B—e,[168] a great original, and a very obliging and civil man, who asked no conditions but that we should not speak of it, because he did not wish it to come to his master's ears that he had been engaged in *sic a profane thing*. We promised strict secrecy; and accompanied by another farmer, Mr S—t, and old B—e, we proceeded to the grave, which B—e described as about a mile and a half distant from the market ground.

We went into the shepherd's cot to get a drink of milk, when I read to our guide Mr Hogg's description, asking him if he thought it correct. He said there was hardly a bit o't correct, for the grave was not on the hill of Cowan's-Croft nor yet on the point where three lairds' lands met, but on the top of a hill called the Faw-Law, where there was no land that was not the Duke of Buccleuch's within a quarter of a mile. He added that it was a wonder how the poet could be mistaken there, who once herded the very ground where the grave is, and saw both hills from his own window. Mr L—w testified great surprise at such a singular blunder, as also how the body came *not* to be buried at the meeting of three or four lairds' lands, which had always been customary in the south of Scotland. Our guide said he had always heard it reported that the Eltrive men, with Mr David Anderson at their head, had risen before day on the Monday morning, it having been on the Sabbath day that the man *put down* himself; and that they set out with the intention of burying him on Cowan's-Croft, where the three marches[169] met at a point. But, it having been an invariable rule to bury such *lost sinners* before the rising of the sun, these five men were overtaken by daylight, as they passed the house of Berry-Knowe; and, by the time they reached the top of the Faw-Law, the sun was beginning to skair the east. On this they laid down the body, and digged a deep grave with all expedition; but, when they had done, it was too short, and, the body being stiff, it would not go down; on which Mr David Anderson, looking to the east and perceiving that the sun would be up on them in a few minutes, set his foot on the suicide's brow, and tramped down his head into the grave with his iron-heeled shoe, until the nose and skull crashed again, and at the same time uttered a terrible curse on the wretch who had disgraced the family and given them all this trouble. This anecdote, our guide said, he had heard when a boy, from the mouth of Robert Laidlaw, one of the five men who buried the body.

We soon reached the spot, and I confess I felt a singular sensation when I saw the grey stone standing at the head, and another at the feet, and the one half of the grave manifestly new-digged, and closed up again as had been described. I could still scarcely deem the thing to be a reality, for the ground did not appear to be wet, but a kind of dry rotten moss. On looking around, we found some fragments of clothes, some teeth, and part of a pocket-book, which had not been returned into the grave when the body had been last raised, for it had been twice raised before this, but only from the loins upward.

To work we fell with two spades, and soon cleared away the whole of the covering. The part of the grave that had been opened before was filled with mossy mortar, which impeded us exceedingly, and entirely prevented a proper investigation of the foreparts of the body. I will describe everything as I saw it before four respectable witnesses, whose names I shall publish at large if permitted. A number of the bones came up separately; for, with the constant flow of liquid stuff into the deep grave, we could not see to preserve them in their places. At length great loads of coarse clothes, blanketing, plaiding, etc. appeared; we tried to lift these regularly up, and, on doing so, part of a skeleton came up, but no flesh, save a little that was hanging in dark flitters about the spine, but which had no consistence; it was merely the appearance of flesh without the substance. The head was wanting, and, I being very anxious to possess the skull, the search was renewed among the mortar and rags. We first found a part of the scalp with the long hair firm on it; which, on being cleaned, is neither black nor fair, but a darkish dusk, the most common of any other colour. Soon afterwards we found the skull, but it was not complete. A spade had damaged it, and one of the temple quarters was wanting. I am no phrenologist,[170] not knowing one organ from another, but I thought the skull of that wretched man no study. If it was particular for anything, it was for a smooth, almost perfect rotundity, with only a little protuberance above the vent of the ear.

When we came to that part of the grave that had never been opened before, the appearance of everything was quite different. There the remains lay under a close vault of moss, and within a vacant space; and I suppose, by the digging in the former part of the grave, the part had been deepened, and drawn the moisture away from this part, for here all was perfect. The breeches still suited the thigh, the stocking the leg, and the garters were wrapt as neatly and as firm below the knee as if they had been newly tied. The shoes were all open in the seams, the hemp having decayed, but the soles, upper leathers and wooden heels, which were made of birch, were all as fresh as any of those we wore. There was one thing I could not help remarking, that in the inside of one of the shoes there was a layer of cow's dung, about one-eighth of an inch thick, and in the hollow of the sole fully one-fourth of an inch. It was firm, green, and fresh; and proved that he had been working in a byre. His clothes were all of a singular ancient cut, and no less singular in their texture. Their durability certainly would have been prodigious; for in thickness, coarseness, and strength, I never saw any cloth in the smallest degree to equal them. His coat was a frock- coat, of a yellowish drab colour, with wide sleeves. It is tweeled,[171] milled, and thicker than a carpet. I cut off two of the skirts and brought them with me. His vest was of striped serge, such as I have often seen worn by country people. It was lined and backed with white stuff. The breeches were a sort of striped plaiding, which I never saw worn, but which our guide assured us was very common in the country once, though, from the old clothes which he had seen remaining of it, he judged that it could not be less than 200 years since it was in fashion. His garters were of worsted, and striped with black or blue; his stockings grey, and wanting the feet. I brought samples of all along with me. I have likewise now got possession of the bonnet, which puzzles me most of all. It is not conformable with the rest of the dress. It is neither a broad bonnet nor a Border bonnet; for there is an open behind, for tying, which no genuine Border bonnet I am told ever had. It seems to have been a Highland bonnet, worn in a flat way like a scone on the crown, such as is sometimes still seen in the West of Scotland. All the limbs, from the loins to the toes, seemed perfect and entire, but they could not bear handling. Before we got them returned again into the grave they were all shaken to pieces, except the thighs, which continued to retain a kind of flabby form.

All his clothes that were sewed with linen yarn were lying in separate portions, the thread having rotten; but such as were sewed with worsted remained perfectly firm and sound. Among such a confusion, we had hard work to find out all his pockets, and our guide supposed that, after all, we did not find above the half of them. In his vest pocket was a long clasp-knife, very sharp; the haft was thin, and the scales shone as if there had been silver inside. Mr Sc—t took it with him, and presented it to his neighbour, Mr R—n, of W—n L—e,[172] who still has it in his possession. We found a comb, a gimlet, a vial, a small neat square board, a pair of plated knee-buckles, and several samples of cloth of different kinds, rolled neatly up within one another. At length, while we were busy on the search, Mr L—t picked up a leather case, which seemed to have been wrapped round and round by some ribbon, or cord, that had been rotten from it, for the swaddling marks still remained. Both L—w and B—e called out that 'it was the tobacco spleuchan,[173] and a wellfilled ane too'; but, on opening it out, we found, to our great astonishment, that it contained *a printed pamphlet*. We were all curious to see what sort of a pamphlet such a person would read; what it could contain that he seemed to have had such a care about. For the slough[174] in which it was rolled was fine chamois leather; what colour it had been could not be known. But the pamphlet was wrapped so close together, and so damp, rotten, and yellow that it seemed one solid piece. We all concluded from some words that we could make out that it was a religious tract, but that it would be impossible to make anything of it. Mr L—w remarked that it was a great pity if a few sentences could not be made out, for that it was a question what might be contained in that little book; and then he requested Mr L —t to give it to me, as he had so many things of literature and law to attend to that he would never think more of it. He replied that either of us were heartily welcome to it, for that he had thought of returning it into the grave, if he could have made out but a line or two, to have seen what was its tendency.

'Grave, man!' exclaimed L—w, who speaks excellent strong broad Scotch. 'My truly, but ye grave weel! I wad esteem the contents o' that spleuchan as the most precious treasure. I'll tell you what it is, sir: I hae often wondered how it was that this man's corpse has been miraculously preserved frae decay, a hunder times langer than any other body's, or than ever a tanner's.[175] But now I could wager a guinea it has been for the preservation o' that little book. And Lord kens what may be in't! It will maybe reveal some mystery that mankind disna ken naething about yet.'

'If there be any mysteries in it,' returned the other, 'it is not for your handling, my dear friend, who are too much taken up about mysteries already.' And with these words he presented the mysterious pamphlet to me. With very little trouble, save that of a thorough drying, I unrolled it all with ease, and found the very tract which I have here ventured to lay before the public, part of it in small bad print, and the remainder in manuscript. The title page is written and is as follows:

THE PRIVATE MEMOIRS
AND CONFESSIONS
OF A JUSTIFIED SINNER
WRITTEN BY HIMSELF

Fideli certa merces.[176]

And, alongst the head, it is the same as given in the present edition of the work. I altered the title to 'A Self-justified Sinner', but my booksellers did not approve of it; and, there being a curse pronounced by the writer on him that should dare to alter or amend, I have let it stand as it is. Should it be thought to attach discredit to any received principle of our Church, I am blameless. The printed part ends at page 153, and the rest is in a fine old hand, extremely small and close.

With regard to the work itself, I dare not venture a judgment, for I do not understand it. I believe no person, man or woman, will ever peruse it with the same attention that I have done, and yet I confess that I do not comprehend the writer's drift. It is certainly impossible that these scenes could ever have occurred that he describes as having himself transacted. I think it *may* be possible that he had some hand in the death of his brother, and yet I am disposed greatly to doubt it; and the numerous traditions, etc., which remain of that event may be attributable to the work having been printed and burnt, and of course the story known to all the printers, with their families and gossips. That the young Laird of Dalcastle came by a violent death, there remains no doubt; but that this wretch slew him, there is to me a good deal. However, allowing this to have been the case, I account all the rest either dreaming or madness; or, as he says to Mr Watson, a religious parable, on purpose to illustrate something scarcely tangible, but to which he seems to have attached great weight. Were the relation at all consistent with reason, it corresponds so minutely with traditionary facts that it could scarcely have missed to have been received as authentic; but in this day, and with the present generation, it will not go down that a man should be daily tempted by the Devil, in the semblance of a fellow creature; and at length lured to self-destruction, in the hopes that this same fiend and tormentor was to suffer and fall along with him. It was a bold theme for an allegory, and would have suited that age well had it been taken up by one fully qualified for the task, which this writer was not. In short, we must either conceive him not only the greatest fool, but the greatest wretch, on whom was ever stamped the form of humanity; or, that he was a religious maniac, who wrote and wrote about a deluded creature, till he arrived at that height of madness that he believed himself the very object whom he had been all along describing. And, in order to escape from an ideal[177] tormentor, committed that act for which, according to the tenets he embraced, there was no remission, and which consigned his memory and his name to everlasting detestation.

NOTES TO *THE PRIVATE MEMOIRS AND CONFESSIONS OF A JUSTIFIED SINNER*

I have tried to be helpful but not over-fussy in glossing the Scots words and phrases in the novel, and so have relied on the reader's horse-sense in dealing with these after a bit of practice. Where a considerable number of Scots words needing a gloss occur in a single passage, I have run the glosses together under a single note cued in at the end of the passage to save space and to encourage readers to read through without flicking back and forth. Quotations from the Bible are from the Authorised Version – i.e. the King James Bible – as read by Hogg and his characters. *OED = The Oxford English Dictionary*.

Explanations of political and theological matters in the novel are offered in the first part of the Introduction, and so for the most part references to these have not been assigned additional explanatory notes here.

1 (p. 3) *reputed*   There is a further allusion to the implied doubt-fulness of Lady Dalcastle's paternity when her father is reported as having 'acquiesced in his wife's asseveration regarding the likeness of their only daughter to her father' (p. 8), and the Old Laird later refers to her son, Robert, supposedly fathered by the Reverend Wringhim, as being 'the third in a direct line who had all been children of adultery' (p. 34).

2 (p. 3) *Baillie*   a town councillor

3 (p. 4) *either of the parties*   i.e. either God or man

4 (p. 4) *bickers*   wooden drinking vessels

5 (p. 4) *saluted*   kissed

6 (p. 5) *Amorite ... Hittite ... Girgashite*   The Amorites, the Hittites and the Girgashites are all named in Joshua 3:10 as peoples who, among others, will be driven out from the lands of the Israelites.

7 (p. 5) *the writings of the Evangelists*   the writings of the original Evangelists – i.e. the Apostles – in the form of the New Testament 'Epistles' of Paul, James, Peter, John and Jude

8 (p. 5) *broad way ... to destruction*   Matthew 7:13: 'Enter ye in at the strait gate: for wide is the gate, and broad is the way, that leadeth to destruction, and many there be which go in thereat.'

9 (p. 6) *sound a nasal bugle*   i.e. snore

10 (p. 6) *Morphean measures*   Morpheus is the god of dreams.

11 (p. 6) *strathspey ... corant*   types of Scottish country dance

12 (p. 6) *skimmer*   skim, glide across

13 (p. 7) *the shackles of the drowsy god*   The 'drowsy god' is again Morpheus, whose victims are commonly said to be 'chained' in sleep; thus 'shackles'.

14 (p. 7) *laird*   landowner of an estate

15 (p. 7) *braird*   the early shoots of a grain crop such as wheat or barley

16 (p. 7) *man of Belial*   In the Bible the phrase 'men of Belial' is used to denote the wicked. See, for example, I Samuel 30:22.

17 (p. 8) *guidit*   treated

18 (p. 8) *take pennyworths of*   take revenge on

19 (p. 9) *lounder*   thrash

20 (p. 9) *wire-drawn*   drawn out to an almost unsustainable thinness, as when ductile metal is 'drawn' into a wire

21 (p. 9) *limb of Antichrist*   Antichrist first appears in the writings of the Evangelists so beloved by Lady Dalcastle and those of her religious temper. Protestant Reformers tended to identify the figure with the Papacy and they refer to the clergy as 'the body of the Antichrist'. Here Lady Dalcastle, who thinks of episcopy as being just as bad as Catholicism, is therefore referring to her husband's religious affiliations as well as to his generally unregenerate behaviour.

22 (p. 10) *Canaanitish woman*   It was the Canaanites who dwelt at Sodom and Gomorrah (see Genesis 13) and so can function here as a byword for morally and spiritually reprobate conduct.

23 (p. 10) *anathemas*   anathema = 'the formal act, or formula, of consigning to damnation' (*OED*)

24 (p. 11) *Moabite*   Deuteronomy 23:3: 'An Ammonite or Moabite shall not enter into the congregation of the Lord; even to their tenth generation shall they not enter into the congregation of the Lord for ever.'

25 (p. 11) *An that be the case ... Here he is*   *an* = if; *an'* = and; *a'* = all; *gang* = go; *canna* = cannot

26 (p. 12) *films*   filaments – i.e. fine threads

27 (p. 13) *on the hip*   at a disadvantage – a term from wrestling. See Shakespeare's *The Merchant of Venice*, 1, 3, 40–1: 'If I can catch him once upon the hip, / I will feed fat the ancient grudge I bear him.'

28 (p. 14) *countenance the banquet . . . a day*   pay for the Christening feast. As the context suggests, the laird's refusal to take on the father's role in the baptism of the child means that a year and a day must pass before an alternative baptismal 'parent' can come forward.

29 (p. 16) *start the game*   to drive the hunters' prey (often hares) from cover into the open

30 (p. 20) *the Canongate*   the 'lower', i.e. eastern, part of the 'Royal Mile' in Edinburgh, which runs from the Castle to Holyrood Palace, the 'upper' part being the High Street

31 (p. 22) *. . . and the Cowgate*   The Cowgate runs parallel to the High Street/Canongate one block south, and they are linked both by a number of streets and by a number of alleyways, or 'closes', in some instances giving access, as here, to open squares between the two main thoroughfares.

32 (p. 22) *abominable weapons of offence*   Throughout the seventeenth and the eighteenth centuries, Edinburgh was infamous, even by the rather lax standards of those times, for its lack of public sanitary arrangements. Human waste was generally just emptied from windows on to the street below (and on anyone unwary who happened to be passing). 'Abominable weapons of offence', therefore, would come easily to hand.

33 (p. 23) *wynd*   a narrow alley

34 (p. 23) *the Castle*   The Castle lies at the western extremity of the old city, at the head of the 'Royal Mile' as it is called. In it was garrisoned a permanent military presence to deal with any civil disorder.

35 (p. 23) *Linlithgow*   an ancient borough approximately twenty miles west of Edinburgh

36 (p. 25) *Set thou . . . down let it go*   This is an extract from Psalm 109, verses 6 to 11.

37 (p. 26) *the Links*   a public open space or park. When Robert recalls this incident (p. 105), he denotes it as occurring 'a little farther to the south' of the previous one: the Links may, therefore, be the area still known as Bruntsfield Links, about a quarter of a mile south of the Grassmarket.

38 (p. 27) *the High Church*   part of St Giles Church in the High Street overlooking Parliament Square

39 (p. 27) *the Grey-Friars*   Greyfriars Church lies about ten minutes walk south of the High Street.

40 (p. 28) *the Parliament-House*   The Scottish Parliament, reestablished in the late 1990s, was dissolved in 1707 by the terms of the Treaty of Union. Previous to that it met in Parliament Square, just off the High Street.

41 (p. 29) *excursion . . . Arthur's Seat*   This episode is precisely located in the still-extant topography of the east end of Edinburgh old town. Arthur's seat is the name given to the hill that rises above the city to the south of Holyrood Palace, which stands at the eastern end of the Royal Mile. To get to it George has to loop round and approach it from the north-east. On that route lie the ruins of St Anthony's chapel and the adjacent well. Arrived close to the summit of the hill, George looks across (in a roughly west-north-westerly direction) towards the city, across the dip and, beyond it, the back of Salisbury crags, a steep escarpment that overhangs the eastern end of the city and what in those days was the outlying village of St Leonards. Any reader with a map of Edinburgh can trace this route, and any interested enough to go there can follow in George's footsteps.

42 (p. 29) *swire*   level place near the top of a hill

43 (p. 30) *Lothian*   'The Lothians' (East, Mid- and West) are the area extending for twenty miles either side of Edinburgh in eastern lowland Scotland. From the point George has reached here one can see right to the eastern extremity of the region.

44 (p. 32) *poltroon*   'a mean-spirited coward' (*OED*)

45 (p. 32) *stinkards*   animals whose defence system involves exuding foul-smelling fluid

46 (p.35) *burning coals of juniper*   See Psalm 120:3–4: 'What shall be given unto thee? or what shall be done unto thee, thou false tongue? Sharp arrows of the mighty, with coals of juniper.'

47 (p. 37) *. . . to the same side*   The Editor's point here is that the young gentlemen are all Jacobites, and so their loyalty to the Jacobite 'side', as expressed in their speeches, toasts and songs, is technically *dis*loyalty to the established regime.

48 (p. 37) *bagnio*   brothel

49 (p. 38) *merks*   marks, the mark being two-thirds of a pound

50 (p. 38) *the North Loch*   This lay on the northern edge of the city, in the area which now lies between the old and new towns. It was drained in the nineteenth century when the railway was built, and the site is now substantially occupied by Waverley Station. It is clear from the context here that communal drying greens were

sited on its southern edge, serving dwellings on the north side of the High Street.

51 (p. 39) *John, Duke of Melfort*   Hogg provides Drummond with an identifiable historical identity. John Drummond, first Earl and Duke of Melfort, was a Catholic who went into exile with James II in 1688. He did have a son called Thomas, who entered the Austrian service, as the Editor later mentions (p. 66). He was related to Lord Craigie, a Lord of Session (mentioned by name, p. 40 and p. 65), who was not his uncle, as the Editor says here, but his grandfather (on p. 65 the Editor is not sure which).

52 (p. 39) *Lord of Session*   what in modern (English) terms might be called a 'law lord'

53 (p. 40) *Charles VI*   Charles VI, Holy Roman Emperor from 1711 until his death in 1740. Previous to this (as Charles III) he was Archduke of Austria and King of Hungary, and it must have been then that Drummond initially joined his service in 1705.

54 (p. 41) *pharisaical*   pharisaic = 'resembling the Pharisees in being strict in doctrine and ritual, without the spirit of piety; laying stress upon the outward show of religion and morality, and assuming superiority on that account' (*OED*). See also Note 79 below.

55 (p. 41) *from . . . of babes and sucklings*   echoing Psalms 8:2: 'Out of the mouth of babes and sucklings hast thou ordained strength . . . '

56 (p. 43) *the Grass Market*   Public hangings took place at the west end of the Grassmarket in Edinburgh.

57 (p. 45) *plack*   a coin of low value

58 (p. 48) *within a good jerkin*   A jerkin is a close-fitting jacket. Bessy's point is that her body is pretty much all she's ever had to call her own, and that any thief would have to extend the usual sphere of his activities to ruin her in that respect!

59 (p. 48) *a' the spoons in Argyle*   Bessy's point here is that Argyll is the home territory of the Clan Campbell, and so 'C' is the initial letter of the name of almost all of the population.

60 (pp. 47-9) *Was I at hame . . . that's my advice* (Bessy Gillies' testimony)   *sic a yelloch* = such a yell; *toom kists* = empty chests; *muckle* = much; *dung dotrified a wee* = struck dumb for a moment ('dotrified' = literally 'stupefied'); *the fer wa'* = the far wall; *tawpie* = scatterbrain, especially as applied to females; *shakel-bane* = wristbone; *hoad-road* = state of chaos; *grumphing* = grumbling; *hayraip* = a rope made from plaited hay, used here as a drying rope

61 (p. 50) *caddy*   carrier. The word survives today in golfing terminology.

62 (p. 52) *stripes*   the marks of a whip

63 (p. 52) *land*   local Edinburgh term for a multi-storey building in a close or wynd

64 (p. 52) *claymore*   a traditional Scottish sword, with a 'basket-hilt'

65 (p. 58) *pillions*   light saddles especially for women riders

66 (p. 61) *Bogle-heuch*   *heuch* = bank; *bogle* = a ghoul or ghost

67 (p. 63) *stock*   'a kind of stiff close-fitting neckcloth, formerly worn by men generally' (*OED*)

68 (p. 63) *dree the weird*   suffer the fate

69 (p. 63) *lend hearing . . . of the woodriff*   Bell Calvert's rather poetic expression needs some botanical explanation. The species of willow called *salix hoffmaniana* has large, markedly ear-shaped stipules, and these are therefore the 'ears of the willow'. The woodriff (*asperula odorata* – more commonly 'woodruff') has clusters of eight (not seven) tongue-like leaves at intervals on the stalk. These therefore can be taken to be the 'tongues of the woodriff'. Bell's sentiment is to the effect that God will, if necessary, give hearing and speech to the 'ears' and 'tongues' of plants in order to expose murder. The general thrust is similar to Shakespeare's, 'for murder, though it have no tongue, will speak / With most miraculous organ' (*Hamlet*, 2, 2, 577–8).

70 (p. 65) *the Tolbooth*   the prison which at that time stood in the middle of the High Street just outside the west end of St Giles's Church.

71 (p. 66) *1715*   'a memorable year for Scotland,' because the date of the first Jacobite Rebellion

72 (p. 68) *single Catechism . . . Effectual Calling*   In the Catechism the question, 'What is Effectual Calling?' requires the answer, 'The word of God's spirit, whereby . . . he doth persuade and enable us to embrace Jesus Christ.' The Catechism was a series of fixed questions-and-answers which children were made to learn, to inculcate in them the fundamentals of religious doctrine.

73 (p. 68) *gowk*   literally, a cuckoo, but commonly used to signify a fool

74 (p. 68) *without the pale of the covenant*   i.e. not included in the elect: pale = paling, or fence

75 (p. 70) *one vessel . . . another to dishonour*   II Timothy 2:20: ' . . . in a great house there are not only vessels of gold and silver, but also of wood and of earth; and some to honour, and some to dishonour.'

76 (p. 70) *There he goes! . . . that thou be'st!*   *Sickan* = such; *aiths* = oaths; *een* = eyes; *bow-kail* = cabbage

77 (p. 72) *Melchisedec* In Hebrews, Chapters 5 and 6, St Paul upholds the Old Testament priest Melchisedec as a prototype of the preacher of the true gospel and the model for Christ's own priesthood.

78 (p. 72) *Apostle of the Gentiles* St Paul

79 (p. 72) *. . . to pray in the Temple* Barnet alludes to the parable of the Pharisee and the publican in Luke 18:9-14: the Pharisee's prayer, which he adapts, is: 'God, I thank thee, that I am not as other men are, extortioners, unjust, adulterers, or even as this publican.'

80 (p. 73) *black stool* seat in church where sinners were made to sit while enduring public rebuke

81 (pp. 71-4) *Well, John . . . as he likes* (Barnet's quarrel with Wringhim) *aw* = variant on 'I'; *ower little* = too little; *aye* = always; *fraze* = noise, palaver; *bannet* = bonnet; *unco* = very (short for 'uncommonly'); *for me* = as far as I'm concerned; *hout na* = oh no; *gibes* = jibes; *yerk* = jerk, pang; *gars* = causes; *better nor* = better than; *maun* = must; *chances* = fates; *juggs* = pillory; *pose* = interrogate; *mense* = honour

82 (p. 74) *the manse* traditional Scots term for a minister's house

83 (p. 74) *Jehu . . . Cyrus . . . Nebuchadnezzar* As King of Israel, Jehu slew Joram, Ahaziah and Jezebel (II Kings 9); in Isaiah 44:28, God says of Cyrus, 'He is my shepherd, and shall perform my pleasure' – Cyrus would later retake Jerusalem for the Israelites and order the restoration of the Temple. Nebuchadnezzar became the instrument of God's wrath against the people of Israel – see II Kings 25 and Jeremiah 21:3-10.

84 (p. 74) *find God a consuming fire to me* from Deuteronomy 9:3: 'Understand, therefore . . . that the Lord thy God is he which goeth over before thee; as a consuming fire he shall destroy them, and he shall bring them down before thy face . . .' 'Them' refers to the Children of Anak.

85 (p. 76) *dominie's* 'Dominie' (from Latin *dominus* = master) is an old Scots term for a schoolmaster.

86 (p. 76) *phiz* old schoolboy slang: short for 'physiognomy' (face)

87 (p. 77) *tikes* terriers

88 (p. 78) *by the slump* in a lump, collectively

89 (p. 78) *. . . as excluding sins* In I Corinthians 6:9ff. and Galatians 5:19ff., St Paul provides dauntingly extensive lists of the kinds of sins which will exclude the sinner from the Kingdom of Heaven. Revelation 21:8, which Robert may consult here, says that 'the fearful, and unbelieving, and the abominable, and murderers,

and whoremongers, and sorcerers, and idolaters, and all liars shall have their part in the lake which burneth with fire and brimstone'; and verse 27 insists that 'there shall in no wise enter into [the new Jerusalem] any thing that defileth, neither whatsoever worketh abomination, or maketh a lie; but they that are written in the Lamb's book of life'.

90 (p. 78) *as filthy rags*   Isaiah 64:6: 'But we are all as an unclean thing, and all our righteousnesses are as filthy rags . . . '

91 (p. 79) *sinful king . . . for a season*   The King of Israel in question is probably Ahab, who 'rent his clothes, and put sackcloth upon his flesh, and fasted, and lay in sackcloth, and went softly' (I Kings 21:27)

92 (p. 79) *the just made perfect*   The phrase comes from a passage in Hebrews 12: 22–3: 'But ye are come unto mount Sion, and unto the city of the living God, the heavenly Jerusalem, and to an innumerable company of angels, to the general assembly and church of the firstborn, which are written in heaven, and to God the Judge of all, and to the spirits of just men made perfect.' This is a central text in Robert's Calvinist theology.

93 (p. 79) *wrestled with God, as the patriarch of old had done*   In Genesis 32:24–30, it is told how Jacob literally wrestled over one night with God's manifestation in the form of a mysterious stranger.

94 (p. 79) *the Lamb's book of life*   See above, Note 89: the image is a recurrent one in Revelation. See also Introduction, p. xiii.

95 (p. 79) *as a brand out of the burning*   Amos 4:11: 'I have overthrown some of you, as God overthrew Sodom and Gomorrah, and ye were as a firebrand plucked out of the burning: yet have ye not returned unto me, saith the Lord.'

96 (p. 84) *as dung to fat the land*   a recurrent image in the Old Testament where the enemies of Israel are left unburied after being killed. See, for example, II Kings 9:37; Psalms 83:10; Jeremiah 8:2, 9:22, 16:4, 25:33.

97 (p. 85) *Finnieston*   a district which then lay west of the city of Glasgow, on the north bank of the River Clyde, but has long since been incorporated into the expanded city

98 (p. 86) *magnanimity*   in its root meaning of 'greatness of mind' rather than its derived sense of 'generosity'

99 (p. 87) *the great preacher*   Gil-Martin refers to the Old Testament Book of Ecclesiastes, which is subtitled 'or the Preacher'. His 'quotation' cunningly conflates Ecclesiastes 9:10: 'Whatsoever thy hand findeth to do, do it with thy might; for there is no work, nor

device, nor knowledge, nor wisdom, in the grave, whither thou goest,' with Proverbs 27:1: 'Boast not thyself of tomorrow, for thou knowest not what a day may bring forth.'

100 (p. 89) *Czar Peter of Russia* Peter the Great of Russia was czar jointly with his half-brother Ivan from 1682–96 and then sole czar until his death in 1725. What prompts Robert's bizarre supposition is that Peter the Great did travel incognito through various countries in Europe in the late 1790s calling himself 'Sergeant Pyotr Mikhaylov'. In early 1698 he was in England and studied shipbuilding at Deptford, downriver from London. By 1704, when Robert meets Gil-Martin, however, Peter was back in Russia leading his army against the Swedes in what became known as 'the Northern War'.

101 (p. 90) *of the moral cast* i.e. Blanchard preaches the possibility of salvation through moral uprightness – good works

102 (p. 94) *Paisley* a borough about seven miles south-west of Glasgow

103 (p. 97) *the Pearman Sike* a sike is a small stream.

104 (p. 102) *Jehu ... Ahab* The allusion is to II Kings 9:6–10, where Jehu receives from God the message, 'thou shalt smite the house of Ahab thy master, that I may avenge the blood of my servants the prophets, and the blood of all the servants of the Lord, at the hand of Jezebel. For the whole house of Ahab shall perish . . . '

105 (p. 103) *Cloud of Witnesses* This refers to the Presbyterian tract, *A Cloud of Witnesses, for the Royal Prerogatives of Jesus Christ; or, the Last Speeches and Testimonies of those who have suffered for the Truth, in Scotland, since the year 1680*. It was, in fact, first published in 1714, later than the date at which Robert claims to have read it.

106 (p. 103) *Famine and Pestilence are my sisters* Robert is alluding to Jeremiah 42:17: 'So shall it be with all the men that set their faces to go into Egypt to sojourn there; they shall die by the sword, by the famine, and by the pestilence.'

107 (pp. 103–4) *Fat the deil ... for your operations* (the gaoler's speeches) *Fat the deil* = What the devil; *yooling* = wailing; *that gate* = in that manner; *rowth* = plenty; *crooning* = moaning or singing loudly; *in-by* = further inside; *kenning* = knowing; *callant* = young man; *fa* = who; *braw* = fine

108 (p. 104) *Gilgal* Gilgal was the site of Joshua's camp before the assault on Jericho (Joshua 4:20), and was where Saul was crowned (I Samuel 11:14–15); but the context suggests that

Robert is thinking of a passage from Hosea 9:15: 'All their wickedness is in Gilgal: for there I hated them: for the wickedness of their doings I will drive them out of mine house . . . '

109 (p. 104) . . . *the heart of the lion*   from II Samuel 17:10

110 (p. 104) . . . *shekels of brass*   The Philistine giant, Goliath, 'was armed with a coat of mail; and the weight of the coat was five thousand shekels of brass' (I Samuel 17:5).

111 (p. 104) *Tophet*   a valley near Jerusalem known as the valley of slaughter, because there Israelites offered their children as burned offerings to Baal (see Jeremiah 7:31–2)

112 (p. 105) *venal prophet*   Balaam: the text that follows is adapted from Numbers 22:29.

113 (p. 107) *flaring . . . flummery*   both words denoting flattery

114 (p. 108) *still small voice*   from I Kings 19:11–13, where Elijah, told by God to stand upon the mountain, is assailed by wind, earthquake and fire, but the Lord is not in any of them. Then after the fire comes 'a still small voice' that asks, 'What doest thou here, Elijah?'

115 (p. 109) *ketch*   a swinging blow

116 (p. 115) *smite him with the edge of the sword*   In Jeremiah 21:7, God promises to deliver the people of Judah into the hands of Nebuchadnezzar (see Note 83 above), 'and he shall smite them with the edge of the sword'.

117 (p. 115) *part of the 10th Psalm*   'Why standest thou afar off, O Lord?' The psalm focuses, as appropriate to Robert's mood, on the character of the wicked man and solicits the Lord's vengeance against him.

118 (p. 122) *pomatum*   pomade, a scented oil

119 (p. 123) *in toto*   Latin = completely

120 (p. 123) *put in requisition*   legal term meaning to require that something be acted upon

121 (p. 124) *writer of the signet*   a solicitor in Scotland with special powers and responsibilities under the 'signet' or royal seal

122 (p. 124) *JAMES . . . 1687*   Hogg's legal document is stylistically authentic for the period. Since an impression of gobbledegook is the point, explanation of the various arcane legal terms would be counter-productive.

123 (pp. 128–9) *Ye sanna . . . rising against you* (Scrape's speeches) *sanna want* = shall not lack; *countit* = considered; *that gate* = of that kind; *the day* = today; *yestreen* = yesterday; *gayan ill-faurd* = very sinister; *tak its swee* = take its course

124 (p. 131) *interest*   here meaning 'self-interest'

125 (p. 133) *Daniel . . . den of lions* Daniel was cast into a den of
lions by Darius for praying to the God of the Israelites, and was
preserved from harm by his faith. See Daniel 6:10-23.

126 (p. 133) *a staunch Cameronian* The Cameronians were an
extremist sect of the Presbyterian Covenanters, named after
their leader, Richard Cameron (1648–80). Although Penpunt,
Scrape's home town, is fictional, it can be supposed to be in
south-west Scotland, probably in Ayrshire, where the more
extreme forms of Presbyterianism had their strongest hold.

127 (p. 134) *Galloway drover* Galloway is the area in the south-
western corner of Scotland; a drover is a cattle-drover, who
herded cattle over often long distances to markets and cattle
fairs.

128 (p. 135) *auld Macmillan* The Reverend John Macmillan (1670–
1753), who was minister to the Cameronians from 1706.

129 (pp. 134–5) *Ye may as weel . . . and ridicule* (Scrape's speeches)
leasing-making = uttering falsehoods; *maun* = must; *whilk o'
thae* = which of those; *luckpenny* = discount paid to the buyer;
feele = fool; *clachan* = small village; *stuff* = insubstantial chatter (as
in 'stuff and nonsense'); *kimmers* = gossiping women; *sidie for
sidie* = side by side; *havers* = fanciful stories, gossip; *ding* = beat

130 (p. 136) *Auchtermuchty* small town in Fife, in eastern central
Scotland. It lies just north of the Lomond Hills, to which
reference is also made.

131 (p. 137) *the Song o' Solomon* also known as the Song of Songs
or the Canticles. It consists of a series of often erotic love
poems, alternately for a male and female speaker, traditionally
interpreted scripturally as expressing God's love for his Church.

132 (p. 137) *the Sidlaw hills* north of the River Tay, beyond Dundee – about 15 miles away from Auchtermuchty – as the crow
flies!

133 (p. 138) *119th Psalm* Psalm 119 is the longest of the psalms,
thus perhaps testifying to the stamina of the church clerk and
the congregation. Verse 77 ('Let thy tender mercies come unto
me, that I may live: for thy law is my delight') does not seem to
have any specific relevance to the entrance of the 'strange
divine' except by way of dramatic irony.

134 (p. 138) *'I will overturn . . . I will give it to him'* from Ezekiel
21:27

135 (p. 138) *. . . sent to the Ninevites* See Jonah 3:1-4: God sent
Jonah to warn Nineveh that it would be overthrown unless it
repented of its wicked ways.

136 (p. 139) *St Johnston*   an old name for Perth. Of the other place names that follow in this passage, Cupar, Newburgh and Strathmiglo are all towns in the same part of Fife as Auchtermuchty; Perth and Dundee are larger cities about fifteen miles distant; the East Nook (or Neuk) of Fife is the stretch of coast, with a number of fishing communities, which lies in the south-east of the county, between Chapel Ness and Fife Ness; and the Grampian Hills mark the northern edge of lowland Scotland and the beginning of the Highlands.

137 (pp. 136–40) *Weel, you see, sir … the stamock again* (Penpunt's story)   *gin* = if; *chafts* = jaws; *shanned* = grimaced; *sauchless* = gumptionless; *cuif* = fool; *bairns* = children; *reards* = cries aloud; *howlets* = owls; *Auld Simmie* = Satan; *dishclout* = literally dish-cloth – a base tool or foolish victim; *till* = to; *his ain ha'* = his own hall; *wad strodge* = would stride; *gizened* = withered, dried up; *cauler* = freshly-caught; *aumuses* = clerical caps; *bodle* = two Scots pence; *the lave o'* = the rest of; *hind* = farm labourer; *lint-swinglings* = flax-beatings; *nooks* = corners; *bridal* = gathering; *corbie craws* = black crows; *east the lift* = out of the sky from the east; *gloaming* = twilight, or half-shadow; *crap* = crept; *bourock* = hovel or rough shelter; *poukit* = preened; *flannens* = flannel garments; *clouted* = clothed; *duds* = clothes; *humming* = humming, droning; *creeshy louns* = fat folk; *thief's hole* = prison cell; *crouping* = croaking; *brae* = hillside; *a' war* = all were; *carl* = fellow; *keust* = cast; *reid* = red; *keek* = peep; *fa' me* = befall me; *nae the waur* = none the worse; *scoudered* = scorched; *het ern* = hot iron; *calm* = qualm; *stamock* stomach

138 (p. 140) *the Saviour's golden rule*   Matthew 7:12: 'Therefore all things whatsoever ye would that men should do to you, do ye even so to them: for this is the law and the prophets.'

139 (p. 142) *the sands o' the linn*   A linn is a small ravine or gorge.

140 (p. 143) *frock coat*   an overcoat with long 'skirts' below the waist

141 (p. 145) *… the kingdom of heaven*   quoting the famous passage from Matthew 19:24: '… It is easier for a camel to go through the eye of a needle, than for a rich man to enter into the kingdom of God.'

142 (p. 147) *pirns*   spools on which thread is wound

143 (p. 149) *Boddel Brigg*   The Battle of Bothwell Bridge, on the River Clyde ten miles or so above Glasgow, was fought on 22 June 1679 between the forces of the Crown, under the Duke of Monmouth, and the Covenanters, resulting in a bloody defeat for the Covenanters.

144 (pp. 145–50) *The weaver's wife . . . deadly point* (episode at the weaver's cottage) *in by here* = come on in; *tak tent* = pay attention to; *fand* = found; *saur o' reek* = strong stench of smoke; *waratch* = wretch, villain; *div* = do; *windelstrae* = a dried stalk of grass (used ironically); *kennin'* = recognising; *rack* = stretch; *fawn inna* = fallen into; *reistit trams* = trapped legs; *wab* = web; *ditit* = foolish; *donnart* = stupid; *burd* = offspring; *howkin'* = digging, poking; *the Auld Ane* = the Old One (Satan); *gayan sib* = close kin; *clapper-clawin* = striking, slapping; *ayont* = beside; *mell* = beat; *slack* = loosen; *circumfauldit* = surrounded; *braidside* = whole side

145 (p. 151) *West Port*   the West Port (or gate) into the old city lay west of the Grassmarket

146 (p. 151) *Mr James Watson*   a noted Edinburgh publisher, and the Queen's printer in Scotland from 1711

147 (p. 153) *The Pilgrim's Progress*   The famous book by the English Puritan preacher John Bunyan (1628–88) had been published in 1678, less than forty years before this phase of Robert's life. It is rooted in the same Calvinist theology as that which underlies Robert's more extreme doctrines.

148 (p. 153) *Chesters*   There are two villages with this name in the Borders, but it is clear from his description of his route after leaving there (p. 163) that Robert is in the one that is about eight miles south-east of Hawick.

149 (p. 154) *Circassian*   'a thin worsted fabric' (*OED*), named after an area that is now occupied by northern-eastern Turkey and southern Russia

150 (p. 154) *Portsburgh*   a district of Edinburgh. As he leaves the city, Robert heads towards England not by the main road that leads to North Berwick and Berwick-on-Tweed (nowadays the A1) but by the inland route to Jedburgh and the Borders (nowadays the A68). Dalkeith lies on that road a few miles south of Edinburgh.

151 (p. 154) *Oh . . . no power to stand!*   Robert begins by quoting Psalm 55:6: ' . . . Oh that I had wings like a dove! For then would I fly away, and be at rest;' but what follows 'fly' in his speech is his own application of the sentiment.

152 (p. 155) *canny*   normal, wholesome

153 (p. 157) *Ellan*   Allan Water runs south to join the River Tweed between Galashiels and Melrose. The Tweed is the main river of the region, running east to the sea at Berwick.

154 (p. 158) *Ancrum*   about three miles north of Jedburgh, just off the main route from Edinburgh south into England

155 (p. 160) *Oh, Tam Douglas ... swallowed up* (the inn at Ancrum) *frayont* = from beside; *cloots* = hoofs; *bedstrae* = straw used as a bed; *take kindling* = catch fire; *cronies* = associates; *brikkin* = breaking; *chiel* = young man; *ye's no lie* = you're not going to lie

156 (p. 162) *the New Jerusalem* the city of God in the next world. See above, Note 89. It is described in detail by St John in his vision in Revelation, Chapter 21.

157 (p. 162) *Redesdale* five miles west of Hawick

158 (p. 162) *Ault-Righ* rendered on p. 167 as 'Eltrive' and on 170 as 'Altrive'. As p.167 clarifies, the name means 'the King's Burn' ('burn' being a standard Scottish term for a small stream).

159 (p. 164) *divot loft* a loft for storing turfs of peat

160 (p. 165) *and cursed ... to alter or amend.* In a last act of spiritual presumption, Robert imitates the end of the Book of Revelation: 'If any man shall add unto these things, God shall add unto him the plagues that are written in this book: And if any man shall take away from the words of this prophecy, God shall take away his part out of the book of life, and out of the holy city ... ' (22:18–19).

161 (p. 169) *plaid* The original plaid, unlike that modern development from it, the kilt, was a woven cloth in which the wearer wrapped himself from shoulder to knee. It tended to double as an outer garment and a sleeping blanket for those who, like shepherds, led an outdoor or itinerant life.

162 (p. 170) *more attractive metal* i.e. something of more interest. The metaphor (derived from the different magnetic – i.e. 'attractive' – properties of metals) comes from Shakespeare's *Hamlet*, 3, 2, 117, where Hamlet thus describes Ophelia to Gertrude.

163 (p. 171) *Mr L—t of C—d* John Lockhart of Chiefswood, who himself contributed to *Blackwood's*

164 (p. 171) *father-in-law* Lockhart's father-in-law was actually Sir Walter Scott, whose home at Abbotsford was only a few miles distant from the area where this part of the action is set.

165 (p. 170) *Mr L—w* William Laidlaw, a servant of Scott's and another *Blackwood's* contributor

166 (p. 170) *Thirlestane* a village just east of the town of Lauder, in Selkirkshire

167 (p. 172) ' *'Od bless ye ... banes'* (Hogg's speech) *stotts* = young bulls; *yowes* = ewes; *after* = afterwards; *foreby* = without; *houk* = dig

168 (p. 172) *W—m B—e* unidentified as anyone within Hogg's actual circle, although an oblique identification with William

Blake has been suggested. See David Groves, ' "W—m B—e , a great original": Blake, The Grave and James Hogg's *Confessions*', *Scottish Literary Journal*, November 1991.

169 (p. 172) *marches*   boundaries

170 (p. 173) *phrenologist*   Phrenology, a science extremely popular in the nineteenth century, attempted to adduce the shape of the human skull as indicative of character. It was pioneered by Franz-Joseph Gall (1758–1828).

171 (p. 174) *tweeled*   twilled

172 (p. 175) *Mr Sc—t . . . Mr R—n, of W—n L—e*   Not definitively identified. In notes for the Oxford University Press edition of the novel (1969), John Carey speculates that 'W—n L—e' is Wilton Lodge at Hawick (about thirteen miles east of Thirlestane), and so 'Mr R—n' should in fact read 'Mr A—n', i.e. James Anderson, who did occupy it in 1824. 'Mr Sc—t' could be one of a number of 'Scotts' residing in that area.

173 (p. 175) *spleuchan*   pouch

174 (p. 175) *slough*   here in the sense of an enclosing wrapping or covering, most commonly used in the more specific sense of a snake's skin

175 (p. 175) *a tanner's*   The point is that tanners in the course of their work effectively tan their own skin, making their bodies proverbially impervious to moisture. In *Hamlet*, 5, 1, 163–8, the Gravedigger makes the same point to Hamlet, claiming that 'a tanner will last you nine year'.

176 (p.176) *Fideli certa merces*   Latin = to the faithful man reward is assured

177 (p. 177) *ideal*   in its root sense of 'in the realm of idea (rather than actuality)' – i.e. imaginary